SPACE NATION

A Novel By

Mike Giesinger

To the lovely, Bianca!
I hope you enjoy the
story.
MWG

Order this book online at www.trafford.com
or email orders@trafford.com

Most Trafford titles are also available at major online book retailers.

Printed in Victoria, BC, Canada.

ISBN: 978-1-4269-2999-1 (soft)
ISBN: 978-1-4269-3000-3 (hard)
ISBN: 978-1-4269-3001-0 (ebook)

Library of Congress Control Number: 2010904279

*Our mission is to efficiently provide the world's finest, most comprehensive book publishing
service, enabling every author to experience success. To find out how to publish your book, your
way, and have it available worldwide, visit us online at www.trafford.com*

Trafford rev. 4/26/2010

TRAFFORD www.trafford.com
PUBLISHING

North America & international
toll-free: 1 888 232 4444 (USA & Canada)
phone: 250 383 6864 ♦ fax: 812 355 4082

DEDICATION

Firstly, I dedicate this story to my Grandma Paluik who, was tired of chasing her rambunctious, 3 year old grandson around her house and had an epiphany to sit me in front of what was considered then, as the improved and new, color TV set. Years later, she revealed to me, the TV series playing that night. She said to me that at least once a week, she was guaranteed an hours worth of peace. I rediscovered, during the early 70's re-runs, the show that got me hooked on anything Sci-fi. Thanks, Grandma.

To Maureen Parker, my Grade 5 and 6 Teacher, eventually, my High-School Counselor and family friend, for encouraging me to keep writing. 'Upward and onward' she used to say. Thanks, Maureen.

To 'The Guys'. Ron, Rob, Dennis, Colin, Dave and Rene. Who first listened to my crazy, wild, fictitious, ideas for a novel. Maybe a movie, with a rockin' soundtrack,("Yeah, right! Have another beer," they would say). They always wanted to hear more. Thanks, guys.

To Mike Oldfield. The most under-rated musical genius of our time. His music inspires me. The first time I became aware of his existence, I was walking past a music store and a poster for "Five Miles Out" caught my eye. I always considered the Grumman Electra, a beautiful plane (still do). On that poster alone, I bought the cassette and listened to it, repeatedly. And I developed a hunger for more of his music. At first, I played his music, softly in the background, while studying for high-school exams. Soon, his music was playing as I locked myself in my room for hours as I wrote. Thanks, for the inspiration, Mike.

CONTENTS

EPIGRAPH

Thucydides showed what war was, why it happened, what it did and must continue doing until Man learned better conduct. The Peloponnesian War between Athens and Sparta was fought for only one reason...because they were powerful and through this fact, were obliged (in Thucydides own words) to seek to increase their power. They fought not because they were different - one a democracy, the other an oligarchy - but, because they were alike. The war had nothing to do with who was good and who was evil. Is democracy good and oligarchy evil?

To ask this question would have been, for Thucydides, to move away from the problem. There was no power representing the good.

Power, whoever exercised it, was the evil one, the demon, the 'corruptor of men.'

Thucydides was the first to recognize (and in any case to express in words) this new doctrine which would become that of the entire world for thousands of years.

Edith Hamilton, 1942

PROLOG

TATTOO

The lone drummer emerged from the tree-covered lane, beating lightly in tune with each step as he continued somberly down the hill of the cemetery lane. After 20 feet, a single bagpiper appeared from the trees, lightly playing the tune of the Tattoo. Marching 20 feet behind him, in 2 groups of 2 with a single piper, leading; 4 more pipers followed, bagpipes at the ready. After they traveled 20 feet, 5 more drummers exited from the trees, keeping in step and in light rhythm of the first drummer. Because of the distance to the grave-site, they all played the beginning of the traditional Scottish folk-song repeatedly,.

The group of drummers traveled 50 feet before the funeral procession finally emerged from the tree-covered lane. The sky was over-cast and a hint of dew hung in the air from the recent rain. Leading the procession were 6 men carrying a coffin high on their shoulders. As the procession continued into the open, the drummers and bagpipers stepped up the intensity of the tattoo, they were playing.

By this time, the first drummer reached the location of the gravesite, followed by the rest of the musicians. Standing approximately 30 feet away from the gravesite, they decreased their tempo, slightly, as the procession crowded around the coffin.

To the crowd, the priest read from the Holy Bible. He read from various passages, examples really, suitable for someone who did great works in one's lifetime. Many stood in somber silence with a few dabbing tears from their eyes and cheeks as the rumbling of the dark clouds above threatened to unleash the last of its moisture on those below. The priest paused, looked up briefly from his bible at the clouds overhead and continued with the last verse.

With his service done, the priest took 2 steps back, the cue for the still-playing, fife and drum to make their way through the crowd to the grave-side. They split up into 3 groups; 3 drummers at the head and foot of the grave, at the periphery of the crowd, while the pipers, also still playing softly, ringed the coffin.

Once the coffin began to lower, they began to play louder, with increased tempo and enthusiasm. The clouds parted and a shaft of sunlight illuminated the grassy knoll that the crowd was gathered on. The pipers and drummers all, raised their heads skyward, playing their loudest and with great passion, as if calling to Heaven to announce the arrival of a great soul. The moment was almost angelic for those in the crowd as a good portion began to weep.

After a few repetitions of the Tattoo, the crowd began to disperse. When all were gone, there stood 2 young men, shoulder to shoulder, with an arm on each other. The music faded and then stopped. The fife and drum retreated quietly, away. Their task, done.

The priest, still standing-by near the head of the grave, stood and watched the 2 brothers as they tried to regain their composure. He approached them and gracefully and patiently escorted them back towards the waiting limousine. Once there, he opened the rear door, allowing the 2 brothers to step in and stopped to look back at the hill before he himself, entered the vehicle. The parting of the clouds still allowed the shaft of sunlight to illuminate the small knoll, as if showcasing the grave-site. The priest allowed himself a slight smirk as he entered the limo; knowing full well that his prayer and request had been answered by God, Himself.

CHAPTER ONE

"..and God said, 'Let there be light."

Marcus Gowan's fascination with the points of light in the darkness of space began when he was a young boy. His father, on a cloudless, starlit night, had pointed out to Marcus and his older brother Glenn, a bright light streaking across the star-field. It was a satellite, he explained. A machine created by men and launched to circle the Earth where it would stay for a long time. He also added that he was one of those men who did such things.

Marcus also learned that night, that those points of light were suns like the Earth's and that each would have planets orbiting them. Marcus was in awe of the night sky and as the moon rose above the eastern horizon, Samuel Gowan explained that Man had, for a brief period in the past, walked on its surface and haven't returned since.

Marcus wanted to go there and beyond. He promised himself that when he grew up, he was going to go there. Watching television news as a child, he knew other men were already working to do that. However, politics and the lack of money always seemed to get in the way. The were the plans for the decommissioning of the 3rd. generation space shuttle fleet and the creation of the next fleet which was twice the size of the 1st. generation and would be capable of not only atmospheric flight but, also able to go the Moon and back. China (the last and only bastion of Communism) had renewed its commitment of sending tiakonauts to the moon. To Marcus, the child, Humanity was venturing out, together.

Although later, as he grew up, he realized that it was competition that compelled those nations.

Years later, Samuel Gowan brought his two sons into the corporation he founded. They turned out to be valuable assets to the company. Glenn started in an entry level position in administration and climbed the corporate ladder in leaps and bounds. His business savvy was almost second nature. His innovative business and marketing ideas became the hot topic and a hot commodity in the business-world before he reached the age of 23. Year after year, he turned out record profits that exceeded those of the year before.

Glenn was recognized as a wonder-boy with the 'Midas Touch'. Any business that was in financial trouble and if it was rumored that he was looking to acquire, that company's stock would increase an immediate 10 points on the stock markets. Competing companies continually courted him to leave his father's corporation, to work for them. Glenn would just smile politely, as if he knew a secret no one else did and say, *"No, thank-you"*.

Marcus, on the other hand, was interested in a totally different aspect of the company: Research and Development. At first, as a child, he accompanied his father to the labs and watched as scientists and technicians worked. His mind was a sponge and he took it all in. Soon, he was working along-side these men helping to do the experiments and creating new devices. As his academic accomplishments surpassed his schooling, he spent more and more time on projects in the labs.

There was only one time when he wasn't in the labs. He entered university at age 14 and came back with 6 degrees, at age19.

He came back with renewed spirit and with that, came new ideas for projects that could only be dreamed of. By age 21, he was in charge of 9 different divisions as Operations Director of his father's company. Samuel Gowan , the board of directors, the shareholders and fellow employees were so impressed at the amount of money being made, that Marcus, at age 21 and Glenn at age 23, found themselves awarded the titles of Junior Vice-Presidents.

Samuel was very proud of his two sons. They worked long hours, especially Marcus. Many times, Samuel and Glenn had to stop by the R&D Facility to figuratively, drag Marcus kicking and screaming away from his toys and gadgets. Long hours indeed.

As the two brothers grew older, the elder Gowan privately wished that they would get a social life. It wasn't that they didn't get along with anybody. Everybody who came into contact with them, enjoyed their company. They each had a type of charisma that was the glue to any friendship. However, he soon realized that what *was* important to the two, was their relationships with their co-workers. Therefore, they had seemed and were satisfied with their 'social' life.

He thought that perhaps, one day, they would each find a girl and settle down.

Samuel Gowan himself was ready to move on. He had wanted to retire and was prepared to let his sons take over. He felt, it was time. He had been at this, most of his adult life. He was the company and the company was he. *Was* him, but not anymore. The company evolved and he just couldn't keep up with the increasing pace of the business. And it now revolved around his two sons. He was beyond the age where most companies would force their senior managers into retirement. No one at this company would even entertain the idea of getting rid of the company icon. He had lived most of his life and now it was time to make way for his sons. It was their turn, now. *Their,* company.

Almost a year after Glenn was made CEO and Marcus, President of Operations, Samuel Gowan died in his sleep. It was determined almost immediately that he had died of natural causes, much to the disappointment of some local authorities, who wanted to suspect foul play.

After the funeral of the richest technologies giant in the world, came the reading of the will. Samuel Gowan had determined that two in charge of such a vast company would only create headaches from top to bottom. He had wanted only one of his sons to helm the corporation he founded and built. However, since he was no longer part of the company, he wanted the brothers to decide between themselves. The other would have to sit things out but, not without compensation. Over the years, the elder Gowan had secretly deposited extreme amounts of personal and company profits into secret accounts in Switzerland, Liechtenstein and the International Depository of the Republic of Cuba. By the time Samuel Gowan handed the reigns of his company to his sons, he had over a trillion dollars socked away.

Ten years later, Marcus Gowan was a very busy man. At the age of 34, he was the recipient of a lot of money. More than he knew what to do with but, he had a few ideas and his father's dream. The first thing he did was build a vast underground complex he named White Alice, under the guise of a diamond mine operation in the frozen tundra wastelands of the Federal Dominion of Canada. Over the previous year, space probes, landsats and comsats were launched from this facility with technology that made all previous stealth technology, ineffective. Technology, his father had acquired so many years before.

As Director Marcus Gowan studied an interactive, electronic cutaway diagram of White Alice Station mounted on his office wall, Assistant-Director Thomas 'Doc' Thorpe entered the office. Doc was older by about 20 years with a hint of grey in his moustache, beard and hair. The two men had met years before when 'Doc' worked as Samuel Gowan's right-hand man. Doc had recognized early on, just how special Marcus was. He noticed upon entering, that his boss' office was colder than the rest of the facility. Marcus often explained, the cooler temperatures helped him to think more clearly while working.

"Hey, Doc. What can I do for you?" Marcus said without turning around.

Thorpe was amazed how mature and confident Marcus seemed. His mannerisms and gestures were that of an older man with years of experience.

"Uh, right. I need your thumb print on these files so we can store them to archives before they are shipped to the South Pacific," as he handed the electronic file folder to Marcus.

"These are the last?" Marcus asked, accepting the data storage folder.

"990 tera-clusters of your personal files. It's the last", Doc confirmed.

"When will the phase six crews be finished? Marcus asked while he applied his thumb to the touch sensitive screen.

"In sixteen hours," Doc replied. "It will take the phase seven crews three hours to transfer the Destiny from hanger bay six to the main launch bay. Countdown is set six hours after that".

Marcus noticed a hard copy printout in Doc's other hand.

"This just came in from our informant at the Department of Federal Defense", Doc handed it to Marcus. "His information states that the military has observed our last three launches. *Visually*. What really piqued their interest is that; although they could observe these launches, NORAD couldn't pick them up on radar", he paused. "That in turn piques the interest of the US government, since it means they don't have that kind of technology." He continued. "They are concerned that the son of a wealthy industrialist is launching satellites, undetected, into orbit. We both know, that government's view that anyone not an ally of the US shouldn't have any space capabilities."

Marcus gave Doc a sideways glance, noticing the sarcasm.

"Since both the U.S. and Canadian governments have a common interest in the defense of the North American continent, the Federal Canadian military will be *allowed* to send a small force to assault, police and investigate the White Alice Diamond Mine."

Marcus looked up from the printout, eyes disbelieving.

Doc recognized that look immediately. "Yeah, I know. I had to read it a couple of times, myself."

"Damn it! Just when we were starting to get this ball rolling," Marcus raised his voice as he walked back to his desk.

Doc went on, "Within the next thirty-six hours…an anti-terrorist response team of the Canadian Federal Armed Forces will be airlifted into the area near the outer perimeter, at the runway, south of the station. Their rules of engagement are to take this complex and I am quoting, "with a minimum of force unless lives of military personnel are at risk."

Letting that sink in, for a few seconds, he continued. "Their secondary objective is to detain, *alive,* Marcus Gowan, for reasons specified by the North American Continental Security Agreement; specifically, suspicion of inciting an insurgency and domestic terrorism and secondly, violations pertaining to the United Nations, UNISPACE 5 Treaty".

Marcus looked up from the printout, eyes wide in disbelief.

Doc recognized that look immediately, "Yeah, I had to read *that* a couple of times, too."

"Damn it, I don't believe this!" Marcus exclaimed as he walked behind his desk. The computer-archive-pad clattered on his desk as he sat heavily into his chair.

It was the first time Doc had ever seen Marcus Gowan upset about anything. He watched Marcus get up from behind his desk and begin pacing the office. He had known him long enough to know that when he started to do that, that genius brain was on to a train of thought that was heading to the station.

Marcus Gowan was in overdrive. When he finally did break his silence, he startled Doc.

"Doc! Have the phase six crews finish two hours before schedule. Really push 'em. They can do it." He paused for a moment. "I want the Destiny placed in the launch bay two hours after that and hold a pre-launch briefing, with the crew, in fifteen. We're gonna' launch before the cavalry arrives."

"Well, I guess that means we'll have to scrap the moon-base projects," Doc said disappointedly.

Marcus stopped in mid-pace. "At least until we've rebuilt in the South Pacific. Now, we'll have to make sure we take as much equipment as possible."

Doc was puzzled and Marcus could see it on his face.

"Why don't we just set the charges and evacuate?" Doc suggested.

"Even if one nano-molecular processor is left behind and found, it wouldn't take very long, for any scientist worth his salt, to figure out how it works. In this world, that would be very dangerous."

That was a fact they both understood. Samuel Gowan had built up much of his corporate empire based on a secret, unknown, undiscovered technology. He had also spent considerable time and effort hiding it from others except those close and trusted enough to take that secret to the grave. Without that secret, the company, the wealth, probes, satellites, White Alice, and the Destiny would be nothing more than a fantasy. The two men knew that that secret could and would be turned into the ugliest weapons the Earth had ever seen.

"Strip the station of equipment and materiel's. Load them aboard the cargo planes and send them to the South Pacific," Marcus ordered.

Doc was silent, staring at the floor, with his right thumb pressed against his lips.

"The evacuation could work but, within thirty six hours?"

"No," Marcus replied. "We are going to do this in *twenty four*. I want those planes loaded and on their way over international waters by the time the military arrives."

There was an expression of horror on Thorpe's face. He was thinking of logistics, manpower, timing, stress....panic.

"Uh, Marc....I..." Doc began, thinking of the volume of work involved.

Seeing his reaction, Marcus put his right hand on Doc's left shoulder.

"Look, Doc. I know I am asking a lot out of you and everyone in this station. I know this can be done. And in doing so, we can guarantee that no one will ever find any evidence of what we were doing here."

Doc felt a slow but powerful surge of confidence build deep down within him. He suddenly realized that, through all this, they could actually pull it off. Alone if need be. By God, if he had to. It was like a brainstorm. When Doc began nodding in agreement, Marcus continued.

"Allright! Now, give the evac-order and have everyone on the job with the exception of the phase six, seven and the flight crew."

"Consider it done," Doc promised. He turned and left the office. Several moments later, the evacuation signal sounded throughout the White Alice Station.

Major Dennis Manning sat sleepily, feet on his desk, reading report after report. He resented being a desk jockey. He didn't get out much. His superiors saw to that. The last thing they wanted, they said, was an experienced and decorated officer to be maimed training others on the proving grounds.

'Well, why would they want me in charge of an anti-terrorist team?' he asked himself.

He knew why. He was an old soldier. Old soldiers had a habit of speaking their minds and not putting up with bullshit. This no-nonsense attitude came from experience and past mistakes; personal and from those of others. His superiors felt he was too old for field duty and after thirty years of service, he should accept the government's retirement package and make way for the 'young guns'. Being behind a desk, he no longer felt useful. He wasn't a combat soldier anymore, he was a paper warrior and his weapon was a damn pen. All his operational experience over the years and his reward was to be a slave to paperwork and Intel reports until they forced him into retirement.

He would have made, at least, Brigadier-General by now if he hadn't told a certain superior officer what he thought of him, years ago.

Manning had been in charge of a troop-squadron when this officer showed up with orders from the Department of Federal Defense. This officer, who held a higher rank than he, was to try a new field training technique that someone, somewhere, dreamed up. This officer firmly believed in the technique. He told Manning so.

Manning's orders were to stand down and observe. When the training techniques were not achieving the results that this particular officer had hoped for, he started improvising in the field with disastrous results that involved several injuries. This officer, faced with a major investigation into his pet project as to cause and fault, went to Manning to enlist him in a cover-up. At first, Manning was non-committal and aloof. He was trying to distance himself, from a command point-of-view. However, when this officer found out that Manning had kept notes of his daily orders and directives, he ordered Manning to make his observations disappear. For the welfare of the Canadian Federal Armed Forces, of course.

Manning was so shocked; he really didn't know what to do. First, he had to pick up his jaw from the floor. He realized at that moment, that this man had no business being an officer, much less a soldier.

The next night, in the officer's lounge on-base, Manning was trying to enlist the help of a few scotches to help him decide how to, strategically, handle the situation. Manning, sitting at the bar, happened to overhear this officer explain, informally, to senior DFD officers, that his training techniques were sound and suggested that blame should lay directly with the entire brigade who were not enthusiastic about the techniques and were (he felt), doing what they could to undermine his training orders. Then he suggested that a few of the men should be singled out and court-martialed to make an example of.

Manning saw red. Those were his soldiers. They were, in his opinion, good people. And they always followed orders. Manning decided right then, what he had to do. He wasn't going to standby and let his soldiers become the scapegoats of a fool. Early Canadian military history was full of examples such as that, already. Manning stood up from his barstool and marched himself over to the table these men were seated at and as if carrying a shotgun, he let the fool have it.

"What village are you depriving of its *idiot,* Sir?" Manning smirked as he remembered.

"I beg your pardon?" a senior officer asked.

"You are out of line, Captain!" another responded.

"I am a combat soldier. Sirs. If you are entertaining the recommendations of a fool, then I don't have a whole hell of a lot of respect for you people in Ottawa," Manning shot back.

The fool tried to separate Manning from the group, "Captain, may I have a word with you?"

However, the highest ranking DFD officer, a Major-General, wanted to hear Manning out.

"Just a moment, Colonel. Elaborate, Captain."

Manning straightened his tunic and told them everything. The blunders, training errors, misleading and vague orders, safety violations and injuries, the incompetence and the cover-up. The result of one man who, Manning stated, had no business being, out in the field.

All eyes bore down on the Colonel.

"Captain," the senior officer announced. "Before we return to Ottawa, tomorrow, I will stop by your office to pick up a copy of those observations. Have them ready."

"Sir. How do I know this issue won't be buried in Ottawa by a bureaucrat?" Manning asked.

The General took a step closer to Manning and spoke so only he could hear.

"Captain. By the time this is done, you and your men will be absolved of blame at the court-martial and I will owe you a marker."

Flabbergasted, Manning could only muster the words "Yes sir." But he at least had a smile on his face.

The DFD officers were getting ready to leave and as he watched them gather their coats and covers, a question popped into his head.

"General, Sir. Who's court-martial?"

The General looked around the lounge, acquired his target, pointed his thumb in the direction of the Colonel and said, *"His."*

Manning looked back at the fool. If looks could kill, he'd be carrying a Howitzer.

Manning went back to his scotch at the bar.

At the court-martial, everything came out as promised. However, Manning found himself facing charges. Insubordination and disorderly conduct.

Even that fool had friends in high places and it was his way of 'sticking it' to Manning. This coward was still trying to escape military justice. The General assured him that this would not happen, although, the insubordination charge was valid since Manning was drinking when he confronted the Colonel in front of the senior officers. It was a technicality that he was off-duty. The General had tried but was unsuccessful in having the insubordination charges dismissed.

Manning considered it a trade-off. At the Colonel's court-martial, he pled guilty to the insubordination charge without advice of military counsel. He admitted it freely even though he only had two drinks that whole night. He wasn't going to lie about it. The judgment against Manning was that he be held over at his next promotional review.

The Colonel, well, things didn't turn out as well as expected. Everything that this officer did was examined with a fine-toothed comb. Everyday was worse than the day before. Even the Colonel's competency came into question. After the first week, Manning felt sorry for that buffoon but, had to remind himself what was at stake. When all was done, the Colonel found himself demoted to the rank of lieutenant and posted to a NATO base in northern Labrador.

Manning just laughed. He thought, they might as well have sent him to Siberia.

He had heard, years later, that he had left the military and after a while, had managed to get himself started in politics. He had heard the fool had gotten himself elected to some city council, in some city in eastern Canada.

Just then, his Admin-Assistant, entered Manning's office, handing him several large, color coded envelopes. Manning went for the 'yellow jacket' marked 'White Alice', broke the seal and emptied the contents onto his desk. He spent a few moments studying the documents and flipping through the satellite photos. These were really good photos, too. Very high resolution and in color. Advantages of having the United States for an ally.

However, one thing bothered him about this file. The photos belied what the preliminary paragraphs suggested. To him, it looked like what it was supposed to be. He took out his magnifying glass and studied the photos more closely.

"Somebody's full of crap", Manning said to himself.

"Beg your pardon, Sir?" Lieutenant David Chen replied, looking confused.

Manning forgot his Chief Administrative Aide was still in his office and realized he thought out, aloud.

"Tell me something, Lieutenant," he showed him the satellite photos. "What do you see?"

Chen studied the photos for a couple minutes and even used the magnifying glass to see the finer details.

"Well, Sir. It appears… to be a mining station, with a camp, various outbuildings and an airstrip, about a mile long, I presume for flying in the work crews." Chen looked up at Manning to see if he got his assessment right.

"Bingo," Manning hesitated as he handed Chen a cigar. "To the American government and the Federal Dominion of Canada, that is an insurgent terrorist training camp in the Arctic Territories."

Chen's eyes went wide as he looked down at the photos once again.

"Who made that determination, Sir?" Chen inquired.

"The powers that be, lad", shaking his head. "The powers that be."

"I'm sorry, Sir. I just don't see it."

"That makes two of us." Manning replied.

Chen was still going through the photos, "Where is the fencing, evidence of patrols? No practice ranges? Nothing that can be attributed to anything, slightly militaristic. Nothing sinister."

Manning watched a realization wash over Chen's face.

"An exercise!" Chen blurted out.

Manning reached for the yellow folder on his desk and waved it in front of him.

"Yellow jacket means 'High Priority' and is stamped 'Interest of Federal Defense'.

"So what do you plan on doing, Sir?" Chen asked.

"Well, somebody up the ladder is going to have explain to me why they think the heir of a now dead, rich industrialist is a threat to continental security," Manning explained as he gathered up the Intel reports and photos.

"Do you think you will get an answer to that, Sir? Chen asked.

"Probably not," Manning sighed. "Won't know unless I try. Right? When did that folder arrive?"

"Fifteen minutes ago," Chen replied. "It was *'Direct Rush'* from the Deputy Minister of Federal Defense."

Manning looked at his watch.

"I would like to hold briefings at sixteen hundred with the CAT team leaders. Please notify them also that we are a 'Go'.

"Yes, Sir. Very well, Sir," Chen said as he stood at attention before proceeding out of the office.

Manning began going through maps and charts when he called after Chen.

"And get me General Huculak on the horn. I'll be damned if we show up at a legitimate work camp, locked and loaded, and end up shooting at a bunch of civilians."

"Yes, Sir!" Chen called back through the open door.

Nineteen hours later, Commander Richard (Tricky Dick) Graham walked slowly down the large corridor that led to the White Alice hanger/launch bays. The insulated wall and floor panels had already been removed and were probably aboard one of the many cargo planes currently enroute to the South Pacific.

'Not much left of the station, now', he thought to himself.

He realized that frost had started to form on the walls and floor. That soon, if they stayed any longer, they would all need arctic clothing to stay warm. With each step, the frost made an audible crunching sound. He knew they wouldn't be at White Alice for much longer, now. Soon they and a great many other people from around the globe would be enjoying more hospitable temperatures in the South Pacific and he quite frankly, couldn't wait.

Smirking to himself, he looked down at his electronic checklist and flight charts as he entered an intersecting corridor and didn't see the loaded, computer controlled, anti-grav cargo cart that hit him.

When Marcus heard about the accident on level 10, he was on his way to the conference room for the pre-flight briefing. He was not looking forward to telling most of the crew that for this flight, they would not be required. The Destiny's shakedown cruise would have to wait for another day.

He was looking forward to it, too. They all were. That, for the first time, the ship's systems would be tested for real outside the confines of Earth's atmosphere. They had tested and simulated realistic conditions and situations for over a year.

When he arrived at the scene, there was a crowd gathered in the intersection of corridors. He was hoping it wasn't as bad as he had heard. After moving through the crowd for a few moments, Marcus set his eyes upon the man lying on the perma-frost floor.

"Hey, Marc," the man moaned. "Guess what?" he gasped for air. "Tried to play chicken with a CGC unit."

Even though Graham tried to laugh at his own joke, the pain on his face betrayed the humor of the situation.

Marcus looked around. "Has anyone called topside for a med-tech?"

Structural engineer, Danny Nguyen, bent down on one knee. "I have, Mr. Gowan. He is making his way down, now."

Marcus made a quick assessment of Graham's injuries. "Well, you definitely have a broken collarbone…..probably some broken ribs, too."

Graham looked up at his boss painfully, stating, "Guess that means we have to abort the flight."

Marcus was about to say 'Yes' when an idea popped into his head. One thing was for sure; the Destiny was going to fly.

"No, not necessarily," he replied.

Graham passed out before Gowan could answer.

Voice Island. A barren piece of rock in the Arctic Territories. Why anyone would build and operate a diamond mine in such an inhospitable place was beyond Dennis Manning. The Gowan corporate empire had applied for and won the mineral rights to Voice Island some years before. Samuel Gowan had ensured that his bid had the highest return to the Federal government and the Arctic provincial government. As far as those governments and their agencies were concerned, there was no downside. Greed and corruption won.

Manning had studied all the Intel there was on Gowan, his family and his business. After resigning from a promising career in the aerospace field, Samuel Gowan began a small business in high technology, mostly in manufacturing. First by building up his small company and then acquiring larger and larger competitors, eventually becoming a modest empire. The one thing Samuel Gowan didn't touch was; businesses dealing in weaponry. While everyone was getting rich selling arms and military-related equipment and technology during various conflicts, he was getting rich elsewhere. Mostly in Asia. From toys to communications, entertainment, shipbuilding, construction, heavy equipment, etc. He had his fingers in it.

At middle age, since he was unmarried, he became the godfather to children of an employee who had no living relatives. When he was asked and accepted to be godfather, he not only proudly displayed their photos in his office; he even babysat for the parents. He was considered 'Family'. Then, the parents died in a terrible auto accident a year after Marcus had been born. Sam thought, that as godparent, it was logical for him to care and eventually adopt both Glenn and Marcus as well. The adoption and foster care agencies agreed and within the year, Samuel Gowan had a family.

Eventually, the boy's were spending as much time at the company as they were at home. They went to school there as did most employees' children. It seemed that the only time they went home, was to sleep.

Samuel Gowan had for many years managed to keep his company off the stock exchanges of the world until one year, he had to finally offer its stocks. By this time, other multi-national conglomerates were beginning to take notice of this upstart company's wealth potential. They began salivating at the prospect of the fresh infusion of cash and assets only to find that once they had taken offensive steps for a corporate takeover, it was they who were on the defensive and were soon assimilated into the Gowan corporate empire. Years later, Samuel Gowan began compartmentalizing

15

his empire into separate units but, still retained 100% control over them. His Empire was still strong, just hard to buy up. Every time a company came along and tried to buy up one of his 5000 separated companies, that company soon found itself under attack and itself facing what Samuel Gowan often referred to privately as, 'extinction'.

Manning was impressed. Had Sam Gowan been a soldier, he thought, he would have made General, easily. This man commanded his business empire like a field tactician.

He put the file down for a moment and reached for his favorite coffee cup not realizing that he had been reading for so long that the contents, was now cold. He got up from his chair and headed for the coffee maker for a fresh, hot cup. A poster on the wall above the coffee maker was Manning's favorite. It displayed a smiling, WWII era soldier holding and toasting a canteen cup to those reading the poster. The caption below said "How about a nice big cup of shut the fuck up". Manning couldn't help but smirk every time he saw it.

On his way back to his office, he noticed a plain white envelope on his assistant's desk. It was simply addressed to Manning in handwritten form and the desk was completely devoid of the piles of documents and files that were usually there. In fact, it was the first time Manning had ever seen the color of the desktop. He opened the envelope and began reading. He couldn't believe what he was reading. He took the letter into his office, and sat heavily into his chair and read it over again.

To: Major D. Manning, Commanding Officer, Federal Canadian Anti-Terrorist Team.
From: Lieutenant D. Chen, Admin. Assistant, Federal Canadian Anti-Terrorist Team.
Subject: Resignation.

Please accept my formal resignation under your command and from the Canadian Federal Armed Forces, effective immediately. I have been offered a promising future as a civilian in the private sector. I wish to convey to you, sir, my gratitude for your fairness, your initiative, honesty, competence and above all, your code of honor. It has been an honor and my privilege to serve under your command. Please accept my sincere apology in not notifying you before we had a chance to speak of this but, this company required my decision immediately. I have made the necessary arraignments with the DFD and I have purchased my discharge papers as per protocol and they should be on your desk within the week. My replacement will report for duty tomorrow

With Gratitude,
Lt. D. Chen (Retired)

'*Short and sweet*', Manning thought to himself. With a smirk on his face, he lightly flung the letter on the top of his desk and just stared at it for a few more seconds. He began to rub his eyes to relieve the hours of tension from the hours of reading. He decided he didn't need to worry about Lt. Chen until after he got back from this mission.

They, were letting him command this mission in the field. *They*, didn't want him to go. In fact, this time they came right out, saying he was too *old* to command a group, *any* group, in the field. He was ready for them, though. He promptly supplied his medical report, psych evaluation, combat readiness report and every single one of his commendations. They couldn't deny him, this time. They tried but, he also, had to cash in all his remaining markers. As always, there was a price. After this, he would have to retire.

Suited him fine, though. He was ready to admit to himself, finally, that he needed a change. After all these years, he realized that he was stagnating in what had become a dead-end job. There wasn't any joy in it anymore. He had served his country since graduating high school and spent his first six years as a trooper. After becoming the youngest officer in the CFAF, he was offered the opportunity to enroll in the US Army War College, Carlisle Barracks, in Pennsylvania. He accepted and when he was done, five years later, he climbed to Command with instructor rating.

Manning wasn't looking forward to retirement. He never looked forward to anything that involved sitting around on his '*Kiester*'. Not unlike the '*big brass butts*' sitting around over at the Department of Federal Defense. '*Oh, sure*', he chuckled to himself, '*some of them were OK*' but, the rest of them were what he would often refer to as the '*Paper Platoon*'. Just a bunch of bureaucrats who's only concern was protecting their jobs.

Lieutenant Robert Stuart arrived at Manning's office door carrying a field pack and assault gear.

"Evening, Sir. I have your gear. You might want to try them on and adjust them before we leave in the morning."

"Thank-you, Lieutenant. I'll do that later, tonight. Is everything set for tomorrow?" Manning began rubbing his eyes.

"Yes, Sir," Stuart hesitated. "We have been allocated four C-280's, one AREA Command vehicle, two Wolverine LAV's and CAT, First Company in full arctic gear." Stuart brought up his left arm to look at his wristwatch.

"Pardon me, Sir. It's already 2200 hours and we have to be on the flight line at 0500. Aren't you going to get some rack time?"

"Rats," Manning exclaimed as he, too, checked his watch. "I lost track of time," he said as he stood up from his chair. He stopped, craned his head towards the Lieutenant and asked, "You wouldn't be interested in being my assistant, would you?"

Caught by surprise, Stuart began stuttering,"Ah..um..well, I thought you had one, already, Sir?"

"I did." Manning picked up the letter Lt. Chen had left and waved it in the air. "He resigned and purchased his discharge papers, today." Manning shook his head. "Best damned assistant, I ever had. He was offered a better paying position as a civilian. I just wished he had talked to me about it, first. I would have talked him out of it. Then again, he probably knew that," he sighed.

There was a moment of silence between the two men. It was obvious to Stuart that Lt. Chen's resignation bothered the Major.

Manning broke the silence with a smirk on his face, "I just thought you might prefer staying clean and dry."

"Thank-you for the consideration, Sir," Stuart chuckled. "I think I'm under-qualified."

"You are," Manning shot back, with a smirk.

"Permission to speak, freely, Sir?" Stuart asked.

"Go ahead," Manning replied.

"Thanks for the offer, Sir," Stuart started. "I'm a ground-pounder. I like it. *A lot.* One of the reasons I joined this unit is that you yourself, are a lot like the troops. You're in the trenches, in the water and mud with us. You'll even eat field rations out on maneuvers with us. You're one of us."

Manning looked up from the combat boots he was retying. He was not aware of the reputation he had earned.

"Yes, Sir! Soldiers are either afraid of you or can't wait to serve under your command," he paused. "The first time recruits hear your name, is at Boot Camp. Everyone learns that you used to command there, years ago. The training grounds has been unofficially named in your honor. Anyway, when you were the CO of the boot camp, you created training specs. and protocols that are still used by the instructors, to this day. Everyone knows you caught a lot of flak and took a reprimand for standing up for trooper safety. After you were re-assigned, the DFD quietly implemented those changes that you started. The didn't have the decency to admit you were right. You are the only command officer, anyone is aware of, that actually enjoys being in the field with us 'grunts'. Personally, that says a lot about your character, Sir."

Manning gave a half-sarcastic smile."

"Doesn't mean I plan on holding hands and singing campfire songs with you, grunts."

Stuart chuckled, at which point Manning chuckled a few times because he caught the Lieutenant completely by surprise.

"That's another reason the men look up to you, Sir. Anyway, I won't waste your time considering the offer. You'll find an Aide."

Stuart stopped for a moment and then asked, "Did you know that the men gave you a nick-name?"

"Who? The troops? I wasn't aware of that?" Manning stopped as he picked up his pack. "Do I really want to know what it is?"

"I think so, Sir," Stuart replied. "It's a badge of honor."

"So, spill," Manning ordered.

Stuart hesitated, "General Hand Grenade, Sir."

Manning chuckled. Puzzled, he asked, "Why, General Hand Grenade?"

"Because, Sir. You are as blunt and decisive as a hand grenade in a china-shop."

"I like it. I really like it," Manning said. "By the way, what's yours?"

"Eight-ball, Sir," Stuart replied.

Manning cocked his head, raising his left eyebrow, "Why Eight-ball?"

He cleared his throat, sat down opposite to the Major and began.

"Well, a few years ago, we accepted a fresh recruit that boasted he was a crack shot and that he wanted the Primary Sniper Position. A position I held at the time. We all knew he was good but, he thought that because he was good, that we should just hand it to him. He didn't realize that he still had to earn the position."

Stuart stopped briefly, staring at the wall, remembering.

"After a couple of weeks of listening to this guy shoot his mouth off, I had had enough. I told him one night in the bar, in front of everyone, to put up or shut up. I told him to pick the range, I'd pick the target and to make it fair, the section that was present, would pick the rifle caliber."

Manning began to realize that this soldier was a lot like his younger self. He could see himself doing exactly the same thing. He wished he could allow himself the luxury of getting to know those under his command on a more, personal level. To find out what makes them 'tick'.

"What was the range?" Manning asked.

Stuart, staring down at his feet, chuckled before looking up at Manning.

"3 'klicks'."

Manning whistled, "And the target?"

"He asked the same question and at first I had no idea until I looked around the bar. I got up from my barstool, walked over to the pool table and picked up an eight-ball." Stuart had a smirk on his face.

"I take it, you nailed it?"

"Dead center, Sir."

"Him?" Manning inquired.

Now a broad smile formed on Stuart's face, "Not even close."

Manning knew that there were only a handful of people around the world who were excellent snipers. He knew of only one man who could take out a target at three thousand meters with a single shot from a .50 caliber Browning machine gun and that guy used to practice day and night to make those kinds of shots.

"Well," Manning said as he looked at his watch, "I need to get to my rack and catch some 'Z's.'"

"Yes Sir. Sorry Sir." Stuart said as he began to leave his CO's office.

Lieutenant!" Manning called after Stuart. Stuart poked his head around the corner of the office door.

Yes, Sir,"

"What was the caliber?" Manning asked.

".308-Super with a slight cross-wind, Sir," he replied, smiling.

Manning let out another whistle. "Very good. Dismissed."

A half-hour after Commander Graham's accident, Marcus arrived at the conference room where the assigned crew of the Destiny were waiting. He went to the head of the table and dropped all the documents Graham had been carrying, not to mention all the materials that he himself had been bringing. The crew had been talking amongst themselves. Some in hushed voices, some loudly. Marcus, still standing, waited until they all quieted down before beginning.

"I assume you've all heard, by now," he paused. "Commander Graham was involved in that accident on level ten."

Marcus looked around the room. Some were seated in chairs; some were leaning against the walls with arms crossed. He continued.

"He'll be okay, but he won't be doing any flying for at least a week and this flight *cannot* be aborted," he announced.

Most of the crew seemed generally relieved that the Destiny would fly. Now that they had digested that piece of good news, he had to give them the bad news.

"As for the reason for the early evac. of this station; the Canadian Federal Armed Forces is sending the Canadian Anti-terrorist Team with supporting personnel to secure this station and arrest me as a possible threat under the North American Continental Security Agreement."

The crew exploded in shouts of disagreement and disbelief. Marcus was taken aback by how upset they seemed by this new information. It was evident, to Marcus, that they still firmly believed in 'The Dream". Everyone knew how important this technology was and how envied they would be if the general population knew of its existence. World governments would vie for its possession. Negotiate for it, steal it, kill, or go to war if they had to. Everything that they were all afraid of, concerning this project was beginning to come true. Power brokers of the world would either take it or suppress it.

Marcus held both hands up to calm the crew down.

"All right, *all right,*" he said softly. "People, please…" The crew continued their tirade of objections and questions.

Doc entered the briefing room, eyes wide at the crew's reaction. Marcus and Doc could only smirk at each other. Still holding both hands up in the air, without saying another word, the crew finally quieted down.

Mackenzie Marsh, pilot, stepped away from the wall so he had direct eye contact with Marcus. He was a tall, thin man who was serious, calm and analytical. He had short blonde, curly hair with an almost invisible moustache. He was older than Marcus by about ten years and was often seen wearing dark sunglasses and an old beat-up, straw cowboy hat. The former Australian test pilot could fly just about anything and had the reputation that if you gave him a brick, he'd make it fly, too.

"Marc, this mission can't fly without the Commander. And I am not qualified to pilot the Destiny alone. I still need someone in the left seat."

Marcus sat down and cleared his throat.

"As you all know, I am also qualified for that position. I've logged in just as much simulator time as Rick. I know more about the Destiny and her systems than everyone in this room".

Murmurs of agreement started to rise in the room.

"I've always been listed as 'relief' on the flight-deck; therefore, I will command this flight. Now, what I'd like to know is, does anyone have any concerns about that or any questions?"

Everybody looked around the room at each other.

"Anything? Anybody?" Marcus asked.

Marsh added, "We will still need this station to receive telemetry and provide support for a prolonged mission."

Marcus sat straight up in his chair.

"We won't be going on the original mission as planned," Marcus announced, which now got the attention of everybody in the room. "Instead we will perform a high orbit insertion to avoid detection by ground based stations and orbital satellites, until the station is rebuilt in the South Pacific. To avoid having to reprogram the flight and nav. computers, those systems will be set to manual via computer assist."

"How long will we be in orbit, Marc?" a voice asked from the rear of the room. Marcus recognized the voice of Bruno Kravakis, Destiny's Engineer. He was one of four people who designed the propulsion system and then the superstructure. If he wasn't working for Marcus, he would have become a successful naval engineer and architect. He was 15 years older than Marcus and the two first met at the university Marcus had attended. They started out student and mentor and left good friends. He had recognized him as a 'hands on' guy who liked hard work and getting right into getting his hands dirty. Once he figured out a type of technology, he could come up with at least five practical uses for it. Almost nothing escaped his technical expertise.

"We'll be in orbit for at least a week. Maybe as long as three weeks," Marcus replied.

"What about the 'Fence', Marcus?" Mac Marsh asked.

Everyone in the room knew about the 'Fence'. It was an electronic detection grid, part of the Satellite Surveillance Network, linked between satellites in orbit around the Earth, which replaced the older, ground-based system. Launched into orbit by the United States Air Force under a 'Black Operations Budget', it was to remain a classified, top secret project under the North American Air and Space Defense Command. In fact, after the demise of the former Soviet Union, NORAD continued to have it operate in secret.

'The Fence' was accidentally discovered when one of the first probes Marcus sent into orbit to study electromagnetic fields between the Earth and the Moon and picked up an EM anomaly in geo-synchronous orbit. Further study by the probe revealed that the anomaly was not naturally occurring, but man-made. It was eventually determined that the purpose of the 'Fence' was to detect, track and if possible identify whatever it was that crossed the electronic line. Coming or going. After that, in order to avoid detection, all probes were set to scan for the 'Fence's' EM signal when passing through it and send out a signal that matched its frequency. Simple electronic counter-measures.

"We will be in a high orbit but, not that high," Marcus replied. "I think ten thousand kilometers will be sufficient to avoid detection from the surface."

He paused for a second.

"Another item I need to inform all of you about…on this mission…we will not need the full crew compliment we originally planned for."

Marcus paused for a reaction. There was none. He continued.

"Mission requirements call for a crew of six. We only have enough mission resources for a short duration flight. As for the rest of you, I need you to help coordinate reconstruction of the station."

He paused again.

"Now, I know you were all looking forward to going into space at the same time and you will. I promise you. This crisis has postponed that. Besides, I think you'll like the climate better in the south Pacific."

"Who's going up, Sir?" a voice asked from the back of the room.

It was Joni Edwards, the computer and operations engineer for the station and specifically, the Destiny. She was hired by Samuel Gowan as a Computer Design Engineer to work for the computer subsidiary of the Gowan corporate empire. She designed and perfected the Diverse Intuitive Logic Computer System for the company which was a project originally started by Samuel Gowan and shelved ten years before. Her innovations were so complex, yet, simple, it was evident that this young, long-haired brunette was clearly thinking outside the box. It would've made Bill Gates look like he was playing with Basic programming, if it would have been made available to the public. To show his appreciation, Samuel reassigned her to Marcus' R&D Facility.

She was originally apprehensive about the transfer but, when she reported for work and Marcus showed her around to the different labs, she was as giddy as a child in a candy store. Marcus knew that she would be a valued asset to 'The Dream'. He gave her Level One security access and the run of the place, even Marcus' office. Marcus told her that if her computer software/hardware system was mass-produced and offered on the open market, it would take the rest of the world 30 years to catch up. Factor in a secret, unknown technology, that number goes up another 200-300 years, just for starters.

"You, me, Marsh, Kane, Kravakis and Kyras", he replied. He paused for a moment. In the silence, he could hear the evac. crews moving equipment in the corridors.

"Now, the military is apparently going to arrive…" Marcus checked his watch, "in about fifteen hours. I want this station evacuated and all cargo planes out into international waters in twelve. Any equipment that we can't take with us will have to be destroyed when the self-destruct devices are activated. However, make it a priority. We all know what would happen if any of this technology were to fall into the wrong hands."

Silence, hovered the room as heads nodded en masse. Everyone understood, implicitly. When the molecular degradation devices were activated, all matter within the perimeter of the station would dematerialize in a cascade effect starting at the center, spreading outward. The devices, which would disassemble anything within the perimeter, molecule by molecule, was not an explosive and would not impact the environment with hazardous chemical residues. Marcus designed it specifically to work in that fashion. No devastating explosion. No concussive shockwave. Matter just faded out of existence as if it wasn't really there in the first place.

"If there aren't any questions or issues, there is a duty roster out on the corridor wall. Your assignments are noted."

He paused as he scanned the faces in the room.

"Work safe and dismissed," Marcus concluded the briefing.

Now motivated by a sense of urgency, the crew of the spaceship Destiny filed out of the conference room. Mac Marsh and Doc remained behind.

"How accurate was that information from our source at DFD?" Marsh asked.

"David Chen's a good man. Very reliable," Marcus began as he stood up from his chair. "He's been in deep cover for a long time. I sent word to him that he is to, 'vacate' his current employment."

Marcus paused and turned to face Marsh.

"You know, he asked for the DFD assignment. Fresh out of high school. Made quite a name for himself, too."

"You kept his identity a secret," Marsh began. "Why reveal it now?"

"Mainly because he's completed his assignment," Marcus stopped, rubbing his chin. "It's crucial that all my sources and informants remain secret until their assignments are complete."

Doc, who had been leaning against the wall added, "It's as much for your protection as theirs."

"Anyway," Marcus continued, "David was unable to give us a precise timetable as to their ETA. He was, however, able to give us a window I can work with. I have two choppers flying patrol eight hundred kilometers South and South-east of here. Those are the two newly designed, hypersonic ones that you were itching to fly, so we'll get fair warning when they come"

"What are their orders once the station is evacuated?" Marsh asked.

"Well," Doc began. "After they are given the word that the station is clear or if they detect the military, they are to relay any info and are ordered to fly non-stop, for any of the six cargo ships heading South in international waters. It'll be a fast but, long flight; they'll be tired. We told them to head for the closest ship but since the choppers don't have to be refueled, we've left that to 'pilot's discretion'."

Marsh looked down at the hard copy printouts in his hand. "Well, I have a few things to do and then, I suppose I better catch a few Z's. Probably the only chance we'll get for a while."

"Good idea, Mac," Marcus announced. "Order the crew to bed. At least six hours worth."

"Same goes for you, Marcus," Doc said. "Don't look at me like that. The last thing we need is the Flight Commander falling asleep as he reaches orbit."

"Ok, ok, Doc." Marcus conceded before looking to Marsh "Just make sure the crew is on the flight deck at 0600 hours."

Marsh waved back acknowledgement as he left the room.

CHAPTER TWO

WIND CHIMES

The flight deck of the Destiny, when empty and with systems powered down, was a place of choice and solitude for Marcus Gowan. Being there helped him to think. It inspired him. He was comfortable there. He, at times, sought solitude there when he felt stressed or needed to re-affirm his vision of the future as he could see it. This was a place he envisioned as the beginning of the realization of that vision.

The flight deck was wide and spacious. It was designed as a two-tiered level flight deck. On the top level, when entering, was the Operations/Science workstation. To the left, against the bulkhead, was the Engineering workstation. To the right of that, and down three steps, was the lower flight deck and the Pilot's and Commander's stations. Every chair and workstation, ergonomically designed. Every line flowed together. Each of the workstations faced forward, with the exception of the side/rear facing Engineering workstation, and were connected to the bulkhead walls on each side of the flight deck. Equipment and components designed as modules so that as the technology changed and improved, it was as simple as pulling out the old and plugging in the new.

Through the expansive, oversized windscreen, he watched the loading teams scurry around the brightly lit, launch bay. The power supplied to it made the windscreen transparent and when switched off, it looked no different than any other part of the bulkhead wall. Made from a special blend of ceramics, titanium and other non-earth materials, it was designed as part of the superstructure of the hull. It was the strongest, densest impact-resistant material Marcus' R&D team had yet designed at the Anti-Grav Facility. The process by which it was made was called Molecular Fusion-forming. It involved melting the desired ingredients to a liquid state in a zero gravity chamber, allowing them to interact as one substance and then form the desired shape. So, if one wanted something that resembled a rock, all one had to do is turn on a power switch and it would become transparent.

The team leader, at the time, called it 'Duraglass'. Even though they sought no compensation for their newly created product, Marcus rewarded them anyway with company recognition and by monetary means. They reciprocated by presenting Marcus with a desk made of Duraglass. The desk was a marvel of modern, if not, futuristic design.

"Computer", Marcus called out, as he descended the three steps to the lower flight deck, "Lights on. Intensity at fifty percent".

The computer responded immediately and although he had asked for reduced lighting, the suddenness by which they came on still caught him by surprise. Wincing, Marcus realized he should have asked for a gradual lighting increase, instead.

"Computer, initiate power to the flight deck and initialize all work stations onboard."

Reaction by the computer was again immediate. All instruments of the workstations lit up and one could detect a low hum as power brought them to life.

"Now, computer. Recognize Gowan, Marcus. Acting Flight Commander of the prototype vessel, Destiny. Verbal confirmation, required."

The male voice of the computer responded, "Computer recognizes Marcus Gowan. Acting Fight Commander of the prototype vessel, Destiny," it paused. "Please state security level and security password."

Marcus could not get tired of that voice. The voice of his father. He missed hearing it even though; he had asked his father to carry a digital voice recorder for over two years so that every word, tone and inflection could be downloaded as part of the interactive processing software of their computer systems. It wasn't until after his father had died that he realized that he had a slight British/Scottish accent. After a bit of tweaking, he made the voice in the recordings sound younger before it was downloaded.

"Commander Marcus Gowan. Security level, alpha. Password, alpha two. Omega," he responded.

"Thank-you, Commander," the computer said. "Access and command and control, granted."

"You're welcome, Dad," Marcus replied under his breathe.

Marcus initiated maintenance diagnostics of each of the workstations beginning with the flight deck and working his way towards the rear of the Destiny. He could have done it remotely from the flight deck but, he felt better going from station to station, ensuring with his own eyes that everything was in order. It was not that he didn't trust the computer to do the work; he just preferred the human touch. He had complete confidence in this technology. It was so reliable and dependable that there were very few things that could compromise or affect it adversely. Since he had taken steps to prevent those issues, it was no longer a consideration.

The Destiny's systems were designed in such a way that power and/or information could be rerouted from one system to another. Everything had built-in redundancies. Even the back-ups had back-ups. All workstation control displays were touch sensitive switches and had keyboard and mouse built-in as part of the workstation; however, they also had voice recognition and interaction capabilities. After an hour and a half, he had completed the systems diagnostics and returned to the flight deck to find Joni Edwards and Mac Marsh at their stations, each with a travel mug of coffee in their hands, busy going over the preflight checklists.

"Good morning," Marcus offered.

They each replied greetings and smiles and went back to their duties. Watching them for a moment, working at their terminals, listening to the beeps and tones, to Marcus was like listening to music.

Turning half out of his seat, Marsh handed Marcus a quantum hyperlink communication headset. It was another one of Marcus' ingenious gadgets. The product of molecular-miniaturization, it packed enough communication components that two people could hold a conversation as far away as the moon with signals and frequencies yet to be discovered. And it would be a very long time before they would be.

"Before I forget, Doc asked me to give this to you. He's topside getting the last cargo plane loaded and ready for take-off."

"Thanks, Mac," he put on and adjusted the headset. "How's the situation, here?"

Joni stopped what she was doing and spun around in her high backed, acceleration seat and handed an electronic clipboard to Marcus.

"Well, we are almost done the preflight checklists. Bruno and Joe are in Engineering initiating the Cryogenic condensers and should have the reactor-quad primed and powered up in about ten minutes. Ron is loading some last minute provisions that I figured we might need in case this takes longer than anticipated. I've also had him running around double-checking some of the systems I have been monitoring."

Marcus eyed each of the items on the list of 'To Do's' on the clipboard. It was in abbreviated form and he couldn't make head or tails of it, although he tried.

"What are you trying to do to me? I hate headaches this early in the morning," he said with a smirk on his face. "After all this time, I still can't read you shorthand."

With a chuckle, looking over at Marsh, she said, "I love being a smarty-pants."

Marsh smirking, "Leave him alone, will ya. We gotta' lotta' work to do."

"Thanks," Marcus said as he readjusted the headset. "At least, you're on my side."

Marsh tried to hold back a chuckle and blurted out, "I have to. You're the boss."

"Ok, Ok. I think that's enough boss-bashing for today," Marcus feigned resignation. "What are we looking at for a launch window?"

Marsh and Joni made eye contact, both independently calculating times of procedures.

"Well, we're holding at zero, now. What do you think, Joni? About 30/40 minutes?"

"That sounds about right." She agreed.

Still readjusting his 'Hyperlink' headset, "I'm going topside for a couple of minutes to see the last plane off and then I'll be back for the launch preflight."

Marsh looked up from display panel, "Ok but, don't take too long. I'll be ready in 15 minutes. Any sooner, I'll recall you on the 'Hyperlink'."

Doc Thorpe was busy shoveling snow into the hopper with the group of men he had assembled. The special equipment was mounted on the back of low capacity dump truck. It was fitted with a magazine of five fiberglass moulds. The raw snow went into a hopper, feeding the molds, which was compressed, color added with a series of dyes placed in strategic locations throughout the mould. Then a light spray of water was added, freezing immediately, after the mould was removed from the human figure to keep it from blowing away in the Arctic winds.

Doc had the moulds designed to look like soldiers, holding rifles in various poses, all facing south towards the small White Alice airstrip. The Canadian military C-280 'SuperHecules' cargo planes would land, offload its troops and equipment, assess the area and notice immediately, Doc Thorpe's 'Snowman Army'. Working away, they all joked and laughed at how they'd like to stay, just to see the reaction of fully armed troops in a shoot-out with twenty snowmen.

Marcus, exiting the emergency stairwell hatchway had to let his eyes adjust to the reduced daylight of the Arctic morning. The Sun, at its apogee, to the south below the horizon, gave the sky an eerie, twilight glow. He could make out activity between him and airfield. He walked the half kilometer to satisfy his curiosity.

The heavy-lift cargo plane was idling on the runway with its rear cargo door open and down. Even though Marcus could see the blades of the ducted fans turning, reflected by the landing lights, he still couldn't hear its powerful, pulse charged engines. The result of one of Marcus' drive to rid the world of the fossil-fueled engines.

The Pulse-Charging Generator was one of those breakthroughs that was almost overlooked had it not been noticed by one of the junior scientists apprenticing under Marcus' team of R&D scientists. He had made an observation during a test, logged it down accompanied with a question, although it eluded him after all this time. One of the senior scientists, going over the logs and test results during a coffee break, was impressed with the logic and obviousness of the question. An investigation to answer that question was launched immediately. The end result; the creation of the more powerful, Pulse Generator. Any station equipment using fossil fuels to operate, was quickly refitted.

Marcus found Doc, done with his project and ready to load the small dump truck aboard the cargo plane. Doc, seeing Marcus' approach, waved a greeting.

"Doc. What are 'ya doin'?" Marcus said in jest, arms out to his side, palms up. "You guys are supposed to be long gone, by now."

With the work crew gathering around, doc replied with a devilish grin, "We're on the way. We're just shuttin' her down, now."

He launched the shovel into the air by its handle where the wind caught it, creating 'hang time' that almost seemed like slow motion, then dropping into and banging against the walls of the back of the mini-dump truck.

"You guys get going. I'm right behind ya'," he ordered to the work crew. He turned to Marcus and then half-turned back to his departing crew. "Just tell the pilot not to leave without me."

They all waved back acknowledgement and headed towards the runway.

"Well. What do you think?" Doc asked Marcus.

"You know that won't slow them down."

"I know," Doc conceded. "At the least, it'll make them think cautiously every step of the way. And that will buy you some time."

They both looked around in silence at their frozen surroundings before Doc continued.

"Marcus, I am not comfortable leaving you and the Destiny unprotected. There is nobody here to slow or distract the military before you get a chance to launch her. From the perspective of the airstrip, it'll look like an armed force is waiting for them." He gave Marcus a grin, "I wouldn't be a good Assistant-Director if I didn't think of these things."

Marcus offered his hand to shake Doc's.

"You're right, of course," Marcus said. "And thank-you, my friend."

"Anytime, Marcus," Doc replied as he turned to head towards the cargo-plane. "Well. I guess I better get a move on. The pilot isn't going to wait forever. I'll see you in Pacifica in a week."

Marcus turned and began trudging up the slope to the emergency stairwell, stopped abruptly and turned.

"Hey," he called out after Doc. "You gave the island a name?"

Doc, walking backwards, chuckled and hollered back, "It was the least I could do."

"Pinto. This is Mustang. Pinto...this is Mustang. You got 'yer ears on'? Comeback."

There was static on the UHF radio channel as helicopter pilot Colin Gallant listened for a response. He didn't like using radio communication when they could've been using the newer, Quantum Hyperlink system. There wasn't enough time to grab even one headset once the evac signal had sounded.

He looked back down at the scanner display screen to reconfirm what his JAFO had been looking out for. JAFO is to a helicopter pilot what a RIO (Radar Intercept Officer) is to a naval fighter pilot. Only the acronym stood for 'Just Another Fucking Observer'. His JAFO, twenty year-old Timothy 'Timbo' Matthews, was a good kid. He trusted the new technology, his pilot and loved to fly in helicopters.

Suddenly, the static was gone on the UHF channel and Gallant knew he had been heard.

"Mustang, this is Pinto. Go ahead," was the response from the second helicopter, piloted by his friend, Olivia 'Ollie' Greene, two hundred miles west.

"Pinto. Mustang. I am reading three red lights," he said as he looked west through the cabin window, trying and failing to magically see the other helicopter. "Repeat, I am reading three red lights. Please confirm."

"Mustang. Pinto. Standby," was the response and then static again. Gallant knew that 'Ollie' would be checking with her JAFO to confirm the flight or declaring it as bogus. If it was bogus, they would continue to scan the horizon for a flight of C-280 SuperHercs, headed in their direction. If it were confirmed, they would send word through UHF radio to White Alice and then head for any of the cargo ships heading south off the continent of North America. Colin didn't have to listen to the static for long.

"Mustang. Pinto. Roger, dodger, that. I say again, we confirm your three red lights," followed by a short pause. "What's the word, Mustang?"

Gallant began flying his ship in a west, southwesterly direction and began increasing power to the rotors. Both helicopters would be increasing speed to supersonic and be over the Pacific in two hours.

"Pinto. Mustang. The word is…" he paused trying to recall what the password was. "The word is 'D-Day'. Repeat. The word is 'D-Day'. Please acknowledge."

"That's a big ten-four, good buddy. I'm clear."

Gallant could hear the inflection of relief in Ollie's voice, now that the waiting, scanning and flying in an orbital pattern was over. Now she too, would be increasing speed to the Pacific Ocean.

As per prearranged protocols, Timbo changed UHF frequencies and began informing the Destiny with a cryptic, situation report. Mac Marsh was supposed to be monitoring the radio on the flight deck, getting ready to launch.

"Roughrider. This is Mustang. Roughrider, this is Mustang," Timbo began calling. "Stampede. I repeat. Stampede. ETA is…"

Captain Larry White was, for the most part, a well trained officer. He began his career in the United States Air force during college under the ROTC program. It was a great opportunity that paid his tuition. Upon graduating, he enlisted directly into the USAF for the required tour of duty. Two years later, he found himself at the North American Aerospace Defense Command in Colorado Springs, Colorado. He became the finest radio scientist NORAD had ever acquired. When his mandatory tour was due to expire after six years, he re-enlisted. Not only because he received commendations and a promotion but, because he was a proud American. He also relished knowing things that the general population of the world did not. Even if it meant he couldn't discuss it with anyone off-base. He was a member of the strongest; best equipped military force in the richest country in the free world.

Today, he was assigned to monitor certain, but specific ranges in UHF channels originating in Canada's high north. There was the normal, usual chatter from the certified, Canadian government licensed, radios and even those were minimal. He rarely had questions about his orders but, this one caught him by surprise. For well over a hundred years, Canada had been an ally. It was a mutual thing. Canada and the United States of America had a common interest in continental security. Especially, after 9/11/2001. He also knew that if it weren't for the Canadian uranium deposits, the Manhattan Project of WWII would have taken longer, which would have hindered the development of the first two atomic bombs dropped on Japan in WWII's Pacific Theater. It would have been more drawn out, costing more American lives. The Canadian military even had personnel serving at NORAD under joint agreement between the two governments.

Suddenly, his computer alerted him to activity on a frequency in the range he set for scanning. Checking to make sure the computer was recording, he called over the 'Duty Officer', Federal Dominion of Canada Air Force Colonel Christopher Bohaychuk. As Col. Bohaychuk joined him at his station, the signal stopped abruptly and continued on another frequency. White turned up the volume so that both professional soldiers could listen in.

"thirty to forty minutes. Comeback." There was slight static as both men leaned closer to the speakers.

And then.

"Mustang. This is Roughrider. Report survey. Comeback." Silence went on a little longer this time before there was a response. The two officers listened intently and could hear a faint, powered hum in the background. Somebody was holding the mic. open before there was an answer.

"Roughrider. Mustang. Three plumbs are indicated five degrees above bubble and alignment is holding true. Please confirm 'Paragraph Eleven'." Mustang clicked off.

"Mustang. Roughrider. Paragraph Eleven, confirmed."

"Roughrider. Mustang. Acknowledged."

Now Capt. White was really confused. Not only were the subjects using Citizen Band Radio lingo but, surveyor's or construction terms as well.

"What the hell was that?" White asked, rhetorically.

"I think," Bohaychuk postulated, "what we just heard was a pre-arrainged coded signal." He straightened up and crossed his arms over his chest. "That sounds like the order that Rear-Admiral Ludwig von Reuters gave, on June, 1919 to the interned German Navy at Scapa Flow. It was an order to scuttle the entire German Fleet."

White looked away from his screen and up at his Duty officer. He treated him like any other officer in charge.

"Sir. Do you know what this is all about?" he asked in a hushed voice.

Bohaychuk quickly glared down at the captain.

"You know better than to ask me that." He softened his facial features. "It's 'Need to Know'. I don't even know. I just report your findings to our superiors," he added.

"Yes, sir. Sorry, sir," he paused. "Shall I put myself on report, sir?"

Bohaychuk looked around to see that no one else was paying attention to them, leaned down closer to the Captain and said, "Tell you what. I'll cut you some slack. However, you do that again on my watch, I will have no other choice. Understood?"

White swallowed hard, nodded and said, "Thank-you, sir."

Turning back to the computer and the task at hand, Bohaychuk asked, "Are you recording this?"

"All of it, sir," White confirmed a second time as he too, turned back to the computer. "What are my orders after the assignment is complete?"

"Deposit the recordings in a sealed envelope and have dispatch, courier it to Washington. Make sure it is addressed to the 'Chief of Staff' and marked 'Eyes only'."

Bohaychuk began to walk away when he stopped mid-stride and turned. White anticipated what he was going to say next.

"Yes, sir. I know. Another officer is to witness the deposit and sealing of the envelope."

Col. Bohaychuk smiled and gave White a 'Thumbs up' gesture, turned and continued on his way.

Marcus had noticed the wind beginning to pick up and send wisps of snow into the air. Once he had reached the entrance of the stairwell that led down to the launch bay floor, he decided to steal one last look at his arctic surroundings.

White Alice was on a plateau between a south facing, U-shaped ridgeline. At the south end, the plateau, then gradually sloped down towards the Arctic Ocean where it flattened out where the airstrip, laid out east to west, was located. He watched as the last cargo plane silently sped down the runway and launched itself into the air. As it gained altitude, the pilot performed a high-speed, low-altitude banking maneuver, heading west. Marcus figured the pilot was trying to use the open spaces between the various islands as cover. That way, they would minimize the chances of being spotted, visually and electronically. Once they were far enough away, the pilot would 'pop-up' to a higher altitude, increase speed and head southwest over the Pacific.

"Marcus," Mac Mackenzie called on the headset. "You got your ears on, mate?"

Marcus adjusted the boom-mic on his headset, "Marcus here. I didn't forget, Mac." He began reaching for the door of the stairwell. "I'm on my way down, now."

"It's not about the preflight, Marcus," Mac paused. "Just got word from Mustang and Pinto. The party has begun."

Grabbing the doorknob and quickly swinging it open, Marcus raced down the stairs taking two steps at a time.

"ETA?" he asked as he hit the first landing, swung around and off to the second flight of stairs in one fluid motion.

"Mustang reported thirty to forty minutes but, they have the wind at their backs. They'll be here sooner than that."

Second landing.

"How far did you get with the pre-flight?" Marcus was going faster.

Third landing.

"About half-way," he paused. "Why?"

Fourth landing.

"Begin Emergency Launch Procedures. Everything else ready?" he asked, panting.

"No." Mac replied. "It will therefore be, anyway."

Marcus hit the bottom of the stairwell. He was going so fast that he banged into the door trying to stop, open and run through the doorway, all at once. He rubbed his shoulder and, slowly and calmly, opened the door. He then ran through the doorway and across the launch bay, his footfalls echoing against the walls.

Running across the expansive bay, he eyed the design of their cooperative creation. The highly reflective surface of the Duralloy skin was like looking at a mirror. The quick look was all he could afford as he ran up the retractable stairs, two at a time, to the main hatch.

"Computer! Close and secure main hatch. Retract stairs." Marcus said as he took a moment to catch his breathe, right arm outstretched against the bulkhead.

The stairs began retracting and the main hatch sealed immediately. The status panel lit up indicating it was secure and locked. In a quick walk, he began heading toward the flight deck and bumped into Ron Kane coming around a corner in the corridor. Tools were sent flying to the deck in three different directions and both men knelt down to retrieve them. Kane was a sandy-haired man, the same age as Marcus and was a firm believer in 'The Dream', as he liked to refer to it. Marcus helped load up the tools cradled in his arms and up from the deck.

"Where's the fire, Ron?"

"Brian and Joe asked me to retrieve these tools from the Tool crib," Kane explained.

"Is there a problem?" Marcus asked.

For a brief second, a puzzled look washed over Kane's face. "Oh, no. Not at all," he blurted out. "It's just in case there is a problem."

"Ok, Paul. I won't keep you. See you later," Marcus said as continued towards the flight deck.

Entering the flight deck, Marcus found Mac and Joni huddled over Joni's operations workstation. Mac was asking Joni to try this or that. Joni would try it to no apparent effect.

"Problem?" Marcus asked.

Joni sighed as she swiveled her chair to face Marcus. "We were checking the uplink with the launch-bay doors when we lost it."

"Which means there is no power to open them," Mac announced.

Marcus' mind raced to figure out what the problem might be. If they weren't pressed for time and be in the situation they were in, he had no doubt they could find a solution. He felt an overpowering need to launch, now.

"Well, one of us will have to check the control room," he offered.

Mac, knowing his boss was volunteering, put his hands on his hips, "Oh no, you won't. I'm going with you."

"What about the pre-flight?" Marcus asked.

"ELP will only take a minute. I just don't like the idea of you running around out there alone in the off chance the army comes busting in."

Marcus was weighing what Mac had said and came to the realization that he was right. Joni looked up at the two men from her chair. Marcus made eye contact with her and she gave him a single nod.

"Ok, let's go," Marcus relented. "Joni, hold down the fort. We'll be back in a flash."

She watched as the two men let through the flight deck hatchway.

"You better, because I can't fly this thing outta' here."

As soon as Marcus' and Mac's feet met the frosted floor of the launch bay, they sprinted to the corridor that led to the stairwell up two floors to the control room. Once they entered the room, it was evident why the controls and the launch doors weren't responding. Since the prefabricated wall panels and structural supports had been removed, the permafrost began to thaw from the relatively warmer air inside the station. There was nothing to prevent the melting walls from collapsing in on the room. Marcus knew this could happen but had thought they would be far and away, long before it would happen. Especially since the Molecular Degradation Charges would take care of the station as a whole. What they saw was that an entire wall and a half, plus part of the ceiling had collapsed on all the equipment meant to operate the launch-bay doors.

"Oh, shit," Mac said in awe of the destruction.

"Mac," Marcus began to say. "I have a feeling that if this is starting to happen in a small room like this......" pointing his thumb towards the room.

"Then sure as Hell, the rest of the station is becoming unstable, too," Mac finished.

Marcus continued, "If that happens, we're doomed."

"Well, as long as the walls in the launch-bay don't collapse, we can still hand-crank them open," Mac suggested.

Marcus began sprinting back to the launch-bay.

"Let's do it to it."

His men were down and out and three of the C-280's were back in the air. Two of the 'Wolverine' MK.IX LAV's were heading to opposite ends of the runway in support of 1st and 4th Sections. As Manning was surveying the terrain directly ahead of his position, he didn't have to watch as the fourth C-280 came in low over the runway to drop the AREA command vehicle out the rear of the workhorse of the Canadian Federal Armed Forces. That didn't stop the four sections of troops from watching this precise maneuver.

The pilot brought the wheels of the double-wide cargo plane to within two feet of the tarmac when a drogue-chute appeared from the rear of its open cargo door. The chute was designed to fill with air, pulling the contents, usually a loaded pallet, out the rear of the aircraft and to slow the pallet down once it was on the ground. For those inside the AREA vehicle, it was always a wild and fun ride. As long as the 'package' didn't roll, which rarely happened on prepared, flat surfaces.

However, this runway had a slight film of ice from the blowing snow, which caused the AREA vehicle to slide further than expected. The ten tons of military armor came to a stop approximately two hundred feet past its intended stop. The crew immediately exited to undo the straps securing the eight-wheeled vehicle from its transport pallet. It took the AREA vehicle two minutes to reach Manning's position. He would use the AREA vehicle as his command/Infantry Support vehicle with 2nd and 3rd Sections while the two LAVs would support 1st and 4th Sections respectively and make their approach/assault east and west of the mining facility.

As soon as the AREA vehicle came to a stop, Manning was on his feet, crouching low, heading to the rear-hatch of the long but, squat vehicle. Inside, the radio-surveillance operator turned from his console.

"Sir. 4th Section reports 'Diamondback.'"

Manning knew then that 4th. Section was in position and ready to proceed. Soon, 1st. Section would send their signal.

"Very well," Manning said as he unfolded the jump seat next to the operator. "Carry on."

The operator turned back to his console and was busy flipping switches when Manning heard an electric motor activate. This was the surveillance part of the vehicle. On the top of steel, retractable mast was a pod full of cameras and listening equipment. Then the motor stopped and the operator turned to the Major.

"Sir, with the winds outside, I can only extend the mast to five meters but, we have a fair view of the station and surrounding area."

After examining the monitor Manning replied, "It'll have to do."

He could see 4th Section a kilometer away on the monitor as if he were standing ten feet away, taking position amongst some snow covered, rocky outcroppings and tailings from underground mining. If he were to walk out and try to spot them by eyes alone, he would not be able to spot them moving about in their winter camouflage.

"OK. Let's see the station," Manning ordered.

The operator panned back and zoomed the camera in on the buildings of the station. Seeing no movement, he moved the camera to the next building. Then, the next. And the next. Still, no movement. The hairs on the back of Manning's neck began to rise. It's one thing to see an industrial operation in full production or even during a maintenance 'shutdown'; it was quite another thing to see such a large complex completely devoid of life.

"Lieutenant, zoom out, please."

As ordered, the image slowly began to zoom out. Watching intently, Manning studied the monitor. At the same time, they both spotted something halfway between them and the station.

"Now, zoom in on that ridge," he said, stabbing his finger at the monitor.

Along a snowdrift, Manning counted ten figures with what appeared to be rifles pointed in their general direction. They were all evenly spaced so that a lucky grenade couldn't catch them all. The fact that they held the high ground and Manning and his men had no cover to make their approach didn't help, either.

"Pan to the east."

The image moved east of the defender's position in which Manning and the operator spotted a second group of defenders on the higher slope forward of 4th Section's position, all with rifles. It didn't look like 4th Section had spotted the defenders through the blowing snow.

The hairs on Manning's neck were getting higher.

"Now pan over to the west," Manning ordered.

It took the operator about ten seconds to find what Manning was looking for. A third group of defenders, entrenched on higher ground, facing 1st Section. However, they had spotted the defenders and took cover behind some rather large, snow covered boulders.

The hairs on the back of his neck were now erect.

"Sir. 1st section sends 'Copperhead'," the lieutenant relayed. "Shall I send the 'Go' code?"

"No," Manning said right away. "Send the 'Standby' code. Let them know we have defenders." He began stroking his goatee. "I want time to come up with some options."

"All Sections, this is Razorback. Sanctuary. Monte Casino. Message repeats. Sanctuary and Monte Casino."

As soon as the message was acknowledged by all sections, Manning asked the Lieutenant to switch to infrared imaging. Both men leaned closer to the monitor. The defenders weren't giving off any heat signatures, even though it was -30 Celsius outside. Even with thermal-abatement clothing, their faces should light up like a Christmas tree. The lieutenant made some adjustments to the monitor and the camera and then looked over at the Major.

"It's not the equipment, Sir. With thermal-optics, we should be seeing them breathing."

Watching the monitor for half a second, Manning replied, "I've got a hunch. Radio 1st Section and hand me that radio."

By the time Manning had the handset; Lt. Robert Stuart was on the horn.

"Eight-ball. Can you still sink one from your angle? Over."

Manning was hoping Stuart remembered the conversation from the night before. Manning waited for what seemed an eternity when he finally heard the microphone click on.

"Pocket? Sir." Stuart asked.

"The closest," Manning smiled, although he didn't particularly care.

There was another long pause. Manning could see Stuart on the monitor looking at the ridgeline forward of his position. Peering over the large snow-covered rock he was using for cover, he analyzed the area for targets and hunkered back down behind the boulder. His radioman nearby, he reached for the handset.

"Can-do Sir," was the reply.

"Do it," Manning ordered.

Again, Manning and the operator watched the monitor as Stuart laid on his stomach and crawled along the base of the rock with his rifle cradled in his arms. As he began sighting in his target, the operator panned the camera back to the defender's ridgeline. Stuart's closest target was now in the center of the monitor and both men watched and waited.

They didn't have to wait for long as the head of the defender exploded in a shower of splinters and chunks. Yet the body still remained in an upright but, crouching position, still holding his rifle.

Manning swore under his breath.

"Lieutenant. Send the 'Go' code," he said, shaking his head. So much for the element of surprise, he thought to himself. Not to mention they had already wasted enough bloody time, as it was. They knew the army was coming. They even had enough time to set up decoys. It was almost laughable.

"All Sections. This is Razorback. Snakebite. I say again. Snakebite."

Manning left the relative warmth of the TRIL, to join the men of 2nd and 3rd Sections. As he came around the rear of the vehicle, the sections were already up and heading towards the station. All had their rifles at the ready, locked and loaded.

"Stay alert, people," Manning hollered over the noise of the cold, arctic winds. "This is not a walk in the park!"

His men spread out even more. Manning's plan was to have 2nd and 3rd Sections make their approach from the south. Any civilians encountered would be taken into custody for interrogation and de-briefing, later. Meanwhile, 1st and 4th Sections would enter the compound, undetected from the east and west to outflank any armed defenders. If they encountered heavy resistance, the MK.IX LAV's would be brought up to the line for fire support with their 25 mm. turret-guns.

When he and his men reached the ridgeline, they all stopped to inspect the decoys. It was at this point that Manning realized they had all been duped by a bunch of snowmen. One of the Privates walked up to the snowmen and kicked it over.

"A fuckin' snowman," he said, disgusted.

Manning surveyed the station from the ridgeline. It sat on an expansive plateau walled on three sides of steep valley slopes. It reminded Manning of a caldera of an ancient volcano with a non-existent south rim. They had come about halfway and the station was so spread out that he doubted anyone could approach, undetected. At least, it looked like 4th Section still had the cover from snow removal operations.

"Hold up, people," Manning announced. "Change of plan."

Rifles ready, all knelt down. He went up to his radio operator and called all teams.

"All teams. Razorback. Plan B."

His contingency plan was to have 1st and 2nd Sections form up with him for the south approach, have 3rd Section double-time it back to link up with 4th Section for the eastern approach and have the two MK.IX LAVs hang back below the plateau ridgeline for artillery support or until they are called up for a more direct show of force.

It took about five minutes for the secondary plan to organize when Manning again gave the 'Go' code and they ascended the ridgeline to begin their approach of the station. No one noticed the large snow-covered, circular depression, directly in their path.

Marcus was winding the hand crank so furiously; his arms and wrists began to ache. His body wasn't used to working this hard, this fast. All that time in the gym didn't seem to help. Then he realized he was using a different set of muscles to accomplish this task. He looked up towards the retracting launch bay doors and realized that his half wasn't even 1/3rd of the way open and that the other half (Mac's half), hadn't budged. He began winding faster, then stopped, panting.

"Mac," he called into the mic of his headset. "What's wrong?"

"Damn crank is stuck," he grunted as he continued to work the mechanism.

Marcus' gaze went from the launch bay doors to the Destiny and back again. His mind was formulating a plan. The last thing he wanted to do was push the Destiny through the open gap. He knew that it couldn't damage the superstructure, if done gently but, forcefully. Only, if it were his last option.

"Mac," he said into the hyperlink as he calculated the angles of his plan. "I need your help with this one."

"On the way, boss."

Marcus could hear Mackenzie's footfalls from across the launch bay. He was running full out. By the time he arrived, Marcus was working the hand crank, once again. After about a minute, he stopped.

Puffing and panting, "Your turn."

The big Australian attacked the crank, feroucisly. Marcus watched in amazement as the older man worked the crank. Marcus half expected smoke to start venting from the gearbox of the mechanism. After about two minutes, the crank came to a hard stop and the sound of the stopping launch bay door hitting its rubber-stops filled the bay. Mac, rubbing his wrists from the jolt of the sudden stop of the crank, joined Marcus who was looking up at the remaining and fully closed launch door.

"What are we going to do about that one?" Mac asked.

Marcus readjusted the boom mic on his headset, "Hold on. Ron! Marcus here. I want you to roll out the MOMEE from its crib to the edge of the cargo ramp platform. I want you to fire up the generators and charge up the coils."

A look of realization accompanied with a smile of approval was on Mac's face. Marcus was going to have the remaining door cut away by using the one piece of equipment that was made for use off-world, the Manned Ore Mineral Excavator/Extractor(MOMEE). Although this was not an easy task, it would take some tweaking and adjustments of the laser lens-emitters and careful control of any high-energy plasma feedback in the charger coils, to fire a considerable distance through an oxygenated atmosphere to cut through solid matter. Designed to work efficiently in the vacuum of space, it was conceived to work in pulses instead of a steady beam. This way, vaporizing through millimeters or meters of rock at a time, could more easily control depth. Although the target matter wasn't really being vaporized, it physical properties were only being changed from a solid to a gaseous form, where it was instantly being siphoned, broken down at the molecular level, separated, refined and reconstituted and collected as individual minerals. The process was called 'Reformation'. Ron Kane was the Destiny's Technician/Mechanic Specialist and the one man who had more firing time on the MOMEE. He logged in most of the time it took to carve out the underground caverns and tunnels of the White Alice Station.

"Then what?" Ron replied.

"One of the launch doors failed to open and it won't budge with the hand cranks," Marcus shivered, noticing the cold arctic air infiltrating the bay. "I need you to cut through it so we can launch through the opening."

Marcus could already hear Kane through the Destiny's corridors, panting. "I'm on it."

Both men moved off to the side of the bay where they could watch the MOMEE at work. Soon the cargo hatch of the Destiny opened and Kane drove the MOMEE to the edge of the ramp platform.

Kane was watching his displays and calling out energy levels and ratios. He had driven the MOMEE to within a foot of the edge of the platform. Of course, the ramp had not been deployed. He rotated the double-armed drill mechanism into an upward firing position that to Marcus, seemed unnatural. It was originally meant to fire downward but,

Marcus had designed specifications so that it could rotate in 360 degrees, vertically and horizontally.

"Sir? I was going to use a 7/8's inch beam width but I think ½ inch should do it more efficiently," Kane announced as he looked over at Mac and Marcus through the duraglass of the MOMEE's cab.

"The charger-coils will need to hold the charge for as long as possible. Half an inch should be good. Make sure you pre-program your firing arc so that it is done in a single, continuous discharge. Agreed?" Marcus asked.

Kane gave the two men a 'thumbs-up' gesture, "Way ahead of you."

Kane then manually pointed the drill along the path it would take as the laser cut through the perimeter of the duralloy and concrete launch door. As he did so, he was also keeping an eye on a simulation program which kept track of the power usage in the charging-coils. If the energy levels dropped below a certain point, the chargers would cut out and the generators would kick-in to recharge and valuable time would be lost. He knew they all had to be out of there, yesterday.

After thirty seconds, Kane called out; "Program and firing arc is locked and confirmed."

"What's your power levels reading?" Mac asked.

Without taking his eyes of the displays, he called, "Charger-coils are at eighty-eight percent and the generators are at forty-three kilowatts." He looked over at Mac and Marcus, "Another twenty seconds."

Out of the corner of Marcus' eye, he could see Mac shiver in the ever-present cold and he, too, shivered. Mac looked down at his wristwatch which was also linked to the timer of the molecular degradation devices. He raised his arm to show Marcus the watch and tapped it twice.

"Ten minutes."

"I know," Marcus acknowledged. "I want to see this, first."

"Charger-coils are now at full capacity and the generators are holding at forty-five kilowatts," Kane announced. "If you would be so kind as to give the word, Sirs," he shrugged as he folded his arms and leaned into the back of his seat. "I wouldn't want to be accused of 'destruction of property'."

"Shut-up, Ron," Mac chuckled. "You're enjoying this."

"Actually, I am," he declared with a wide, goofy grin on his face.

Marcus, chuckling at the banter between the two, interjected. "Ron. Consider the 'word' given."

Kane hunched over the joystick and gave out a macabre chuckle like that of Dr. Frankenstein's assistant, Igor.

"Yeath, mathter."

All Kane had to do was pull the trigger on the joystick and the onboard computer would swing the arms attached to the laser drill in its pre-programmed firing arc, taking out the launch door along its perimeter.

"Watch your eyes, people," Kane warned. "Laser drills a firing."

Mac and Marcus put up their hands to shield their eyes from the intense laser light.

As if like lightening, the beam of the laser suddenly appeared. It wasn't like in the movies where lasers shot out like bullets from a gun. It was a single, thin focused beam of light that moved as the drill mechanism moved. And it cut through the second half of the launch door like a hot knife through butter. White, hot molten slag from the duralloy and concrete, fell to the floor.

Mac commented to Marcus, "All we need now, is the popcorn."

Major Manning peered through the opening in the ground. 2nd Section had reached the opening first and stopped in their tracks. Manning seeing this, wondered what the bloody, Hell they were doing. Then he noticed that they were bathed in light from below. They were sitting ducks if the defenders had a half-decent sniper. He and 1st Section finally reached the opening and without looking down, he snapped at his people.

"Cover!"

The soldiers responded immediately by either flattening out or kneeling down. That's when Manning first looked over the edge. His eyes just about bulged from their sockets. He saw a large deep cavern carved into the perma-frost. In the middle of it, sat what appeared to be a rather large craft. Only the design was unlike anything he had ever seen. From this height, it was not unlike an aerodynamic, rectangular box. It was sleek but, bulky looking. Manning was trying to figure out how something that massive got down there when a large door opened at the rear of the craft that they could all see from their position. A large, eight-wheeled industrial vehicle appeared and drove to the edge of the craft's rear platform. At the end of two, large manipulator arms at the forward end of the vehicle was a large cylindrical device with tubes, wires and hoses connected to it. The vehicle was not unlike an industrial front-end loader. Manning could see an operator at the controls, inside the cab.

The first signs of life since their deployment.

Then, the most peculiar thing Manning had ever seen, happened. A thin line of light appeared, emitted from the cylinder, shining skyward to Manning's right. The beam of light passed through the platform he and his two sections had taken cover on, sending vibrations throughout as it moved along the rear and to the left. Those who were kneeling flattened out immediately. Some of the troopers looked over at the Major to see his reaction. The look on Manning's face was as fearful as the look on theirs.

Then the platform moved. Not side to side, nor back and forth. It moved down. Manning realized too late that the platform was becoming a giant slide. He could hear and feel the concrete cracking and breaking up. Through his boots, he could feel the vibration of metal twisting and then snapping. As the right side of the platform fell to the cavern floor, soldiers, equipment and gear slid and/or tumbled. The fight for self-preservation became the paramount concern of every man and woman in the two sections.

They had about twenty feet left in their slide to the bottom when the rest of the platform gave way and fell to the cavern floor. By the time the left side of the platform hit the floor, Manning and his people slid another ten feet and they fell the remaining ten feet.

Manning, who landed square on his back, had the wind knocked out of him, as did much of the troops. He tried to get up and then his world went black.

Ron Kane was watching the operator's panel as the drill did its job. The one half of launch-bay door had successfully fallen way from the Destiny. When the operation was complete, he began shutdown procedures. He successfully powered down the pulse generators before they could recharge the charger-coils when he finally looked outside the cab to see the damage he had wrought. The launch bay floor was littered with bodies.

"Oh shit," he whispered.

He could see Mac and Marcus making their way towards the injured on the floor. Some were moving and some were not. Ron was so stunned, all he could do was just sit there and watch. Where did they all come from? There wasn't supposed to be people up there. There wasn't supposed to be anyone near the station, at all. He was watching Marcus checking the injured and as he did so, what appeared t be unconscious soldier, began coming to. A feeling of foreboding began to enter his mind as those who remained unconscious, just laid there.

Marcus suddenly stood up erect and looked over at Kane. Both men made eye contact. To Kane, it felt like Marcus could see into the very depths of his soul. Marcus' facial features had the look of compassion.

"Its not your fault, Ron," Marcus said softly into the headset. "No one could have foreseen this."

"I....I.." Kane stuttered.

Marcus needed Kane focused and back on track. He would get him to start task by task.

"Ron, I need you to situate and secure the MOMEE back inside the cargo hold and give us a hand boarding these people in the Mess bay."

Kane threw the big machine into reverse. "On the way, boss."

He reversed the MOMEE into its cradle in the cargo hold of the Destiny. He opened the door of the cab and jumped to the deck. He went to the cradle control panel, engaged and locked down the wheel clamps. Although the Destiny created its own gravity field, they didn't want to take chances having heavy equipment bouncing around the hold when there was turbulence during flight. He closed the cargo hold's exterior and inner doors, shutdown the panel and ran through the corridors to the main hatchway.

When he reached the main hatch, the first soldiers carrying soldiers were climbing the retractable steps.

The first pair, a woman carrying an unconscious soldier over her left shoulder and an assault rifle in the other, barked at Kane.

"Where can I put him?"

The scowl on her face was frightening. Kane supposed she could scare the bark off of a tree with that look. Then Kane saw past that look and decided that with everything she was carrying and the combat uniform she was wearing, she was hot.

"Uh, ship's Mess-bay," he sputtered. "First corridor on the left, up one flight of stairs, turn 180 degrees, second door on the left."

She hesitated for a second, long enough for him to catch the name patch on her winter camouflage parka and then she staggered down the corridor with her cargo. Her last name was Rozinski.

"Uh, I can show you, if you like," Kane offered.

"Fuck off!" she grunted. "I got it!"

"Yep," Kane concluded softly to himself. "Hot and dangerous."

He then turned his attention to the other soldiers who were coming up the hatchway steps. Those who were not carrying the injured, were carrying

47

their equipment and/or rifles. He directed those to follow the first pair and as he did so, began counting rifles and sidearms.

"What the fuck do you mean, they're missing," replied Lieutenant Andre Dechene, Team Leader of 3rd and 4th Sections.

His radioman removed the headset from beneath his helmet. "Lieutenant Pardo in the command vehicle was survielling the buildings and when he panned the camera back to 1st and 2nd Section's position, they were gone."

Dechene rose up from his kneeling position and gave the hand signal for all to hold their positions. Kneeling back down beside his radioman, he asked for new orders from the command vehicle. Listening intently for a few seconds, the radioman then put his hand over the mouthpiece.

"He said to 'Hold'. He is going to try to extend the camera another meter to see if can spot them."

He removed his hand from the mouthpiece, "Understood." He looked up at Dechene, "He says, he'll get back to us."

"What the fuck is going on?" Dechene cursed under his breathe.

Major Manning was in a dark place. His conscious mind was fighting to escape the darkness and the depths of unconsciousness. He was barely aware of the activity and voices nearby. His awareness in this state was almost dreamlike. Instinctively, he didn't like the lack of control he had in this state. He fought for control. He fought to wake up.

His eyes finally slammed open. He was dazed, confused of his surroundings. Disoriented, he couldn't understand where he was or why. Sitting up and looking around, he tried to see if there was something nearby that was familiar. It was all familiar...somehow. Rifles, packs and soldiers.

'OK', he thought to himself.

Broken ruble, large cavernous room and a very large aircraft. It was all too slowly coming back to him. As he was trying to piece the jumbled puzzle of his mind together, he watched two civilians going around to groups of soldiers. His soldiers, he remembered. His soldiers were picking up their gear, the injured and weapons and hurriedly boarding the aircraft. He felt there was something wrong with that picture.

The two civilians now spotted him just sitting there amongst the debris and started making their way to him. He didn't recognize the older man on the left but the younger man on the right was familiar. His face had the look of concern. Manning had never seen that look on that man's face before. He couldn't place the name with the face. He had the vague feeling that he had seen or studied that face on more than one occasion.

And like a ton of bricks, he remembered. Everything. His life. His job. His mission. His duty.

"Gowan, he whispered under his breathe as the younger man stopped mid-stride, as if hearing him. Manning quickly stood up, drew and aimed his sidearm.

"Stop!" he ordered, almost shouting.

The older man stopped, raised his hands and then stepped into the line of fire, shielding Marcus Gowan.

"Major," the older man addressed him, "please put that away."

"Step out of the way, son," Manning warned.

"We haven't got time fo.." the older man began to explain.

Manning interrupted, "If you don't step out of the way so I can see his hands, I'll shoot."

"You wouldn't," the older man exclaimed.

"I will," Manning stated.

From behind the older man, Marcus Gowan spoke up.

"No Sir. You won't."

Marcus Gowan put his hand on the older man's shoulder and stepped out from behind him. He slowly walked towards Manning with his arms spread out from his sides, palms up.

"You, Sir, are a man of honor and duty. You have served this country with distinction and integrity. Morally, you would never fire upon an unarmed person."

Manning realized that Gowan was right. He was simply reacting. Reacting so quickly, that he scared himself. He began to lower his sidearm, now dizzy from the sudden, adrenalin-fueled rush to his feet. He could feel his heart racing and the beads of sweat forming on his forehead. He felt like passing out.

Marsh and Marcus saw the Major's face turn white as a sheet and before his legs buckled from beneath him, they each caught him by each arm. Manning still conscious, pressed the muzzle of his handgun into Marcus' ribs.

Marcus looked down at the weapon and then into Manning's eyes.

"Major," he said. "If we don't get out of here in the next five minutes, we will all die here when this facility self-destructs."

Manning, hearing the words and seeing the seriousness of Gowan's face and taking into account that these two seemed to be helping his people out of harms way, nodded silently and holstered his sidearm.

As the two men helped walk Manning over the ruble and debris that was the launch bay door, Marcus quipped, "Besides, you can arrest me later."

After several minutes of unsuccessfully trying to raise 1st and 2nd sections via radio, the decision was made to pull back.

Lieutenant Dechene was now back at the command vehicle with 3rd and 4thsections. He wanted to see what the camera operator could see from the vantage point of the camera atop the mast. After several minutes of scanning the various buildings for activity and any sign of the missing squads, the camera zoomed in on what appeared to be an extremely large hole in the tundra. He estimated the size of the hole to be 400 to 500 meters in diameter.

"Is it possible they repelled into that hole?"

Lieutenant Pardo shook his head, watching the monitor, "If they did, two of our troopers would still be guarding the opening." Panning the camera along the closest edge, "I don't even see anchors for the ropes."

Dechene sat back in the jump-seat and stared distantly at the interior bulkhead of the command vehicle. This was supposed to be a simple assault/seizure/arrest(ASA) mission. 'By The Book', classic assault. This was so far, anything but, textbook. He was wondering if 1st and 2nd Sections fell into that hole or if they entered it deliberately. If they fell into it, it was unlikely they all did. If they entered deliberately, they would have sent word back, somehow. He was out of contact from his superior and without command support. He was the senior officer on the ground and he had to make a decision. This was now becoming a search and quite possibly, a rescue (SAR) mission.

"I think me and a couple of guys are gonna' have to go up to that plateau and check it out," Dechene announced.

Pardo nodded, "I'll keep the camera on you the whole time."

"Thanks, Snoopy," Dechene said as he slapped him on the shoulder and left the command vehicle.

Dechene picked the first four troopers he saw and they began trudging towards the ridgeline of the plateau. He had the rest of the two remaining squads fan out to cover their ascent to the ridgeline. Once they arrived and it was determined to be clear of hostiles, Dechene would hand-signal the two squads to approach the plateau in a broad formation.

With the slight slope and the snow-drifts, running with packs and gear, it took the five men about five minutes to reach the ridgeline. After stopping just below its crest, they caught their breathe and spread out. Dechene took out his binoculars from inside his winter camouflage parka and poked his head over the ridge. There was no movement from the buildings. The hole in the tundra was lit up from within in the arctic twilight. From his position, the distance was perhaps fifty meters. Ducking back down, and facing the two remaining squads, he gave the hand signal for them to make their approach. He then looked around in the snow to confirm that 1st and 2nd Sections had indeed come this way. By the time he finished looking for other evidence as to the disappearance of the first two squads, 3rd and 4th Sections had reached the ridgeline and taken up firing positions, scanning the plateau for any threats.

Looking to his left and then to his right, Dechene finally spotted the radioman for 4th Section and gestured to him to join him, which he did.

"Ask 'Snoopy' if he can see anything else out of the ordinary from those buildings," he said as turned back to the ridgeline of the plateau. The wind-blown snow had created a haze a foot above the plateau so Dechene had to stand on his knees with his binoculars. He took comfort in the thought that if he couldn't see clearly, he himself, couldn't be seen clearly. He crouched down beside the radioman who had the rear access panel of his pack radio open.

"What's wrong?" Dechene asked.

"Radio's dead," he replied. "Everything inside looks OK, just no power."

"The cold affecting the batteries?" he offered. "You drop it?" he accused.

"No way," he answered. "The batteries and radios are tested at temps colder than this. And you can throw these babies out of a moving vehicle doing sixty and they'd still work."

"What, then?" Dechene inquired.

The radioman shrugged his shoulders and shook his head. "Beats me. It was working before we got up here."

"Go check 3rd section's radio," he ordered.

51

Three minutes later, Dechene's radioman returned crawling on all fours to keep below the ridgeline.

"Same problem," he announced.

'This isn't happening', Dechene thought to himself. First, the mining station appears to be deserted. Second, the CO changes from Plan A to Plan B. Then, half the CAT force and the CO go MIA. Now, the radios stop working.

He wanted a better look at this hole in the ground. Bringing the binoculars to his eyes, he stood up this time and surveyed the entire plateau. There was still no sign of the other assault teams, anywhere. There was absolutely no sign of any mining personnel, either.

'This is the high Arctic', he thought to himself, *'where the fuck, could they go?"*

He was now better able to see the outline of that hole in the tundra. Between the gusts of blowing snow, he thought he could see part of a steel girder. Then again, he thought he was seeing things. He blinked his eyes a few times and refocused.

They all felt it before they heard or saw it.

The tundra shook beneath their feet and Dechene, for a moment, thought it was an earthquake. Then, they all heard the muffled sound of multiple rocket motors firing. Still holding the binoculars to his eyes, Dechene instinctually crouched a little, looking for what he thought were the rocket-propelled grenades heading for their positions. Then, something briefly obstructed his field of vision and was gone. Putting a scowl on his face, looking away from his binoculars and looking from side to side, he tried to find who was out of position.

Nobody had moved. The rocket motor sound was now louder.

"What the fuck, is *that?"* he barely heard one of the troopers say slowly.

Dechene returned his eyes towards the binoculars and the hole; only he saw the same thing as before. A hole.

"Its fuckin' huge," another soldier said.

"Holy shit," said another.

Dechene still couldn't see anything. "What are you 'numb-nuts' talkin' about?"

There was a cold silence from the nearest who heard him and Dechene had the feeling that all eyes were on him.

"Uh, look up," his radioman suggested.

Looking up over the top of his binoculars, what he saw seemed almost impossible. The craft was long, bulky and almost aerodynamic looking. Its highly polished skin reflected its surroundings like a mirror. Dechene could even detect a slight glow from its surface. The craft, which seemed to levitate atop hot plumes of rocket motor exhaust, began pivoting on its axis and Dechene could see what appeared to be the front of the craft. He raised his binoculars again but couldn't see any discernable cockpit windscreen.

"Fuck a Canuck duck," he said slowly, dumbstruck.

As his mind was trying to register what his eyes were seeing, he hadn't noticed that the nose of the craft had begun pointing skyward to the southeast. He did notice, however, that the intensity of the glow increased to the point that he had to take his binoculars from his eyes. From his peripheral vision, he could see that some of the troopers from both squads had stood up. Some had even lowered their weapons while others cocked and locked theirs, held at the ready.

Then, the most peculiar thing happened. The combustion gases from the rocket motors ceased and the deafening sound was replaced by silence carried by the cold arctic winds. Dechene was expecting the strange craft to plummet to the earth, no longer supported by the obvious power of its rocket engines. It continued to hover, defying gravity.

Then, for a few milliseconds, the craft seemed to wobble and lurch forward. Just long enough for the human eye to detect and then, it disappeared. The sound of rushing air was heard by all and all eyes were fixed on the wall of snow approaching the ridgeline of the plateau. Some had managed to duck down below the ridge or turn away from the wave front of snow and ice. Those who were still standing were propelled, sliding, rolling, or tumbling down the slope. Dechene was one of them.

After coming to a stop and realizing that more than half of the two squads were out of position and exposed, Dechene ordered everyone back up to the ridgeline. It took them all about twenty seconds to regain their former positions. After taking a quick head count, he grabbed his binoculars to peer over the ridgeline to see any other activity coming from the mining facility.

He couldn't see anything. Just, whiteness.

The mining facility was gone.

He lowered his binoculars to see if snow obscured the lenses only to find them clear. Looking in the direction of the mining facility, his eyes beheld the largest hole in the ground that he ever witnessed.

Like an excavation, he could see the different layers of dirt and sediment. He peered over the rim and down into the bottom of the crater. To him, it looked like someone had taken a giant ice-cream scoop and scooped out the entire plateau. There were no signs of explosion, fire or debris.

Feeling awestruck, Dechene sat in the snow and contemplated the day's events. The section was now talking amongst themselves in hushed murmurs, attempting to sort out what they, too, witnessed. He was relieved to see that the command and two support vehicles hadn't 'disappeared'. He decided that if he were alone, this would be the point where he would question his own sanity.

CHAPTER THREE

'AERODYNAMIC'

The Destiny was now pushing MACH 8 and accelerating. 'Pushing' was a misnomer. Actually it was more like 'pulled'. The Gravity-Distortion (GD)-field projectors created and projected a gravity-well to a focal point in whatever direction they happened to be pointed at. Being that the projectors created and focused an artificial gravity distortion field a certain distance away from the ship and the mass of the ship being lighter, meant that it would always 'fall' towards the gravity-well. The more power put to the projectors or the more projectors working in unison, the faster the fall into the gravity-well. Because the projectors would never reach the distortion, it was akin to hanging a carrot on a stick in front of a hungry horse to get it to move.

The energy requirements for the projectors were provided by not one but, four powerful reactors located in the engineering hold amidships. In fact, the Destiny was built around this hold and the projectors. These four reactors were set within a rotating ring known as the Reactor-Quad and provided all and more of the Destiny's energy requirements. The added bonus was that it also created an artificial magnetic field outside the ship and an artificial gravity field within. The magnetic field would protect those inside from any harmful radiation just like the Earth's own magnetic field. The gravity field not only kept those inside firmly planted to the deck but, while the ship was in motion, it dampened the g-forces to a constant 1G. While the Destiny was maneuvering at low or high speeds, the sensation of motion was completely, non-existent. No one could tell if they were in motion, unless they looked out a window or saw outside from on a monitor.

Mac and Marcus had chosen to fly the Destiny on a course that would take them south-east down the middle of the Davis Strait, between Baffin Island and Greenland. The Destiny shot out of the strait in minutes at an altitude of one hundred meters. Looking through the forward windscreen of the flight deck, the ocean waves and icebergs passed below them as a blur.

By the time Ron Kane entered the flight deck, the Destiny was already at the southern edge of the Newfoundland Basin. Both Mac and Marcus were watching their displays.

"Coming up on thirty, North. Well within the 'Triangle', " Marcus announced.

"Stand-by for ascension," Mac warned. "Five…four… three…two… one…now."

Mac and Marcus pulled back on the flight controls and at the same time, each with a hand, one on top of the other, increased power to the throttle controls. The view from inside the flight deck went from the familiar view of the earth and sky to the sky completely filling the windscreen.

At MACH 25, the Destiny immediately went vertical at 90 degrees and climbed. To those onboard, there was no indication of movement. Only those on the flight deck or in engineering were aware of the Destiny's velocity and orientation. In mere seconds, she was flying through, past and leaving earth-bound clouds behind. In a few more seconds, the shade of the blue sky was becoming discernibly darker. Then, one hundred eighteen seconds from when she first started climbing to space, the Destiny broke atmosphere and continued for another few seconds until Mac and Marcus eased the speed back on the throttle controls.

Marcus looked up from his displays and stared through the windscreen at the full moon lit up by the sun. The rest of the flight-deck crew joined him. For a moment, there was complete silence from the four as they took in the sight that beheld them. Even though it was nearly a quarter million miles away, the brightness and the detail of the features, once out of the Earth's atmosphere, mesmerized them.

Marcus was the first to break the eerie silence.

"Joni, what was the elapsed time of our ascent?"

Stealing one last long look at the Moon, she finally turned away to look at her displays, "From one hundred meters to our current altitude of one thousand kilometers, elapsed time comes to….one hundred twenty seconds and our speed was MACH 25."

"Talk about going ballistic," Kane muttered across the aisle from Joni.

"You ain't seen nothin', yet," Mac hinted.

"I'm tracking a lot of objects in orbit and most of seems to be junk and debris," Joni announced. "Some are even inactive satellites."

"Anything we need to be concerned about?" Mac asked.

"Only if we stay here."

"The magnetic field we generate would deflect any small debris, anyway," Kane commented.

Marcus interjected, "But, not the larger, dead satellites. That's why the Destiny can also emit a defensive barrier for short periods, in case of collisions."

Joni's instruments started to light up accompanied by audible warning sounds. She turned to them and began reading the information on her displays. Everyone turned to her and waited for her report.

"Exterior sensors were just tripped. I am showing three RADAR locks and one by LIDAR."

"Source?" Marcus asked.

"Cataloging," Joni announced as she worked at her terminal. "I see one RADAR and the LIDAR coming from two satellites in orbit and the remaining two from the surface. Wait a minute…..one is mobile." She keyed up more information from her displays and began to scan for the last RADAR signal.

"Confirmed!" She said excitedly. "US Air Force fighter jet is tracking us and flying in a circular holding pattern, over the Atlantic."

"Put it on my overhead, please," Marcus asked. "Number two."

As she transferred the information to his station, Marcus reached up above his head a grabbed a monitor set into a socket in the overhead instrument panel. After unlocking from its cradle, he extended it down so it was right in front of him by way of spring loaded, hinged arms, like a periscope. He pushed it further away from himself so Mac could also see the information.

They both read the information, seeing the correlations, they were even watched the scans of the fighter as it flew its circular pattern.

"Are you thinking what I'm thinking?" Marcus looked over at Mac.

Mac stroked his chin and made eye contact with Marcus.

"That, maybe, he's got a little birdie with teeth under that wing? I got money that says he does. Do we hang here and find out?"

"I don't think so." Marcus declared.

Mac turned to Joni, "Send out a corresponding carrier signal on the same frequencies. Make us invisible. We're gettin' outta' Dodge."

Mustang was playing 'catch-up'. Pinto had a two hundred kilometer lead on Colin Gallant's and 'Timbo' Matthew's chopper. He had to fly over the top of Prince of Wales Island and across the southern part of the frozen McClintock Channel and over the south-eastern portion of Victoria Island to close the distance.

By the time Mustang caught up with Pinto, they had both crossed over Melville Sound in seconds. Within minutes they were over Contwoyto Lake and heading for Great Slave Lake at an altitude of 200 meters. Their airspeed remained a constant MACH 3.5 and they flew in a close but staggered 'Loose Duece' formation. Although, both choppers were equipped with certain, stealthy, electronic counter-measures, if they were detected, whoever would be tracking them would only see a radar return, the size of crow.

After flying into the northern end of the province of Alberta, both choppers gained altitude to over-fly the Caribou Mountains before dropping down to enter the Peace River valley-basin. They continued this route until, over the small enclaves of Peace River, Grimshaw and Berwyn, turned west and prepared to fly over the Rocky Mountains. When the sonic boom was heard in these communities and homes shook and windows shattered, the inhabitants at first thought it was caused by an earthquake. It was even heard as far south as the provincial capital of Edmonton.

Within the hour, they had crossed over the 'Rockies', the City of Prince George, the B.C. Coastal Mountains and finally, over the waters of the Pacific. Once over the Queen Charlotte Sound, at 130 west, longitude, they turned south and dropped down to an altitude of 20 meters above sea level.

"We're making good time, aren't we?" Timbo asked over the intercom.

"You bet," Gallant replied.

Timbo, who had been sleeping in the back, joined Gallant by sitting in the right-hand co-pilot's seat. Gallant decided to give him a rough time.

"You know how to fly this bird?" he asked.

Looking down at the flight controls and the instrument panel, Timbo hesitantly replied.

"Uh...no."

"Well, only a certified pilot gets to sit in that seat and if you touch anything, I'll bash your fucking teeth in," he said as he craned his head to make eye contact with Timbo. "You read me, JAFO."

Timbo could see through that insane pilot look he was getting and responded with a gruff, fake Scottish accent.

"Aye, aye. Captain Blye, Sir," giving the pilot a comedic salute.

Timbo watched the other chopper ahead of them and admired its configuration. The absence of its main rotor belied the fact that it was indeed, a helicopter. Normally, in its 'helicopter' mode, the main rotors would be visible, providing the lift required keeping it airborne. However, during supersonic flight, the rotor would be shutdown, the telescoping rotor blades would automatically retract and small delta-wings would extend from the lifting body of the fuselage. Also, while flying in the 'Loose Deuce' formation, Mustang's flight navigation system could link, via computer, to the Pinto's and vice versa. Whatever speed and course of the Pinto, Mustang would match it instantly. Although, Gallant kept his hands on the flight controls at all times, it was almost like flying by auto-pilot. If either of the two linked craft identified a collision hazard, the navigation system would plot a course to avoid it. At supersonic speeds, at their current altitude, that gave them about a five second warning.

"What's our ETA to the Yankee Rose?" Timbo asked.

"2 to 3 hours," Gallant replied after looking at the clock on the overhead panel.

The two choppers popped up to 100 meters to momentarily avoid an oil tanker in their path. They were crossing the shipping lanes for ships arriving or departing Vancouver or Seattle. With every ship or boat they had to 'hop' over, the sonic boom was breaking glass, in their wake.

The Yankee Rose was an old automobile cargo ship that, in its heyday, used to make its freight runs from the manufacturing plants in south-east Asia to the auto markets of North America. For years, she carried hundreds of thousands of cars and trucks of almost every make and model until her decommissioning.

As she was being sold for scrap, Marcus Gowan bought her, among others and immediately had her in dry-dock for re-fit. Officially.

Unofficially, she and other freighters like her were being modified to accommodate human cargo (passengers really) as well. These would be the people who Marcus had met with personally that agreed with and believed in his 'dream'. The promise of a new life and a new beginning, in a new world with a new technology to back it up. People from all walks of life, cultures and regions wanted desperately to be a part of what he offered.

While in re-fit, these ships were outfitted with small staterooms to accommodate families. Cargo areas included for their belongings were also built. Before the 'Exodus', these freighters still made their respective shipments so as not to attract attention. Work done on these vessels were done by Gowan company employees and they, too were offered the opportunity to leave the poverty, chaos and uncertainty of the real world and join those who wanted to make a difference in their lives. Between shipments, these ships would first take on supplies needed to construct this new world on the island in the South Pacific Ocean. After unloading the supplies, they would 'sail' at top speed, for their next pick-up/delivery run.

The Yankee Rose was making her final run with three thousand families and as much supplies as she could carry aboard. She was speeding at 100 knots, thanks to her new propulsion system and redesigned hull, for that small island. Gallant had described it as such when he first saw the drawing of it superimposed on a globe of the world. That view changed when, given an opportunity to fly in a survey team to the island, he discovered just how big it was. They spent three weeks on that island and he thought he had seen it all. He didn't. It was too big. When he returned, he and his family made the decision to join the others and make the island their new home. His family was now on the Yankee Rose and he couldn't wait to join them.

Captain Martin 'Smash' Reddikop had launched his F-151C Strike Maverick into the air so fast, he almost made his Weapons Systems Officer (WSO) puke up his morning's breakfast when he pulled back on the joystick to near vertical. His call-sign was awarded to him by his fellow pilots because, as they saw it, he was always buying a new car to replace the previous one he smashed up.

"Whoa! What are you trying to do to me, man? Leave me behind? He complained.

"Narc, you are behind," Smash replied to his Weapons Systems Officer (WSO). Narc was Lt. Declan Reese and as a young black man growing up in the Underground district of Atlanta, Georgia, he saw a lot of people come under the influence of the drug and gang world. Before he enlisted in the USAF, he was a narcotics cop for three years. He could see a drug deal going down a mile away. He left because he didn't feel he could make a difference anymore.

They were already at Angels Thirty, meaning thirty thousand feet, and still climbing out of Bush, AFB in Florida. They were heading for a preprogrammed waypoint two hundred miles east over the Atlantic. Their orders were to scan, by radar, for a satellite in a decaying orbit, being tracked by NORAD and USACOM (United States Atlantic Command). As a P.S., they were told in the rushed preflight, that the general consensus was that the satellite would impact the middle of a major city in Europe. His orders were to vaporize the target. Under the port wing of his F-151, was the Orbital Defensive Ordinance (ODO-5C). This was a missile designed and produced to bring down satellites in low-earth orbit for the USAF's Space Operations Squadron (SOS). It was twenty feet long and almost two feet wide and packed five hundred pounds of blast plasma explosive for a warhead. It was the next best thing to a nuke. It wasn't required to hit its mark but, home in on target and let the proximity sensor do the rest.

Once they achieved Angels Seventy, they leveled out and proceeded to a waypoint and scanned for the target. They would receive additional tactical radar information to download into the guidance system of the ODO from USACENTCOM. Also they would simultaneously link it to those sources so it could triangulate while enroute.

"Final uplink from SOS Command received and downloaded into the ODO," Narc announced. "Radar is locked and tracking."

"Copy," Smash replied. "Rally-point is two minutes down-range. Warm–up the guidance system," Smash ordered.

For the next minute, Narc did as ordered and completed his task. That gave him some time to star-gaze. At this altitude, the Moon was especially bright and he studied the features he could see. For occasions like this, he stuffed a compact monocular telescope in the pocket of his flight-suit so he could try to see the finer details. Of course, it was nothing like a real telescope, but it was better than the human eye on the ground.

For a moment, he spied the Sea of Tranquility, hoping to see a glint of sunlight reflected off the hardware from the first landing, so many decades ago. He knew he would never see it but, tried anyway. He resorted to studying the details of the craters and for a moment, he just immersed himself imagining what it would be like to fly just a few hundred feet above them. He knew he would never get that chance.

The on-again, off-again space program of the United States had only effectively become a non-goal. With so much capital required, Congress had become reluctant to fund such an idealistic venture. For many decades, scientists pleaded with the public and the politicians for the backing to go back to the Moon for its resources. To turn planet Earth back into the paradise that God had intended. But, with the domestic problems, natural disasters and the constant terrorist attacks at home and abroad, Congress felt the money was best spent down here, than up there.

Until China entered the picture.

China had been launching 'Taikonauts' into orbit for years with the proven and reliable Russian Soyuz platform and had even maintained a small orbital space station for about ten years. What nobody realized was that the Chinese space program was slowly building experience and expanding their program to include not only a landing on the moon, but a permanent base as well. They purchased the blueprints of the Russian space shuttle 'Buran'(Blizzard) and spent considerable amount of time making improvements to its design. And then, they launched it into orbit.

The result was a beefed up version of the original design. It was wider, longer and deeper. It had a crew compliment of six with an emergency compliment of twenty. In its oversized cargo hold, it could carry whatever could fit. And more. The 'Chairman Mao', however, would never re-enter Earth's atmosphere. It lacked, on purpose, the heat resistance for re-entry. It was a true and purpose-built spaceship.

The Chairman Mao was built for the sole purpose of shuttling supplies and personnel between the Earth and the Moon. Its course would take it once around the Earth to load supplies or cargo, journey to the moon, offload/load resources, round the Moon on its way back to Earth. Round trip was six days. Once, every six weeks, while in Earth orbit, the crews would rotate. There were eight crews in all and that meant that each crew would fly about once a year.

This was not only done for the health and welfare of the crews as well as giving them the chance to be back on Earth to break-up the monotony of a long mission, it was also done so that their Communist masters could keep an eye on them once they were back home. In case they had a sudden change in idealism before their next rotation. Especially, when on the Chairman Mao's maiden voyage, the political officer barricaded himself inside an airlock to keep two mutinous crewmembers at bay, when someone, unknown, jettisoned him out over the dark side of the Moon. The entire crew was held responsible, tried and executed.

"Narc," Smash said looking into the rear-view mirror, breaking his concentration. "What are you spying?"

"Just the Moon, Sir," he replied as he put the monocular back into the pocket of his flight-suit.

"We are at the rally-point. Standby," he announced as he began to bank the interceptor in a wide turn to the south. "Any word from USACENTCOM, yet."

"Not so far, Sir," Narc responded as he checked the communications display. Normally, they would have received permission for a shoot-down in mid-flight and it seemed like someone was taking their time. This, however, was not a normal sortie. The rules of engagement (ROE), was the same but, with a small change. They were to await for the final order once they reached the muster point and no one could tell them how long that might be.

Finally, Narc's monitor alerted him to a flash-message from TACC (Tactical Air Control Center). He opened the electronic text-message and read it out, aloud.

"Message received. Whiskey Flight has a 'go'. Repeat. We have a 'go'."

"Copy that. Master-arm is on," Smash replied, checking his status displays. "Release countdown set. Standby."

Smash squeezed the trigger on his joystick and after two seconds, both men could feel the interceptor become lighter as the ODO was automatically released from the rails under the port wing. Three seconds after that, they watched the ODO as it climbed at hyper-sonic speed towards the heavens.

As 'Smash' was flying the Maverick, 'Narc' was watching the telemetry downlink from the ODO. It was already traveling at Mach 12 and would soon exceed Mach 25. Its course was holding true and closing on its intended RADAR and LIDAR locked target. Telemetry was showing that the first-stage of the ODO's booster was expended and jettisoned and he waited for second-stage ignition at Angels 200. Not long after he received confirmation of second-stage ignition, the ground RADAR stations lost their lock on the target.

Although 'Narc' wasn't alarmed by this, he was surprised. It had only happened in simulator training and he had learned that this could happen in a real situation. He also learned to compensate for this since he knew he still had the help of two orbiting satellites plus the onboard RADAR of the ODO.

As he was adjusting his equipment to track the target, he caught a glimpse of the telemetry and noticed that it wasn't falling towards the Earth as he had seen so many had done in the past. This target was actually stationary. All kinds of things began to enter his mind as to why they were about to shoot down something that was anything but, falling. He gave his head a shake and put it all out of his mind. Orders were orders.

Then, both satellites lost their lock on the target.

"What the…" 'Narc' exclaimed.

"What's the matter?" Smash inquired.

"The ground stations and the satellites lost their target-lock, Sir," Narc announced.

"And the ODO?"

"Still has a lock and closing the distance," Narc replied. "As long as it stays within its field of view, it'll continue to track all the way in."

And then, the ODO lost its target-lock.

"Son of a Bitch," Narc called out. "Sir! The ODO has lost target-lock. It no longer sees the target."

"Malfunction?" Smash asked.

"Couldn't tell ya, Sir," Narc said, shaking his head. "One minute it was just sitting there and the next, it just disappeared."

"You mean 'it was falling', don't you." Smash corrected.

Narc paused, "No Sir! I read the telemetry. Its orbit was not decaying, it was stationary.

Smash hesitated. "Well, never mind that, for now. Are you still receiving telemetry from the ODO? And what's it doing, now?"

"We are still receiving and it's looking for a target it can't find," Narc replied. "She's starting to fly wild."

Smash had to make a decision. Let the ODO keep flying in search of the target or send the abort signal that would order its self-destruction. The last thing anybody wanted was the wrong satellite to be taken out.

"Send the abort signal. We're done here," he decided.

"Sending signal. In three, two, one. Look to two o'clock high." Narc announced.

Both looked up through the canopy glass into the starlit sky. A half-second later, they witnessed a bright flash as the ODO self-detonated.

Smash began pointing the F-151 west towards Florida.

"Whiskey Flight to Kingpin," Smash called out on the radio. "Whiskey Flight is inbound.

'Something's wrong', Marcus thought to himself as he watched the moon pass by in the first two seconds. Looking up at the main engines display, he could see that power distribution was in the red. In bold letters across the display flashed the word, 'Overload', accompanied by an audible alarm.

Bruno Kravakis was on the ship wide intercom, "Flight deck. This is the engine room. We are showing a power surge on our panels. We have to reduce power and shutdown the reactor-quad."

Joni rerouted communications to the Hyperlink headsets so that their guests in the Mess hall didn't listen in.

"Roger that, guys," Mac calmly replied to engineering. "We see it."

"Mac," Marcus called out. "Speed?"

Quickly checking the displays, he blinked his eyes before checking another display for reactor and engine outputs. He called out velocity.

"Point nine," he paused, "past light speed."

Marcus gave Mac the strangest look. Mac could see the young genius mind at work. He had an almost vacant, blank look. When one carefully watched his eyes, you could tell his mind was in overdrive. This time the look lasted about three seconds when a look of realization washed over his face.

"I know what I did wrong," Marcus announced as his fingers began flying over the flight console.

Mac watched his displays as Marcus worked furiously to halt the Destiny's velocity.

"Marcus, we're not decelerating".

"Engine room, here," Kravakis said over the headsets. "Our panels are indicating a fused accelerator relay from the reactor-quad to the projector amps. Tachyon indicators are in the red. Energy flow from the quad *is* at a controlled rate. However, we can no longer divert that much energy back to the reactor since the relay is fused. We are going to try using a manual Regulating Sequencer to shunt the plasma to another relay back to the reactor quad".

"How long will that take?" Marcus asked.

"We have to suit up," Joe Kyras cut in. "About a minute or two. You'll know it when we're done."

"That's all you got," Mac interrupted, "Flight controls are frozen. And Mars is coming up fast."

Looking down at his displays, Marcus could indeed see that Mars was coming up and if the Destiny wasn't on a collision course, as was indicated, they'd probably skim the upper atmosphere. It was going to be that close.

He felt like a heel. While setting course and speed, he was in such a rush to vacate White Alice that he must have inadvertently misplaced a decimal point and also forgot to delete from the computer the Destiny's ground speed once the had achieved orbit. When in space, one can no longer rely on the speed of the ground passing under you when it is no longer there.

In view of his own self-judgment, a crucial mistake. Or so he thought.

"Standby. Collision Alert!" The Destiny's computer announced.

"Bruno, how much longer?" Mac asked over the Hyperlink.

Static and the noise of the power of the reactor quad could be heard through the headset as Kravakis answered.

"Wait one."

"You have less than that," Joni added.

What seemed like an eternity for the three on the flight deck was actually no more than ten seconds. They watched as a distant point of light slowly emerged as the Planet of War grew increasingly larger in the windscreen of the flight deck.

Mac commented, "At this speed, objects are definitely closer than they appear."

"What do you mean?" Joni asked.

"Meaning, what we are now seeing, is the light of Mars from a few seconds ago and by the time we realize we are too close, is when we'll have already impacted on the surface."

From where Marcus and Mac were sitting, they could tell Joni was becoming increasingly nervous of the Destiny's approach to the Red Planet.

Finally speaking up, she asked, "Shouldn't we get to the escape pods?"

And then, the Destiny came to a dead stop.

"And what?" Mac asked. "Bail out of a perfectly good spacecraft," he chuckled. "I don't think so."

"you know what I meant," she accused with a smile.

Mac just chuckled, letting her know that he did.

"Ok," Marcus said. "Paul, let's see where exactly we are. Joni, I want a full diagnostics of primary and secondary systems. Mac, check our flight control systems. Primary, secondary, auxiliary, emergency backups and even the manual systems. I want to know why we were frozen out." Marcus began speaking into the Hyperlink, "Bruno, Joe; check main propulsion and main power for damage in case there is something else I caused to fuse or fail other than what we know."

Everyone agreed and got to work. Marcus rose from his seat and joined Kane at his work station.

"We cut it real close, Boss," Kane commented. "We were two tenths of a second away from drilling into the surface of the planet." He brought up a 3-D spatial representation of their location in the solar system onto his main monitor. "We are currently twenty thousand kilometers away from Mars and drifting towards it's gravity well."

"Can you show me the path we took to get here?" Marcus asked.

"Sure," Kane replied as he brought up the appropriate information on screen. The trajectory showed the Destiny's position from Earth orbit, accelerating passed the Moon, and continuing on until they reached their current position.

"So close, yet, so far," Kane murmured.

Marcus was surprised to hear those words from a no-nonsense, practical young man like Ron Kane.

"When have you had time to study philosophy?" Marcus asked.

"Murphy's Law 101, from Doc," Kane replied.

Marcus chuckled, "That figures."

"You know, it wouldn't take much to go into an orbital maneuver at this distance," Kane suggested.

Marcus thought about it for a half second. Ron was right, of course.

"What is our rate of descent into the Mars gravity well?"

Calling up the scan logs they both could see the raw data. A quick calculation, cross-referenced, gave the conclusion.

"A half meter every twenty-four hours," Kane replied.

"Well, let's wait until the damage control assessment and we'll make a decision, then," Marcus said.

"Fair enough," Kane agreed.

"The camera in the keypad to the Mess-bay door," Marcus stated. "Activate it. Let's see what our quests are up to, shall we."

Once Kane activated the camera, the monitor showed groups of soldiers tending to the wounded. They watched for a moment and Kane spoke, "They have no idea of where they really are."

"Nope. They don't." Marcus slapped Kane twice, lightly on the right shoulder, "Come on. Let's go help."

Marcus looked over to Mac and Joni as he began to walk off the flight deck.

"Keep an eye on us on that monitor. Just in case."

Mac glared at Marcus. "Where do you think you're going? Your place is here, *Commander*. They'll try to arrest you. Maybe, take you as a hostage."

Marcus didn't even look back as he left the flight deck.

"I am going to negotiate their surrender."

Ron Kane followed, stopped at the hatchway and looked back at Mac.

"He knows that they're the ones with the guns, right?"

Manning was helping the medics with the injured. The only serious injuries seemed to be one broken leg, a broken arm and a dislocated shoulder. Everybody, though, were nursing various bumps and bruises including Manning and the medics. In all, they got off pretty lucky. He was actually surprised to find that no one had suffered head injuries. It was obvious everyone had their helmet straps secured.

Lt. Stuart approached Manning and asked to speak to him privately. Both went into a vacant corner of the Mess-Bay. Manning stared at a vacant wall, with his poker face as Stuart gave his casualty report.

"Captain Svanda has a badly broken left leg just above the knee. We've tried to set it as best we could and ease his pain but, without proper medical attention, he'll lose the leg."

"Understood," Manning replied in a hushed voice

"Corp. Marchand's broken arm is set and splinted. We popped Private Vogel's shoulder back into place. They both say they are ready for duty, Sir."

Manning slowly turned his head and scanned the room until his eyes met with Stuart's and in a hushed voice said, "Mandatory rest period for all three. They're wounded. Treat them as such."

And then, Manning's poker face softened, "Maybe, in a few hours, Vogel can join the rest of us."

"Yes, Sir," Stuart agreed. "I would also like to set up a kill-zone at that door. That way we can hold this room on our terms. May I?"

Manning did another quick look around and agreed. "Good thinking, Lieutenant. Two, three-man teams on either side of the doorway. Flip the tables over for cover. Move everybody else back, deeper into the room." Manning turned to the galley and then back to Stuart, again in a hushed voice. "Take two and make sure the galley doesn't have a back door. I don't want to get caught with my pants down, again."

"We won't let that happen, Sir," Stuart replied as he looked over the shoulder of his CO and directed two troopers to check out the galley. He then organized the fire-teams for the main door. Stuart returned to Manning's side.

"Sir. Where are we? What is this thing we're on? Stuart asked quietly.

It was the first time Manning had the luxury to think about it, other than the mission's objectives.

"I haven't a clue, Lieutenant," he admitted. "But I know this. None of **this,** was included in the intel, I read last night." Then a realization occurred to him and he looked at Stuart.

"Gowan said something about self-destruct charges. Did he mention it to you, as well?"

"Yes, Sir. He did," Stuart replied.

"I wonder why we haven't taken off, yet?" Manning said.

"Maybe it was just a ruse to lock us up in here," Stuart suggested.

Manning disagreed, "If I was gonna' lock someone up in a room, I'd take the precaution of first relieving them of their weapons."

"Couldn't hurt to try the door, then," Stuart suggested.

Just then, the two troopers appeared from the galley and reported that although there was no back door, there was three large, food locker rooms marked 'Dry', 'Fresh', and 'Frozen'. All were about half full.

"At least they can't starve us out," Manning quipped. "Lieutenant, go try the door."

As Stuart approached the Mess-bay door, the troopers on either side of the kill-zone pointed their weapons toward the ceiling. He looked for a door knob that wasn't there and then noticed the motion sensor on the wall beside the door at the right height that a knob should be located. The door slid open when he got within 2 feet of the door. He quickly examined the motion sensor and discovered light and lock/unlock switches to the mess hall.

Out of his left, breast pocket, he unfolded a telescopic engineer's inspection mirror and crouched down. He slowly poked the mirror past the doorway and looked down to what seemed to him to be a long corridor. Moving to the opposite side of the doorway, he spied the other direction. Another long corridor but, this time he also spotted the stairway they all climbed to get to the mess hall. Folding up the mirror and putting it back into his breast pocket, he moved away from the door, depressed the lock button and watched it to make sure it closed as he walked away.

"That's one, long corridor, Sir," Stuart reported back to Manning.

"Any movement?" Manning asked.

"None that I could see," Stuart replied.

Manning stroked his grey goatee and stared at the floor, deep in thought for a moment. He was deciding whether or not to escape their current confines or try to take over the aircraft they were on. If they tried to do either while the aircraft was in the process of take-off, damage to the plane could result in disaster. Act now and run the risk of a crash or wait until it was in the air and try to take it then.

"You thinking of taking the plane, Sir?" Stuart asked.

"I am," Manning confessed. "And in the process, we could get everybody killed. We'll wait until the plane is airborne and then we'll assess the situation."

Marcus and Kane were on their way to Deck Five when they made a detour to the Infirmary on Deck Three. They grabbed as many medical kits as they could carry and proceeded to the Mess Bay. They were carrying so much that, once in a while, they had to stop to pick up a dropped kit or two.

Once they arrived on Deck Five, Marcus stopped to peer down the long corridor to see if the soldiers had left the Mess Bay to reconnoiter or to set up a sentry point. The corridor was clear. Marcus was the first to expose himself in the corridor as the two walked slowly towards the Mess Bay.

"Ron, stay behind me," he whispered. "If they jump out suddenly, don't move and follow my lead. Ok?"

"Yes, Sir," Kane replied.

The two of them had traveled about half the length of the corridor when Mac Marsh warned them on the headsets.

"Marcus, Ron. Our guests in the Mess-Bay have set up a kill-zone just inside the hatchway and they locked the hatch."

Marcus had stopped and replied into the headset, "Did anyone leave the room?"

"Nope. But, they did stick their noses out to take a peek up and down the corridor."

"Did they see us coming?" Kane asked.

"Naw, mate. They did that while you were still in Infirmary."

Marcus continued walking down the corridor with Kane close behind. Once they arrived at the hatchway to the Mess Bay, they placed all they had carried on the deck, carefully and quietly. Standing up, the two examined the hatch and it's panel. Both could see that the panel's computer display indicated that it was indeed, locked.

"What, now? Over-ride the controls?" Kane asked.

Marcus grabbed Kane by both upper arms and gently placed him against the wall, right of the door and it's panel.

"Stay out of sight. When the hatch opens, I want you to lock it open."

Confusion was on Kane's face.

"How are you going to get them to open the hatch?"

Marcus smiled and turned to look at the hatch.

"Easy. I'm just gonna' knock on the door."

Manning, Stuart and a couple of troopers were sorting out the preliminary details of taking the plane when everyone heard the knock at the door. The six soldiers who were in position but, had taken a more relaxed stance, cocked and locked their weapons. The sound of chambered rounds into the breaches of rifles was unmistakable. At first, everyone else froze, until there was a second knock at the door. Then, everybody had a weapon in their hands. Manning motioned Stuart to the door. When he got there, just in time for the 3rd set of knocks at the door, he unholstered his sidearm.

"Who is it?" Stuart asked, half singing in a high-pitched voice. For those who didn't chuckle at that, it brought a smirk to the faces of the rest, including Manning.

"Marcus Gowan," was the reply through the door.

That pretty much wiped the smiles off of everybody's face, Stuart had noticed as he shot a look towards Major Manning who gave him a single nod.

"I am going to open the door," he said as he looked to the six men with weapons trained on the door. "There will be six rifles pointed at you. If you have any weapons, discard them, now."

"I came unarmed and with medical supplies," came the reply.

Stuart depressed the unlock button on the panel and the electric motors activated and the door slid open to reveal a lone male, hands up, palms facing forward. He made eye contact with Manning as he stepped through the doorway. Stuart grabbed him by the collar, pressing his sidearm hard into his neck and forced him to his knees.

"Hands on your head!" he ordered as he quickly checked Marcus for weapons. After he was satisfied there were no concealed weapons, he tugged on his flight-suit to make him stand and marched him over to Major Manning.

The whole time, Marcus and Manning never broke eye-contact. Manning had been concealing his un-holstered sidearm against his right leg and as the two came face to face. He holstered it.

"Marcus Gowan, I presume?" Manning said.

"Major Dennis Alexander Manning. Pleasure to finally meet you, Sir." Marcus replied, hands still on his head.

Manning's eyebrows squinted, "How do you know my name?"

"I know a lot about you, Sir. And of your men, of course." Marcus admitted.

"You know, of course, that is classified information. How did you acquire such information?"

"I can't reveal that, Major. Not right now," Marcus said.

"Very well," Manning conceded. "Marcus Gowan. You are hereby under arrest under the North American Continental Security Agreement, Section Five, Paragraph One. You will be detained until you are handed off to the appropriate authorities whereby you will be interrogated by representatives of both the Canadian and American governments. Do you understand?"

"I have one question, Major."

'This ought to be good,' Manning thought to himself. "Go ahead."

"How do you propose to 'hand me off' to 'said' authorities, if you can't deliver me?"

Manning was puzzled by that question. For a second, he thought he was dealing with a cocky, arrogant wise-ass. Did this man not realize that he had all these personnel, artillery and air support to transport him back to civilization to face, guilty or not, charges of being a terrorist? Gowan knew they were coming for him. He had prepared for them and tried to run. Gowan had even tried to trick him into thinking all of their lives were in danger in a ruse to lock him and his soldiers into a room on some type of large aircraft. But, Manning had him, standing right in front of him.

"Simply by turning custody of you over to the government in Ottawa," Manning said.

"Let me ask this question, Major," Marcus paused. "How do you plan on getting me there?"

When Marcus Gowan asked that question, Manning witnessed a seriousness in his eyes that was unmistakable. His voice belied the immaturity of his age. It was obvious he didn't think Manning could deliver him to the Canadian capital.

"We're all going to take a *nice* little plane ride in one of four C-280 'SuperHercs', where you will be bound and gagged, for your own safety of course, all the way back to Ottawa." Manning said sarcastically.

"On Earth, right?" Marcus asked.

"Of course, you idiot!" Manning blurted out. He was beginning to form a very low opinion of this man. How anybody felt he was a threat to Continental Security should have his competency re-evaluated.

Marcus leaned closer to Manning without taking a step and lowered his voice so that only those close by, could hear.

"Major. We're not on Earth." Marcus revealed.

Manning didn't believe Marcus. "That's insane."

Marcus slowly took his hands off his head and lowered his arms and chuckled, "Perhaps but, it's the truth."

"We haven't even left the ground, yet," Stuart tried to justify.

"Actually, Lieutenant, not only have we left the ground, we've left the planet, traveled twenty million miles and are now parked in near orbit of Mars," Marcus replied.

All those within earshot just froze. Some watched with mouths agape, some swallowing hard in disbelief. The result was the same. Silence. Manning's and Marcus' gaze met and the two men tried to size each other up. Manning trying to figure out if the man before him was lying or, as incredulous as it sounded, actually telling the truth. Marcus, confident the Major was a just and fair man, and would make the right decision. Marcus decided to give a peace offering.

"Major, I know you have wounded and we've brought as many med-kits from the Infirmary as we could carry. I want to offer our assistance to your wounded," he asked.

"We?" Manning asked.

"One of my crew is just outside the hatch. He is unarmed and he is one the best mechanics, I have. And he is an excellent medic," Marcus explained while watching the hatch. "So, I really don't want one of your soldiers, to accidentally shoot him. Can he enter to render medical assistance?"

Manning looked over at Captain Svanda who was now unconscious, probably from shock. He nodded to Stuart to give the order.

"You six, at the entrance," Stuart called out. "Stand-down, secure your rifles."

The six soldiers who had been guarding the entryway, stood up immediately, switched on their safeties and stepped away from their previous positions.

"Ron!" Marcus called out. "You can bring in those med-kits, now."

All eyes were on the individual as he slowly appeared, arms cradling several med-kits. He stopped to survey the Mess-Bay before actually entering. Stepping through, he began to hand out the kits until joining Manning's medics huddled around Captain Svanda.

Manning turned to Marcus

"Let me get this straight. You claim that we are not on Earth but, in space. Orbiting Mars…."

"Near orbit of Mars," Marcus interrupted.

"That's impossible," Manning concluded. "By conventional means, it would take almost a year to get to Mars."

"Yes. By conventional means," Marcus agreed, adding nothing more.

Stuart and Manning looked at each other. It was obvious that Marcus Gowan was admitting that this 'aircraft' was not powered by conventional means. They looked at Marcus and waited for an explanation and back at each other.

Manning's eyes narrowed as he looked back at Marcus.

"Prove it."

Manning wasn't expecting the response he received from the young man standing in front of him.

"I thought you'd never ask," Marcus said as he turned and headed for the open hatch of the Mess-Bay. "Follow me, gentlemen."

CHAPTER FOUR

Riding on Freedom

Pinto and Mustang had been flying for a while without encountering any more ships by which their auto-navigation systems had to continually pop over them. Gallant had gotten accustomed to traveling at MACH 3.5, even if they were only flying at half the speed the modified choppers were capable of. Even though this was, technically the first time they flew this fast.

For months, the helicopters were tested extensively in the Wind Tunnel Facility at the Gowan R&D Division. Every system and component was tested in the extreme. By the time the tests were completed, they knew what the helicopters could and couldn't do. When it came to actually flying them in the real world, they were restricted to speeds of no more than 100 knots so as to not to arouse suspicion of a far more capable airframe.

To prevent erosion due to friction at hypersonic speeds, all leading edges were coated with an ablative material which burned off. After 1000 hours, those leading edges would be subject to recoating, which the onboard computers would log. Marcus Gowan had even toyed with the idea of installing the new Auto-Maintenance and Repair systems on-board but, realized that would restrict the helicopter's speed and lifting capabilities.

Mathews was still sitting in the right seat but, listening to music on his portable player and staring out the side window. Gallant nudged his shoulder and he popped out his earphones.

"I didn't touch, nothin'," Timbo said.

"Just seeing if you're still awake over there," Gallant offered. "What are you listening to?"

"E.L.O. , " Timbo replied.

"Who?" Gallant asked.

"Not the 'Who'," Timbo replied. "E.L.O. Electric Light Orchestra."

"Well, pipe it through the speakers. Let's have a listen."

Timbo hooked up his portable player to the main console and cued up the song and informed Gallant of the name of the tune.

"I think you'll like this one. Its their version of Chuck Berry's 'Roll Over Beathoven'."

They both listened as the song opened in the familiar classical theme of orchestral music and then, suddenly, the rift of an electric, lead guitar. At these speeds, Gallant felt the rock and roll music was quite appropriate. After that song was over, another, Wings, 'Rockestra', Judas Priest's 'You Got Another Thing Comin' and Joe Satriani's 'Surfin' with the Alien' continued. To Colin Gallant, Timbo had picked music which suited flying. Speedy and adrenilin-rushed.

"Standby," the auto-navigation computer announced. "Collision Alert. Climb initiated."

Timbo turned off the music.

Pinto and Mustang promptly began climbing up to 80 meters above sea level but, instead of closing formation as they had done so many times before performing this maneuver, the auto-nav. system made them separate by 100 meters. A lone shape appeared on the horizon and as it grew larger, Matthews and Gallant could recognize the silhouette of an aircraft carrier.

Flying at MACH 3.5, at a climbing altitude of 60 meters, both choppers just cleared the flight deck of the aircraft carrier by 10 meters with their paths taking them forward and aft of the carrier's command island. Since the carrier was making her way to her home port of San Diego, California, air operations had ceased and most of the 'Deck Crew' was preparing the mighty vessel for her homecoming. Combat Air Patrols (CAP) had even been suspended. A few of the deck crew members, who saw the two dark shapes approach from the north, low over the water, had yelled out a warning as they began running to the opposite side of the massive carrier, thinking that they were inbound air-to-surface missiles. Although there was no jet or rocket motor noise from the over-flying choppers as they passed over the flight deck of the carrier, the Doppler-effect of the trailing sonic boom shattered, if not cracked every armored glass window on the carrier's island. The two fast moving shapes continued their course south, again, dropping low over the ocean waves.

Timbo quickly looked out the co-pilot's side window just after they passed over the aircraft carrier.

"What was that?" he said aloud.

"That was a US Navy, MacArthur Class, MegaCarrier," Gallant replied.

Just then, their instrument panel let out a warning alert. The automatic defense system, Ship Self-Defense System(SSDS), had reacted quickly. It was a self-contained missile defense system strategically placed about the mighty warship and worked in conjunction with other defensive systems and hit their targets 99.5% of the time.

"Shit!" Gallant exclaimed as he sat bolt upright in his seat. He put his hand on the chopper's joystick and engaged the radio.

"Pinto. Mustang. Missiles in the air!" He called out to Olivia in the other chopper.

'Ollie' responded almost immediately, "Copy! We see four. Tactics?"

Gallant didn't have a lot of time to devise a clever way to get the two choppers out of this predicament. He had to 'wing-it'.

"Disengage auto-nav. Full power climb to 5-5-0," Gallant offered. "Let's see if they can keep up."

The two choppers were now flying almost side by side. Gallant and Timbo looked over to their right to see Ollie and her JAFO looking back. To Gallant, she was a fair-skinned, long-haired brunette, beauty. Ollie engaged her radio.

"Twenty seconds to impact. We gotta' do this now!" she said.

"You first," Gallant ordered. "We'll draw them off and away from you."

Without another word but, with a single nod, Pinto climbed and accelerated to MACH 7. Timbo was watching the scanner to check on the four missiles as they homed in. The two which had locked on to Pinto, had now locked on to Mustang.

"Give me the good news, JAFO," Gallant asked.

"All four, locked on. Five seconds," Timbo called out.

"Hang-on! Let's go ballistic." Gallant warned Timbo as he simultaneously pushed the throttle handles all the way forward and pulled back and to the left on the joystick. Gallant wanted make sure he put as much distance between him and Pinto. The two were now being pressed into their seats as they continued to climb at almost 70 degrees to starboard.

Gallant called out to Timbo, "Where are my missiles, JAFO?"

Timbo, as much as he could, from the G-force of the climb, stole a look of the scanner.

"Two are still on our six," he took a breath. "They're lagging behind."

Gallant leveled off Mustang at 50,000 feet and looked down at the scanner. Pinto was 500 kilometers west and the two remaining missiles were still two kilometers below and 5 kilometers behind. Gallant thought that they would have expended their solid rocket fuel by now. He decided not to take any chances. He would wait for them to climb to match Mustang's flight level. He had another trick he could try.

""Timbo. When they get within a klick, we're going to power dive. I want you to call out our altitude in one kilometer increments," Gallant instructed. "When we get to 3 kilometers, I'm gonna' pull up. Hard. Those missiles won't be able to do the same."

"Will do," Timbo acknowledged.

Gallant eased the throttles back to MACH 3. Timbo looked over at him with a concerned look.

"Just letting them catch up," Gallant offered.

They watched the gradual approach of the missiles in silence. One of the missiles seemed to drop back. Gallant concluded that it spent all of it's fuel. When the last remaining missile came within the predetermined one kilometer distance, Gallant pushed the joystick forward and put Mustang into a steep dive. The missile followed.

"Fifteen," Timbo called out, right away. "Speed. Three point nine Its still on our six."

Gallant considered, briefly, increasing speed. Until....

"Ten, nine, eight, seven, six, five, four, three...."

Gallant yanked back on the joystick as fast and as hard as he could. The effect was immediate. Both men could feel the G-force on their bodies as the chopper barely skimmed the waves of the Pacific Ocean.

One second later and three kilometers behind them, unable to follow it's quarry, the missile slammed into the water and exploded.

"We're clear," Timbo announced. "No other hostiles in the air."

"Dumb-bombs," Gallant muttered as he pulled back on the throttles. "What do you say we ease the speed back and link-up with Pinto."

Diego Guzman realized he was a man who knew too much. Sometimes, that scared him. He was a self-made Multi-millionaire who had sold his automated robotics company to Glenn Gowan two years before. Glenn Gowan had even insisted that he remain as the plant's manager. It was the 'windfall' of a lifetime that he had been striving for all his life. And he cared what direction the company would take after he gave up control of it. He was forty years old, a widower and felt fulfilled in his life's accomplishments. He had a good, comfortable life. But, he needed challenges.

One day, his life changed. He met Glenn's brother, Marcus. Diego, at first, thought Marcus was a bit eccentric for his tastes but, as the two talked, he realized he was more mature than he looked and that they both had common interests. Not long after that, Marcus confided in Diego, his secret, his dream. And he was intrigued.

Marcus made him an offer that was out of this world. Literally. Marcus told Diego not to accept the offer right away and asked him to think about it for four or five days before giving an answer. Diego sat on the fence for three of those days and the decision was made late one night when watching the late-night news. There were reports after report of chaos and violence in the streets all over the world. If it wasn't the food riots, it was the water riots or the constant energy crisis. The muggings, car-jackings, armed robberies, extortions, kidnapping and the killings. Not to mention, the battles raging between the various countries in the world. Democratic nations implementing marshal law to curb the violence.

He decided on the fourth night that he would accept Marcus' offer. He was driving home from the plant and realized that he had driven through six police checkpoints to travel two miles to his home. All vehicles sent out a radio signal that allowed them uninterrupted passage through the checkpoints, but since he worked late in his office and it was after dark, the police were stopping all vehicular traffic. At one point, he was questioned by a bad tempered, frustrated cop who obviously was having a bad day. Elapsed time was 2 hours. America, he concluded, had become a police-state and the Founding Fathers of Liberty and Freedom would surely be turning in their graves.

Tonight, as he closed the front door, he double-locked the door designed to prevent home invasions which were now a common occurrence. He disarmed his home security system which employed a retinal scan panel built into the wall. He walked into his kitchen, threw his mail and advertising flyers on the kitchen table and opened the refrigerator door and took out a bottle of water. Standing there, looking at the food in his fridge, he decided he was no longer hungry.

He decided to go up to his bedroom on the second floor and as he did so, the motion sensors in each room turned on lights as he entered and off as he exited. When he entered his bedroom and the lights came on, he turned on his desktop computer to check his e-mails. He didn't immediately notice the large, quartz-like clear crystal, sitting on his nightstand, glowing blue. He stared at for a few moments.

'Finally,' he thought to himself.

He felt like a giant weight had been lifted of his shoulders. The wait was over. And now he was faced with the dilemma of what to do next.

After he accepted Marcus Gowan's offer, he was given the crystal. He was told to keep it nearby and safe for when it came time to leave his world behind, all he had to do is touch the crystal to receive a message after it began to glow blue. He took it home and placed it on his nightstand beside his bed.

Often, he found himself studying the crystal. It's transparency revealed no batteries or electronic hardware. It was about nine inches tall and four and a half inches in diameter and weighed about five pounds.

He approached the nightstand cautiously and gently touched the top of the crystal with two fingers. A holographic image of Marcus Gowan appeared.

"Diego, my friend," the smiling image began. "This pre-recorded image of me has been activated via satellite in orbit. This recording can only be accessed by your DNA alone and can only be viewed once after which, this crystal will disintegrate."

The image paused.

"The time for our exodus has arrived. You and hundreds of thousands of others are currently making their way out of their home countries. Make your way, at first light, to the LA Marina and board the converted ferry 'Firenze'. She will shuttle you and others, who have received a similar message to a rendezvous point, two hundred fifty miles out to sea. Take only what you know you can carry. Company employees will arrive in two days to box up the rest of your belongings and have them shipped to you. I must also re-iterate the importance of being discreet on your way to the marina. Draw no attention to yourself and you'll have no trouble at all. Call the video-phone number below this image to notify the crew that you are enroute to the Firenze. They will know to expect you and will not leave without you unless absolutely necessary. Godspeed, Diego, my friend."

The holographic image faded and the crystal's blue glow began to change to green, then clear. Then the glow ceased and the crystal simply and abruptly fell apart to the carpeted bedroom floor like a column of water. Diego was startled and had taken a step back. Liquid splashed all over his nightstand, the side of his bed, and onto the floor. He bent over and touched the liquid on his nightstand and at first smelled it, rubbed it between his fingertips and then, tasted it.

"Huh, salt-water," he concluded.

He stood up and walked over to his closet and began to extract two medium suitcases and a backpack and piled them at the doorway of his bedroom. He began to take clothes out of his closet and dressers and piled them on the edge of his bed opposite of where the crystal had disintegrated. He decided the contents of one suitcase would contain a week's supply of clothing, the second would contain miscellaneous electronic gadgets and his backpack would carry his camping and survival gear.

He spent an hour packing at which point he decided to carry them to his front door and then try to get some sleep on the sofa in the living room. First, he needed to make a videophone call.

After the third ring, a young brunette's face appeared on the screen, "SS Firenze Pacific Tours. This is Annette."

"Hello, Annette," Diego began. "My name is Diego Guzman and a friend of mine booked me for a tour, tomorrow morning. I'd liked to confirm my booking and time of departure."

"Certainly, Mr. Guzman," she looked away. "I'll just check your name on the manifest," she was typing keys on a keyboard of a computer that was just out of view. It took about five seconds.

Yes, Mr. Diego Guzman," She looked back at the videophone with a pleasant, warm smile. "Your booking is confirmed and departure is scheduled for 10 a.m. Do you require transportation to the marina, sir?"

"That would be nice, Thank-you," he accepted.

She typed again on her computer, "Allright. The shuttle van will pick you up at nine a.m. How much luggage will you be bringing with you?"

"Two medium suitcases and one backpack. And please, call me Diego."

She smiled at that, "OK, Diego. I'll see you on the Firenze in the morning, then."

Diego smiled back at her, "Goodnight, Annette. He ended the call, fluffed up a throw-pillow on the sofa and made himself comfortable. He set the alarm of his wrist-watch and loosened his tie. Laying back, closing his eyes, he hoped he would be able to get some sleep.

Major Manning and Lt. Stuart followed Marcus up to Deck 3. Manning was counting entranceways to different rooms of whatever it was they were in. He still hadn't made up his mind to believe anything Marcus had told them. Manning's situational awareness was telling him they were facing the rear of the craft as they headed down the corridor. Marcus stopped at a large hatchway and pressed a button on the panel. The double-layered doors of the hatch opened accompanied by a yellow-strobe warning light. Manning read the ID markings on the bulkhead, 'DECK 3 EXTERIOR HATCH, STARBOARD SIDE'.

"What, exactly, are we doing?" Manning asked.

Marcus had entered the hatchway and began handing out what appeared to be spacesuits and helmets to Manning and Stuart from the equipment lockers inside.

"Well, I figure the only way I am going to get the two of you to believe anything I've told you, is to get you to experience it, first-hand."

He paused as he turned back to the lockers and extract a pair of boots for each of them.

"We, the three of us, are going for a space-walk on the outer hull," he concluded.

Manning saw Stuart's jaw drop as they looked at each other.

"I'd just be happy to look out a window," Stuart said to Manning.

Marcus stopped rooting through the locker and stood up, chuckling.

"Look," Marcus began to explain to Manning, "The only way I am going to convince you both, beyond a reasonable doubt, is to show you. If I show you a window and you are debriefed once you are back home, you won't be able to say for certain that we are in space. Your superiors will claim you were duped into thinking you were in space. Therefore, I will show you, firsthand,"

Marcus turned to Stuart.

"And you, Lieutenant, will accompany us. Not only to bear witness but, to ensure the safety of your commanding officer from a 'terrorist', like me."

It took Rob Stuart about half a second to realize that Marcus had a sarcastic sense of humor as he returned to the equipment lockers. Once he gathered everything for the three of them, he activated his headset and called for the Destiny's engineer.

"Bruno. This is Marcus," he paused. "I need your help at the starboard exterior hatch."

Manning and Stuart just watched Marcus as he listened intently with his hand raised to the earpiece of the headset.

"No, Chief," Marcus replied. "Everything's fine. I and two others are going EVA to check the hull and I need your assistance suiting up."

Another pause.

"Thank-you, Chief," Marcus said as he turned to the two soldiers and handed each of them an EVA suit.

I want the two of you to watch and do the same as me as I put on my suit. They go on tight but, will loosen as the suit is pressurized to fifteen psi but, won't blow up like a balloon."

Marcus depressed a latch against the wall where an electric motor revealed a bench which folded out from it. He sat down and continued his explanation of the spacesuits.

"The material the suits are made of, are of a unique fabrication process. I won't bore you with the details but we were originally designing a diving-suit that would be able to handle pressures of depths of around two to three kilometers during our archeological dives near the Guiana Basin of the Atlantic Ocean."

Marcus paused and stood up as pulled up the bottom of the suit to his waist. Manning and Stuart also stood up as they struggled to pull up the bottom half of their suits.

"What archeological dive, was that?" Manning asked. "What ship were you diving on?"

Marcus, seeing that Stuart was still struggling with his suit, began to help him. "Oh, it wasn't a ship, Major. It was a structure."

Now skeptical, Manning stopped. "In the water? What kind of structure?"

Still helping Stuart with his suit, Marcus just turned his head to look Manning in the eye.

"It was a building, Major. A really big, building," he said and turned back to his task of helping Lt. Stuart with his suit.

Stuart had stopped trying to put on their suits, "I don't understand. What building would be in the Atlantic Ocean?"

Marcus had paused and even hesitated to reveal any more information while continuing his task of helping Stuart and then realized that both men were still waiting for an explanation. He stopped for a moment.

"Well, the building is called the Temple of Archives and in it contained all the records of a now extinct society," Marcus finally revealed. "And it also contained technological records as well."

Manning thought that either Marcus Gowan was very good liar or this story was just too fantastic not to be believed. Then again, he didn't believe Gowan about being in space and yet, here the three of them were, suiting up getting ready to walk in space. Either they were going to walk back out amongst the rubble of the cavernous hanger bay or they all would be….

"Who built it and how do you know it was called the 'Temple of Archives', Manning asked.

Marcus succeeding with helping Lt. Stuart with his suit went back to his own and began to answer the Major.

"It took us a while to figure out the language. It would be considered today as more ancient than ancient Aramaic. The name of the structure is inscribed into the stone fascia of the entrance." He gestured to the two soldiers to put on the upper half of their space suits. "As to who built it, they referred to themselves as 'The Children of The Law of The One'. Loose translation; 'The Chosen of God'.

Manning looked over at Stuart as he was helped by Marcus to put on the upper part of the space suit. "You want us to believe that, there is some ancient building on the bottom of the ocean containing ancient records of some lost society?"

When Manning's head came through the neck of the suit, Marcus stopped and looked him in the eyes, "You don't have to believe anything I say, Major. You asked."

Marcus checked over and closed the seals on Stuart's suit before moving to and doing the same for Manning's suit.

"You're talking about Atlantis, aren't you," Stuart asked.

Manning watched for Marcus' reaction.

"Yes. I am," Marcus said matter of fact.

"Atlantis is a myth," Manning stated. "Stories made up by some long dead philosopher. Scholars and scientists alike, have pondered and searched for it and no one has found any definitive proof that it ever existed."

Marcus had succeeded in putting on his own upper part of his EVA suit and when his head popped through the neck, he replied, "Until now."

All three men had not noticed the approach of the Destiny's Chief Engineer, Bruno Kravakis. Listening to the end of the conversation, he immediately began double checking the seals on the three EVA suits. Marcus introduced everybody.

"How about a tour of the Engine Room," Stuart asked Kravakis.

Not even looking up, a big smile broadened on the Chief's face and he replied, "That's up to the 'Skipper'."

Manning looked over at Marcus Gowan and the two men made eye contact at which point, he quickly raised and lowered his eyebrows.

"You?" Manning asked.

"Me," Gowan confirmed, nodding once.

"I didn't know you were a pilot as well," Manning commented.

"You mean, it never said anything in my intelligence file about being a pilot," Marcus corrected with a smile.

Manning's eyes narrowed. He was trying to figure out how Gowan knew what would be in that file or how he would know there was even such a file. Marcus interrupted his train of thought.

"Major. If I were in your shoes, I would want to know everything about the objective including intel gathered from other sources. I suspect you would be as, 'methodical'."

Manning thought that he had to, at least, acknowledge that explanation. It made sense. He eased his facial features and Gowan recognized this. Marcus had succeeded in diverting suspicion away from the fact that he knew what was in his own dossier.

"You guys ready for your helmets?" Chief Kravakis asked as he handed them to each man.

"Do as I do and as the Chief checks the seal, watch and double check with him. Doing that is meant as a safety precaution. We look out for each other," Marcus instructed. He then slowly put the helmet on, locked the seal at the collar and then toggled the on-switch for the life-support system of the EVA suit which was located on the panel built into the chest of the suit. Manning and Stuart watched as Chief Kravakis checked over Marcus' suit and when he was satisfied, patted the suit twice on the right shoulder and gave Marcus the 'Thumbs-up' signal that everything was 'OK' on the outside of the suit and he reciprocated that everything was 'OK' inside.

Kravakis turned the two military officers, "Who's next?"

Stuart stepped forward, "I am, Chief."

The same routine was followed for both men and when all three men were ready to enter the airlock, Kravakis activated his headset to give final instructions.

"The Skipper knows this but, you two, don't. Anytime there is an EVA, you will be monitored at all times, audio-visually. It's a safety procedure. Your boots are magnetic capable and is activated by the control panel on your left arm marked 'Mag Boots'. The boots only require five pounds to dislodge from the hull and as you can see, the magnetic strength can be increased or decreased. The other buttons on the arm panel are the environmental controls for your suits," Manning and Stuart brought their left arms up to their helmets as the Chief continued his instruction.

"Air pressure; increase and decrease. Suit temperature; increase and decrease. As well, the helmet glass has auto-tint features that will protect you from direct sunlight," he paused. "Are we copasetic?"

All three men gave a, 'thumbs-up', affirmative.

"Good. Step through the airlock and activate your boots before decompression has cycled." The three men turned and stepped through the airlock and turned to watch the inner airlock door close. "It's your show now, Skipper."

Marcus gave the Chief the 'Thumbs-up' through the dura-glass window of the airlock door. Chief Kravakis then headed back to the Engineering Bay.

"The moment of truth, Gentlemen," Marcus said as he initiated the decompression cycle. An alarm sounded and additional, amber strobe lights lit up the airlock. Marcus could see that Lt. Stuart's breathing had increased and before anything else, he looked him directly in the eyes and put his right hand on his left shoulder. "Calm down, Lieutenant. Slow, deep breathes. You're a parachutist, right?"

Stuart nodded his head inside the EVA suit.

"Remember your first jump? You were nervous, right? Remember how easy the jump seemed afterward?"

"I puked my guts out after I pulled my chute," Stuart admitted.

Marcus chuckled, "So did I after my first jump. Keep your eyes on the hull."

Stuart stole a look over at his CO who had a smirk on his face

"And don't puke in your suit," Manning said.

Marcus, now himself smirking, turned and depressed the outer hatch release button and watched the hatch slide open.

Kyle Latavish piloted his private luxury submarine, 'Angelique', carefully towards the mouth of the harbor. He was surprised to see the completed dockyards. He was told not to expect much in the way of civilization when he arrived. He was told that, as a new nation everything was being started from scratch. As he continued further into the harbor, he could see that construction of a small city was evident. To the west, he could see a large tent and shipping container city and some activity there as well. He knew that he and the three families he offered to bring with him would most likely be staying on the submarine for a while.

The 65 meter submarine was a marvel of modern technology. Even though she was of a simple but, luxurious design, she supported the latest in navigational and wave stabilization aids. She was worth a hundred million dollars brand new, Kyle Latavish had purchased it for a quarter of that, second hand from a now bankrupt multi-millionaire. Its power plant was a one megawatt fuel-cell propulsion drive which took water from the sea and through the process of electrolysis, split the hydrogen and oxygen atoms to convert them into heat and power from the fuel-cells with the only byproducts being pure, drinkable water and pure oxygen.

Six year old Caitlin Stone was suddenly at Kyle Latavish's side.

"Are we there, yet?" she asked, jumping up trying to look out the bridge/conning tower windscreen.

"Yes, Luv," he replied. "Would you like a look-see?"

"Yes, please," she said.

With one hand still on the helm, he bent down and quickly picked up the precocious little girl who saw land for the first time in two weeks.

"Doesn't look like an island," she said.

"No, it doesn't," he agreed. "It's a big island. In fact, it would take a long time just to walk all the way around it."

"Wow!" she replied.

"Wow, indeed." he chuckled.

There was a moment of silence between the two of them as the yacht continued slowly, deeper into the harbor. The radio suddenly came to life as the harbor-master called the slowly approaching sub. Latavish put the girl down, responded and identified the sub as the 'Angelique' and gave the clearance code. The harbormaster directed him to make for the small marina on his starboard side on the western side of the harbor.

Caitlin looked up at Kyle, "Are you a pirate captain?"

Kyle looked at her, puzzled.

"No, luv. Why do you ask that?"

"Cause you talk like a pirate. Kinda' funny." she replied.

Kyle laughed, "I'm English, luv. I was born in London."

"Still sounds funny," she said.

"Well, luv," he began. "You sound funny, to me."

"Like what?" she asked.

"Oh, I don't know. Like a duck, maybe."

She laughed, "No I don't. Do I?"

"No, luv," he smiled at her. "Just kidding."

"Do you like playing captain?" Caitlin asked.

"I like playing music," he replied.

"I like music," she announced.

"Me too, luv," Kyle said. "Tell you a secret; I can even make music, too."

"Wow," she said. "Can I learn to make music, too?"

Kyle looked down and the little girl was swinging her hips and rolling on her heels. The innocent look in her eyes made her look like the poster-child for cuteness.

He figured that given that the attention span of a six year old was likely pretty short, he could probably promise her the moon and she would likely be fairly happy with that.

"Sweetheart, You can do anything you want to," he agreed. "Why don't you go below and tell your parents, we have arrived."

"OK," she said as she skipped across the deck.

Kyle briefly toyed with the idea of teaching music to children. He felt too young to teach music. He was still enjoying composing and recording.

Kyle Latavish had composed and sold his first song to a rock & roll band when he was twelve years old. The song earned the band 'Song of the Year'. Even though he had sold the rights to the song as well, he received the recognition and the confidence to continue to compose for six years while learning to play every musical instrument he could get he hands on.

At age nineteen, after a year of vocal lessons, he created his own commercial recordings. He, however, did not like the sound of his own voice and decided to stick to instrumental/dance compositions. He became quite renowned and accumulated a large, worldwide fan-base. At age twenty-four, he conceived of the 'Army of Rock' which involved one thousand guitars playing a set of compositions in an acoustically perfect valley in Ireland. The guitar rifts emanating from the valley was inspirational, beautiful and powerful. The event, called 'Supreme Overload' was recorded, filmed and sold commercially worldwide making it the best selling and most creative musical compositions created that year.

There were those before him who were given labels, when it came to the music styles with which they created like; the 'King of Rock & Roll', the 'Prince of Pop', the 'Boss' or 'Badboy' of Rock & Roll or even the 'First Lady of Country Music' and the like. Ever since that event, six years before,

Kyle Latavish has been known by the media as the 'Supreme Overlord of Rock & Roll'.

There was no doubt about it, he was famous. And he was rich beyond his wildest dreams. He was as recognizable as the teenaged King of England. Only Latavish had more paparazzi following him around, invading his private life. The final straw came when a photographer broke into his studio on his estate in Scotland, stole the latest recordings he had spent months working on and sold them to a tabloid newspaper which turned around and put them on the Internet for free, for the world to download. He was furious.

So he sued. He had the money by which to do it. He was told by his team of lawyers that if he won, and they believed they would, it would be a precedent setting case. Latavish instructed the lawyers to "swarm like sharks at a feeding frenzy". In the end, after a year, he and his team of lawyers won a ground-breaking case that not only penalized the tabloid with initial damages in the multi-millions but they also had to pay hundreds of millions in punitive damages which he, in turn, gave to charities involved with the poor in third-world countries. The tabloid newspaper and it's parent-company, went bankrupt. Glenn Gowan, CEO of the Gowan corporate empire, bought the parent-company and all it's assets. And that is how he met Marcus Gowan.

The two became fast friends. Marcus conceded that he, too, was a fan and Kyle admired him for his quiet, low key work with the poor and disadvantaged. Kyle had wanted to continue creating music without the notoriety but felt discouraged in doing so. One day, Marcus called his friend and asked him to travel to his lab as he had created a new tool which would enhance a musician's ability to make 'beautiful, almost angelic music' and he wanted Kyle to test it. Kyle was initially skeptical but privately, hopeful and excited. Anything to get him back on track, to create wonderful music again. The music he composed made his spirit soar skyward. He confided to Marcus once, that he would love to go into space or even on the Moon to play in zero-G and that the music contained in him was just waiting to burst out. He felt as if his music was from his very soul and that believed he was touching the souls of those who listened. He could feel it within himself. Based on that, Marcus Gowan created the Neural EnhancingTransmitter that relayed the feeling part of the brain and tied it directly to the instrument being played. By the end of the first day of testing, Kyle's musical block was gone and he felt the need for the music inside him to escape.

After a bit of tweaking and adjustments, they called it a day and Marcus gave his friend a tour of the complex. Kyle had to admit that, some of the things in the labs quite frankly, freaked him out.

Marcus asked for secrecy of the things he saw and Kyle agreed. Marcus then made an offer Kyle just simply couldn't refuse.

"Kyle, you once expressed a desire to play music off-world, but you want to live life like a normal person," Marcus asked. "Still feel that way?"

"I did and I do," Kyle confirmed. "What are you asking?"

"What if I told you that some time in the future," Marcus began. "that a space-faring nation will be created on this planet, inhabited from a select group of people from almost every nation and from every walk of life, poor included. Going into space will be as easy as taking a commercial jet airliner."

Kyle just gave Marcus a weird look. Marcus continued.

"You will be able to make the music you want and have all the anonymity you want."

"What's the 'Catch'."

Marcus paused for a moment, "The catch is that, I must ask for secrecy not to divulge this to anyone and that you will have to leave this part of your life behind. In time, you will still receive the recognition and accolades for the music you will undoubtedly create, without the negative attention a person of your stature seems to attract. Your life will be rewarding and you'll have purpose and meaning."

Kyle laughed, "What. Are you in contact with aliens or something?"

Marcus chuckled, "No. Nothing like that at all. All I can tell you at the moment; is that a short time from now, there will be a nation that will ensure the survival of the Human race from extinction on Earth. I would also like you to be a part of that nation."

Kyle looked at his friend directly in the eyes. The seriousness of this man was uncanny. Each of them just stared at each other for what seemed an eternity.

"Extinction from what? Aliens?"

"Same thing that wiped out the dinosaurs. Comets, asteroids," he shrugged his shoulders. "Possibly from ourselves."

"I see," Kyle said trying to reassess his relationship with his friend.

"The point is that, for the first time in the history of recorded time, Humanity has the ability to not only wipe itself out but, to save itself from or prevent it's own extinction. I have the means by which to do this."

"Why not share it with the world?" Kyle asked.

"You've seen the technology in my labs." Marcus said briefly looking down at the floor and back into Kyle's eyes. "Experienced for yourself what it could do for you to improve your God-given gift. That technology would be perverted into weapons of mass destruction and make life on planet Earth a lot worse than it is already."

Even back then, Kyle was ready to accept the offer, to jump at the chance. To be able to make the music he wanted without always having to be constantly worried of the fact that his life was under a microscope. Marcus had sensed this but told his friend to sleep on it.

And he did. For one night.

He went to Marcus' lab the next day and told him he would accept his offer but, on one condition; that he receive full disclosure.

Marcus Gowan agreed and Kyle was flabbergasted, speechless at what was planned. Marcus Gowan was a man in a unique, if not historic position. It took Kyle a full week to process what he was told. In his opinion, this was the single most important thing to happen on Earth since the life, death and resurrection of Jesus Christ. And he wanted to be apart of it, too. A new life in a new world was just too, damned attractive.

That was a year ago and he hadn't looked back since. He quietly got his affairs in order, sold all his assets and also helped Marcus Gowan acquire provisions for those who arrived on the island after the 'Exodus'.

And now, here he was at the end of one journey and the beginning of another. He took great comfort in knowing that he was not alone in exploring new horizons.

As he approached the Fresco City's Marina, he spotted a perfect berth to tie up his submarine.

CHAPTER FIVE

'AGNUS DEI'

Major Manning was doing everything he was instructed. Marcus Gowan was telling him and Lt. Stuart to take slow and deliberate steps as they moved about the hull of the ship. Gowan was even walking along, both hands on each of them to make sure the two were doing OK.

"That's it," he said, watching each step they made. "Slowly lift the heel and slowly take your next step. Any fast movements, you risk launching yourself into space and *that,* would not be a good thing."

"I think I'm getting the hang of this," Stuart admitted.

"Same here," Manning agreed.

Marcus released his hold on the two soldiers and watched them as they watched their steps. He watched and followed them until they were all on the topside part of the hull.

"Ok, gentlemen, stop." Both men stopped and straightened up from their walk. He paused for the longest time, looking to their gold-shielded visors before finally speaking. "Now, turn around."

Both men turned together slowly and their eyes beheld the first heavenly body other than the Moon. The two men just stared at the red planet. Even at this distance, it was larger than the size of the Moon as if being gazed upon from the Earth. In space, the color and the details were so vibrant that it seemed, to at least Manning, it was too good to be true. He put his gloved hand to his helmet and rubbed the glass with it. He heard Marcus chuckle over the intercom.

"It's not a trick, Major. I assure you," Marcus said.

Manning turned to the approaching Marcus who now stood beside him. "Just checking."

"Well. What do you think?"

Lt. Stuart spoke up first, "If this is a hoax, you sure went to a lot of trouble."

All three men laughed at the comment and then Manning spoke.

"That is amazing. I feel awed and so small at the same time."

"My first time was watching the Earth from lunar orbit. I felt the same way." Marcus admitted.

Manning turned to Marcus, "You do this often?"

"Half a dozen times, so far," Marcus confirmed. "First time I've been out this far, though."

"And what, exactly, do you plan on doing out here?" Manning asked.

"Ensure the survival of Humanity, colonize, explore," Marcus offered.

Manning and Stuart just stared at the man who had taken them 'topside'. Marcus avoided eye contact with the two professional soldiers and continued to watch the planet Mars.

"You think I must be mad, yes?" Marcus plainly said.

Manning bluntly said what first came to mind. "Deluded, maybe."

"Believe me, Major," Marcus chuckled. "I am anything but, that."

"Others would beg to differ," Manning countered. "My superiors would claim this is all the result of a madman. That *you,* are still a dangerous man and a threat to the world community."

"I am only a threat to those who would want events, such as this, to be kept from the public consciousness of the world. That, with certain technologies, which would revolutionize life on Earth as we know it, a person could become powerful. That such a man in possession of such technologies is also a man in possession of incredible power. A man with that much power could endanger and possibly attempt to conquer the world. All I want to do is to go into space and prove to everyone that going there will be as easy as flying your own private aircraft."

Manning's baiting of Marcus Gowan had failed. He was hoping to get an idea of this man's real intentions. It was obvious that he possessed incredible technology and power and such a man could be tempted to seek to increase his power. There were plenty of examples in history of these men. Marcus Gowan had passed his first test.

"What do you mean by 'easy'," Stuart asked.

"Well," Marcus started. "To get out here, you didn't apply, go through an extensive interview process so others would determine whether or not you have the 'Right Stuff' to be out here. You didn't require years of specialized training. And you didn't sit on several hundred thousand tons of rocket fuel for hours before an aborted or successful launch to *maybe,* get as far as Earth orbit."

"Oh," Stuart had said. "I thought that was the easy way."

"Not anymore," Marcus smiled as he looked at the two. "Look at it this way; you two now hold the record for humans to have ventured this far from Earth."

That brought a smile to the two officer's faces as they realized the truth of the statement. The furthest manned expeditions from the Earth, had been to the Moon, first by the Americans, years later, the Russians and now the Chinese. They both looked around their surroundings. Manning turned and saw a yellow, bright sun for the first time outside the confines of the protective atmosphere of planet Earth.

"To activate the telephoto lens of the helmet glass," Marcus said to Manning. "Just say; 'Magnify view, maximum.'"

Manning did so and was taken aback as he viewed through the magnified, filtered lens. The details of the sun seemed so exact, even at this distance. He could see the faint outlines of sunspots and solar flares. The corona was even apparent.

"What is the total magnification," Manning asked Marcus.

A computer voice answered inside his helmet. "Magnification is currently set at one thousand percent of normal."

Intuitively Manning asked, "Set to normal, please."

The response was immediate and for a couple of seconds, Manning was disoriented as his eyes tried to adjust. Marcus saw this and grabbed his left arm to help him stabilize his stance.

Stuart had done the same thing, only he wasn't looking at the sun.

"Hey!" he said excitedly. "I can see the Earth and Moon from here."

The three stood there, for moments at a time, in silence, just viewing their stellar surroundings. Manning was so shocked as to the vividness and brightness of the stars, he didn't notice the haze that was apparent, across the darkness of space. It was like a thick, cloudy line that stretched far from his lower left to his far upper right. Looking away to the planet Mars and then to the upper hull of this spacecraft on which he and Lt. Stuart were standing, he had to admit, finally, that they were exactly where they appeared to be and that this was clearly no hoax. Standing here, in a spacesuit on the hull of a spaceship, gazing amongst the stars touched his soul. He felt the overpowering sense of peace. He looked over at Marcus, who had said nothing but, had been watching the two soldier's reactions to their surroundings. Marcus was wearing a pleasant frown on his face as if he were aware of what Manning had come to realize. He looked back to the hull of spaceship and realized that he really couldn't tell how large it was without a frame of reference. He began slowly walking to the far edge to look over what was the starboard side of the ship and looked down. Even though he saw even more stars, he became slightly nauseous. He closed his eyes and slowly turned around and kept his eyes on the hull as he rejoined the other two.

"What is that cloud over there," Manning inquired.

Marcus turned and looked up as Manning and Stuart stepped beside him. He turned from his left to his right.

"Well, we are looking towards the center of the Milky Way galaxy. Our home galaxy. That is its inclination in relation to us. Our star system is located close to the outer edge of the Milky Way."

"How come we can't see this from Earth?" Stuart asked.

Marcus summarized the explanation with one word, "Atmosphere.. pollution..."

Stuart understood the answer immediately. The diffusing effect of a polluted atmosphere for stargazing on Earth is difficult enough with large telescopes, let alone with the human eye. Even when there are no light sources nearby, it is still a challenge to acquire the best viewing locations. In space, there is no atmosphere present. The three men stared up and took in the sight which beheld them. Manning turned slowly to Marcus.

"We have to talk."

"I'm listening," Marcus replied without turning from the heavens.

"Although I can think of no other place to discuss what I have to say of the subject, I prefer to do so, inside."

Marcus Gowan turned to Manning and looked to his tinted visor of his suit's helmet and then nodded.

"Alright. Lets go."

The reception area was lavish yet sparsely dotted with large potted plants, here and there. The man was sitting patiently on the well worn and well cared-for sofa. As he checked his watch, he realized he had been waiting for about ten minutes, now. Unconsciously, he began staring at the receptionist who was going about what ever it was she was doing. Her desk was made of mahogany wood and had a riser so he could only see her from the neck up. Between typing on her computer and the occasional shuffling of paper, he surmised that she probably had a hand-gun under her desk and a bank of monitors underneath that desk riser watching him. Her phone buzzed and she calmly answered it. He couldn't make out what was being said from her end, so he looked back down at his watch.

"Agent Tobin," the receptionist said as she hung up her phone. "He will see you, now."

"Thank-you," he said as he rose from the sofa and picked up his briefcase and began making his way to the double mahogany doors that led to the inner office. Upon entering, he realized that the inner office was much more lavishly appointed than the reception area. The smell of cigar smoke and the slight odor of brandy was apparent. The lights were off and the room was lit only by sunlight from a bank of three large windows and a single lamp set to one side of the desk at the rear of the office. He could barely make out a silhouette sitting in the leather -padded chair.

"Come in. Come in, Agent Tobin," the silhouette encouraged. "Please, sit down."

Agent Tobin found a comfortable chair in front of the desk and placed his briefcase flat on the small end table beside it. He could see the man behind the desk more clearly now. He was a tall, thin man, clean shaven with short, grey hair. He was a handsome man who Tobin suspected was and still turns women's heads.

"Would you care for a brandy before we get started," the man offered.

"No. No, thank-you, Senator," Tobin declined.

"Very well," the Senator said as he sat erect in his chair. "Right now, you are trying to figure out why you have been asked to report to me on this matter of Continental Security."

"Well, Sir," Tobin replied. "Actually, I am trying to figure out how senator of your tenure and low-key stature is the man who is the one pulling the strings behind the Continental Security Agency. However, I suspect that there is more to the CSA than you want people to know."

"I was right about you Agent Tobin," the Senator admitted. "You are smarter than your superiors give you credited for." The Senator sat back in his chair. "Of course, the CSA is just my cover. I am going to tell you something that must not leave this office and it will always be denied and will never be confirmed."

The Senator paused for a moment, articulating his thoughts.

"I am, part of an organization that monitors technological advances throughout the world. Technologies that could tip the balance of power from one nation, to another. If a technology is deemed dangerous and a threat to this nation, or even beneficial, it is either acquired, in one form or another, discredited or stomped on, as if it were a small fire of crumpled paper. The point is, throughout history, there have been certain technological advances in all fields that have kept Human progress moving forward. Those historical advances evolved and now the United States of America is the master of all those technologies. I, and the group which I am apart of, want to keep it that way. Have you ever read about the discovery of the two scientists who tested that a cold-fusion generator as a viable energy source in the mid 1990's? The group I work with was, back then, responsible for putting out that fire."

Tobin looked at the Senator quizzically, "Are you telling me cold-fusion is a viable power source?"

"Oh, yes." the Senator replied enthusiastically. "Until it was discovered that the by-product of cold-fusion was weapons-grade Tritium. Imagine, just about everyone in the world making a cold-fusion generator on their kitchen tables and having weapons grade nuclear material as a waste product. And I'm not talking about miniscule amounts, either."

Tobin thought about that for a moment. "I see what you mean."

"I'm glad that you do," The Senator said as he put out his cigar in a large crystal ashtray. "There are plenty more examples of which I won't bore you with. Suffice to say, the group I'm associated with, is large, far-reaching and has many resources on which it can rely on. It's an organization that has a higher security clearance than that of the CSA, CIA and the NSA. In fact, *we* are the real spooks."

Tobin sat there quietly listening to the story spun by the Senator. If he hadn't been here, hearing this tale, he would have assumed this to be fiction.

"Senator, why are you telling me this? I thought I was here to bring you up to speed on the Marcus Gowan situation."

"You're a rising star within the CSA. You are the analyst who put the pieces of the puzzle together on the Galveston insurgent group last year. You prevented a lot of civilian deaths tracking their activities and netted us a gold mine of intelligence." The Senator stood up from behind desk and headed for the office windows. "From now on, you'll be writing your reports and assessments for us. You will also be making presentations to my group. In the future, you may even brief 'The Committee'. For the time being, you'll still be working from the CSA but, you'll be paid by us."

He turned from the window and made eye contact with Tobin.

"Does this shock you, Agent Tobin?"

"No, sir," Tobin replied. "It's unexpected but not shocking."

"We expect your acceptance of this opportunity.." the Senator began.

"...and you would not have offered it to me if you knew I wouldn't have accepted, either," Tobin finished.

The Senator smiled widely, clearly impressed at Tobin's forward thinking.

"Exactly."

"Then, I accept."

"Good," the Senator replied as he sat back down at his desk. "Then, bring me up to speed, son."

Tobin turned to the table he had placed his briefcase and opened it to retrieve a red file folder. "At 0930 hours, eastern time, anti-terrorist response teams of the Federal Dominion of Canada were inserted on Voice Island containing the White Alice Diamond Mine Facility owned and operated by Marcus Gowan. These elements consisted of one platoon of four squads, about 60 men, four C-280's and three light armored vehicles. Now there is some confusion as to what happened after they began their advance on the facility. Two of the squads are MIA and...."

"MIA?!" the Senator exclaimed. "What about Gowan? Did they get Gowan?"

"I'm getting to that, sir," he said as he looked up and then down to continue. "When the other two squads realized that half their force was missing, they regrouped and began to advance the facility, only to discover that the facility had disappeared."

"Disappeared?" the Senator asked.

"As I said, there is some confusion on our part as to the details," Tobin explained.

"What are the 'details'? Let's here it, anyway," the Senator ordered.

Tobin flipped through a couple a pages and found what he was looking for. "Well, after the two squads regrouped, they were within sight of the mining facility and were getting ready to do two things; take the base and then look for their missing squads."

He paused for a moment, looking for a particular statement. "Here it is. According to a... Lt. Dechene, a large craft, he called a 'UFO',only because he couldn't identify it, launched from out of nowhere and suddenly disappeared. The two remaining squads found themselves out of position and when they recovered to take the facility, they found it no longer existed."

"Explain," the Senator asked quizzically.

Tobin handed him two 8x11 color satellite photos.

"First one is the before and the second is the after photo. I figured, a picture's worth a thousand words."

The Senator briefly looked at the first picture. It was evident to Tobin that he had seen that layout before. But, when he flipped to the second, his eyes went wide. Tobin too, had studied the second photo. What was once what appeared to be a sprawling industrial mining facility, was now, nothing more than large hole in the ground. If there was any question that the three-sided caldera was once an ancient volcano, it certainly looked more apparent, now."

"Casualties?" the Senator asked.

"The two aforementioned squads are MIA. A short, preliminary search was conducted before the remaining elements were ordered to evacuate. No sign of them was found."

"Was there any contact between Marcus Gowan and his brother, Glenn?"

"The last contact that we know of; was almost a year ago when Marcus signed over his rights to their father's company to Glenn."

"Where did this occur," the Senator asked.

"Apparently, in Glenn Gowan's office."

"Surveillance?"

"We had audio and visual set up but, there was so much interference, we couldn't get anything."

"You're sure that's what he was there for?"

"Pretty much," Tobin said. "We tried to get someone on the inside who would be 'cooperative' but, we were unsuccessful. It was announced publicly in the newspapers the next day."

"Anything of the base left?" the Senator asked.

"Apparently nothing, Sir. Being that this all occurred on Canadian soil and there are sovereignty issues involved, the CSA was going to send a covert investigative team from our side of the border to survey the area."

"That's been scratched," the Senator said quickly. "I'll be sending you. In disguise."

"Senator, I'm an analyst," Tobin began to explain. "I have no field training whatsoever. There are qualified field agents who can.."

"A field agent doesn't know what you know. I need someone on-scene to assess certain evidence and report back directly to the members of our organization."

Tobin couldn't argue with the logic. It made perfect sense. He looked at the Senator questioningly, "What evidence am I looking for?"

"Technology of any kind. Or evidence, thereof." The Senator rose from his chair, approached Agent Tobin and gestured to the door. "Now, if you'll excuse me, I have a meeting at 'State' that I cannot miss. Report back next week and remember, dress warm. I hear its deathly cold at this time of the year, even during the day."

Tobin left the Senator's office slowly with his briefcase and overcoat. Walking down the hallway, he muttered to himself, "I hate the cold."

Thomas 'Doc' Thorpe stepped off the ramp of the cargo plane in time to see the flight crew exit the aircraft to stretch their legs. It was a long flight and he sympathized. Sure, they occasionally left the cockpit to walk and stretch, but now they were no longer restricted to the confines of the aircraft. The flight of cargo planes had made good time reaching Pacifica. In fact, his plane was catching up to the rest until he asked the pilot to make sure theirs was the last to land. He explained to the flight crew that he wanted to make sure that all planes were safe before they were. They agreed.

A burgundy-colored SUV pulled up to him and the front passenger door opened before it came to a full stop. A young black woman exited and made a bee-line for Doc.

"Doc," she waved as she approached. "Hi. Welcome. How was the flight?"

"Cindy," he gave her a hug. "It was long. How are things progressing here?"

Cindy Gates, Operations Director, was Thorpe's point-woman on Pacifica. She had been on the island for eighteen months organizing logistics before the 'The Exodus'; construction, infrastructure, communications, receiving new arrivals and shipments, etc.

"Slow," she announced. "A week of rain finally stopped yesterday. Family housing is about 2/3rds complete. Hence; the temporary sea-container city to the west. Power grid is up and running. Hydroponics greenhouses are in full production. The open-ocean fish-farm stations are producing 11 metric tons of fish, monthly. Water and Recycler plants are completed and running. Food synthesizer and processing plants will be operational by the beginning of next month. That won't be a problem since as of yesterday, inventory shows we have enough food to feed everybody for over a year. Comms network, will be running by the end of the day, tomorrow."

"Where is Angela Teslin?" Doc asked. "I was expecting her to meet me."

Angela Teslin was Cindy's Operations Manager and had worked closely with Doc, Cindy and Marcus on the preparations for the island's infrastructure. She was the same age as Marcus Gowan and was his biggest supporter and promoter.

"She is currently returning from Colani City," Cindy replied. "I told her I would meet you when your plane arrived."

"What about the space flight facility?" Doc asked.

She took her boss by the elbow, shaking her head and began to head to the SUV. "You realize that we weren't expecting your evac and arrival for another three months. Its about 70 percent complete. We will still have comms up by tomorrow. We've tried to raise Destiny via individual Quantum Hyperlink. Nothing. Have you tried?"

"I did." Doc admitted. "Couldn't raise them."

A look of horror came across Cindy's as she put her hand over her mouth. "You don't think they were still at White Alice when.."

Doc put his hands on her shoulders to calm her, "No, no. I received telemetry when they launched up until thirty minutes after."

"Maybe something happened in orbit," she wondered.

"That's why I need comms up A.S.A.P." he was now leading her towards the SUV. "I need to use our satellites to use the scanners to look for them."

They both got into the back seat of the SUV and the driver began to drive off the tarmac of the airport.

"What do you have supplying the power grid," Doc asked.

"We have the wind generator farm on the south side of the island, the ocean-wave generator farm off the west coast and the geo-thermal generating station ninety kilometers south of here. We have a bit of a problem supplying the docks in the harbor," she admitted. "Power grid is almost finished there but, supply is at a minimum. Kyle Latavish just arrived and he's offered the generating power of his private submarine to supplement demand."

Doc remembered Kyle Latavish. A famous musician who was also a poet and arm-chair philosopher, in his opinion.

"How much power can he provide?" he asked.

"Believe it or not, about one megawatt."

Doc was taken aback, "How big is this sub?"

"Its huge. It's the most luxurious thing I have ever seen." she replied. "However, that introduces problems of its own."

"What's that?" Doc asked as he grabbed the back-seat hand hold to steady himself as the SUV rounded a street corner a little too fast.

"The generating power of the sub is meant for just that; the operation of the sub. Bringing the rev's up to generate one Meg. for a long period increases wear and tear and she is powered by a fuel-cell engine that draws its fuel from the seawater."

"What does Kyle have to say about that," Doc asked.

"He says he doesn't care but, until his house is ready, he and the families he brought will stay on his sub."

Well, Doc thought to himself, if he didn't care, who was he to argue.

"When can we expect the dock problem to be resolved? He asked.

"Tomorrow afternoon, at the latest," Cindy responded.

"New arrivals status?" He was concerned for the people who had arrived and the ones that were enroute.

Cindy began pressing buttons on her computerized clipboard.

"Currently, there are approximately 1.3 million people on the island and approximately six hundred thousand now enroute. We estimate that .08 percent won't be able to get out of their home countries either because they couldn't make the rendezvous or they changed their minds."

"When the comms are online, for those who still want out, maintain contact. Those who have changed their minds, well, that's their choice."

"I concur," Cindy said.

Doc paused for a moment trying to think of something he knew he was forgetting to ask about.. He stared out the side window for the longest time. He knew Cindy was waiting for him ask about something else. He was so preoccupied with worry about the whereabouts of the Destiny and her crew. He knew they were up there, somewhere. Losing contact was supposed to be for a short time. But, not this long.

"What about the surplus ships? Where are they?" Doc finally remembered.

"We have fifty six converted freighters here in the bay awaiting transfer to join the two hundred twenty one currently at Colani City on the west coast. They are scheduled to be on the move tonight so we can receive the last of the new arrivals in the next couple of days."

"And the salvage crews?" he inquired. He was asking if they were ready to begin taking all those converted freighters apart for dismantling and recycling. This would be the trigger industry that would start an economy.

"Salvage crews are preparing. They are currently coming up with procedures for the removal of any and all hazardous wastes for recycling and/or destruction.." she was interrupted.

"What hazardous wastes? I thought they were removed when the ships were converted?" he suddenly spoke up.

"They have been," she replied. "When we start purchasing decommissioned freighters and tankers from around the world, we are going to need an aggressive hazardous waste removal procedure to deal with the toxic wastes."

Doc remembered. He and Marcus formulated a plan to purchase the decommissioned freighters and tankers of the world to recycle them. Originally, this was being done in India and Bangladesh. The industry was called 'shipbreaking' and they were being purchased, towed thousands of miles only to be run aground and dismantled on the beaches. This employed thousands of locals and created many spin-off businesses. However, when he and Marcus went on a covert fact-finding tour of the area, they found that there were no environmental controls; because there was no enforcement. Safety standards were non-existent and every day they were there, he saw evidence of work-related injuries and heard of at least five fatalities.

When United Nations investigative teams arrived to respond to reports of hazardous waste dumping into the Indian Ocean, they discovered that the Indian and Bangladeshi governments had for decades, looked the other way. The reason the government officials and agencies had done this, was because the salvage industry employed thousands of people in the impoverished region. The investigative teams had discovered that although the salvage companies were UN certified, audit documentation was either falsified or most cases, non-existent. They also discovered that the entire coastal region in the area had effectively become toxic from years of illegal dumping.

The World Health Organization was called in to investigate and to help. They were soon overwhelmed by the magnitude of the sick and dying from the decades of toxic dumping. The shear volume of acute and chronic illnesses was enough for the UN and the WHO to jointly declare the entire region an ecological disaster area. The salvage companies in the region lobbied the Indian and Bangladeshi governments to invoke sovereignty claims, to publicly deny and later downplay the full extent of the damage to the coastal region. They tried but, even doing so, seemed like a sick running comedy that turned into what seemed like a Shakespearian tragedy to the rest of the world.

Marcus felt for these people and he didn't want them to be victims of their environments. So, he began recruiting the locals. He met with some initial resistance but when they realized they could immigrate with their families and provide a better quality of life, he successfully recruited ninety percent of the workforce. With the vast financial resources afforded to Marcus, top dollar would be paid just to prevent the toxic wastes from being dumped into the oceans. Once immigration and relocation was complete, his medical teams cured them of their various ailments. And now, with retraining, a majority were living and working in the City of Colani on the west coast of Pacifica.

"We're almost there," Cindy announced as she began looking out the windshield. Doc looked up to see what she was referring to. They turned a couple of corners, went through two intersections before he realized what it was, she meant.

The building was the shape of a pyramid about ten stories tall constructed of Pallasite asteroid rock and Duraglass. Pallasite was the most beautiful of asteroid rock they had yet obtained. It contained olivine crystals set in a nickel/iron matrix. Believed to have been formed at the core/mantle boundry of a large asteroid or planetoid where the iron from the core would mix with the olivine crystals from the mantle. The result was a metallic sparkle effect of the stone, resembling a sparkling, black marble. Doc stood beside the vehicle, mouth wide open, shoulders low on his frame and clearly impressed. The massive building was flanked by young elm and oak trees. The landscaping had the effect of showcasing the building.

"Wow!" he said.

"I thought you'd be impressed," Cindy said as she stood at his side. "Final finishing was completed two days ago."

"You must have had those guys working around the clock, you slave driver," he kidded her.

"A little," she smiled as she confessed.

"Is this the Administration Building?"

Cindy began walking up the granite sidewalk towards the Duraglass entrance. Doc followed.

"You bet," she said, half turning. "What do you think?"

"Its looks better than the blueprints," he said as he watched the building as he approached. He found he couldn't take his eyes off of it.

"I honestly didn't think it would be finished by now," he admitted. Already, they had walked for a considerable distance and he realized they hadn't even covered half the distance, yet. All around, were small pathways that led to park benches and picnic tables set beneath trees, bordered by flowered plants.

When they both finally reached the Duraglass vestibule and entered, Doc realized the interior was as just as impressive as the exterior.

"I never saw this on the blueprints."

Cindy giggled, "Come on, Doc. I'll take you up to the operations floor."

As Doc followed Cindy, he took in the atrium of the main entrance. Potted plants, flowers and benches were everywhere. The mood and feel of the area was quiet, peaceful. He entered the elevator with Cindy, still spying the atrium. It was a quick ascent to the seventh floor and when the elevators opened, the entire floor was a hub of activity. It completely betrayed the quiet and serenity of the main floor. It reminded Thorpe of the bull-pen of the New York Stock Exchange. They skirted the perimeter of the activity to find, on the other end of the floor, the quiet Situation Room.

The room was exceptionally large, with slanted exterior Duraglass windows facing north. They had entered through a set of Duraglass double-doors flanked by Duraglass walls. To one side, on the wall was a large flat-screen monitor surrounded by a bank of relatively smaller ones. On the opposite wall was a full color, geographical map of the world and of the island nation of Pacifica. There were a couple of computer work stations in the room but, was mainly dominated by the large Duralloy conference table centered in the middle of the room.

Doc approached the table, put his luggage on the corner and kept going until he reached the window. What he saw was the layout of the land all the way to the harbor. The area was large and went on for miles.

He was amazed at how far away both the airport and the harbor was. The land rose slightly from the ocean to this location which he estimated the distance to be approximately 8 kms. Most of the land was untouched, covered mostly with grasses and very small shrubs. Anywhere there was a human presence, trees were planted. He spotted a round-bulbous hill area to the west of the tent city. It was about 15 km. away and rose higher than his current location on the 7th floor within the pyramid.

"What is that hill, over there," he pointed as he turned to Cindy. She joined him and looked in the direction of his pointed finger.

"Oh. That's Police Point. I have a team there survielling incoming ships from the peak," she explained. "They relay that info to the harbormaster to give him the heads-up. Anything else they see, is relayed here to Operations."

"How did you come up with 'Police Point'?

"I can't take credit for that one," she said. "The team that's up there came up with that. Someone had to name it something."

"Include that on the map," he said.

Cindy took out a felt marker and walked over to the map wall and in small letters, wrote the words 'Police Point'. When she turned around, she found Doc had begun to go through his bags to change his clothing. Startled, she walked over to the Duraglass wall that overlooked the operations room. She touched one of the buttons on the panel near the double-doors and the entire wall went white obscuring the view inside the situation room.

"I'll give you five minutes to change and then we'll go up to your office," she said as she opened the door and left.

A few moments later, she returned and Doc was freshly dressed.

"What about emergency services," He asked while he was rolling up his sleeves.

Cindy was ready for that question.

"Emergency services was up and running from the first day we landed. We have fire suppression crews strategically placed through-out all three population centers. There are also small police forces to tend to the needs of the public. We have three hospitals operational and fully staffed. Search and rescue teams are on standby to respond to any calls that may come through here. HAZ-MAT teams are also set and ready to respond."

Doc was leaning against the conference table, with his arms crossed, listening.

"Coastal patrols?"

"None yet," she said. "We do however, have 30-ft open boats fifteen kilometers out to guide the incoming ships into each of the harbors. Once we have comms to uplink to our satellites, we won't need them to guide those incoming ships."

"And the 'A-D Grid?" he asked. The Anti-Detection Grid was integral to the island being the best kept secret in the world. In an age of global mapping and surveillance via satellite, it was important to keep the island invisible since the day it first broke the ocean waves. Samuel Gowan was the first to realize that an island would appear here months before it occurred. The ocean-floor survey team, that were investigating the possibility of harvesting mineral nodules, discovered the slow ascension of the ocean floor. Samuel Gowan had the team scan the phenomenon in great detail. Once he analyzed the data, he not only determined that the ascension would continue but, that its rate of ascent would increase. Immediately, he initiated steps to prevent its discovery. This involved setting up the A-D grid which not only hid the island visually but also from orbiting land-sats which routinely scanned the earth. Effectively the entire area was a dead-zone. He also had anti-gravity and anti-magnetic projectors set up in the water surrounding the rising mass, preventing the displacement from creating tsunami's which would result in massive destruction around the Pacific Rim. And when the island ceased rising, it was kept in place and operating.

"Running perfect since day one. Its operating at 98 percent efficiency resulting in 100 percent effectiveness."

Doc began stroking his chin and then finally extended his right hand to Cindy who, hesitantly, grabbed his hand.

"Cindy Gates," he said shaking her hand. "You have done an exceptional job here and it hasn't gone unnoticed. Everyone knew that this would challenge you. Marcus and I knew you could do it. And after living and breathing for this island for the last eighteen months, I will authorize for you, two months vacation. You deserve it."

She let go of his hand and gave him a hug, "I was beginning to think this was a thankless job." She let go of her embrace, "Actually, I enjoy this job very much. Thank-you, Doc. I would also like to take a leave of absence, for a year or two. I want to spend time with my family and I think Angela Teslin would be best to replace me."

"Request, granted. How's the family doing?" he asked out of the blue.

"Good," She replied. "Unpacking the house is an 'in-progress' thing. The kids are helping and they have made friends on our street, already. Henry is busy at Search and Rescue Headquarters, getting his people settled in and the equipment set up."

"Everyone is happy to be here?"

"Oh, yes." she said. "The air is better. The land is better. The people. The environment. Everything..."

"What is the general consensus and morale of those you have come in contact with?"

"Morale is great," Cindy began. "Whatever hesitation and uncertainty these people had during their journey, certainly diminished upon arrival. Consensus is; people are happy to be here. In fact, I would characterize it more as, excited."

Doc was pleased. After what seemed to him to be an eternity of hard work and preparation, things were going more smoothly than he and Marcus could have hoped for. To him, it seemed like he had worked at full speed ahead to achieve this goal. And, for a moment, he was tired and had thoughts of 'what to do next?'. It almost seemed unnatural that the culmination of all everyone had worked on, was all but, complete. He looked around and took stock of his surroundings. The realization that he and a great many others had made it to this place, astounded him.

"Would you like me to take you up to your office?" Cindy said, interrupting his train of thought.

Looking around again, he replied. "You know, I would kind of like this conference room to be my office, for the time being. Will that be OK?"

"You're the boss. Use it for however long you like." She began to leave the office and before she did, she smiled and said, "Call me on the Hyperlink if you need me."

CHAPTER SIX

CALM IS IN THE AIR

Flying at 20,000 feet, the C-30 Tanker was holding station 250 miles south of the 19th. Carrier Task Force which had 6 days earlier, rounded the tip of South America on its way to Pearl Harbor. It had been refueling fighter-planes of the combat air patrol (CAP) from the aircraft carrier USS Lexington. Those who served aboard her, affectionately referred to her as 'Lady Lex'.

The MacArthur Class Mega-Carriers were the latest addition to the US Navy arsenal. They were twice the size of the previous Roosevelt-Class Super-Carriers, carried four times the fire power and manned by 3000 more personnel than the previous generation. The Mega-Carriers could also land two and launch eight fighters simultaneously. Unheard of in carrier-based air power history. There were only 2 old Roosevelt-Class carriers left in the fleet and they too, were soon to be de-commissioned.

The Tanker had received the last two fighters of her sortie before heading back to the Lexington. Both fighters eased into position from behind to hook up to the drogue lines and take on fuel. It was a fairly routine maneuver when, the fighters, received an urgent message from the Command/Information/Control (CIC) of the Lexington. She was tracking 2 unidentified, fast moving aircraft, flying in tight formation at low altitude. Although, it posed no threat to the Lexington and was moving quickly away and out of her defensive perimeter, the orders were to track and if possible, identify the unknown aircraft. Even though they had taken only half the fuel they had intended, the pilots accepted their orders without question and disengaged from the tanker and when they were at a safe distance from it, engaged the 'super-cruise' of their fighter's engines.

Traveling at a top speed of MACH 3, at Angels 20, it took the fighters about ten minutes to catch up to the two unknown aircraft. At that altitude, they were flying in the clouds, occasionally making visual contact, flying from one cloud bank to another. Their radar could see them regardless.

"What do you think, Jako?" the wingman said to his lead.

Captain Neil (Jako) Jackson was silent for the longest time. He was trying to glimpse the two aircraft while at the same time fly and read his instruments in his cockpit.

"They're moving at MACH 1 at Angels 2. Pretty fast for small aircraft. They're pretty far out from land, too."

"You think they're flying with spare fuel pods?" the wingman asked over the radio.

"Can't tell from this height," he replied as he looked over at him. "We have to go down to the 'deck'. Check 'em out."

"I got your 'six', his wingman stated.

"Tally-ho," Jako said as he began putting his plane into a dive with his wingman, Simon 'Sawbones' Bransen following behind.

Both planes made a gradual, passive descent as opposed to a fast, aggressive one. The purpose of this was that in case their approach was detected, the pilots would be confused as to what the slow, rear approaching aircraft were doing. It was an approach in timidity, implying an act of non-aggression. All they wanted to do, really, was to 'eyeball' the unidentified aircraft and report back. They couldn't afford to do anything else or they would have refuel in mid-air just to make it back to the Lexington. The last thing a pilot wanted to do was to explain to the Commander of Air Group (CAG), is why they ran out of gas and had to punch out of a $100 million aircraft as it splashed into the drink. One had to have good reasons for doing so. Running out of fuel, was not one of them.

Once they reached Angels 10, they briefly, re-assessed their progress to see if they had yet been spotted, before continuing their descent. They had not. They had kept their radar and LIDAR systems on passive and would not switch them to active unless they took a more aggressive posture. Captain Jackson was beginning to think this was going to be a piece of cake.

Mustang and Pinto had, for the last while, been enjoying a leisurely flight as they flew to make contact with the freighter, Yankee Rose. Climbing to 2000 feet above sea level and slowing to just over MACH 1, gave them the best opportunity to spot her more quickly and make final approach to land on her upper deck. Upon making UHF radio contact with the Yankee Rose, her captain would reduce speed to accept the two inbound helicopters. However, Colin Gallant was beginning to think that finding and making contact with the Yankee Rose was no longer a priority.

"What are they doing, Timbo?" he asked.

His JAFO, Timothy Matthews, was working the scanners to answer his question.

"Trying to sneak up on us," giving his analysis. "They've come down to 10,000 feet from twenty. I think they're trying to see if we spotted them, yet."

Karl clicked on the mic on his joystick, "Ollie, standby to disengage auto-nav and start up your main rotor. We'll get them off your back so, that we will have their complete, undivided attention"

Timbo looked through his side window to see Olivia 'Ollie' Greene wave back acknowledgement. Although it was obvious she understood what Gallant was planning, Timbo did not.

"She's ready," he relayed. Just then, the scanner gave out an audible alert. Looking down, Timbo could see that they had, at last, found the Yankee Rose. She was due south just this side of the horizon.

"Yankee Rose," Timbo confirmed. "Dead ahead."

Now, Gallant realized they had to act fast. It wouldn't be long now before the two US Navy fighters spotted the Yankee Rose and realize this was what Pinto and Mustang were headed for. They had to draw them away from the freighter and lose them at the same time. He knew he could do one, the other was going to be tough.

"Timbo," Gallant began. "Make contact with the Yankee Rose. Tell her to begin reducing speed and prepare to receive us. Tell 'em we have un-invited guests"

Immediately, Timbo made contact with the captain of the freighter and explained the situation. Once informed, Captain Dorcas agreed to make preparations to accept the two helicopters.

"Yankee Rose is ready," Timbo said.

"Good," Gallant replied. "This is what's going to happen. We're going to drop down to the deck and engage the main rotor. That won't give those fighters much room to maneuver. Flying slower, with our main rotors operating, we'll be able to out-maneuver them so they won't be able to get a radar lock. The whole time we'll be making our way in the direction of the Yankee Rose. We'll cover for Pinto until they land."

Timbo had moaned during Gallant's explanation.

"It's a good thing we had G-force compensators installed on these choppers last month."

Gallant was going over his controls, making preparations for changing the helicopter from fixed-wing to a rotary-flight profile. "You can say that , again."

Gallant looked past Timbo through the side window, at Olivia Greene piloting Pinto.

"You ready, Ollie?" he said when he clicked on the mic.

"Set," she replied, looking back at Mustang.

"Standby," he ordered. He looked down at the scanner to see the indications on Timbo's screen that were the two US Navy fighters. They had matched speed with Pinto and Mustang at 10,000 feet. They both sat and waited for them to make their next move when, they began to make their slow descent from behind.

"OK, here we go," Gallant said to Timbo while at the same time clicked on his mic. "Pinto. Go."

On that command, both craft disengaged from auto-nav and began their nose-down dive to the ocean surface. The fighters followed suit. They knew they had been spotted. When Pinto and Mustang pulled up at 100 meters, their main rotor-hubs were spun-up to maximum rotation which enabled the rotor blades to extend and provide primary lift and maneuverability for the helicopters. Once the fighters were within visual range, they were surprised by the fact that instead following two fast moving aircraft, they found helicopters.

The two fighters were maneuvering, from behind, to slide their fighters cautiously to the outside of each helicopter. Finally, matching speed and flying side by side to each helicopter, the fighter pilots were able to lay their eyes on the pilots they were sent to investigate. They were in the process of attempting radio contact with no success.

Gallant, finally, looked over to the fighter pilot flanking Mustang, acknowledging his presence. The two could see the whites of each others eyes clearly. He grinned and gave the fighter pilot a double-fingered salute.

The eyes of the fighter pilot had the look of confusion and he, too reciprocated with the same two-fingered salute.

Gallant looked forward, down to his instruments, over to Pinto and finally back to his flanking fighter. He grinned devilishly from ear to ear and then, made his move.

Changing the pitch of the main rotor, Mustang came to a virtual standstill. Caught by surprise, both fighters went evasive and began to climb. With such an act by Mustang, they didn't know what Gallant's intentions were. They had to assume it was hostile. Gallant began flying Mustang due north to keep the fighters attention. They had spotted that other aircraft carrier earlier, changed course to avoid her and he knew that this was where the fighters came from. If he made it appear that he was headed for it, they would have to eliminate any threat before it even got close to it. He added as much speed as he could without the rotors automatically cutting out. This was a safety feature designed into the helicopters. As speed increased, the rotors would cut-out and the aerodynamic lift of the air-fame and the power of the engines would take over.

Flying at MACH 1.2, it took longer than expected for the fighters to follow and catch up. At 200 feet, with the fighters hot on his tail, Gallant suddenly turned the helicopter 180 degrees and climbed back to 2000 meters. Both fighters had to break formation to avoid him when the chopper flew in-between them in the opposite direction. Now heading south-east away from the carrier, Gallant was convinced that Pinto had enough of a lead to make it to the Yankee Rose safely. He just had to keep the fighters occupied, a little longer. This time, the fighters were coming up fast. When they were almost on him, again he dramatically reduced speed and watched the fighters shoot by. Timbo let out a laugh and looked over at Gallant.

"Alright! Somebody who can fly!" he yelled.

All the while, he brought the chopper back up to maximum rotor-speed and began chasing the US Navy fighters for about ten seconds. They both broke formation to take evasive action in opposite directions from each other. By the time they realized it, they should have just stayed the same course and slowed down. This time it took a full minute to catch up. When they did, Gallant banked the chopper into an almost perfect 90 degree, right angle turn to port and again, the fighters shot by, unable to match the high speed turn. This time turning in unison, the fighters spotted their quarry which was now holding a steady course heading south-west. The lead pilot, not wanting to be fooled again, told his wingman to hang back to take over pursuit in case he lost the advantage. Matching speed once again, he was behind and to the left of the helicopter. Instead of another trick to pull on the US Navy fliers, Gallant just held his course, further confusing them. For the longest time, Captain 'Jako' Jackson just followed the helicopter, waiting for it to make the next move. Just when he thought nothing was going to happen, the helicopter abruptly, reversed direction and went the other way.

Now he was getting frustrated. This guy was pulling every trick in the book and out-foxing them every time.

Gallant was having fun and Timbo was enjoying the ride. He was careful to make sure the fighters didn't interpret his tactics as too aggressive thereby resulting in retaliation. The most he wanted to do was frustrate them with his shenanigans. The last thing he wanted, was to be fired upon. With each maneuver, Mustang was closer to the Yankee Rose. Again, with both fighters right on his tail, Colin Gallant formulated another plan.

"Hey, Timbo," Gallant said. "Target the wingman with the auto-nav, hack into their flight-control wireless network and get ready to engage it."

This crazy, 'are you out of your freakin' mind' look appeared on Timbo's face. It then disappeared to be replaced by a huge grin, once he realized what Gallant was planning. "Cool."

"Just be ready," Gallant ordered.

Ten seconds later, Timbo reported that the auto-nav had successfully 'linked-in' and he was ready.

Gallant wasn't sure if this was going to work. He had pulled off so many tricks, he was sure they would be wise to anything he might try. If he waited too long, they would be sure to be ready.

Just then, their radio crackled to life. It was the voice of Horace Dorcas, captain of the Yankee Rose.

"Mustang. Mustang. Mustang. Yankee Rose here. Pinto is in the corral."

The radio message did not repeat. Now, they could disengage from the fighters and fly directly to the freighter. But, Gallant still wanted to try this last trick.

"Get ready," he ordered.

He again, changed the pitch of the rotor so that it not only slowed the helicopter down on a dime but, abruptly made it climb. The fighters shot by and Gallant noticed they reacted more quickly this time. But, not quickly enough. As the fighters flew by, Gallant gave the order to engage the auto-nav and the helicopter instantly matched course and speed with the wingman in a tight, parallel formation just below the fighter. For the longest time, the two fighters, with the lead out in front, flew in a leisurely search pattern looking for their quarry. Gallant offered his hand to Timbo for a high-five which, he accepted.

"How long can we fly like this?" Timbo asked as they both looked up through their overhead windows to study the underside of the US Navy fighter. Up close, it was larger than it appeared.

"Until we get spotted. Then again, I don't suppose anyone would try to shoot at us when they see us this close to one of their friends," he mused.

Timbo looked over to Gallant. "That's right. I never thought of that."

Just then, the lead fighter had applied its airbrakes and slipped back beside Mustang. Gallant could clearly see that he was communicating where the target now was.

Gallant looked from the lead fighter to Timbo. "Oops," he said and he looked back to the fighter that found them. Since the auto-nav system was flying the helicopter like an auto-pilot system would, he put his hands up to his head, thumbs in his ears, palms showing, fingers out-stretched and stuck out his tongue to the lead fighter pilot.

The wingman then began evasive maneuvers to try to shake the tailing helicopter but, try as he might, couldn't lose them. Gallant was enjoying the tactics the wingman was trying to employ but, Timbo was not, as it became obvious that at some point during the flight, he had loosened his seat restraints. He was busily trying to tighten them.

"Ok, Timbo," Gallant announced. "Get ready to disengage auto-nav."

By this time, both fighters were making a power dive to the ocean surface. Figuring out that the helicopter was somehow linked to the fighter, loosing it with unpredictable maneuvers would be impossible. So, they would get rid of it by 'skimming the deck'. With the helicopter below the linked fighter and by skimming the surface of the ocean, they would force the helicopter into the water. It was a tactic that Gallant predicted and would have tried, if the roles were reversed.

At 1000 meters, he ordered Timbo to disengage the auto-nav and as soon as the main rotor was safely clear of the fighter, he half-barrel rolled the helicopter and inversely flew in the opposite direction of the fighters; a 'split-S' maneuver, descending to the deck. Righting Mustung, Gallant performed a long turn to port and they began, once again, heading for the Yankee Rose, ten miles away.

Timbo could see on the scanner that the two fighters were fifteen miles away and closing. He indicated to his pilot that he was worried that they wouldn't make it. Gallant assured him they would. Then, an audible alert sounded on the instrument panel.

"They're trying to lock on with radar," Timbo announced.

"Oh no, they won't," he replied as he jerked the joystick hard, turning the helicopter to starboard. He began performing a zig-zag pattern that would eventually bring them to the Yankee Rose. The problem with that tactic, Gallant understood, was that the intervals of the turns could become, predictable. He did his best to keep those intervals and his altitude, as random as possible.

In the distance, they could see their destination. A few more zigs and a couple of zags and they would be on the upper deck of the Yankee Rose.

"Tell me where they are, Timbo!" Gallant ordered as his zagged Mustang.

"Flying straight behind us. Zeroing in!" he replied as he braced himself for the zig that Mustang performed.

This time, instead of a zag, Gallant performed three right angle turns which really threw off their pursuers who, had to take a wide high-speed turn to get back behind the hunted. With the Yankee Rose now twenty miles away, Gallant had to reduce speed to make their final approach and landing. Gallant decided that now, they had to make their final approach to the freighter. There was no longer any point in trying to hide their destination. He had to take the risk that, one; they wouldn't shoot them down and two; wouldn't fire on the Yankee Rose once they landed.

Timbo, who had been watching the scanners and relaying the whereabouts of the two fighters to his pilot at all times, warned, "They're coming back for another run. Fast and on the deck."

"We're almost there," Gallant said quickly, confident they could make the freighter before the fighters were on top of them.

Coming up from behind the Yankee Rose, Gallant really had to work the cyclic controls of the helicopter to slow down. The freighter was at a virtual dead-stop. Only the momentum of the freighter's weight propelled it through the water. He could see where Pinto was sitting on the topside deck and the spot where someone had hastily spray-painted an 'X' for Mustang to land. Several people were also there, watching, from a safe distance, the incoming helicopter. As Mustang came in hot, Gallant did his best not to overshoot his designated LZ (landing zone), hover, descend quickly and land as light as a feather.

As he began shutting down main power to the rotor, they both heard the fighters fly over them and looking to port of the ship, watched them fly off and climb. Getting out of his seat and moving to the passenger/cargo compartment to open the main hatch, he descended the four steps to the upper deck of the Yankee Rose. There, he was met by tall, thin man with red hair, beard and moustache sporting a simple merchant marine cap.

"Permission to come aboard, Sir," Gallant said as he extended his hand.

Captain Horace Dorcas accepted and shook Colin Gallant's hand. "I was watching you boys on the scanners. That was some *unbelievable* flying you did," he said with southern US drawl. "Mighty fine!"

Just then, the two US Navy fighters re-appeared, flying high and slow over the Yankee Rose, both waving their wings as if saluting their adversary while flying north.

"They're honoring you, son," he said. "You're a worthy opponent."

Captain Dorcas and Gallant turned to a laughing Timothy Matthews as he exited the helicopter.

"What's so funny?" Sandhu asked Timbo as he joined the two.

"Bingo!" he announced.

Captain Dorcas looked at Gallant and back at the still chuckling JAFO. "Bingo?"

"Yeah, Bingo! As in 'Bingo fuel'," he chuckled again. "I scanned their fighters. They're low on fuel. They have to return to their carrier. A couple more minutes of evasive action, there's no way they could have kept up with us."

"Well, if that don't beat all," Captain Dorcas said. "They was about all played out, Mr Gallant. At least, you boys had yourselves some fun with some of America's best."

A big grin appeared on Colin Gallant's face, "I suppose I did, didn't I?"

Captain Dorcas put his arms around Gallant and Timbo's shoulders, laughed and began leading them to the other side of the helicopters. And Gallant saw that his son, daughter and wife were among those on the topside deck watching the impromptu air show. Finally, he embraced his loving family.

Marcus was escorting Major Manning and Lt. Stuart through the many areas of the Destiny. Starting in the rear cargo/equipment hold, Manning was impressed as to the size of it and of the amount of equipment stored there. The heavy equipment was locked and secured to the deck.

117

Manning asked about the vehicle he saw earlier in the cavern; was it a weapon?

Marcus took both men over to the vehicle to better explain to them and better yet, convince them, of its intended use. Allowing them to actually sit in the cab, he was able to show them how the machine worked and what it was able to accomplish. Manning decided to rephrase his earlier question.

"Can this technology be turned into a weapon?" he asked.

Marcus regarded the question and the questioner for a moment. He had already shown the two men much and had been open about his intentions more than he should have been. Manning asked an honest question and he deserved an honest answer.

"I won't lie to you. Its possible," he said after a long moment.

"As a professional soldier, I can think of a dozen applications, off the top of my head," Stuart somberly added.

"The purpose of this machine is for mining," Marcus defended. "Specifically, asteroid mining. Not for war. We would never allow it."

Marcus' statement took both men by surprise. The least they expected was for him to say that some part of the technology could be used for defensive purposes. And they said so.

Marcus just looked at the two and said, "Against what? A bunch of rocks?"

Manning couldn't argue with the logic of the man and Marcus passed his second test.

Next they found themselves heading back to the mess bay. A couple of soldiers had come out and were standing around in the corridor. Two of them approached the three.

"They had a camera on you the whole time and piped it into the mess-hall. What was it like, Sir?" one of the troopers asked Lt. Stuart.

"What was 'What' like?" Stuart asked.

"Walking in space," the other trooper said excitedly.

Manning stepped forward and said with serious look, "It was out of this world."

Just then, Ron Kane stepped out into the corridor followed by two more troopers carrying the injured Captain Svanda on a stretcher, an I.V. solution of Saline dripping through a thin tube to his arm.

"He's gone into shock," Ron Kane explained. "We're taking him to Infirmary. His leg is hemorrhaging and he needs surgery, now."

"I thought you were just a medic? Manning asked.

"Oh I am. Our Infirmary is fully equipped. State of the art," Kane said and looked at the stretcher-bearers. "C'mon. We gotta go now." Kane turned and proceeded up the corridor at a fast pace with the troopers carrying Svanda.

Manning looked into the mess-hall from the corridor and realized he had nearly thirty soldiers in a relatively small area. All were nursing minor injuries. His first concern was for them. He was responsible for them. He had to get them back safely home. And then, he realized, he had to get them back to Earth.

"Well," Manning said. "This is your spaceship. We're your guests and we will cause you no trouble at all."

"Understood," Marcus said.

"However, I need to get my people home to their families."

"Believe me, we'll get you and your people home," Marcus assured both men as he began walking up the corridor.

Both officers followed. Marcus began explaining the problem with the propulsion system and that their current location near Mars was in fact, a fluke. That his people were working on the problem and that once a solution was determined, homeward bound, they all would be.

They arrived at the Infirmary where Svanda had been placed on the surgical bed inside the surgical bay and Kane was attending him. Manning and his men watched through the observation window as Kane worked fast on the Captain's swollen, injured leg. The leg of the trousers had been cut open to reveal bare skin. Several devices were laid atop the limb with Kane periodically checking their status and removing one or more devices for other ones. After announcing the repair of the fracture, he informed his audience that Svanda's arterial injury was also repaired and he would now drain the hemorrhage. Manning watched Kane insert an I.V. into the leg which was attached to a clear plastic container. Blood began draining from the swollen leg immediately. Kane then prepared an injection-spray gun and approached the unconscious Svanda.

"What is that?" Manning asked Marcus of the device.

"Its called an injector," Marcus explained. "Instead of using hypodermic needles and the disposal of them, that device does away with that. Injections are administered at high pressure through the skin with almost no sensation of it being done."

"What is he injecting?" Lt. Stuart asked.

Marcus depressed the intercom to the surgical bay, "Ron. What medication are you giving him?"

Kane looked up abruptly and replied, "A concoction of anti-coagulant to eliminate blood clots, pain-killers and a muscle-relaxant. He should be up and around in twelve hours and able to return to full duties in forty-eight."

Manning looked over at Marcus. "That's not possible," he stated. "I've seen people out of action with that kind of fracture for as long as six weeks."

"Its possible," Marcus replied. "With all the medical technology we have at our disposal, we are now able to return a person back to normal health faster than was previously possible."

"But you can't cure cancer, can you?" Lt. Stuart asked.

"Actually," Marcus started. "We do have a cure but, it can only be administered once a person has become diagnosed in its early stages of the disease. And that includes all forms of cancer."

The two officers just stared at Marcus, saying nothing.

Marcus did a double-take of the two men looking at him.

"C'mon guys," acting as if taken aback. "Its better than nothing."

"Don't misunderstand," Manning said, turning to face Marcus, stoking his goatee. "Why not share the cure with the world? Do you realize how many lives can be saved with that knowledge?"

"To answer your second question, first," Marcus began, stepping into a standing huddle with the two soldiers. "I do think of those lives that could be saved. Everyday. And it bothers the hell out of me. I want to share this with the world. The reason why I can't, is the answer to the first question. To cure a person of that disease would require the use of technology that the medical community will probably not develop for another hundred years. Its that far ahead. Imagine all those scientists and researchers, around the world who would be unemployed, overnight."

"It, too, could be turned into a weapon, couldn't it" Manning asked after interpreting Marcus Gowan's response.

"Potentially, it could be turned into a biological weapon, yes," Marcus admitted.

By this time, he had led them to an upper deck that took them to a narrower corridor that ended at a closed hatch. He depressed a button on the panel located on the bulkhead to the right. The door opened to the right via mechanical assist. Marcus stepped through first, then Lt. Stuart and then the Major.

Manning saw that he was standing on a two-tiered flight deck. In front of him was acceleration chair positioned in front of an L-shaped console that looked directly below to the lower level. LCD panels and touch screens were everywhere at the workstation, including, those that were mounted on telescoping hinges on the wall and on the ceiling. To his left, against the wall, was what seemed to be the Engineer's workstation. This workstation dominated the rest of the space of the upper part of the deck with blue LCD monitors everywhere. The young lady sitting there didn't see the two soldiers enter through the hatch as Marcus had blocked her view. It was only when she heard movement behind him that, she shifted her position in her seat and saw them looking around. She looked up at Marcus with a puzzled look who in turn gave her a slight nod and a re-assuring look on his face meaning that everything was Ok. Marcus turned back to the two officers.

"This gentlemen, is the flight deck of the Spaceship Destiny," he announced.

Mac Marsh, too busy to notice that someone, let alone three people had entered through the hatchway, jumped out of the pilot's seat and stood straight up and looked back to see who Marcus was speaking to. He did this so abruptly, the two soldiers, who hadn't noticed him before, instinctually reached for their side-arms. Marcus immediately moved beside the two men as if to temper their reaction.

"Major. Lieutenant," Marcus spoke softly and controlled. "You haven't been formally introduced to my pilot and First Officer, Mackenzie Marsh."

"G'day, Mate," Mac hesitantly waved, giving Marcus the same look that Joni had.

Marcus, turning to Joni, "And this is my Flight Operations Specialist, Joni Edwards."

"Hello," she said as she waved. Both men nodded.

Manning looked forward through the expansive windscreen by which he could see the blackness of space and the brightness of the stars. He had never seen a windscreen as large as this. It was as wide as the flight deck and was long enough so that all workstations on the upper and lower part of the flight deck could take in the view ahead. His eyes looked down to the lower flight deck and observed the pilot's and co-pilot's stations. Marcus invited the two down to the lower level.

Descending down to four steps, Manning and Stuart were able to get a better look of the outside environment.

"You have quite a view," Manning said.

"Best view on-board, other than the observation lounge," Mac commented.

Stuart who had been staring at Mac was trying to remember where he had seen the pilot before when he finally remembered.

"I remember you," he said finally. "Weren't you the Aussi test-pilot that broke the record for the fastest circumnavigation of the world?"

"That was when he was young, cocky and thought he was invincible," Marcus interjected.

Mac shot Marcus a look. "I am invincible."

The four shared a short chuckle and then finding themselves gazing out into space were lost in their own thoughts for a brief moment.

"Space is there and we're going to climb it, and the moon and the planets are there, and new hopes for knowledge and peace, are there," Marcus quoted aloud.

Manning looked over at the young man.

"I've heard that before. Who said that?"

"President John F. Kennedy, in the early 1960's," Marcus replied without looking away from the windscreen.

Marcus let them take in the view in their own silence for a few moments. He knew that at least, in Major Manning's mind, he would be processing the situation and would start asking questions. Patience, in this case, was a virtue and a necessity.

Manning looked over to Marcus again and began to ask.

"Why have you allowed us onto the bridge?"

"To show and to prove to you, that while you are aboard the Destiny, you'll have full access to all areas. That you can, trust us."

Manning smirked, "You know, because you said that, means I shouldn't trust you."

"I know," Marcus agreed. "but our actions, I believe, has said volumes about us. The fact that we could have left you in that launch bay to die and the fact that one of your seriously wounded is now recovering in the Infirmary, is not part of a ploy. Just because someone else claims I am a terrorist with little or no or even, fabricated evidence doesn't mean, I am. Just make up your own minds."

"We could take this ship, by force," Manning suggested.

Marcus realized Manning was not only a combat tactician; he was a chess-player as well. Marcus countered.

"You could but then, who would get you back to Earth? And if you did, I would set this ship to self-destruct long before you figured how to get the Destiny, under-way."

Manning looked over at Rob Stuart and then over to Joni and Mac.

"Even with your own people aboard?" Manning re-grouped.

Marcus was prepared for that, "Actually, if it were possible for them to escape, everything would be done to ensure that. If there were no hope of re-taking the Destiny, and there was a possibility that this vessel could fall into the wrong hands, any one of us could set the self-destruct. Everyone understands the ramifications of how this technology could, and would be miss-used."

"And you wouldn't miss-use that same technology?" Lt. Stuart countered.

"No," Marcus turned to the Lt. and said, flatly. "All through history, Humanity has invented and progressed in all things. We have become the masters of our world. We have created many beautiful things *and* are capable of a great many horrors. If I may quote Pope Paul VI's commentary on the emergence of atomic weapons, it certainly applies to this situation. 'Two conditions render this historic situation of mankind: It is full of tremendously deadly armament, or in this case, technology, and Humanity has not progressed morally as much as it has scientifically and technically.' I won't let that happen."

Manning was surprised that this young man seemed to be much more mature than his age. The more he heard this man speak, the more gradual his respect for him increased. He was trying to fight that respect, fighting his instinct to trust. His bull-shit detector wasn't going off. His whole demeanor and those of his crew was, non-defensive. They seemed helpful, open and honest.

"How are you going to prevent the miss-use of this technology?" Lt. Stuart asked skeptically.

A smirk appeared on Marcus' face, "All in due time, gentlemen. I'm not prepared to reveal that, just yet."

"You know you are considered a terrorist and a threat to continental security," Manning said. It was as much as a question as a statement.

Marcus looked at the floor and nodded at the same time.

"I know," he said as he looked Manning in the eyes. "I am certainly no terrorist but the reason I'm a security threat is because of this technology. I have been labeled that by the 'powers that be'."

Manning, who began looking away, shot Marcus a serious look. That statement struck a chord with Manning. It was as if they both were the underlings of the same system.

Marcus continued.

"Major. What if I were to tell you that as a result of this technology, my father, brother and myself, each, have been approached by individuals who, from time to time, representing one organization or another, asking us to 'share' our technology. When we denied possession of it, we were implicitly threatened, economically and physically. The first time they approached my father, he was able to (with the help of this technology) track them back to their organization. He had them so scared, they didn't approach him again for 15 years. Every once in a while, they'd try placing a mole within the company, to get information. One day, we had nearly 50 CIA and CSA agents file their resumes with us."

"How do you know they were Central Intelligence and Continental Security?" Lt. Stuart asked.

"Because, we interviewed them as if we were interested in hiring them and during the interview process, we were able to utilize certain technologies that were able to positively identify them. To them, the interview seemed to go on longer than it actually did. As if they were missing time. And then, a very small and invisible and auto-decaying GPS chip was placed on their clothing. From there, they went back to their real homes and we were able to track them from there. More often than not, they went back to report to their real employers. You see, the only new employees we get, are the ones *we,* approach. And they are not necessarily the best and the brightest. Although, they become that, in the end. Anyway, the only threat I represent, are to those who already have possession of the same technology and have decided that one; its too valuable to share with the world, and two; its too dangerous to share with the world."

Manning considered Marcus' words for a moment.

"Who else has this technology?" Manning asked as if knowing the answer.

"Certain elements of the US Government," Marcus responded. "You heard the rumors of Area 51and S-4?"

Both men nodded. The Groom Lake, Nevada Air Force Base was the focus of UFO conspiracy groups for decades. An area so large and so secret that even the US Congress decreed that the mountain ranges that ring it, off limits.

"Its no rumor," Marcus announced. "It exists. The world's worst kept secret is maintained in the best secured and largest military installation in the whole world."

Manning and Stuart looked at each other and then at Marcus.

"Your talkin' about UFO's and alien technology, but…" Manning began.

Marcus interrupted, "Yes, I am."

Manning and Stuart stared at Marcus in silence. Manning, himself, was waiting for the punch line that wouldn't come. He looked up at the young lady, Joni Edwards who was now leaning against the stair-rails. There was no hint of a joke on her lips or in her eyes.

"You're saying, that this spacecraft is alien technology?" Manning asked.

"No, not exactly," Marcus began to explain. "The Destiny was built with alien technology that was reverse-engineered. After that, it becomes terrestrial technology. It took a some years, but we figured it out, in the end.

Manning began shaking his head. "You know, I hear you saying the words and I just can't believe my ears."

"How long did it take to build this ship?" Lt. Stuart asked.

Joni Edwards spoke up, "From the moment we finalized the blueprints, electronically, to the day the last systems were installed, 18 months. However, once we get into mass production, we could turn out one of these ships every 300 days."

Manning's eyes just about bugged out of his eye-sockets.

"You plan on mass producing these ships?"

"Only as required," Marcus admitted. He paused for a moment trying to think of a way in which to reveal his dream. He knew that there would be no way in which they could be stopped. Not out here, in space. Events were now set in motion for completion of all the hard work expended by him and his brother, the people in his employ and his father before him.

"Only as required? For who?" Manning asked.

"For the nation of Pacifica."

Now Manning observed a very interesting reaction and it didn't come from Marcus Gowan, himself. Joni and Mac gave Marcus a look as if they had never heard that place before. Manning was sure Marcus had made his first mistake. And just when he was about to let his bull-shit detector guide him, Joni approached her commanding officer.

"You finally named the island," she said as she gave Marcus a quick hug.

Mac Marsh stretched out his right hand.

"Its about time, mate. Calling it the 'Island' was getting old."

"Sorry. I can't take the credit," Marcus conceded. "Doc came up with the name and I thought it was a perfect fit."

"Whoa," Manning interrupted. "Wait. Can someone kindly tell me what you are talking about?"

Marcus chuckled and gestured to Joni and Manning to the upper flight deck.

"Joni. Might as well show them," he said.

"In for a penny, in for a pound?" she offered as she began climbing the steps.

Mac sat back down into the pilot's seat as the four, Marcus, Joni, Maj. Manning and Lt. Stuart went to the upper level. Joni sat at the Operations workstation and on one of the displays, on telescoping hinges, she brought up an archived satellite image, taken from orbit. The image Manning and Stuart saw, which took up most of the screen, was that of an island surrounded by a large body of water. The island, set diagonally on the monitor, was roughly, square shaped with the exception of the bottom left corner of the island which had a more rounded shape and the upper left corner which was more elongated. Cutting across the island, from left to right of the screen, were two mountain ranges which bordered a high plateau valley.

"What are we looking at, here?" Manning asked.

"Beautiful, isn't it?" Joni turned to Manning, her face, beaming and turned to the monitor, "Top of the screen is north, bottom is south, and east and west, respectively. The island has a temperate climate similar to that of the North Island of New Zealand except at the higher elevations, where snow is beginning to hard-pack into what we think will eventually become pockets of glaciers. The valley between the two mountain ranges contains a dry desert plateau. Vegetation at the lower elevations, we are seeing the beginnings of warm temperate coniferous and mixed forest including mid-latitude grasslands."

"How big is this island?" Lt. Stuart asked. "And what is its relation to the rest of the world?"

Joni touched her keypad and the picture on the monitor zoomed out to reveal the size and location of the island on the underside of the Earth.

"The island has an area of almost a million square kilometers and is located in the South Pacific Ocean half-way between New Zealand and Chile in South America, and a thousand kilometers south of the Gambier and Pitcairn islands."

"Dear God," Manning exhaled. "That's as large as Alberta," he said referring to the Canadian province.

"How long has that island been there? How could no one know it was there?" Lt. Stuart asked.

Marcus leaned against the workstation, scratching his head as he began to explain.

"Well that was actually the hard part. You see, all through-out the Pacific Ocean, there are seismic and tsunami sensors that record the slightest movement of underwater sea-floor activity. Forty years ago, my father, Samuel Gowan, realized from data from his underwater expeditions, that a large mass was rising from the sea-floor. After the first initial push and resulting tsunami and after the NOAA investigation teams had left, my father moved in and set up a series of tsunami containment generators and mass dampeners. The purpose of that equipment was to prevent detection of the rising mass and to prevent the destruction that would result all around the Pacific Rim."

"What about the displacement of the water?" Manning asked.

"Two years ago, it was determined the island was no longer rising. We were able to finally siphon off the remaining displacement, then." Marcus explained.

"To where?" Manning inquired.

"The Moon," Marcus stated.

"How the hell did you get it there?" Manning asked incredulously.

Marcus smirked, "It just so happens that my father's company owned a fleet of decommissioned oil tankers which were cleaned up, converted to carry sea-water and as more were decommissioned and became available, they were simply lifted into space and emptied into a deep crater at the south pole of the Moon. There it froze and it would be available for our use in space later on."

Manning looked over at Lt. Stuart and asked, "Is it me or does this all appear just a little too, routine to them?"

Stuart nodded.

"I'm sorry, Major. Lieutenant," Marcus conceded. "I guess from your point of view, it would appear that way. In the last ten years, we set out and have accomplished so many great things. Things that Humanity, should have done and should be doing. For the benefit of all Mankind. When you're out here, in space, and you see with your own eyes, the Earth, the planets and the sparkle of the stars outside the confines of Earth atmosphere, it changes your perspective. We are so much better and bigger than our petty, earthly differences. We are not meant to stay on Earth, forever. Its in our nature to explore beyond our environment. Mankind has proven that for centuries. The next logical step is to reach for space and establish ourselves here. Well laid plans and resulting accomplishments begin with one thing; a dream."

"Your dream?" Manning suggested a guess.

"It began with my father," Marcus admitted. "As a child, I could not understand why we weren't out here already. Couldn't understand why the Apollo missions to the Moon of the early 1970s, were cancelled and why a presence wasn't established there. Couldn't understand why we only orbited Mars, never to return, except sending a bunch of robots. It seemed so simple, then. As I grew older, I began to understand the whys but, thought, it shouldn't make a difference. We should still be out here. We should just, go. And if we were out here, maybe those societal, economic and environmental issues would be solved. Humanity should be sprinting to its long-term future involving our activities in space, like our ancestors were about making a new life in the 'New World'. And we would have been well established out here by the end of the twentieth century. I think we've waited long enough. Out here, we are capable of so much and we *can* make a difference."

"Look," Manning began, apologetically. "I am not here to judge you. My mission was to bring you in, to face charges of conspiracy and terrorism. When it comes down to it, at the end of the day, I follow orders."

"Questionable orders?" Marcus hinted.

Manning tried to read the young man's poker face. Tried to read if this man knew the doubts and questions he had raised with his superiors.

"What do you know about questionable orders?" Manning asked, suspiciously.

"Major, I see the conflict on your face when you speak of your orders. Its obvious to me, that you and your men are not getting the same from further up the food chain."

"We're soldiers," Manning re-iterated. "We do our jobs."

Marcus held up his hands indicating he didn't want to argue, "I respect that, Major. Don't get me wrong. I now why you were sent in to apprehend me; because of this technology and this ship. If it became public knowledge how easy it is to create this technology, everybody would be breaking orbit. This technology would change the face of life, politics and economics, the world over. Those who have power over others, would lose it."

"But, you don't seek the same power?" Manning asked.

"No. I am a scientist and a researcher. Just a dreamer. And *that,* is where I am happiest. I don't think I'd make a very good politician."

"And why wouldn't you?" Manning found himself asking. "It's only logical that you would. You are the one who's responsible for all this. You, of all people, would be the logical choice for the job. You're the one with the dream. You're the one who made all this possible. Look at another dreamer, Nelson Mandela of South Africa. He started out as just another activist fighting for the rights of his people, lands in jail and suddenly becomes famous because others carried on his cause in his name. Years later, after the fall of the political system that put him there, he not only gets released, he becomes the President of South Africa. Again, I say, Why not?" Manning couldn't believe he was saying this.

Marcus looked over at Joni who returned his gaze.

"I think you found an outside advocate, skipper," she smiled.

Manning felt his face turn red, blushing. He looked over at Lt. Stuart who looked away, trying not to acknowledge what was said so his commanding officer wouldn't feel embarrassed.

I'll put it to you, this way," Manning was careful to explain. "Yes, I did question my orders. Yes, I and my people had reservations about our objectives concerning a civilian industrial operation. And when I didn't receive a satisfactory answer, I called in a few markers and I was warned not to pursue, any further, inquires of the legality of the orders. Then, all of a sudden, our orders were no longer coming from the Department of Federal Defense, they were coming direct, from the Continental Security Department. At that point, we could no longer question our orders."

Marcus nodded and smiled at Manning, "I appreciate your candidness, Major." Walking over to the engineer's workstation, he flipped a switch to an indicator light that was blinking. After a brief moment checking the status panel, he continued.

"Major, we all understand the job you were tasked with and hold no malice towards you or your people. However, when we return to Earth, we won't be returning to Canada. For obvious reasons."

"I understand that," Manning said.

Lt. Stuart gave Manning a sideway glance.

Manning caught his subordinate's look. "Don't give me that look, Lt."

Stuart straightened up and looked away, "Sorry, Sir. Its just that we haven't completed our mission objectives and.."

"Lieutenant. Given our current situation," Manning said looking around the flight deck and then nodding towards the windshield glass, "and our current location, I'd say our mission is a scrub. Wouldn't you agree?"

Lt. Stuart looked out into space and considered the words spoken by his commanding officer.

You are correct, of course, Sir," he agreed.

"Good," Manning said as he turned to Marcus. "Mr. Gowan or should I say, Commander Gowan. We will take our leave and check on our people and try to get some rest. If you need us, that is where we'll be."

"And Major, Lt., if you need us, you know where to find us, or simply call us on the ship's intercom." Marcus reciprocated.

Marcus and Joni watched the two soldiers exit the flight deck and when the door sealed behind them, Mac came from his station below and Joni asked, "What are you thinking, Marcus?"

Marcus, who had been staring at the hatchway, answered.

"I was thinking that we may have gained an ally."

"You really think he's given up on the idea of arresting us," Mac asked climbing the steps to the upper level.

"He has to," Marcus said quietly. "According to international law, specifically, high seas law, he would be breaking that law if he tried."

Joni had a puzzled look on her face.

"But, we are in space, not on the high seas."

"That law applies, even here, in space. The United Nations Treaty on the Exploration and Peaceful Uses of Outer Space, the UNISPACE 5 Treaty, states that this ship is the sovereign property of the nation that claims it, that being Pacifica. Canadian law has no jurisdiction here."

"Pacifica isn't a member of the United Nations," Joni observed.

"The Federal Dominion of Canada *is* a member of the UN and has to abide by international law, even space law," Mac explained.

"Oh, I get it," she said.

"I just hope the Major does," Mac said.

"Oh, he does. He has no choice," Marcus stated.

CHAPTER SEVEN

'MASTERMINDS'

The limousine pulled up to the parking area located a hundred yards from the steps of the State Department. It was an area created after the various terrorist attempts on the building over the years. Security around the building had been beefed up to ensure the safety of the those who worked there. One terrorist cell had once orchestrated the placing, on each side, 18-wheeled trucks packed with shape charges in an attempt to devastate the entire building. The terrorists, driving the 18-wheelers made a crucial mistake. They hadn't done their homework. Six months earlier, the DC municipality decided that traffic around the State Department Building should be one way to alleviate road congestion for a construction site 3 blocks away. The terrorists, faced with a mission failure, found themselves with trucks, filled with explosives and at any moment, facing discovery, facing away from the intended target. The nearby buildings across the street, on each side, were obliterated but, the State Department only suffered blown-out glass from the concussion. Instead of rebuilding the destroyed buildings, it was determined to establish a buffer-zone around the building, complete with obstacles for vehicular traffic.

The Senator had quite a walk but he always enjoyed it. Kept him healthy, he believed. After passing through the half-dozen security check-points, he found himself inside going through yet another check-point. He proceeded to an elevator off to the side which was originally installed for those who were wheel-chair bound. After entering and allowing the doors to close, he put his brief-case down and searched his left pant pocket which he extracted a single key. He inserted it into the top key-hole on the instrument panel, turned it clock-wise twice, counter-clockwise once, extracted it and put the key back into his pocket. The elevator began to descend.

It was 60 seconds before the elevator came to a stop and the doors opened to reveal a long hallway with various doors flanking each side. The senator walked down the hallway to the third door on his left and entered.

"Sorry, I'm late gentlemen. Traffic was especially heavy, today," the Senator explained.

"Maybe you'd like to explain what the hell is going on. Why isn't Gowan in custody, yet?"

"Relax, Dean," the Senator said as he put his briefcase on the conference table and unlocked the snaps to open it. "One way or the other, he'll no longer be a concern."

"We were supposed to have him by, now," another man, pounded his fist on the table.

The Senator's blood pressure was beginning to boil.

"I said, relax!" raising his voice, passing out folders to each of the four men in the room. "This briefing is 'Above Top Secret' and is not to be discussed with anyone below Level 1B Clearance."

"What we want to know is, what happened up there?" another man said, apologetically.

"Well, Frank," The Senator replied. "That's what we're trying to figure out."

Each of the men in the room accepted the folders and opened them. They sat in silence studying the aerial photos.

"What are we looking at, Senator?" the man, Frank asked.

The Senator, still standing at the head of the conference table, hands in his pants pockets began to explain.

"Those satellite photos were taken six hours ago. That crater is what's left of the diamond mine operation the Canadian military was to assault. It is 200 hundred feet deep and almost a mile across.

"My God," a man dressed in a US Air Force Colonel's uniform, gasped. "Casualties?"

"Approximately, 30 MIA's," the Senator revealed. "All Canadian personnel."

"What is the preliminary information?" the man Dean asked.

The Senator cleared his throat. "Early this morning, four squads of the elite arm of the Canadian Federal Armed Forces was airlifted to the mine's airstrip, where they disembarked and took up positions to seize the complex. This is the sketchy part. At some point, the commanding officer deviated from the assault plan. After that, we have no further info that is reliable to report here. We do know, is that the two remaining squads linked up to continue the mission while at the same time, re-contact the other two missing squads. However, as they were about to approach the complex, several soldiers observed the launch of an unidentified craft which subsequently, disappeared."

Two of the men shook their heads and Dean said something to the Colonel at which the Senator didn't hear. The Colonel nodded and the Senator continued.

"The ranking officer, after determining the craft was gone and posed no threat to the remaining force, prepared to advance on the complex. Only. It was no longer there."

"Gowan blew it up?" Frank asked.

The Senator shook his head, "According to the personnel on the ground, there was no explosion nor is there evidence of an explosion. It just wasn't there anymore except this huge, hole in the ground."

The Air Force Colonel stood up, "About the same time, this morning, NORAD intercepted radio-com traffic between 2 helicopters flying in an orbital patrol south of the complex and what would appear to be communication with the facility, itself."

The Colonel produced a small tape recorder and pushed play for all to hear. After the excerpt played out, the Colonel turned off the player and slid it down the length of the table to the Senator.

"I assume this is the original, no copies made?" the Senator asked as he picked it up and placed the device into his briefcase.

"That is correct, Sir," the Colonel confirmed.

"And what of the two helicopters?

"We lost track of them, Sir," the Colonel admitted. "They too, disappeared."

"How the hell do you flyboys loose track of anything in the air?" pounding-fist man blurted out.

The Colonel, still standing but, at ease with hands behind his back, looking down disgusted at the belligerent individual, calmly replied, "How does a person like you, thinks that tie goes with that suit." He turned to the smirking Senator and answered the posed question. "Sir, we don't know how we lost them. We're still trying to determine that."

"Fair enough, Colonel," the Senator said. "Tell us about the Air Force sortie over the mid-Atlantic."

The other three men sat forward in their chairs, waiting and listening intently.

"Roughly 45 minutes after the Canadian personnel were inserted on the ground at the diamond complex, we detected a fair sized, unidentified vessel in a stationary orbit. An Air Force, F-151C Maverick, specially outfitted with an orbital defense missile; a satellite killer, was dispatched to shoot it down. As the missile was homing in on the target, there was a series of malfunctions that prevented acquisition of it and the ordinance had to be destroyed before it acquired an unintended object or re-entered the atmosphere."

"Define 'fair sized vessel'," the Senator asked.

"As long as a football field and half as wide."

Frank whistled and sat back in his chair.

"What 'kind' of malfunctions did the missile suffer," Dean asked.

"There were four independent sources tracking it, including the missile and for some reason, all four lost target lock."

"What about the pilot and his weapons officer?" Frank asked.

"They can be trusted. 'Top Secret' was all over this sortie. And their 'Non-Disclosure Agreements' are up-to-date."

The Senator looked around the 4 walls of the conference room in silence before finally speaking up.

"So. What do we know so far? One; Marcus Gowan has possession of the same technology we have had since 1947. Two; that he, like us, has reversed engineered the same technology to produce a spacecraft and most likely has produced other technologies to support systems and infrastructure. Three; he has developed technology that can evade detection by conventional methods. Four; possession of 'weapons of mass destruction'. Five; there is a real possibility that with this technology, he may have just left the Earth, never to return."

"What makes you say that?" Dean asked

"Just less than a year ago, Marcus Gowan visited his older brother, Glenn and legally signed over his half ownership of the company. Many of their industrial operations were shutdown and apparently sold off as well as about 800,000 people worldwide were laid off in Glenn Gowan's corporate restructuring plan. He got his affairs in order."

"Let's hope," Frank stated. "Are we sending a team up to investigate the mine site?"

"Not a team but, I have sent, covertly, a pair of eyes to investigate the area and assess the situation for further containment. I'll provide you all with a situation report by the end of the week."

The fist-pounder spoke up, sarcastically "Somehow, I don't think we've heard the last of Marcus Gowan. We should have taken care of this problem 40 years ago."

"Like *you* were supposed to, when you had the chance, Charles?" the Senator shot back.

"That wasn't my fault!" Charles grumbled as he, again, pounded his fist on the table. "Somehow, Samuel Gowan found out about our 'hit' on him. After that it was out of our hands."

"For the benefit of the rest of you in the room, Charles and the Gowan family have some history," the Senator began as he watched Charles lean back as if sinking into his chair. "You see, Charles was the senior field agent in charge of eliminating Samuel Gowan as a possible threat to what was then, US Homeland Security. Sam Gowan found out about it somehow, and because Charles chose not to abort, like he should have, Gowan almost exposed the operation, a whole network of field agents, our paid civilian debunkers and skeptics and of course, our organization. We were forced to agree upon a truce negotiated by Gowan's team of lawyers."

"What sort of proof did he have?" Dean asked.

The Senator looked over at Charles and said, "Video evidence."

The other 3 men stared at Charles leaning back in his chair, saying nothing.

"Well, with that said, you all can understand why Charles has developed a rather unique, personal connection to this problem. Because of his knowledge of the Gowan situation, he has been kept apprised of any recent, relevant, developments from time to time."

"So, what do we do now?" Frank asked the Senator.

The Senator began collecting the folders from each of the men and placing them into his briefcase.

"If this is the last we've heard of Marcus Gowan, then so be it. I won't loose any sleep over him. However, I think he has just gone under the radar and we'll pick-up on him, soon enough. And once he does, we'll take him and get him to tell us everything and then make him 'disappear'. And there is still the issue of what happened to the two helicopters. Colonel, I want them found. They would have a range of, what? 300, 350 miles?"

"Possibly as much as 600, if they had extra fuel pods mounted," the colonel replied.

"Find out," The Senator ordered. "This meeting is adjourned."

Diego Guzman settled himself into his seat and began going through his backpack in search of a book he had brought along to read. He knew he probably wouldn't start reading it right away anyway since he was up early to catch his ride in the shuttle van to the marina. He thought he might require a power-nap to rejuvenate himself. Then again, as excited as he was to start his new life, he doubted he would be able to. Finally finding the book by feel in his pack, he extracted it.

Placing the Holy Bible in his lap, he looked up to see other people finding seats for the voyage. Stewards were busy taking people to their seats. He didn't recognize anybody but knew that they too were looking forward to their new lives. He observed that a few new arrivals knew each other as they waved to acquaintances or friends. He was alone but wished his late wife could be here. It had been 5 years since she died and he still felt the pain of her absence. More than anything, he felt guilt. Guilt, because she had died alone.

He had been at work, that day when armed intruders had broken into the attached garage of their home. Thinking that the house was empty with the owners at work, they began to ransack the place. When his wife, who had called in sick that day, awoke to the noise and went to investigate, confronted them. The automated home security system alerted local law enforcement to the intrusion, who were given automatic access to the premises. Police found Rosa Guzman unconscious from a single gunshot wound to the abdomen in the upstairs hallway. The Coroner listed cause of death as abdominal hemorrhage. She 'bled to death'.

The home security system had recorded everything and was even programmed with voice and face recognition software. The culprits were caught within a week. The trial lasted 2 days and the jury returned a verdict of guilty, within an hour.

He turned to the only thing that comforted him in time of need, the Holy Bible. His faith kept him sane. As he began to read through Exodus, he didn't notice a brunette who seemed to recognize him and began to approach him. Although he didn't look up at who was taking the seat in front of him, he couldn't help but notice the pair of nicely defined and shapely calves of a woman over the top of his bible. Trying to read the passages, he tried to ignore the woman as she began settling in.

"Diego? Diego Guzman?"

Diego looked up from his bible to see a woman standing before him, smiling.

"Annette!" he smiled back, offering to shake her hand. "Pleased to finally meet you."

"I was hoping to see you on-board." she said. "Did you have any trouble getting here?"

"Oh, just the usual searches at all the security check-points we had to go through to get here."

"May I sit with you?" Annette asked and then paused. "Or did you have a companion?"

Diego moved over one seat. "By all means, please. And no, I'm traveling alone."

Annette took the seat he previously occupied and made herself comfortable. Diego felt a little uncomfortable sitting this close to what he considered, a beautiful, young woman. He slid over as much as he could, out of her personal space. She noticed.

"I'm sorry," she said as she scooted over, away from him. "I don't bite. I nibble." And then she laughed an infectious laugh that Diego, too, began to laugh. She looked down at the book sitting on his lap. "Oh, you read scripture. I think that's a wonderful read."

"Its actually helped me through some pretty rough times," he said looking down at the bible and brushed the face of it as if it was dusty.

They sat in silence for just a moment. Both were watching the various goings-on inside and outside the ferry. Diego felt as he was a child again trying to gain the courage to ask a girl to the school dance.

"So, how did you come to be involved in all this?" Diego asked as he looked into Annette's eyes.

"About 10 years ago, I was in rehab," she began. "I was a meth-addict and the program I enrolled in, was run by one of the Gowan companies. I was really messed up. Anyway, I volunteered myself for an experimental addictions treatment program that they suspected was near 100 percent effective. Only it couldn't be administered on US soil."

"So which country did you have go to?" Diego asked, intrigued.

Annette giggled, "Not a country. As I said, not on US soil."

Diego looked at her face blankly, thinking.

"At sea? On a ship?" he guessed.

"Uh, huh. One of the cruise lines is owned by the Gowans. Samuel simply booked the cruise ship strictly for addicts, medical staff and of course, psychologists and psychiatric staff to deal with behavioral issues and after 4 weeks, we came ashore, changed people."

Diego regarded her words for a moment. This was a side of Samuel Gowan he had not heard of before.

"So, you're cured?" he asked.

Annette shook her head, "Oh, no. I'm an addict. I'll always be an addict but, I'm clean. Its more of a behavioral problem. At least for me. Each person is what they call 'case specific'. Once the physical addiction is dealt with, then you move on to the psych stuff and really deal with that."

"So, you've been straight for 10 years?" Diego asked.

Annette sat back, "Yes. And the treatment worked so well, I even quit smoking cigarettes."

Diego chuckled at that. He remembered how difficult it was for him to quit smoking. It had taken several attempts over a period of two years but he finally succeeded. But, a treatment that was near 100% effective? It sounded like a miracle. Or a fantasy. Much of this, however, would seem to be a fantasy to the average person.

"What was involved in this treatment?" he asked.

"Well, all I can recall is that it involved an injection. Later, I learned that it was some new wonder drug that not only inhibited the effects of what a person was addicted to, it actually reversed the effects at the cellular level, in a matter of days, depending on the length of the addiction. While the drug was working, that's when the case-workers assisted."

"On your cruise, how many people failed?" Diego inquired.

"None," She said. "All on board were given a very public status report onboard of the effectiveness of the drug and the treatments. When we disembarked, every last one of us had succeeded. It was like having a meaningful second chance at life again. One, not to be squandered."

"That's impressive and good for you for seeking help," Diego commented.

"Why, thank-you," Annette replied. "Now. Your turn. Tell me how you got involved in all this."

Diego began to fill her in about the robotics company he had started, first in toys and then evolving his company into specialized industrial equipment. He told her that he made a point of staying away from anything that could be used for military applications even though there was money to be made in that lucrative market. He was rich enough. He just didn't see the point of being, richer than rich. He explained that after the death of his wife, Marcus Gowan, the son of Samuel, who he had business dealings with for years, offered to purchase his company and then approached him with an offer for a new life. He explained that although he would have normally scoffed at such a proposal, there was something to the offer and when he pressed Marcus for more information; Marcus could only offer pieces in return. But to Diego, it was enough to take the chance.

"And so, here I am," Diego finally said.

"Well, Just so you know, Diego. I'm glad you took the chance." Annette confided.

Just then the P.A. system of the ferry clicked on and for a moment, nothing was said. The passengers who were mostly all seated, quieted down to hear the announcement.

"Ladies and gentlemen. This is Captain Farrell. My crew and I would like to welcome you aboard the ferry S.S. Firenze. If you have any requests, our stewards will be happy to assist you. Our route today, will take us within sight of Catalina Island and past San Clemente. We are scheduled for a 'Whale Watching' expedition but, we all know our final destination. That being said, just to make sure you're aware, we'll be linking up and docking with the cruise liner, Majestic Empress, in six hours. She'll take you the rest of the way. We'll start off at speeds a ferry of this size is expected to travel at and once we're in international waters, we're going to kick things up a notch or three. Just for your info, the Firenze will be making the journey to the South Pacific at a slower pace since she still uses fossil fuel propulsion. The Cafeteria on deck 2 will be open in 90 minutes. Departure will be within 5 minutes. Again, welcome aboard and enjoy the ride."

Noise and excitement levels began to rise on the deck as passengers began talking amongst themselves. When the ferry began moving away from the dock, they all quieted down once again while watching out the expansive, wrap-around deck windows which gave everyone a great view from the sides and forward. The Firenze sailed slowly and smoothly through the marina, careful not create the large waves the ferry was capable of at start up speeds.

Annette looked over at Diego, "Do you have any ideas for your new life on the island?"

Diego looked back and found himself looking deeply into Annette's hazel eyes. He found himself mesmerized for a moment before responding.

"I, uh..well, I thought I'd figure it out once I got there. Actually, all I've ever known is computer and robotic systems. I've built some pretty impressive machines and got rich doing it. But, the machines. They were very durable and reliable. I love designing machines. Stick to what you know, right? What about you? Thinking of a career change?"

Thinking for a moment, she made a kind of funny face, "Oh, I don't know. I thought I would start my own business or work for someone else in a management position, or something. I won't know until I get there."

"What can you bring to the table?" Diego asked.

"Architectural PHD from Stanford with a BA in Design Engineering." she stated.

Diego just looked at Annette, mouth agape. Here was someone who was working for a ferry company, totally over-qualified and beautiful, to boot.

She giggled, "Diego, close your mouth."

Diego quickly shut his mouth, blinked once and said, "Wow." He looked her over again and asked, "How did you manage that? I mean, you're so young. You'd have had to have been going to college while being an addict."

"Well, just after finishing my treatment, I enrolled in a program at the Gowan Learning Institute. At the same time, I was enrolled in Stanford's Distance Learning Program. Anyway, at the Gowan Institute, I was given an implant that increased my learning abilities."

Diego gave Annette a quizzical look, "What kind of implant?"

"Nano-technology, that's all I know. Its injected directly into the blood-stream and attaches itself directly to the learning center of the brain. It is absolutely amazing on how fast and what you can learn."

"How safe is it?" Diego asked.

"Very safe," Annette replied. "The information learned, is permanent. Its like having photographic memory."

"That's absolutely amazing," Diego stated. "How does it work?"

"Oh, I don't know, exactly. But, it was explained to me once that if you took an illiterate person and inject him with the implant, in 5 days, that person will be reading at an undergraduate level."

Diego thought about that for a moment. If a person had no previous knowledge about something, or wanted to learn something, it was conceivable that the same person could be retrained.

"So a person could be retrained?"

"Oh, yes," she said. "I even picked up 3 languages."

"Spoken or written?" Diego asked.

"Both," she said.

"What languages did you learn?"

"French, Russian and Mandarin," she replied. "I plan on learning Spanish, German and Italian as well."

Diego chuckled, "At that rate, you could be an interpreter."

"Oh, no," Annette said suddenly. "I just wanted to see if I could learn other languages. You know, to be able to converse with people from other countries. Besides, with this kind of technology on the island, interpreters won't be needed. And I'll tell you a secret, I kinda like designing things, too. I like creating things."

"Well, I'll hire you," Diego blurted out.

Annette laughed aloud and gave Diego a light punch to the shoulder, "Yeah, right. You're funny, Diego."

Diego put away his bible, placing it into his back-pack. "No, no. I am quite serious, Annette. I need a good designer and what better way to get started than as a designer, working for me. Come on, look. Try it for 2 months and if you don't like it, you can go off and find something else you do like."

"You don't even know if I'm any good. I don't even know the first thing about robotics." Annette felt on-the-spot.

"You have a PHD. That's all I need to know. Mechanical architecture is not that different from structural. I'm not asking you to design the software. Leave that to me. And if you are as good as you say, you could end up as my principle designer. So, what do you say?"

Annette was silent for the longest time, considering Diego's offer. She looked around the passenger deck and it was obvious to Diego that she was lost in thought. He waited in silence, patiently.

"Alright," she said suddenly. "Yes. I accept your offer."

Diego just smiled and offered his right hand. "Good. Welcome to my world."

Annette smiled back, took his hand and shook it.

CHAPTER EIGHT

SHABDA

Major Manning had called for his troops to gather around him in the Mess-bay. Those closest to him chose to sit on the floor with those in the rear, standing. All eyes were on him, waiting for the noisiest to quiet down.

"Listen up!" Lt. Stuart ordered. Those who were talking, stopped suddenly and looked forward.

"Thank-you, Lt. Now, this is a situation report! As some of you have overheard and passed it on. It is no rumor! We *are* on-board a spacecraft and we *are* in space. We are currently drifting in space near the planet Mars!" Manning paused for a moment. He watched for their reactions. Some were had smiles, some stared blankly, ahead.

"The reason why we were taken aboard this spaceship was because at the time of our insertion, they were evacuating. The complex was set to self-destruct and we were in harms-way. These people saved our lives, as they are right now, saving the life of Capt. Svanda. They didn't have to. They could have lifted off and left us there to die. You're the luckiest, sorriest, sons of bitches I know."

That produced laughs and chuckles from the troops. One of the soldiers seated before him raised his hand and asked, "Why the luckiest, Sir?"

"Because you're alive and you're all astronauts, now," Manning replied. "The sorriest, because you didn't even know it."

That brought comments and murmurs of agreement amongst the troops. Some did high-fives, some were smiling, some just stared blankly, ahead.

"Now!" Manning continued. "We are the guests of the crew of this ship. You will afford them every courtesy and you will follow all commands stated by the crew, unless you deem them, questionable. In that case, defer to myself or the Lt. We are not going to take this ship and we are not going to arrest and detain Marcus Gowan. It is my professional opinion that he and his people are not the terrorists as was claimed. If this were Canada, we would still follow orders and complete our mission. We are in space. United Nations Space Law applies to us, here. As Canada is a member nation and a signatory of that treaty, for us to try to take this ship, claimed by another nation, specifically named, Pacifica, we would be breaking that law. World opinion at the UN would turn against Canada, especially if questions were raised about where the orders originated from. Being that Canada is a partner in NORAD and Continental Security with the United States, that would prove embarrassing to the US Administration and any silence from the Chancellor or the US President would be perceived as collusion."

Manning stopped for a moment and paced a little.

"Now, you all know me. I hate politics and politicians but," Manning paused as a majority of his troops nodded in agreement, "I can see the political fall-out from this, a million miles away. No pun, intended"

Again, they all nodded in agreement.

"In the future, when you are all debriefed, I want you to remember this. You are following my direct orders, in this matter. In debriefing, you can even repeat everything I've said here. You won't be held responsible for anything that you're ordered to do from this moment on. It's also for your protection from persecution and that of your families."

Manning paused for a moment to let the ramifications of what he just said, sink in. He didn't want the 'powers-that-be' to manipulate and ruin the lives of good, professional soldiers. Someday, they would all leave the military and the last thing they needed was a black mark on their service records. Over the years, he had witnessed many examples of this, happening to other soldiers, some deservedly, most not, and he was determined not to let the same happen to these people.

"I can also see the scapegoat in all this, in the end," Manning announced. "And you're all looking at him. I am prepared for that and will accept that."

"I've never heard of, what did you say, Sir? Pacifica?" One of the soldiers asked.

Lt. Stuart stepped forward, "It's a new nation in the South Pacific. The island itself rose from the ocean floor, just like the land-masses off California and Baja, was discovered and as difficult as it sounds, hidden by the Gowan's. That's the short version."

"Are we being held on-board against our will, Sir?" another soldier asked.

"No," Manning said. "I have spoken to Marcus Gowan, he holds the rank of Flight Commander, and he has allowed us full access to the ship, within reason."

"Are they going to take us home, Sir?" said another.

"Yes but, not directly. If they were to take us back to Canada, they know we would have no choice but, to arrest them. Commander Gowan has promised to get us home. Most likely, to a neutral country that doesn't have extradition treaties with the US or Canada."

"When, Sir?" asked another soldier to the rear.

"Soon," Manning replied. "They are currently experiencing engine problems. As soon as they rectify that, I've been assured that we'll be underway for Earth."

Manning's face went suddenly blank as he looked over at Stuart.

"I don't believe I just said that."

Stuart nodded, "Shape of things to come, Sir."

"How is Captain Svanda?"

Manning looked over to Stuart and smiled. It was perhaps the best news of this mission. The prospect of losing people in an accident and not in actual combat was always troubling to him.

"He just got out of surgery. He'll be fine. They are keeping him in the Infirmary for a while, for observation. Anyone who wishes to visit him, is free to do so. Nothing has been said contrary to that." Manning explained.

"Can we see Mars, Sirs?" a young blonde female Private asked.

"Yes you can. There are windows you can look out but, I'm unsure as to where they are located."

Master-Corporal Vincent Rojas stood up from the crowd. He was a large, stocky, muscular man whose weapon was the general-purpose machine-gun (GPMG). One had to be strong enough to carry not only the weapon itself but its ammo as well.

"Sirs," he began. "What do we do, in the mean time?"

"We'll all be staying here, in this room, so stake out a spot. That's where you'll be sleeping. Stand down, clear, clean, secure your weapons and catch some Z's. That's an order."

Manning glanced over to Stuart, who nodded, knowingly and stepped forward, facing the two squads.

"That concludes this briefing. Dismissed."

Manning stroked his goatee and moustache as he stood watching his people scatter throughout the room. He was lost in thought as Lt. Stuart, standing at his side, followed his gaze.

"Well, you just confirmed what they thought of you, Sir," Stuart stated.

"Confirmed what, Lt?" Manning said, still gazing off in the distance.

Stuart broke away from his gaze and looked over to his CO.

"You care what happens to them. Sir."

For the longest moment, Manning stared at the floor and didn't respond. It was an observation that he never gave himself the luxury to consider before. And it was something, as an officer, he was supposed to deny. At least, officially.

"Of course, I do. But, if you let them know that, I will personally ring your neck."

A big grin slowly appeared and grew wider on the Lt.'s face as he snapped a salute.

"Yes, sir! Understood, Sir!"

Manning returned the salute to which Stuart held his until his CO disengaged his.

"All right, you suck-up. You're dismissed."

Eighteen hours later, Doc Thorpe was sitting at the table of the conference room on the operations floor. Beside him, was Acting Operations Director, Angela Teslin. The relays for Hyperlink Communication was finally online and the two were working to locate and establish contact with the Destiny. Angela rose from her chair and stepped away from her portable, networked computer to approach the large monitor that was the palisite wall. Looking at the different information displayed on the monitor, she began to massage her own neck muscles. She was studying a graphic representation of the Moon and its relation to the Earth. Listed in between, were all satellites and spacecraft orbiting both. Every once in a while, she would touch the screen icon of a satellite she suspected could be the Destiny. Doing this would list the registered country, name or acronym of the satellite or spacecraft, its orbital path and its purpose.

Frustrated, she whispered, "Where are you?"

Hearing her rhetorical question, Doc too, rose from his laptop and joined her at 'The Wall'. He began to message her neck muscles for her.

"Why don't you take a break," he offered. "You've been at this for five hours. Why don't you go outside and take in some of that South Pacific sunshine. Then, you'll be able to take a fresh look at this."

Angela stood silently, looking at the displays, occasionally closing her eyes at the relief she received at the hands of Doc Thorpe.

"Perhaps, you're right. But, I'll feel so guilty trying to relax when I know there is work to be done. We have to find Marcus."

"You know, if I didn't know better, I'd say you have a crush on him," Doc said as he continued to massage Angela's neck.

Angela pulled away and turned to face Thorpe, "So what if I did? Is that so wrong?"

Thorpe observed that she said this not defensively but, as a matter of fact.

"I won't deny it. But, its not what you think. Its not a physical attraction. I have no illusions about who he is and what he and we, are doing. What he has envisioned has the capability of saving this planet and us from ourselves. He is a man with great vision. What he has to offer, is something Humanity hasn't had in a long time. The belief in our own humanity. Its not just that. Individually, he has given us the ability to believe in ourselves. That, we can make a difference. And I can't name anyone in recent history who has instilled that kind of belief in any of us."

"Everyone feels that way. However, with you, it seems like so much more," Doc said.

Angela looked worriedly into his eyes for the longest moment. It was an observation about herself that she never thought about, let alone, put into words. She knew he was on the right track but, not on the mark.

"I have to admit, I am in awe of Marcus," she revealed. "And as unhealthy as it may sound, I could sit and listen to him all day. Its pure admiration and professional respect that, I have for him. And I know, it could be nothing more than that."

Doc regarded her statement for a moment. He, like everyone else, felt as she did. She was just the first to vocalize it.

"Look," he began. "If it helps, I'm worried too. I've had the opportunity to not only sit and listen to him for days on end but, plan and implement with him as well. He has given us such an opportunity, our lives before seemed, well…empty."

Silently, she nodded and looked down at her feet. She sighed heavily. "Maybe I should take a break."

"Yes. Please do before you start pacing the floor. You start doing that, and even I'll get nervous."

Recognizing that he was joking, a smirk appeared on her face.

"Ok," she relented. "I'll agree to 15 minutes outside and.."

Doc interrupted.

"I don't want to see you back here for 25 minutes. It will take you 5 minutes to and 5 minutes back. I want you to take a full 15 minutes to relax and clear your head."

"But,.." Angela began to protest.

"That wasn't a request," Doc said firmly. "Go on. Get outta' here."

Her hands went up as if she were surrendering while she turned on her heels and headed for the Duraglass doors of the room. It took her the five minutes to reach the picnic tables located 50 meters from the pyramid-shaped administration building. She sat down heavily and for a moment, stared blankly at the flowers that ringed the cobblestone pad the tables sat on. She detected movement to her left and saw the groundskeepers walking wheelbarrows full of potted plants towards a flower garden they had previously prepared. She found it ironic, that with all the advanced technology they had at their disposal, there were things that still required human hands to accomplish certain tasks. It reminded her of a conversation she once had with Marcus Gowan.

One day, she had hypothesized the use of one technology to accomplish a task without the presence of a human master to oversee its completion. Marcus tried to explain to her how impractical and inefficient the use of that particular technology would be. Not understanding what he was getting at, he explained bluntly and humorously, how ineffective it would be to teach a robot how to clean a toilet or sweep a flight of stairs. That the technology is a tool and not meant as a replacement of the human hands that would use it. Only then did she understand. Only then did she realize how smart and wise, Marcus Gowan was.

The next thing she noticed was the path of the Sun as it hung in the sky. Having spent most of her life in the northern hemisphere, she now had to remind herself that she was looking north and not south. She imagined for a moment, looking at her surroundings as if she were still in the northern hemisphere. The Sun would have risen to her left in the east and fall to her right in the west. She wasn't homesick. She just tried to imagine the differences. Observing the shadows being cast by the various, newly transplanted trees, she took the time to calculate what time of day it would seem, if she were in the northern hemisphere. She estimated that it would seem to about 7 p.m. in her hometown of Helena, Montana.

Her thoughts returned to Marcus Gowan and the Destiny. With all this great technology, finding the Destiny was like finding a needle in a haystack. She tried to imagine the possible things that could've gone wrong but none of her reasons made any sense. From what she knew and was told by Doc Thorpe, after extensive testing and no shakedown cruise, Destiny was unanimously deemed, space-worthy.

She tried to think of all the satellites and probes that had been launched from White Alice in the last two years. She wondered which one's sensing capabilities would be more efficient to find the Destiny. Immediately, she ruled out the astronomy and radio telescopic satellites. They were ill-equipped to start a search pattern. It would be like looking for that needle with a pair of binoculars with the lens two inches from the haystack. Next, she thought of the probes on the lunar surface and orbiting satellites but, realized they were focused on the Moon. Mars was another consideration and the situation was the same as the Moon. She felt that that was too far to look.

She looked up briefly at an over-flying cargo helicopter with a 20-ft. sea-container slung under its belly. Although its new engines were whisper-quiet, she could hear the main rotor slicing through the air. She knew its destination was the wind-farm generating station on the south side of the island. The container was full of spare parts that she had arranged for delivery. She made a mental note to check its transit progress in an hour since the container had a built-in GPS transceiver.

Then, an idea struck her as if she were hit by lightening. She instantly stood up straight and looked to the sky. There *were* probes that could find the Destiny. She knew they weren't in position yet, as they still had a few months before they reached their final destination.

"IPS," she said under her breath and in a flat run, headed back into the Administration Building.

It took her almost a minute to get back to the conference room where Doc, upon seeing Angela back early, checked his wristwatch. Before he could say a word, she held up her left hand and gasped the acronym for the Inter-planetary Positioning Satellite System. Like the Global Positioning System which employed orbiting satellites around the Earth, IPS was meant to track spacecraft traveling through the Sol star system. Onboard, as well, were Hyperlink communications relays and sensor/scanning pods.

He immediately turned on his heels and went to his laptop, entered a couple of keystrokes. This brought up a computer representation of the Solar System on 'The Wall'. Just beyond the Pluto/Neptune orbital plane, in quadrants, were four probes. A few more keystrokes brought up the location of six more, three above and three below the Sol System, evenly spaced in flat, triangular patterns.

"These six are still enroute to their final destinations. ETA is two months," he said reading the information off the large monitor.

"Can't we send a signal to pause the flight to do a quick scan and then they can continue on?" Angela asked trying to slow down her breathing.

Doc thought for a moment while staring at 'The Wall'.

"Once the arrays are deployed, they can't be folded back. And they'll have to continue on their programmed course at a slower pace. But,.." he said with one finger in the air and the other hand quickly typing. "..at least we'll get their general location." He hit one final keystroke and the phrase 'Transmission Sending' flashed across the wall monitor. He stood up, hands on hips and looked at Angela. "Now we wait."

"How long before we get confirmation?" she asked.

"It'll take about ten minutes for them to come to a complete stop," Doc estimated. "Another five to deploy the arrays and ten more for them to run a systems and diagnostics check. Confirmation will be immediately after that and then we can send the command code to start a search."

"I feel better, now," Angela said as she let out a heavy sigh of relief and sat down in one of the chairs.

"Why don't you go finish your break," Doc offered.

"Oh, no you don't," she said, crossing her arms. "I am not going to miss this, now."

This time, it was Doc's turn to put his hands up, feigning surrender.

"All right, all right. Suit yourself," he agreed. "Lets get to work on the search parameters."

Agent Tobin stepped out of the Canadian Forces Seagull helicopter seconds after it touched down on the tarmac of Voice Island. The sun was just peaking above the horizon and the air was cold and crisp. Dressed in Canadian military duty fatigues and arctic parka with a back-pack slung over his left shoulder, he headed to a large field tent, 200 feet away. He flipped the hood of his Arctic parka over his head to protect his ears from the wind. He estimated the strong wind-speed to be close to about 20 to 30 mph and thought how incredible it was how any humans could live, let alone work in such a climate. A few times, as he trudged through the snowdrifts, he thought the wind gusts were going to knock him over.

Reaching the tent, he entered the vestibule section and noisily stomped his feet to loosen the snow clinging to his boots. He entered the tent to find about ten soldiers, male and female, either working at laptops, charts or standing by the lone stove providing heat. Tobin happened to make eye-contact with a female Major standing with a Lieutenant at the stove, warming their hands with metal cups of coffee. The Major gestured Tobin over and dismissed the Lieutenant. Tobin gave the Major a salute while at the same time, handed him, his orders.

"At ease, Captain," the Major said as she opened the packet. After reading Tobin's orders, she opened the stove door and placed the papers on the flame and closed it.

"Ma'me," Tobin began. "I would like to request a couple of your personnel to assist me with my investigation."

Looking Tobin in the eyes, the Major placed her metal cup on the stove, "Our orders come from the same place, Captain. What are you looking for, specifically? Maybe what you're looking for, could give us a clue as to what happened here and where our missing personnel are."

Tobin had to act quickly. He couldn't risk his true mission, let alone his true identity.

"Department of Federal Defense was quite specific about my orders, It's 'Need to Know', Ma'me. I'm sorry. I just need a few of your people and then I'll be on the next chopper outta here."

The Major regarded Tobin for a moment. "Allright. Agreed. Next chopper arrives in two hours. I want my people back then and you on that chopper when it leaves. Is there any gear that you require?"

"I brought my own equipment. However, I'll need some climbing gear. I want to descend into the 'pit'."

Activity in the tent stopped and heads turned at that. Tobin couldn't but help notice all the eyeballs looking in his direction. He turned to confirm his suspicion. The Major waved everybody back to their respective duties.

"Did I say something wrong?" turning back to the commanding officer.

"We are not sure as to the stability of the pit wall. I have given a standing order that no-one is to approach it. Personnel safety is my responsibility. I can't allow it."

Tobin realized he needed to be assertive but, low-key. He stepped closer to the Major and spoke quietly.

"Major. I'll be the only one entering the 'pit'. You read my orders. My security clearance is higher than yours. I am sure you received, prior to my arrival, orders to assist my investigation." Tobin could see the Major's face turning to anger as her features tightened and reddened. Tobin spoke again to talk the Major down before she could get started. "Look, Ma'me. I don't want to get into a pissing contest. But if I have to, I will. And when all is said and done, it'll be you on that chopper, possibly facing charges of obstructing my investigation. I would rather have cooperation instead of confrontation. Can I have that cooperation? Ma'me."

The Major turned to take her cup from the stove, took a sip, and looked back at Tobin.

"Ok. You win this one," the Major acquiesced. "However, you risk personnel safety just a little, or if I even think you have. I'll have you cuffed and gagged and I'll throw you on the chopper, myself. We on the same page, Captain?"

"I am, Ma'me," Tobin agreed.

"Good. Take whoever you can find and stay the hell out of my way," the Major ordered.

Giving the Major the last word, Tobin saluted her and left the tent where he muttered 'Bitch', to himself.

Stepping out of the tent, zipping up his arctic parka, pack over his shoulder, he observed what appeared to be the hangar and airport control tower a short distance away. He could tell there was no heat in the hangar as the main doors were wide open. The same could not be said for the single tower and it's small adjoining building. He could see Canadian soldiers coming in and out of the rear door. He began trudging towards the structure. The wind gusts seemed to have gotten stronger and at times seemed to change direction. To Tobin, the wind seemed to bite at the exposed portions of his skin. Only once he was inside the building, did he feel the relief of warmth of portable heaters. Looking around, he found a group of soldiers huddled over a small heater, warming their hands.

"I need volunteers to assist in the descent of the 'pit'," Tobin announced.

Four of the ten soldiers turned and stepped forward. So, Tobin accepted all four. He instructed them as to his intentions and within 15 minutes, Tobin was at the plateau ridge looking down into a massive and deep hole. Ten minutes after that, after putting on the climbing gear, he began his descent. He noticed how smooth the pit wall was. He tried, momentarily, to hypothesize as to what could cause such a massive hole that would be naturally occurring. He couldn't think of anything. He continued to lower himself deeper.

About two-thirds of the way down, now, he stopped to take a series of pictures. It was then that he noticed a hole, cut into the side of the crater wall, roughly ten feet by ten feet, twenty feet to his left. After snapping a few pictures from his vantage point, he tucked the camera inside his parka and took out his radio and informed the soldiers above of his intensions to investigate.

It took him about five minutes to swing over to the hole and jump down onto the floor. The first thing he noticed was that it seemed to be a corridor and that for a mining operation, it seemed to be too small. Following the corridor, he couldn't but, help notice how smooth and straight it seemed. He took out a laser-pointer and held it against the wall so it shined deeper into the corridor. He did the same for the floor. It amazed him how square all the angles were. His first thought was that it was a maintenance or utility shaft. But, other than the frost-covered foot prints, there was no evidence of equipment that would be used in such a mining operation. Taking out a flashlight, he followed the tunnel deeper.

At the end of the tunnel was a wide opening to a large room the size of a double-car garage. To his right, against the wall at the rear of the room, was a frost-covered steel table. A workbench. Above the middle of it was what appeared to be a peg-board with hooks for assorted tools. It was bordered with cabinets. He began opening the cabinet doors to see if any tools or equipment was left behind. They were empty. He turned around to re-inspect the room with his flashlight, in case he missed or didn't spot something that would indicate what this room was used for. When he didn't see anything obvious, he turned back to the workbench. Although, the light from his flashlight wasn't shining directly on the peg-board, he could make out faint outlines from under the frost.

Taking his gloved hand, he swiped the peg-board to clear the frost. Underneath, were the outlines of various tools and the nametags associated with each. He read the tags and observed each out-line and was puzzled as he could not recognize ever seeing tool outlines or their names like these. He decided to clear the frost from the rest of the peg-board, took an overall picture and then took individual pictures of each outline and tag. After taking more pictures of the room and the corridor, he reached the opening to the crater, hooked up the rope to his harness and radioed the four soldiers above that he was going to continue his descent. When the lines went taught, he began his climb down, carefully watching for any other openings in the crater wall.

Once down at the bottom of the crater, he found that it was covered with ice with a fresh, thin layer of slushy water. Standing there for a moment, looking down at his boots in the slush, he was trying to figure out where the water was coming from. He walked around, still connected to the ropes, making sure to not tangle himself, when he stopped and looked closer at his boots. Before, the slush barely covered the soles and now, there was fresh water inching to the ankles of his water-proof arctic boots. He could see a small trickle spreading out. He followed the trickle of water which appeared to be coming from the center of the crater. He could see, in the middle, a slight but, obvious bulge in the center. He realized pressure was pushing the ice upward and at that, a thunderous crack resounded throughout the crater. Ice splintered and fractured up into the air. Large chunks of ice pushed up and rolled over on the surface. Then, the water started to bubble out. And not just a trickle, either. If it wasn't for the chunks of ice the size of houses, it would be a geyser.

It was at this point, Tobin realized why and where the water was coming from. He was below sea-level and somehow the water was forcing its way through the soil. As a child, he once dug a hole on a beach and when down deep enough, couldn't, until his father told him, understand why or where the water was coming from.

'Path of least resistance,' he remembered the quote of his father.

He clicked on his radio as he ran, headed to the crater wall, "I've got an emergency, down here! Get me outta here. Now, now, now!"

Twenty feet up the wall, water at his heels, the ropes finally went tight. With the extra pull from above, it seemed to Tobin as if he were running up the steep slope, the water now, far below him. With ten feet to go till he reached the ridgeline, he stumbled and fell. Moving slower, he was finally pulled over the ridge where he fell hard on the other side and came to a stop.

A Master-Corporal pulled him to his feet. The other three soldiers had basically, grabbed the ropes and ran down the slope towards the tarmac in an effort to save him.

"Thanks," Tobin gasped between labored breathes, patting his hand twice on the Master-Corporal's shoulder. He thanked the other three when they re-joined them.

The five of them looked over the ridgeline to see the crater now almost half-filled with sea-water. Tobin looked for the corridor entrance only to realize it was now under water.

"Wouldn't have believed it if I didn't see it, with my own eyes," one soldier said.

Tobin said nothing. If these men had taken their time, he would be dead. He just instructed them to gather the gear and report back to their previous post, inside the tower to warm up.

As they trudged back down toward the tarmac, Tobin could see the Major, standing outside the tent, hands on her hips, watching. Realizing that the Major would have heard the call for help on the radio, all Tobin could think about was the warning the Major gave him. He knew he had overstayed his welcome.

Tobin took comfort in the fact that he, at least found something, although not much, to take back to the Senator.

"I'm telling you. The linear mitigators, in the accumulator is what caused the surge in power through the amplifiers and then directly to the GD projectors," Joe Kyras, standing beside Bruno Kravakis, said to Marcus and Mac Marsh in an impromptu meeting in engineering.

"Not the inputs from the fight deck?" Marsh asked.

"Right," the big man, Joe Kyras, confirmed. "And the reason why the flight controls were frozen, was because once we entered what Bruno calls, 'phased' space, no amount of inputs could change our course."

"Once in 'phased' space, our velocity and course was 'locked'," Bruno added.

Joe was tall and muscular. Often, he was referred to as 'Tank' and those who knew him well, knew he was nothing but, a big teddy bear. He was a machinist/mechanic by trade but, dabbled in other engineering fields, as well. Marcus had met him one day when his father's limousine broke down. This tow truck, just happened to see the limo pulled over to the side of the road and Leland stepped out of the cab. At the time, it seemed that the cab was too small for its driver. Although, he couldn't tow the Limo, Kyras tried at first tried to get the vehicle running, unsuccessfully. Then, he offered to get a proper, more capable tow truck and at the same time drive Samuel Gowan and the young Marcus home. All, at no charge. Even though, the elder Gowan tried to pay Kyras, he still refused saying that for one; he couldn't restart the limo and two; couldn't tow it either. He added he could fix anything. Samuel had asked him what he was doing being a tow-truck driver. Kyras had replied that he was in-between jobs and that some of his previous jobs weren't enjoyable places to work. So, Samuel offered him a job instead and promised him that it would be one; enjoyable and two; rewarding.

"How," Marcus asked. "Can you show us?"

"We already have it up on the monitor, over here." Kravakis led them over to the engineering workstation. "In the accumulator, power for the amps are channeled between the linear mitigator nodes. The high energy plasma is precisely 'tuned' (focused), between as they pass by each node of the mitigators. Power is boosted by a factor of two for each one it passes, as shown here."

"Ok," Marcus agreed, understanding.

Kravakis pressed a button on the keyboard which displayed another graphic over top of the other.

"This is what actually occurred," Kravakis said as he turned to see the look of surprise on Marcus' face. "You can see that the plasma was actually drawn to the nodes in the insulated accumulator and began bouncing and ricocheting off of each of the linear mitigator nodes in a geometric pattern before finally channeling out to the amplifiers and then to the projectors. This was not a problem for the reactor-quad as it was not a drain on consumption. In fact, we dare say, the surge in power to the projectors quadrupled exponentially, each time it bounced off a given node."

"Why did the accelerating relay burn out and not the nodes?" Marsh asked.

"Ahh," Kravakis said, impressed with the pilot's understanding of the propulsion system. "Because the accelerating relay was drawing all that increased power and passing it on to the amplifiers and then to the projectors. Hence, the power surge. At this point, tachyon particle build-up was off the chart and was being drawn off from the quad along with the plasma. We both knew there was a problem once the glow from the reactor-quad was brighter than usual. Even though, it could handle feedback of a significant quantity, it was never meant to handle the magnitude of both the plasma and the tachyon particles interacting as one. By using the regulating sequencer, we were able to divert the tachyons back to the reactor-quad to contain them before the entire system began to overload.

I'd even hazard a guess that we were moments away from a catastrophic amplifier explosion."

Marcus was still looking at the monitor. He turned to Kravakis and Kyras

"Could we duplicate what happened?"

Kravakis just stared at Marcus. And then, the biggest grin, Marcus had ever seen, appeared on his face. He briefly looked over at Kyras and looked back at Marcus.

"Yeah, we think so. We're already working on a solution to strengthening and enhancing one of the spares. It's gonna take a couple more hours to beef it up and we can't guarantee it won't burn out again."

"and the tachyon feedback?" Marcus asked.

"We've installed two regulating sequencers, one to do the job and the other to control tachyon flow to the distortion amplifiers. We have to build from scratch, a kind of tachyon buffer system complete with containment capabilities and an injector assembly. For the time being, you'll have to relay to us, the speed you'll want to maintain. We'll need you to call out percentages in power utilization."

A confused look appeared on Marsh's face as he looked from Marcus to Kravakis and back to Marcus.

"Just hold on a minute, mate. You wanna try that, again?" he looked back to Kravakis, his Australian accent, more pronounced. "Are you telling us, that we could integrate those modifications and we could go faster than the speed of light, anytime we want?"

"That's exactly what I'm saying," Kravakis agreed. "Up until now, we have achieved only twenty percent the speed of light, without introducing the tachyons to the projectors. Now, we've surpassed that by a country mile. I have to admit, I would rather study and test this, a lot longer before implementing this kind of change."

"Besides, we don't have a choice," Marcus interjected. "There is only enough food on-board for a month. It would take us almost three months to get back to Earth with the Helium3 thrusters. Those soldiers probably only have field rations for three days."

"If you can't feed the troops, we may have to re-christen this spacecraft, the 'Bounty'," Kyras joked.

"Have you completed your inspection of the rest of the propulsion system?" Marcus asked.

"We have on the major components," Kravakis confirmed. "The others will have to wait until our modifications are complete and then I want to double and triple check the entire system with computer diagnostics."

Joni, who was listening and had remained quiet on the Hyperlink headset, interrupted.

"Marcus. Incoming voice transmission from Earth"

All four men looked at each other, puzzled.

"EM radio?" Marcus asked.

"Nope," she replied. "It's Doc. He's transmitting from Pacifica."

"Damn," Marcus cursed. He looked at his watch and realized how much time had gone by. That fact, that he had forgotten that the 'Exodus' was almost completed.

"Ok, Joni. Tell Doc, I'll be there in a moment," he said as he turned to Kravakis and Kyras. "I'll go to the flight deck, update Tom and I'll be back after that to help with the mods."

"Take your time, Marcus," Kravakis offered. "We're in no rush."

Marcus left and walked briskly toward the flight deck. He stopped briefly, at the Infirmary to check on the injured soldier that Kane was caring for. It appeared as if the soldier was being released. A couple of fellow soldiers were there as well. Marcus was keeping an eye out for Manning. He wanted to invite him to the flight deck. As he was about to climb the last flight of stairs to the flight deck, he saw Manning exit the washroom or head, as it was known. Marcus waved him over to follow him. The two of them found Joni at her Ops workstation, talking.

"Hang on, Doc," she interrupted herself. "Marcus is here."

"Doc!" Marcus said immediately and loudly. "What'd ya want?" he looked at Manning and made the expression on his face, as if laughing, silently.

"You didn't check in with us and we lost the telemetry link," Thorpe replied. "We've been looking for you."

"Well," Marcus began. "Greetings from Mars, Doc." Then his tone turned to the more serious. "We've been, uh, dealing with issues, up here."

"I wanted to ask about that. What are you doing way out there?"

"Propulsion systems malfunction. Only this is turning out to be beneficial," Marcus said. "Where are you transmitting from, by the way?"

"From the seventh floor conference room of the Admin. Building. Why?"

"No reason," Marcus admitted. "I knew the space center wouldn't be complete, yet. Listen. Joni will be sending all our telemetry data, soon. I want you to have the propulsion engineers and scientists to pay particular attention to the specs for the new modifications we will be installing. I want their thoughts and any and all concerns."

"Joni," Doc said through the speaker. "when-ever you're ready. Transceivers are standing by."

"Another thing, Doc," Marcus said as he looked over at Major Manning, who was now sitting in the chair at the engineering workstation. "Remember that concern you had about the Army busting into the mine before we were ready to launch?"

There was silence before Doc replied. "Yeah, I do."

"Your snowman army didn't slow them down as much as you had hoped."

Marcus saw a look of realization form on Manning's face, who pointed at the speaker, mouthing the word 'Him?' Marcus silently nodded.

"What are you saying, Marcus?" Doc asked.

"Standing beside me, is Major Dennis Manning. Onboard, are two sections of the Canadian Anti-Terrorist Team. Say 'hello', Major."

Manning leaned closer from the chair to Joni's workstation to be heard and not seeing the microphone, simply said hello.

"Marcus. How?" Doc replied.

Marcus explained the events leading up the launch. The power failure. The collapsed rooms. The stuck launch doors and the injured soldiers on the launch bay floor. The reason for evacuating and saving them.

Doc was silent for a moment.

"What would you like me to do, Sir" Thorpe asked his boss.

Marcus knew he could count on Doc to anticipate him.

"Access one of the telecommunication satellites, place a call to the Canadian Chancellor. Notify her that her missing soldiers are safe and that she should expect another call from us as to the location for their safe return. Answer any questions she may have, except your location. I don't want that to get out, just yet.

"You know, her staff is gonna freak that we can access her private phone in her office, on our terms," a female voice could be heard, chuckling.

Marcus smiled, recognizing the voice of Angela Teslin.

"Angela. I want you to make that call. She'll be more receptive. These people have families that should be notified they are safe."

"Ok, Marcus," She agreed. "I'll make it happen."

Manning stood up and approached the Ops console, addressing Angela.

"Angela. This is Major Manning. The Chancellor's staff will want to authenticate what you will be telling her. When you are asked for confirmation, just say 'What The Fog Has Wrought'. That will confirm the message could only have come from me and that we are alive and safe."

"Understood, Major."

There was a moment of silence when Doc finally spoke through the speaker.

"So gang, What are we looking at for a time-table for your return?"

Marcus returned the moment of silence, deep in thought.

"We're just starting the mods., now. That should take the rest of the day, maybe two. Another day to install and do the necessary testing, find and fix any bugs we find. Then we'll get underway for our trip back to Earth. Five minutes after that, we should be in orbit."

"Excuse me. Did you say, five minutes? Doc asked.

"That's correct. That's the nature of the malfunction," Marcus confirmed. "We think we can duplicate what happened and incorporate it into the propulsion system. You know the old saying, 'most discoveries are usually made by accident'. That's why I want our people to look closely at the propulsion telemetry and our specs for the mods."

"I'll get them to look at it right away, Marcus," Doc promised. "Is there any thing else?"

"How is the 'Exodus' going?" he asked as he looked over to Manning.

"It's going well," he replied, sounding positive. "Do you want the blow-by-blow now, or do you want us to transmit a situation report to you?"

"Transmit a sit-rep. I'd like to go over it. Not too detailed. I'm not going to have a lot of time."

"It's already done," Angela announced. "Uploading now."

"Link established," Joni confirmed. "Ninety kilobytes confirmed received."

"Joni, transfer the data to my digital notebook," he said referring to the electronic document storage device networked to the computer systems.

"Done," she said after a couple of seconds.

"Doc, we'll keep the telemetry downlink active. Contact us at your leisure. We'll notify you before we 'weigh anchor'."

"Understood. Pacifica signing off."

Marcus turned and descended the steps to the lower flight deck to retrieve the notebook. Coming back up, he stood beside Manning, thanked Joni and gestured for Manning to follow him as he began leaving the flight deck. Manning was a little puzzled. He wondered why Marcus Gowan was leading him off the flight deck. Did it have something to do with the information on the electronic notebook? Where was Marcus leading him to?

Marcus led Manning the observation lounge. To Manning's amazement, the lounge was huge. There were rows of forward-facing seating for perhaps two hundred people. What really got his attention was the large, observation windows that gave a 180 degree field of view, forward of the ship. Already, he could see, a few of his personnel, seated in the seats, looking outwards. Finding empty seats in the first row, just left of the center aisle, Marcus gestured for the Major to take a seat. Marcus handed him the digital notebook and then seated himself. The notebook, about an inch thick and the size of a clipboard, had a liquid crystal display with a file listed. Manning began to read the first page.

"What am I looking at?" Manning asked. "Why are you showing me this?"

Marcus, staring out the window ahead, turned to Manning.

"This spacecraft, is not the work of just a few people," Marcus began. "It's the result of untold millions of hours of hard work and sweat. The people, who helped, come from all walks of life, all classes, and many cultures. On Pacifica, there will be a representation of the peoples of the Earth, at least of those who wish to participate."

"You mean," Manning interrupted, "those, to whom you've made the offer to."

Marcus regarded the grizzled, military officer.

"True," Marcus admitted. "Not only the rich. The privileged. The powerful and not necessarily the elected," Marcus said as he gazed out the window. "I have extended my offer to the poor, the less fortunate/lesser advantaged, the persecuted and the wretched, huddled masses. And yes, there is a catch. But, what they gain in return is much more valuable, than what they leave behind. Give a man a fish, he eats for a day. Teach him to fish, he eats a lifetimes worth. They gain a new sense of purpose, direction and a high self-esteem and in this life, they get to make a difference in their world."

Manning looked down at the notebook. He pushed the button at the bottom which enabled it to display the next electronic page. As he skimmed over each page, he became aware that this was no small scale effort of just a select few. Hundreds of thousands of people were involved and were now enroute to this island in the South Pacific. Infrastructure was either in place or nearly completed. Emergency services were fully operational. Power grids, active. Industries of all types initiating start-up. Food production, firmly established. All in all, Manning noticed one thing that was missing.

"There's no mention of the status of your military," Manning stated as he handed back the digital notebook.

Marcus accepted the notebook and smiled at the Major.

"That's because we don't have a military."

Flabbergasted, Manning just looked at Marcus, mouth agape.

"Really, Major," Marcus said. "Why do you look so surprised?"

Manning shook his head and looked down at his clasped hands, "I'm sorry. It's just that with all this wonderful and amazing technology, I thought that you would do whatever, to ensure a base of power."

"And you thought, those means would be best accomplished with a military?"

"That would be a reasonable assumption," Manning agreed.

"Don't get me wrong, Major. The nations of Earth need their militaries. I realize, it's of vital importance to their national security. And Pacifica will also, need a military. But, not for the reasons you think."

"And what reasons would that be, Commander?"

"Couple years after WW II, two spacecraft, two 'Flying Saucers', crash landed in south-eastern New Mexico near Roswell. Now, the 8th. US Army Air Force collected those ships and all evidence of debris associated with the crashes. And after a well publicized and convincing series of denials and the enforced cover-up and resulting disinformation, everything was shipped off, never to be seen again, outside 'Top Secret' circles of the US military. And I happen to think that was wrong."

"1947," Manning began. "was the beginning of the 'Cold War'. Even I can appreciate the need for secrecy in a time of international tensions."

"As can I," Marcus agreed. "However, that information was almost officially disclosed after the 'Cold War's' end. In the end, it was decided to be kept secret. An event so significant, that it would rival the resurrection of Christ, Himself. What I'm trying to say is, that, through that acquired technology, the US military became more powerful than the atomic weapons they possessed, at the time. And no matter how much each successive US President tried to limit those powers, it only caused those who contained it, to bury it even deeper."

"All militaries have civilian over-sight. Even in the US," Manning countered.

"Yes, they do," Marcus agreed. "Only to give that same political, civilian oversight the perception that they are the ones in control. Why do you think that for over 50 years, the Director of the CIA has always been a former, four-star General of one armed service or the other."

That made Manning think. He knew that since 9/11 in 2001, terrorism against the US at home and abroad and against the other democratic nations of the world, had caused the civilian populations to hand over broad powers to their respective militaries and police forces. What freedoms the people gave up, in the name of safety and security. He remembered the latest attack.

Terrorists had purchased six mothballed freighters and filled them with high explosives. Then, they sailed the ships for the harbors of the six richest nations of the world. Pearl Harbor had become the victim of its second sneak attack in history. The cities of Portsmouth, Vancouver, Hong Kong, Le Havre were decimated. They had chosen cities with, smaller, enclosed harbors for maximum effect. The blast waves had the equivalency of low-yield, nuclear explosions. Tens of thousands killed, hundreds of thousands injured. Untold billions of dollars in property damages. Tokyo was spared when the terrorists had tried to detonate their floating bomb in Shinigawa Bay when, it failed to do so. Even though the terrorists tried to manually detonate the ship, even trying to set the ship on fire, they decided to turn the ship around and head for Uraga Strait and then to open sea. The harbor pilot, had radioed a warning to the harbor-master before he was killed. The Japanese Defense Forces, already aware of the almost simultaneous attacks in other countries, realized the importance of this piece of intelligence trying to get away. They managed to disable the freighter's rudder, 8 kilometrs offshore. The terrorists kept the small boats of the boarding parties of the Japanese Navy at bay, for an hour until the Captains of two destroyers decided to try an old-fashioned, high-speed boarding.

They maneuvered their ships to come along side, port and starboard, sandwiching the freighter between and have the armed boarding parties overwhelm the terrorists. The plan worked. The gun battle onboard the freighter lasted for 45 minutes and killed three, wounding nine JDF personnel. Fifteen terrorists were killed and six wounded were taken prisoner.

Even though the governments of those countries that were attacked wanted a crack at interrogating the live prisoners, Japan claimed sovereignty.

Even though, those countries had suffered from the attacks, China had suffered the most deaths and the most damage. China was the loudest and wanted the prisoners to be handed over to them, exclusively. A flotilla of warships was even steaming to Japan, when the Japanese Empress, a skilled diplomat, brokered a deal of intelligence and interrogation sharing with the affected nations but, on Japanese soil.

Third world nations were not immune, either. Large tanker-truck sized bombs were detonated outside schools, churches, synagogues, certain mosques, sports arenas, hospitals and the odd government building, in the coordinated attacks.

Any support and sympathy the terrorists had previously enjoyed, vaporized with the bombs they detonated. They were no longer terrorists. They were now, anarchists. Most of the terrorists were turned over to the police and security forces by their supporters. In some countries, they were hunted down by the public, only to receive mob and vigilante justice.

The man responsible for conceiving and organizing the attacks was identified. Afghanistan-born Abdul Hammed was a self-proclaimed follower of Osama Bin Laden and felt that even his hero didn't go far enough. His organization attacked, killed and assassinated anyone with impunity, who didn't share his personal, religious views and whatever mood he was in, at the time. He even claimed that Allah, spoke to him and commanded him. Both the mainstream and the fundamentalist Muslims eventually, referred and considered him and his organization, as a cult. The first, to be so identified as such, by the Islamic religion.

The world backlash following the attacks caused Hammed to go into hiding. For two years, no-one could find him. Every once in a while he would send video messages to various news media to let his followers know he was alive and that they should continue to carry-on his cause. But, nobody was listening. They were either dead, imprisoned or so appalled at the level of deception and destruction of this man, they no longer supported or sympathized with his views. He was viewed, in the Muslim world as a crackpot or evil incarnate. With each taped message, various intelligence organizations were able to increasingly zero in on his hiding place.

And then China found and confirmed his hiding place.

On some un-named atoll in the Lakshadweep Island Cluster, just west of the southern tip of India, was where Hammed had sought refuge. The atoll was the furthest away from the main cluster by about 80 kilometers and was so small, that it could only contain the closest of his followers and their families. The Chinese Navy dispatched a single 'Sun Tzu' (updated version of Russia's Typhoon V) Class nuclear submarine to the Arabian Sea.

A message package was couriered to the atoll, addressed to Hammed. At first, the message was not accepted by anyone on the Island and as the perplexed courier was about to board his small boat back to the mainland, someone accepted the package for Hammed and promised to pass it along. The Chinese government message conveyed to Hammed that his location was found and that they were the only ones who were aware of this and that "2 envoys would arrive soon to intercede to negotiate to his terms of a truce".

At midnight that night, Hammed was to accept the terms by building 2 huge bonfires, on the north shore, the other on the south shore of the island. The Commander of the submarine waited patiently as he watched through the periscope, 5 kilometers south of the atoll. Onboard as well, was Wang Bin, Fleet Admiral of the Chinese Navy. Just before midnight, both bonfires were detected via Chinese spy satellite, in orbit. At 12:05a.m., two cruise missiles broke the surface, simultaneously heading towards the island, and detonating with a combined 2 megaton yield at 100 feet above sea-level. It was rumored, that Fleet Admiral Wang Bin was the one man onboard who gave the order to fire the missiles and that he carried those written orders issued to him in person, from Beijing.

The atoll was vaporized.

At the same time and as a parting shot, China launched five cruise missiles armed with neutron warheads over the China/Afgan border into the Battu Kush region. Their target, the small village of Kishnar, 60 kilometers south of Chu-il-Mara, birthplace of Hammed and still a stronghold of support. What the blasts didn't kill immediately, the ensuing radiation, made it a certainty.

Publicly, the nations of the world condemned China in a general assembly meeting at the United Nations Building. And the protests were short. Secretly, behind closed doors, they congratulated China for ridding the world of such evil. A large portion of the populace of the world, even agreed and accepted China's decision. Wang Bin even ascended to Chairman/President, while still an active officer of the People's Navy.

"In times of crises, decisive military thinking is required," Manning tried to defend.

"Come on, Major," Marcus countered. "Even I can hear the tone of doubt in your voice."

"Commander Gowan," Manning tensed up. "I am just an old soldier who follows his orders and is unconcerned with what his superiors are up to. Unless, the safety of my personnel are in jeopardy. That's how it works. They lead, I follow."

Marcus remained at ease and relaxed in his chair, "Major, I'm not questioning you or your personnel's loyalty." He took a more conciliatory tone, "Look. All I am trying to do is explain why we're doing what we're doing."

"Ok," Manning conceded. You have my attention."

"Fifty years ago, my father witnessed the crash landing of an alien spacecraft in northern Canada. He immediately recovered it and transported it to a warehouse where he studied it, for years. He was able to access its onboard computer which enabled him to repair it and also provided him with certain technologies that could hack into any Human-made computer system, undetected. My father determined that the aliens, were studying our technological progress through our means of communications and computer databases. And since the crash, he was acquiring both information and creating new technologies. The bonus of him becoming the richest man in the world didn't hurt either."

"What about survivors," Manning asked. Didn't their people send out search and recovery teams to rescue them?"

"There was only one survivor and he informed my father that there would be no rescue because his spacecraft had traveled from the future and the crash was engineered to occur, so that my father would then be able to recover the spacecraft."

"You mean, the crash was meant to happen?" Manning asked

"Oh, no." Marcus said. "Not supposed to happen but, engineered. They wanted to change the time-line they knew. You see, in the future, these aliens realize they are becoming extinct. Although we don't exist in their future, they will be able to determine through small samples of genetic material, the two races are genetically compatible."

"What do you mean," Manning stopped Marcus. "we don't exist in the future?"

"According to their historical data, I've seen," Marcus began. "a hundred years from now, they cease observing us and the aliens return to announce themselves, on Earth, 1500 years from now, They had calculated when Humanity would be mature enough to accept the existence of extra-terrestrials. They discover, half the planet is covered in ice. What cities remain, are only ruins. And not one Homo Sapien, anywhere. It took the aliens a while to figure out what had happened. War. Two hundred years from now, we will destroy ourselves in a senseless, no-win war. Mutually assured destruction."

"Why would they be interested in Humanity when we are already dead and gone." Manning said, thinking he found a hole in Gowan's story. "Why wouldn't they approach us, now?"

"That's because they won't realize they are going extinct for another 2500 years," Marcus replied. "In order for them to ensure their future and ours, they decided to go into the past and change their history and our future. They knew it was a one way trip; that they would be stranded here."

"How do you know that, all this," Manning looked gestured to their surroundings. "won't result in the same thing they were trying to prevent?"

"The data included a concise history of Earth up until their departure and a small, new nation in the south Pacific was not mentioned anywhere. However, the risen landmass, the resulting and devastating tsunamis and the resulting destruction along the Pacific Rim coastlines were mentioned. Political tensions over who claimed the landmass was the precursor to that future war."

"You mentioned a single survivor. What happened to him?" Manning asked.

"He lived at our estate and he died when I was13," Marcus remembered. "We named him Socrates. He was the best teacher I ever had. Anyway, he taught my father everything about how the spacecraft worked; the systems, the computers, propulsion systems, etc. He and my father worked very closely on building the business empire."

"Why would the alien help a human become rich?" Manning asked.

"It wasn't the 'wealth' that he was helping 'per se'," Marcus began. "What he was helping in was; the acquisition of knowledge, technology and information through means that are considered 'hacking'. From that information from the future, my father was able to determine what stocks to buy, sell or hold on to. You see, the aliens have been observing us for tens of thousands of years. Since the beginning of our use of tele-communications and computers, they were able to learn much about our technological progress. What they didn't expect, was our utilization of computers for everything in our daily lives. To them, the wealth in knowledge about how Humanity viewed itself, was a gold-mine. So then, they were able to learn more about us. From that information, they were able to calculate when the best time for 'first contact' with the Human race would be. 1500 years from now. Only, from Socrates' information and perspective, we'll already have been extinct for 1300 years."

"So," Manning began to inquire, "What you're saying is that the aliens want our DNA to help them survive?"

"It's not as simple as that," Marcus admitted. "These aliens, of this time period, are evolving to the point that they can no longer produce children as they once did; like Humans. They conceive through invitro-fertilization and their children are born in gestation pods. This has had a grave effect on their physiology. They are no longer able to bear children, naturally. And in the future, through evolution, will be not have the capacity to create offspring. But, that is not the only reason they need us."

Manning just looked at Marcus, waiting for him to reveal the other reason.

"These aliens are a wasteland, devoid of emotion," Marcus began. "Or at least, they are becoming that way. They are more susceptible to instinct and impulsiveness. The single greatest thing that holds their interest in us the most; is Human emotions. It is unlike anything they have seen or experienced for themselves. Emotions like, grief, guilt, happiness, sadness, spirituality, compassion, creativity. How a police officer can, in one second, shoot-to-kill and wound someone who endangers his or someone else's life and the next second, try to save that life. We are apparently, unique. And the key to their future. And before you make assumptions about how Humanity would be changed, don't. It is only their species they wish to change."

"What about all those stories of abductions and claims of DNA samples taken," Manning questioned. "Wouldn't the aliens have those in storage, somewhere?"

Marcus looked out the window, "You'd think. The aliens of this time period are actually taking samples but, they are analyzing them. Not storing them. In fact, the only samples they are storing, is plant and animal life."

"Why is that?" Manning asked.

"Ecology, in the future, has been destroyed on their planet," Marcus began. "Right now, they are using up the last of their planet's natural resources and are just recognizing the fact that they are facing an eco-disaster. According to Socrates, Earth has such a wide diversity of plant life, climates, animal life, and even Humans; it's unheard of, in the known galaxy. Earth, that beautiful pearl, is truly unique. The samples they have collected, are being used to jump start the ecology of their planet. Socrates saw a lot of similarities between, what he called, 'the end of nature' of his planet and what Humans are doing to the environment on Earth."

Manning's military thinking kicked in, "So they're taking from our planet, to save theirs?"

Marcus, aware of Manning's line of thinking, decided to cut him off, "It's not what you think, Major. They're not uprooting whole forests. Remember, they have had thousands of years to study the Earth and they have a better understanding of planetary dynamics and the biology of our plant and animal life, than we do. All they need is a few samples to make forests of their own. Besides, who's gonna stop them. They can't be detected. They're rarely spotted, visually. Unless, they want to be spotted."

"What about the United States?" Manning suggested. "They could stop them."

"They've been trying, for decades," Marcus chuckled. "They haven't shot one down, yet."

"Why hasn't the USA tried to contact or make a deal with them for access to the planet?" Manning asked.

Marcus looked down, interlocked the fingers of his hands and cracked his knuckles, "The US did send their own envoy to contact the aliens and after repeated radio transmissions, they received a 4-word response. That response was, "One world, one voice," repeated in all the known languages. Meaning; that the aliens would only deal with a *unified* Earth. They consider the USA, as but one faction among many. They will not deal with one, while leaving out so many."

"Well, I guess that leaves you and your people to make contact."

"Nope," Marcus disagreed. "Again, Pacifica would be considered but one faction, among many. They won't have anything to do with us."

"I see," Manning said, stroking his goatee.

Marcus sat in shared silence with Manning as the two men watched empty space, outside. Marcus could see that Manning was trying to make sense of what he had been told. He knew Manning's view of the world had just changed. He was trying to come to terms with it. And then...

"Tell me more of the City of Atlantis," Manning asked.

Marcus thought for a moment, trying to decide where to begin.

"Atlantis wasn't a city but a continent and was, until 10 500 BC, the strongest, most advanced nation on Earth. It was at one time, previously, the center of all Human existence on Earth. At around 28,000 B.C., 2 factions existed. The 'Children of the Law of the One' and the 'Disciples of Vane'.

They co-existed in a society much like own; those who would subscribe to opposite political groups or ideologies. Conservative or Liberal. Democrat or Republican. Democracy or dictatorship. The 'Children of the Law of the One' believed in the oneness with God and every great philosophy that glorified Him. That, when God created Humanity, it was Man that sought out Him to enter into 'The Covenant of Life', here on Earth. That, we could prove to God that we were worthy of His creation. To be the caretakers and custodians of the 'Divine Creation' known as planet Earth. To glorify, magnify and up-hold, the 'Supreme Will of God'."

"The 'Disciples of Vane' formed just before the first cataclysmic disasters which struck Atlantis. They believed that although Humans were created by God, Humanity was left to develop through evolution on Earth. And they believed that God left us to our own devices, our own fate, never to return. They believed that since He was no longer around to oversee how His creation evolved and developed, Humanity was given free will and had free reign over what we could do here on Earth. It was their belief that all things were for their gratification of the senses and did not entertain ideas such as ethics, morality and conscience. Even if that meant destroying the environment around them to further Human progress. That Humanity was the true masters of our own destiny."

"Technology on both sides progressed significantly over thousands of years when the 'Disciples of Vane' decided to turn their technological achievements and experiments towards the planet, itself. There were.. disastrous consequences. The main one of which; was the increasing instability of the fault-line which bisected the continent of Atlantis. They were witness to the eventual splitting of the continent into 2 distinct landmasses. Atlantis and Poseidon. Despite the warnings and stern objections from the 'Children of the Law of the One', the 'Disciples of Vane' continued to target their technology on the Earth. Eventually, the instability was such that it caused the 2 landmasses to sink beneath the waves. In our ancient history, the Atlantic Ocean was known as the Sea of Atlas. Long before then, it was known as the Sea of Atlantis."

"And they didn't survive, did they?" Manning postulated.

"As a matter of fact, they did," Marcus revealed. "*We,* are their descendants. They sought refuge in colonies on the unsettled continents. Europe, Asia, North Africa, North and South America, Australia. Of course, the largest concentration of refugees were in North Africa and Europe."

"Well, who built the pyramids on the Giza Plateau in Egypt? The Atlantians or the Egyptians?" Manning asked.

"Oh, it was the Egyptians," Marcus confirmed. "But, they relied on Atlantian knowledge, expertise and technology. You see, there were already emerging, less advanced human cultures elsewhere in the world who had long before, seceded from the Atlantian culture to seek a more simple and non-technological way of life. The Atlantian refugees believed that, by integrating themselves into these cultures, they would absorb those cultures into theirs and become the new Atlantian society. As a result, it was the Atlantians who were assimilated into those cultures."

"You got all that from that underwater structure?" Manning asked.

"That, and from the pyramid we discovered in the Yucatan Peninsula," Marcus declared. "The records found there, pretty much corroborated the information from the Atlantian structure."

"There was a second Atlantian 'Temple of Archives'?" Manning exclaimed.

Marcus smiled and hesitantly began, "Actually, there are a total of six. The two, we've found, one in Egypt on the Giza Plateau, which the Egyptian Government has been aware of since the late 20th. Century . There is one in the water just off the coast of Japan, which hasn't been properly mapped, yet. The ancient Library of Alexandria contained duplicates of the Giza records. Of course, that was destroyed thousands of years ago. And the last is on the Moon, which one of our probes, recently discovered."

"The Atlantians were on the Moon?" Manning asked, surprised.

"Even the Moon," Marcus confirmed.

Manning whistled. This revelation changed his personal view of history. No longer was Humanity of modern times the first to reach the Moon. To know that another ancient, human civilization had made it there, amazed him. It astonished him .

"Why wouldn't the Egyptians want to excavate the Atlantian records at Giza?" Manning asked.

Marcus sat straighter in his chair, "You know the old saying about, 'You can lead a horse to water….'"

Manning finished, "but you can't make it drink. Yes, I've heard it, before.'"

Marcus continued, "The Egyptians have always claimed that it was their ancient ancestors, who were solely responsible for the conception, logistics and the construction of one of the Seven Wonders of the World. Knowing that so many magnificent structures are standing in only one place on Earth and will continue to exist for thousands of years more, makes the site, unique. Today, Egyptians look toward the Giza Plateau and are filled with national and cultural pride. Revealing such information now, would only accomplish how the world views the Egyptians and how Egyptians view themselves. Politically and culturally, the harm would be devastating. Archaeologically, historically, it's a cover-up. Who am I to burst their bubble?"

Marcus, reading Manning's fidgeting body language, sat forward in his chair.

"Major, I know this is a lot to take in. We had years to come by this information. Then again, Socrates was a big help piecing together and understanding all the raw data."

"The aliens were around at the time of Atlantis?" Manning blurted out.

"Ever since the Atlantian's first use of nuclear and laser technology, 30,000 years ago," Marcus replied.

Manning's eyes went wide, "Just how advanced were the Atlantians?"

"By today's standard, way more advanced. We know they achieved spaceflight. We know they made it to the Moon and set up a semi-permanent base, there. We also know they were in contact with the indigenous inhabitants of Mars."

Manning shot Marcus a look, "But, Mars is a desolate wasteland incapable of supporting life as we know it?"

"It is, now," Marcus responded. "About the same time Atlantis was facing its final destruction, an asteroid struck and destroyed Mars' moon. Debris rained down on Mars for centuries. What the debris didn't destroy on the ground had the effect of ripping away the planet's atmosphere. The only evidence left is now orbiting the planet. Fragments we call, Phobos and Deimos."

"Wh-what about survivors?" Manning asked. "Surely, they would have taken steps to ensure evidence of their existence?"

"They didn't get the chance," Marcus said. "It happened that quick. From what we have been able to determine, half the population was wiped-out almost immediately. Those that did survive, realized they were about to suffocate. Steps were then taken to save those they could. The majority sealed themselves in deep caves and caverns. The rest, decided to seek safety, off-world."

Marcus just stared at Manning to let him piece the puzzle together.

"The Martians, are the aliens you spoke about?" Manning postulated.

Marcus smiling, knew that Manning didn't get it and that he was about surprise him, yet again.

"No, Major. With their own spaceships, they sought refuge, on Earth."

Manning stared back in silence, unblinking.

"And I suppose they too, integrated into our society?"

"Not exactly. They wanted to keep their society, heritage and lineage distinct from Humanity. They sought refuge in some of Earth's deepest caves and caverns in some of the remotest areas of the Earth. Now, some did venture out and inserted themselves into our society. And those that have, helped the progress of Humanity, mainly in the sciences; behind the scenes. They do this to better gauge Humanity so that one day, when the time is right, when all of Humanity is united, they can announce their presence and ask for our assistance in bringing the rest of their people to Earth or go home."

"I thought they had spaceships to journey to Earth? Couldn't they take all their people?"

"They had only a handful of spaceships and could only take the chosen few. They weren't much more advanced than the Earth is now."

"And their spaceships, where are they now?" Manning asked.

"We can only assume they were dismantled to further their survival on Earth."

The two men sat in silence, staring out the lounge windows, out into space. It was a lot for Manning to hear. What Marcus Gowan had told him was even challenging how he viewed Earth's future. All of what he heard, all of what he had seen, was too elaborate to be a lie. He tried to make sense of this, newly discovered history. To make it fit, within his mind. He leaned forward and put his head in his hands, massaging his forehead. Marcus, patiently waited for Manning to assimilate what he had been told. Manning, trying to assimilate it. Marcus could sense Manning was trying to decide what to do with the information he now possessed. Manning looked over to Marcus.

Marcus added, "Now, what I've told you so far, is only part of the real story, you realize."

"There is more?"

"Much more, my friend," Marcus admitted.

"I can't keep this under my helmet. When I return to Canada and I'm debriefed, I will have to inform my superiors. You realize this, right?"

"As I would expect you to," Marcus agreed. "The reason I have chosen to disclose this information, is two-fold. One; I am not or ever was, a terrorist. I want your superiors to know, exactly, what we were doing at White Alice and that Canada, as a nation, could have been a nation surpassing all others, leading the way, *peacefully,* into space. Reaping the rewards *and* the benefits. That, all we have done, was to not waste anymore time, getting into and establishing a firm foothold in space. Humanity has always been curious of what was beyond the horizon. And to again, quote Kennedy, *we,* are making the 'Climb' over that next hill. I want them to pass on the knowledge, to other national leaders, that there will be one nation on Earth that is not satisfied with staying on what Konstantin Tsiolkovksy referred to as the, 'Cradle of Humanity'. That while they're down there, fighting over petty differences and what resources are left, we'll be standing on higher ground. We have a nation as a base of operations. We have technology that supports us. And we are not out to rule the world. We want to be left alone; therefore, we will leave them alone. Even if the Earth faces certain disaster, they can take comfort in the knowledge that the Human Race, will continue."

"And two?" Manning asked.

Manning watched a broad smile appear on Marcus' face which puzzled him.

"Two; I would like to extend the offer for you, to immigrate to Pacifica."

Manning was shocked. This was something he didn't see coming. And then he realized that with all the information Marcus Gowan had told him, he was being...*prepared.* There was no other reason for him to disclose such information.

"How do you know I won't end up spying on you and Pacifica for my superiors?"

"Because, you're not the type, Major," Marcus said with certainty. "As you've eloquently put it, you are a soldier. You're no spy. And if I've read you right, you are a devoted student of military history and a professional when it comes to battlefield combat. You read the lay of the land and you adjust tactics, accordingly. Everything about you is quick and decisive. A spy works in the shadows, biding his time."

Manning thought for a moment, realizing that what Marcus had said was not untrue.

"What would I do?" Manning asked

"How about, 'General of the Pacifican Defense Service'?" Marcus replied.

As many times as he has, Manning had to make the effort to close his open mouth.

CHAPTER NINE

FLYING START

Kyle Latavish had been walking for hours with his electric, acoustic guitar case slung across his back, carrying his small amp in his right hand along a dusty gravel road which seemed to go off into the distance, forever. Occasionally, an automated freight truck would pass by, carrying a load of assorted fruits, vegetables, grains, soybeans to take to the various processing plants or to market, kicking up clouds of dust.

The area was named the Great Plain Region for a reason. As Latavish understood it, this was the region which Marcus had deemed off-limits, for agricultural development only. It was to be used exclusively for farming as the conditions were considered ideal. Fertile soil, rain at night, hot temperatures and sunlight during the day. Genetically-enhanced food, advanced production techniques, advanced storage capabilities. He had once heard Marcus muse about making any surplus available to the poorer nations of the world, for free. He had no doubt that Marcus already had a plan in the works to do just that.

He continued south for quite some time when he spotted his destination, off in the distance. The Highland Hills at the foot of the Barrier Mountain Range. He knew he had a few more hours of walking to get there, when a pick-up truck passed him, slowed and stopped ahead of him. He approached the driver's side, the lone occupant, a barrel-chested Samoan, smiling.

"Brudda! Where you bound?" he asked.

"The Highland Hills," Latavish replied.

The big Samoan looked off into the distance and whistled. "That's another twenty miles, bru. It'll be dark by the time you get there."

"Really," Latavish said as he shielded his eyes from the sunlight and looked into the distance. "I thought is more like five miles away."

"C'mon, jump in, bru," the Samoan said. "I'll take ya the rest of the way."

"Thanks," Latavish said as he put his guitar and amp in the box of the truck. As he climbed into the passenger side, the driver introduced himself.

"Name's Ben Kono," he said as he shook Latavish's hand. "Friends call me 'Tiny'."

"I'm Kyle Latavish," he replied. "I appreciate this."

Tiny held onto Latavish's hand longer than expected. Latavish was puzzled for a second.

"The, Kyle Latavish!" Tiny exclaimed. "The *musician,* Kyle Latavish!"

Latavish was, for a brief moment, unsure if he should answer.

"Aye," he said with an almost embarrassed smile at being recognized, yet again. "The one and only."

Tiny let go of his hand. A big, wide smile on his face. "Oh, Man! I am such a big fan of yours!" Tiny put the vehicle into gear and it silently accelerated down the gravel road.

"You?" Latavish asked. "Like my music?"

"Oh, yeah, bru!" Tiny was ecstatic. "Your music has helped me through some tough times in my life. For me, it had a centering effect on my personality. I think you are a musical genius, and believe me, I've heard music from all over, bru."

"Where you hail from, Tiny?"

"Hawaii," he replied. "Born and raised. Former sugar-cane farmer until the 'blight' wiped out the entire Hawaiian crop. Lost my shirt and almost lost the farm, but thanks to the Gowans, they bought it, paid off my debts, paid me ten times what it was worth and made me the offer for my family and I to immigrate here."

"You weren't anywhere near Pearl Harbor when those terrorists blew up that ship, were you?" Latavish asked.

Tiny was silent for a moment.

"Naw, bru. Farm was on the big island. But, my granny was in a home, overlooking the harbor. I just hope she went quickly."

"I'm sorry for your lose, Tiny," Latavish offered. "I hope she didn't suffer, either. Were you close to her?"

"She raised me and my brothers after our mother died. Cancer. She took us in at great financial cost, she didn't have to, and raised us right. My brothers and I took care of her after we finished school and gained employment," Tiny reminisced, tears welling up in his eyes. "She lived a life of luxury after that. In fact, it was my granny who bought me your first recordings."

"She, too? Was a fan?," Latavish asked.

"Bigger than me, bru. She listened to your music 24/7. All 365."

"I'm sure she was very proud how well, you and your brothers turned out."

"Oh, we know she was," Tiny agreed. "We always remember how she lived, not how she died. And we instill those same values in our families. That is how my brothers and I pay tribute to the memory of her."

For a moment, Latavish was silent as he briefly looked out his door's window and then looked over at Tiny as he navigated the gravel road. Tiny looked back at the smiling Latavish.

"Bru, what you grinning at?" Tiny chuckled.

"I, too, shall pay tribute to your Granny. And to you and your brothers honoring her," Latavish announced.

Tiny's eyes went wide open, "You'd do that, bru?"

"The least I could do for my fans, especially for one who gave you the gift of music appreciation," Latavish offered.

"Then, bru," Tiny began. "You are invited to stay at our farm until you are ready to go back to Fresco City."

"Oh, no. I wouldn't want to impose."

"Naw, bru. No trouble at all. My brothers and I operate a corn/lettuce farm at the foot of the Highland Hills. You can do your hiking during the day, play or compose your music and then you'll have a place to rest your head at night. Unless you had other plans."

Latavish looked over at Tiny and patted the big man on the right shoulder, twice.

"Tiny, I would be honored and it would be my pleasure to stay with you and your family, mate. Thank-you,"

The two men were silent for a while when Tiny broke the silence.

"So, Mr. Latavish. How did you meet Marcus Gowan?"

"Tiny. Please, call me, Kyle," Latavish asked, smiling at new friend. "I met Marcus through his brother, Glenn. Glenn purchased a media parent company that went bankrupt after I sued them for theft of some of my music."

"Yeah, bru." Tiny replied. "I remember that. Two billion dollars. You gave all that money to charity, didn't you?"

With a smile on his face, Latavish replied, "Aye, that I did."

"That was good karma, bru," Tiny began. "You helped out a lot of people and I believe, I, am in the company of greatness and I feel I'm the fortunate one, here."

"Marcus Gowan is the one with greatness," Latavish added. "Without him, all this would not be possible. Everything happens for a reason, I believe."

Tiny agreed, "Exactly! Amen to that, bru."

After twenty minutes driving down the gravel road, Tiny turned the pick-up truck off onto a road bordered on either side by a massive forest of cornstalks. Latavish knew that if he were looking for the farm's entrance, not knowing where to look, he would have missed it. The cornstalks were the tallest he had ever seen. Almost, obscenely tall. And it wasn't just the height that he noticed. It was the amount of ears on the stalks that made him sit up and take notice. He knew that stalks normally produced 3 to 5 ears but, he estimated 20 or more on one cornstalk, alone. Even the stems were the size of small trees.

"My God, those are big," Latavish commented.

"Yeah, bru," Tiny chuckled. "Genetically-selective engineered produce. The wave of the future. Marcus Gowan's answer to Thomas Malthus' theory of population and food supplies."

"Thomas who?" Latavish asked.

"Thomas Malthus," Tiny said. "World's first political economist. Died in the early 1800's. He theorized that although population grows at a geometric rate, food supplies only grow at an arithmetic rate, unable to provide for the increasing numbers of the population as time goes by."

Coming to a T-intersection in the road, Tiny turned the truck to the right.

"I've heard of genetically engineered but, not genetically-selective. What does that mean?" Latavish asked.

"It's the ability to select only certain genes of a given plant and enhance it's ability to produce food, or make the stalk stronger to resist wind or the weight of the food being grown. Double its ability to convert photo-synthesis. Double its CO_2 intake/O_2 output. Draw moisture from the atmosphere. Take in only half the water necessary. That sort of thing."

"That's what you've done, here?" Latavish inquired.

"You bet, bru," Tiny confirmed. "If I wanted, we could have ears growing from the ground to the very top but, the stalks would be so big, my machinery wouldn't be able to cut them down and we'd loose about 25 percent every time we harvested."

"That, is amazing," Latavish declared.

The truck emerged from the 'corn forest' into an open field containing domed, concrete structures. It wasn't until the truck came to a stop at one of them, when he noticed these buildings were in fact the homes of Tiny and his brothers and their families. The buildings stood alone for each family and from the looks of the balconies, were two-stories tall. Children ran towards the truck to greet them and calling out for 'Daddy' or 'Uncle Tiny'. After formal introductions to the entire family, Tiny directed Latavish to look at the hills just south of the farm. They gazed up in silence, Latavish, with a smile on his face.

"Grab your gear, Kyle. I'll show you to the guest room and in the morning, I'll take ya up there."

Latavish walked with Tiny, back towards the truck, "Sounds good to me, bru."

Agent Tobin was glad to be back in Washington. Glad to be back in civilization. Glad to be back where it was warm. He still felt chilled after spending all that time north of the Arctic Circle. And it was a dry-cold. He didn't notice just how warm it was until he had experienced the cold of Canada's north. With the slight breeze, it felt almost like being in a blast furnace.

He made his way to the office building which held the Senator's 2nd. office, one block from the Capital Building. Upon entering the vestibule, he noticed and appreciated the building's air conditioning system but, it reminded him of that cold Canadian air. Making his way to the elevators, he wondered if the Senator would be in, this early in the morning. He assumed the Senator would keep 'Bankers Hours'.

Upon entering the Senator's office, he detected the slight odor of cigar smoke. The Senator was 'in'. The receptionist was at her customary post who greeted and informed Tobin to go straight into the office, the Senator was expecting him.

"Mr. Tobin," the Senator said as the agent closed the office door. "Please, come sit down."

"Good morning, Senator. Thank-you." Tobin went straight for the conference table where he placed his briefcase and opened it to empty it's contents.

"I hear you had a close call, up north," the Senator asked.

Tobin stopped and just stared at the man taking a seat at the table, "How could you know that?"

The Senator smiled and said, "I have my sources. You don't get where I am without them." And he said nothing more.

Tobin went back to emptying his briefcase, "Well, yes. I did have a close call. And although, I had to end my investigation prematurely, I was able to gather some evidence."

"What happened?" The Senator asked.

Tobin handed the Senator a small set of 8x10 photos, "These are pictures of the crater. The first is of the top of crater. Second is of the bottom, looking down. The other two were taken at the bottom, one looking up and the last was done looking across to the other side. Just after that last one was taken, sea-water, leaching through the soil at the bottom, began pushing up and out. It was a mad rush, just to get out."

"Judging from these," the Senator began. "The pictures doesn't do justice to the actual size."

"No, Sir." Tobin agreed. "They do not. The crater is massive and deep. There was no evidence of an explosion and no radiation. Only a few out-buildings remained but, they only contained a few tools and some miscellaneous industrial equipment and parts. I did, however, find an undisturbed corridor about halfway down the crater wall. It is now underwater."

"Did you find anything interesting?"

"Depends on what you classify as, interesting," Tobin stated. He handed the Senator several more pictures. "These are photos of the corridor. It is perfectly straight and perfectly square. From the mining consultants I've talked to, it's unheard of unless you were building an underground bunker of some kind."

"Where does it lead to?" the Senator asked.

"At the end, around the corner is a large room. It appeared to be some kind of maintenance area. Again, all angles are perfectly square. Nothing was in the room except, this," Tobin said as he handed him the photo.

The Senator examined it, "Looks like a workbench."

"It is," Tobin confirmed. "But, that's not the unusual thing about it."

"I don't understand."

Tobin handed him another photo of the workbench, with the frost removed from the pegboard. The Senator looked closely at the nametags of the outlines, not being able to make them out. Tobin handed him the photos of the close-ups of each outline and nametags. Tobin watched the Senator's face for recognition of the items. Either the Senator had a great poker-face or he truly, didn't recognize anything in the photos.

"Now, I've asked around and nobody has ever heard of the tools or the equipment that would be on that pegboard."

"I'll have somebody analyze these." the Senator said. "Maybe they can figure it out."

Tobin handed the Senator the photos and a folder of his report.

"Anyone question why you were there, doing a separate investigation?" The senator asked.

"Not, really," Tobin replied. "But, did get some resistance from the commanding officer who wanted me to throw her a bone as to why I was really there. I promptly told her mine was bigger than hers."

The Senator chuckled, "You're full of surprises, Mr. Tobin. I wanted to see how you reacted to being challenged"

Tobin smiled for the first time in the presence of the Senator.

"The Major is your source," Tobin stated.

"Mr. Tobin, the best way to find out about a person is how they react under duress. You passed."

"I don't know if I should be angry or grateful for being set-up, Senator."

"Tisk, tisk," the Senator said flippantly. "It's nothing personal. It's the nature of the business."

"What do you want me to do now, Senator?"

"I'll need you to go back to Canada," the Senator announced. "I want you to make contact with Glenn Gowan. Find out what his brother was doing on that island. What impression he has of his brother, now that he isn't involved with the company, anymore. Was he forced out or did he leave of his own volition. His state of mind. Anything, you can gather."

Tobin gave the Senator a puzzled look.

"Why would he tell us anything?"

"Word has it, that the two were fighting for control of the company. That the older brother had the support of the Board of Directors. I want to find out how accurate that intel was."

"How shall I approach him? Covertly, posing as someone else?"

"No," the Senator replied. "That's been tried, unsuccessfully. No, go as yourself under the auspices of the CSA. Record the conversation so it can be transcribed, later. I'll trust you to work out the details of making contact."

"I doubt he'll be receptive to meeting anyone from the CSA. Asking about family."

The Senator leaned back in the chair, "How good are you at innuendo?"

"Pardon me?"

"How good are you at implied threats?" the Senator asked, more specifically.

"I'm better at being blunt and to the point," Tobin admitted.

"Well, if you have to use threats, implicit or explicit, in order to get Glenn Gowan to open up about his brother, I'll back you up. However, I want info that is off the record. The best way to achieve that, of course, is without the use of threats. Again, conduct your questioning as you see fit."

With the Senator watching him, Tobin thought for a moment, staring off into the distance before finally nodding in agreement.

"Good!" the Senator said. "I'll have official CSA travel orders delivered to your apartment tonight and you can leave in the morning. You'll be on a CSA jet that will be wheels up by noon, tomorrow. Once you are in Toronto, you can make whatever accommodations and arraignments you like. The jet will wait on standby for your return trip."

"That'll give me some time to rest and repack," Tobin said. "Did you want me back before your next meeting with your committee?"

"Only if you've accomplished your task. Its not important to rush this. Take your time. Whatever intel you are able to gather, can be given to the committee at a later time."

"Will I have a local contact in Toronto, to assist before I contact Gowan?"

"All that will be in the intelligence packet on the jet." the Senator said.

"Senator," Tobin began. "I think these assignments are going to compromise my position at the CSA. This morning, I stopped at my office before coming here. My team leader dragged me into her office and asked me why she received documents upgrading my security clearance. Clearance that was considerably higher than hers."

The Senator just smiled, re-lighting his cigar.

"Actually, it's the CSA that is compromising your position with us," he exhaled smoke. What did you tell her?"

"I told her it had to do with a special research request from the White House and that I had already said too much."

"Very good, Mr. Tobin. I'm impressed," the Senator sat forward. "Look, we need you right where you are. That way, you can gather intelligence for our needs. Soon, you will have your own section, with your own, small staff."

Tobin decided it was time to push the envelope and bait the Senator.

"Well you better tell me what I'm supposed to be keeping my eye out for or I just might miss something vitally important. And I don't think you and your committee would be very happy about that," Tobin explained.

The Senator looked Tobin unblinkingly in the eyes and regarded him for what seemed a long moment. Then a wide smile appeared and gave way to a laugh. Tobin was unprepared for this reaction and returned a puzzled look.

"Bravo. Agent Tobin," the Senator began to clap his hands. "Bravo. Trying to get full disclosure. I'll have you know that such tactics won't work with me. I've been doing this for far too long. But, you are right. Full disclosure is in order in this case but, not yet."

Tobin wasn't quite satisfied with that and sat back, heavily in his chair, "If not now, when?"

"Everything we do, is contemplated, calculated and discussed before a consensus is reached," the Senator revealed. "In our line of business you know that, for me, to unilaterally disclose certain information to those without clearance would jeopardize my position and ultimately, our goals. Just because you have the security clearance, doesn't automatically mean you are privy to all of the projects, we have out there. Everything, each project, is compartmentalized. Timing is everthing. And right now, is not the time for you to know the details of the intel we are asking you to gather. Am I being cryptic and clear enough?"

Tobin nodded, "Of course, Senator. I didn't mean to sound as if I were making demands. Its just that, it's somewhat frustrating that I'm being asked to look for something without being told what it is. Like, I'm the last to know."

The senator smiled, "You are the last to know. In this case, at least. The 'Committee' needed someone to look at this with a fresh set of eyes. That's you. If you are able to piece together what we suspect and confirm it, independently, then we are on the right track and that will determine our next course of action. Only then, will I be able to give you full disclosure."

Tobin gave the Senator a puzzled look, "After I find out for myself, what's going on or after the 'Committee' decides what to do?"

"After your return from Toronto," the Senator confirmed. "Based on your findings, you'll be making the presentation to the 'Committee' and you'll have to know everything by that time."

Tobin nodded, "Well, that'll give me the incentive to find whatever it is, I am being tasked to look for."

"That it would," the Senator agreed as he stood from his chair at the conference table and offered his right hand to shake Tobin's.

Tobin accepted the hand-shake and realized the Senator had deposited a small business card with a single phone number on it, into his. Tobin stared at him, blankly.

"In case you find something and have the need to discuss it," the Senator said.

Tobin simply nodded, put the card in the breast pocket of his shirt and turned towards the door of the office. He knew it was time to dismiss himself. He nodded to the receptionist as he exited and as he entered the corridor, wondered if he should need a sweater this time, in Toronto.

Canadian Chancellor Sheila Conway looked around her office as people began entering and taking seats on the two sofas positioned around a larger than normal coffee table. Each person was being admitted by her secretary, Bob Simon, who would indicate silently to her, with a show of fingers, how many were left to arrive. The last person arrived and had to stand as there was no more seating available. All eyes were on the Chancellor, awaiting the announcement for the reason for the abrupt meeting. From behind her desk, she turned her chair to the group and began.

"Last night, I was working late when I received a video-call on my private line," she said as she watched for a reaction from her staff. "That line is so my teenaged children and ex-husband can call me at any time. They are the only ones I have given that video-phone number to, since that line was installed. Since, you all are the only ones who have knowledge of the existence of that line, I have called you to this briefing. What I want to know, without consequences, did anyone here, give out that number or let slip, that number?

All those present, shook their heads in unison, with genuine perplexed looks on their faces.

"Who was it?" a balding man at the end of the sofa on the right asked. He was holding an unlit tobacco pipe in his right hand.

"She said her name was Angela Teslin and she was calling on behalf of the Pacifican Government and that she had a message to relay in a separate call, today. That it concerned a Major Manning of the Canadian Federal Armed Forces."

The Chancellor's Chief Aid, sitting to the left, sat forward to get her attention.

"Forgive me, Chancellor. I don't believe there is a country called, Pacifica."

Chancellor Conway held up her hand to her Aid, signaling to wait and looked over to the Minister of Federal Defense. "George. Who is Major Manning?"

Defense Minister George Boudreaux began handing out photos of the man in question, " He's a hot-headed, arrogant old man," he spat.

Everyone in the room stopped in their tracks and stared at the Minister. The off-hand comment had taken them all by surprise. Realizing that he said what he did out loud; he apologized to the Chancellor and then began reading from the personnel file he brought with him.

"Dennis Alexander Manning entered military service at age 16 with the consent of his father. Spent a year as a regular trooper before being nominated for acceptance into the Federal Canadian Military College in Winnipeg, Manitoba. Graduated top of his class, with honors four years later, at the rank of Lieutenant, junior grade. Years later, deployed to Baja, USA as part of the US/Canadian contingent to prevent General Zamora's government forces from retaking Baja after their request for US annexation was granted. He received a battlefield promotion to Captain which was upheld upon returning home. Saw action in North Korea when dictator Jun Inn launched his attack against South Korea. Later, his battalion was part of UN forces that held the defensive line of South Africa at the Messina Frontier. He and his brigade received the US Congressional Medal of Honor and the South African Golden Leopard for the defense of Trichardt Bowl Area, where they came to the rescue of an armored convoy caught in an ambush. Out-numbered 20 to 1, Manning and two hundred troopers dispatched over three thousand combatants, while managing to evacuate eighteen hundred Americans and South Africans. Ninth Brigade of the Federal Mobile Light Cavalry has been nicknamed by the Americans, 'The

Bowl Area Brutes'. Was invited, specifically, by the Pentagon to attend the US Military College, Carlyle Barracks in Pennsylvania. After returning home, he spent several years as commanding officer of the Canadian Federal Armed Forces Recruit Training Center in Saskatchewan."

The Chancellor noticed that her Federal Defense Minister seemed to be unsettled for a moment, seemed to fidget in his seat and make it look as if he was reading ahead on the papers before him. And then he continued.

"He was court-martialed for drunken insubordination and received a pass-over at his next promotional review. He has been in command of the Canadian Anti-Terrorist Team for the past five years and has been deployed on various CSA missions within country, all classified."

"And what mission is he currently deployed on?"

Looking around the room, Boudreaux hesitated.

"Chancellor," he began. "There are those present who don't have adequate clearance for a proper briefing…".

"George. I know you are newly elected Member of the Federal Parliament and that because your constituency in Quebec helped win us a majority government but, when I ask a question like that, I expect disclosure," She was giving the junior minister her best poker face. "Especially when *I,* have taken steps to ensure the integrity of Federal and Continental Security."

Embarrassed, he nodded, "Of course, Chancellor. Forgive me. Canadian Federal Security and the Continental Security Agency have for the past while, been investigating a diamond mine in the Canadian North on Voice Island. Apparently, several rocket launches were observed and when Canadian Federal Security asked NORAD to provide trajectory data, there was no evidence of such launches. The mine operation is owned and operated by Marcus Gowan."

"The industrialist's son?" the Chief Aid asked. Boudreaux nodded affirmative.

"Continue," Chancellor Conway encouraged.

"Senior Analysts determined that the mine was a front for domestic terrorism and that since there was several rocket launches, the mine and its owner, failed to secure the proper permits and notifications, both under Canadian and International law. Lots of stuff went in, few diamonds came out. According to the Department of Federal Taxation, the mine was operating well into the black; apparently making significant profits. Intelligence reports, confirmed from various sources, that Gowan was buying up tons of dismantled and obsolete weaponry and equipment, transporting them to Voice Island. His official import declaration stated that he was purchasing them as scrap to be melted down. Permits for a small scale smelting operation is evident. Canadian Federal Security and the CSA believed it wouldn't take much to reactivate the weapons."

"Did any of these weapons leave the island?" Sheila Conway asked.

"Not to our knowledge, Chancellor," Defense Minister Boudreaux hesitantly replied. "It was suspected that he was merely stockpiling them. Two days ago, four sections and three Wolverine Light Armored Vehicles, led by Major Manning, were flown by C-280 to Voice Island to deploy and detain all personnel, including Marcus Gowan under the Continental Security Agreement."

Chancellor Conway slowly turned her office chair toward the windows behind her which had the heavy curtains drawn closed. She rotated the chair 360 degrees and faced her staff but, looked directly Boudreaux.

"Why wasn't I briefed about this, beforehand?" she said as the tone of her voice changed. "Why was I not told by CFS and/or CSA that this, Marcus Gowan represented a possible threat to continental security?"

"Chancellor, there wasn't time to brief you before sending the Canadian Anti-terrorist Team," Boudreaux began. "From the on-the-ground surveillance, senior analysts felt that we had to 'contain and secure' the mine before the seasonal storm-fronts prevented us from doing so."

Holding eye contact with Boudreaux for a long moment, Chancellor Conway could tell she made him uneasy asking specific, to-the-point questions. He was withholding something.

"What does this mine look like? Where are the photo's?"

After quickly finding the photographs, he rose from his seat to hand them to her. The first groupings of pictures were taken with a telephoto lens, possibly from another island. Then, she was looking at a series of satellite photographs with a one meter resolution, stated at the bottom. Occasionally, she would use a magnifying glass to better see minute details. After another moment or two, she came to another series of pictures which left a confused frown on her face. Several times, she went back and forth in the folder before holding one photograph up for all to see.

"George. What am I looking at here?" she asked, sternly.

Boudreaux cleared his throat and looked, nervously at the other faces in the room before addressing the Chancellor's query.

"I was getting to that, Chancellor. That is what's left of the White Alice Diamond Mine. We suspect some type of self-destruct device was used to create that hole in the ground. The mine is completely gone."

Taken aback, the Chancellor shook her head, "And why wasn't I informed of that, in the beginning?"

"I'm sorry, Chancellor. I wanted to give you the details, first."

Chancellor Conway looked away from her Defense Minister and back at the 8x10 pictures, "Has the commanding officer, this Major Manning, filed his After-Action Report, yet?"

When her question was met with silence, she looked up to see Boudreaux generally surprised that she was aware that such reports would be filed. He looked down, seemingly embarrassed.

Uhm…well…." Boudreaux began.

"Well, George? Did he file his report?" she asked again.

"No, Chancellor," Boudreaux quietly replied. "He and approximately thirty personnel are MIA."

Chancellor Conway stood quickly from her chair.

"WHAT!?"

The Chancellor's exclamation got everyone's attention. Most were shocked at the Chancellor's display of shock and anger. She put her hands on her desk and leaned forward to admonish her defense minister.

"And when, in God's name, were you going to tell me that? Or, were you going to leave that information, out of the briefing?"

"M-M-Madame Chancellor, I assure you, that…." Boudreaux began nervously as his French accent became more noticeable .

"George! Please, don't refer to me as Madame, Miss or Ms.," she corrected him on protocol. "Male or female. Whomever, is elected to this office is always referred to as 'Chancellor', only."

Boudreaux simply nodded.

"Now, continue," she urged, politely.

"Chancellor, I assure you that it was not my intention to omit information or mislead you," he began to explain. "However, I was only prepared for a one-on-one briefing."

Sheila Conway considered his posture for a moment and came to the conclusion that she put enough of a scare into the junior minister that would make him think twice in the future, about withholding information.

"So, we have people who are 'missing', no confirmed deaths. Correct?" she asked.

"Yes, Chancellor."

"Among the missing is the commanding officer?"

"Correct, Chancellor."

"Marcus Gowan and all his people are missing, as well?"

"That is the current assessment, Chancellor."

"Tell me, Minister Boudreaux," she said, quickly. "Who dreamed up this action? Who implemented it and who gave the 'green light'?"

"I was contacted by both, the Directors of CFS and the CSA. Both asked me to implement the plans they proposed and they both, gave the green light."

Obviously pleased with the response that was given, Sheila Conway sat back down.

"Thank-you, George. That wasn't so hard, now was it?" her tone softened and she didn't expect him to answer.

"No, Chancellor," he replied. He gave her the impression that he was 'brown-noser'.

"However, that changes, as of today," she began. "From now on, if it happens on Canadian soil, it is to go through this office and only green-lighted by the Chancellor, alone."

"With all due respect, Chancellor, I told both directors that you were in British Columbia campaigning for the 'NO' vote on the referendum of annexation by the United States. They quoted Clause 54, under joint jurisdiction of both nations, of the Continental Security Agreement, where neither the US President and/or the Canadian Chancellor could be reached for consultation, urgent decisions would be made, in their absence, by the directors, jointly of both nations," Boudreaux defended himself.

Chancellor Conway looked to her Chief Aid, "Bill. Did you receive any calls regarding this issue?"

Her Chief Aid, leaned forward on the sofa, looked up and replied, "Chancellor, I received no such notification."

Chancellor Conway stared at Boudreaux, saying nothing.

"I'm sorry, Chancellor. I was mislead," he offered.

"I'll be contacting the Director of the CSA to voice my displeasure of his actions and asking for the resignation of the CFS Director. I hope, I have made myself clear on the matter of Canadian sovereignty," she stated.

Heads bobbed in agreement around the room.

"Good," she said, satisfied. "Now, about this video call that I'm expecting, any moment," she asked. "Any thoughts?".

"We could do a security check on this Angela Teslin," someone offered.

"And the message she wants to relay concerning Major Manning?" Chancellor Conway asked.

From the group, all she got was blank stares.

"Maybe she wants to offer an explanation to what happened to our soldiers at White Alice," Boudreaux offered.

"Possibly," Chancellor Conway agreed.

The man with the unlit tobacco pipe spoke up. "We should prepare ourselves for the possibility that, they may be dead and she wants to notify us of that fact. Offer an explanation as to the how's and the why's. Offer an apology."

Everyone in the room stared at him, either shocked or glad he was the one who said what they were all privately thinking.

"Now, let's not get ahead of ourselves," Chancellor Conway said. "We have no evidence that suggests that. Am I right, George?"

"You are correct, Chancellor," Boudreaux confirmed. "According to a...Lt. Dechene, who was the most senior officer left, contact was lost with the two sections just before the mine 'disappeared'."

"What do you mean, 'disappeared'? the Chief Aid asked. "He meant, 'self-destructed', didn't he?"

Boudreaux shook his head, "According to Dechene, and confirmed by his own men and by an investigative team, on site, no explosive residue was found. Quite frankly, we lack sufficient information to conclude what happened."

Chancellor Conway saw some of the quotes made by Dechene in the informal, preliminary report.

"There was an aircraft seen taking off before the mine disappeared?"

"Apparently, but the descriptions given of the aircraft make it physically impossible for such a craft to fly," Boudreaux began. "Investigators believe weather conditions contributed in the erroneous size and configuration, described by the witnesses."

"How big are they saying it was?" Chancellor Conway asked.

The Minister of Federal Defense hesitated before answering.

"They claim the aircraft was the size of a football field and it, too, disappeared before their eyes."

That statement was met with shaking heads of disagreement and the odd exclamation of 'impossible'. Chancellor Conway, however, was silent. She looked at her watched and realized it was near the time that she would be receiving the second vidphone call from Angela Teslin.

"What about the families of the missing personnel?" Chancellor Conway asked. "What have they been told, George?"

"Not a thing. The remaining personnel were immediately flown to Canadian Federal Base, Suffield in southern Alberta for debriefing and quarantine, until we can sort this out."

"Who made that decision?" Chancellor Conway asked.

"I did, Chancellor," Boudreaux replied, waiting to get chewed out by his national leader.

"There's hope for you, yet. Good job, George," she complimented him.

A smile appeared on the Federal Defense Minister's face as he sat back down on the sofa. There arose an eerie silence in the office. The Chancellor again looked to her wristwatch before speaking.

"In one minute, I will be receiving the video call from this, Angela Teslin," Chancellor Conway announced. "I am having the call traced. I'm curious who she is and where she'll be making the call from. I'll try to keep her on the line as long as I can in order to accomplish that. While I'm speaking with her, you all may also ask any questions that come to mind. Anything, to lengthen the call for the trace."

She received silent nods from the group gathered in her office.

Then the video telephone rang and the large LCD monitor hanging on the wall activated with the text; 'Incoming Video Call'.

"Ok," she said with her finger hovering above the receive button. "Here we go."

When the monitor was activated, the image of a woman, with long, brunette hair appeared. Behind her was a bank of windows and outside those, was clear, blue sky with a few wisps of cloud.

"Good morning, or in your case, afternoon, Chancellor Conway," Angela Teslin began.

Good afternoon, Ms. Teslin," she replied. "I've asked my senior staff to join me. Is that alright?"

"Of course, Chancellor. Hello, gentlemen," Angela replied.

"Ms. Teslin, earlier you spoke of a message you wanted to relay concerning a Major Manning. I have since been informed that the Major is currently on a very important and highly classified mission. The fact, that you have identified, one of our members of a classified, military organization means, you could be arrested under the Continental Security Agreement."

Angela was seen chuckling to herself and quickly stop. This confused Chancellor Conway as to the source of the humor.

"I'm sorry, Chancellor. Please, forgive me," suddenly serious. "I know all about Major Manning's mission to the White Alice Diamond Mine on Voice Island."

Chancellor Conway, who had been slightly reclined in her office chair, sat bolt, upright, "How did you come across that information?"

"There is only two plausible ways I could know that information, Chancellor. One, you have a government leak and let me assure you that you do not."

"And two?" Chancellor Conway asked.

"Chancellor," Angela began. "I work, for Marcus Gowan."

Chancellor Conway looked over to the gentlemen in her office for some sign of recognition and found none. She turned back to the image before her.

"I see," she replied. "And where is Mr. Gowan, at this time?"

"I will reveal that in just a moment," she smiled.

"And what did you have to say concerning Major Manning?"

"I've been asked by Marcus Gowan to contact you and inform you that Major Manning and his team are safe and although there were some minor injuries sustained by his personnel, all are unharmed."

"What kind of injuries?" Chancellor Conway inquired.

"A few scrapes, bumps and bruises," Angela could be seen reading from a list on a clipboard. "Two received broken limbs, one requiring immediate surgery. The other had his limb set and his bone was repaired as well. They are expected to fully recover with no lasting effects."

Chancellor Conway opened her mouth to ask for more details of the wounded, when Angela, continued.

"Major Manning said there is an authentication code that would confirm that they are, indeed okay and that the message could only come from him. He asked me to ask you, to express to the families of the troopers that they are all, okay."

"And the authentication code is…?" Chancellor Conway asked.

"Well, it wasn't a code per' se, but a phrase, really. And it is; quote "What the fog has wrought", unquote," Angela looked up as she finished.

Chancellor Conway looked over to Defense Minister Boudreaux, who was looking into Manning's personnel file. Finding the section, he immediately looked up, made eye contact with the Chancellor and nodded twice, confirming the phrase as authentic.

Nodding back to her defense minister, Chancellor Conway addressed Angela Teslin.

"Now that we have that out of the way, please inform us of the whereabouts of the Major and his team, Marcus Gowan and which medical facility the two soldiers were admitted to."

"Well, Chancellor. This is going to sound rather, unbelievable and I'm going to have to ask that you and your staff, hold all questions until I have finished."

"Allright, continue," she agreed.

Angela cleared her throat before beginning.

"At the same time of the Canadian Anti-Terrorist Team's deployment at Voice Island, all mine personnel were evacuating. Major Manning had unknowingly led his team onto half of the horizontal launch-bay doors, which had failed to open. In the launch bay below, was the prototype spacecraft, Destiny. Unfortunately, the remaining half of the launch-bay door was cut away with Manning and his team, unknowingly, still in position on it. As the mine was set to self-destruct, Marcus Gowan chose to board those soldiers on the Destiny to prevent their deaths. As I said before, injuries were sustained and medical aid provided, on-board. As to their whereabouts, Chancellor; all I can say is that they are currently, off-world. Also, that all of your people will be returned to you, immediately after the Destiny enters orbit. Of course, you may expect their arrival in a yet to be determined, neutral country."

Angela, finished with her prepared statement, paused.

"Do you have any questions, Chancellor?"

Chancellor Conway sat unblinking at the image of Angela. She didn't know what part of the story to believe. She felt outrage welling up inside her. She looked over to her senior staff, who looked at her with as much uncertainty.

"Ms. Teslin," she began, tersely. I do not appreciate this 'fiction', you have conveyed. Now, I've accepted your call on the basis of courtesy and in return, you have lied to me."

"With all due respect, Chancellor," Angela countered. "The only reason you decided to accept this video-call; is so that you can trace it back to its origin."

Chancellor Conway's poker face, faded.

"Allow me to help you with that," Angela offered. "The results from your trace will reveal that this is a direct video link to your office, originating from a communications satellite in geo-synchronous orbit. Your trace will not be able to go further than that. As for me telling lies, I assure you that

I have told you the truth. Really, Chancellor, how would I know Major Manning's authentication code?"

"I don't know," she replied, regaining her composure. "But, the story you just told us could only be an invention to hide the fact that our people may, in fact, be dead. And, that you're trying to buy yourselves some time, before you reveal the truth."

Angela Teslin could be seen looking to someone off camera who suddenly got her attention. "Excuse me, Chancellor. An acquaintance of yours, wishes to speak with you." She suddenly stood from her chair and removed herself from before the camera.

The man placed his hand on the back of the chair before sliding into its seat. He thanked Angela, now off camera, before looking and smiling back at the image before him.

"Hello, Sheila. How've you been?"

"Tom," she whispered, flabbergasted. Confused, she was suddenly aware that those in the room had heard her exclamation and now all eyes were on her. Her look towards them confirmed this. She cleared her throat and looked back at the former boyfriend from years ago.

"Uh, I..I'm fine. And you?" she replied.

Thomas 'Doc' Thorpe looked around his own surroundings, "I'm good."

A sense of nostalgia began to come to mind that she couldn't shake. For her, this was the first time since entering politics that she had seen any one from her university days, especially her former lover. After three and a half years together, they both realized their respective degrees would take them in separate directions in life. It was an amicable break and she always held a special place in her heart for Tom Thorpe and what he had meant to her. She was elated and apprehensive to see him, again.

"Chancellor, can we speak...privately?" Doc said, clasping his hands, leaning towards the camera of the monitor.

Chancellor Conway slowly looked back at the people in her office and thought for a moment. She wanted them in on this call but, she too, wanted to speak with him, in private.

"Clear the room," she ordered.

The Chief Aid was about to protest when everyone else stood up to leave the office and he decided to follow. He was the last to leave and he closed the door behind him.

Thorpe reciprocated by asking Angela to leave the conference room.

Chancellor Conway turned to the image of Doc Thorpe. He looked older yet more distinguished. He was still handsome.

"You look well, Tommy." She offered.

"As do you, Sheila," he replied. "Congratulations, on becoming Chancellor. I knew you could do it. You accomplished your goal what, three years ahead of schedule?"

"Two, actually," she confirmed. "But I don't know how much longer Canada will exist as a nation if British Columbia votes for annexation by the US. If that happens, US territory will extend from the Arctic Ocean to the State of Baja. After that, the Yukon will most likely consider annexation, then Alberta and Saskatchewan, so on and so on, etcetera, etcetera….."

"I'm sure you'll be able to figure it. There is no-one else better for the task," doing his best to elevate her ego. He always could do that when she seemed a little down-trodden.

"Tommy," she began, appealing to the intimacy they once held for one another. "What *is* going on? I have sovereignty violations to deal with; accusations of conspiracy and insurgency, military personnel are missing. Give me a 'snapshot'."

Chancellor Conway had used the phrase that they once used between themselves, in private, when they wanted to inform the other of something that they could not otherwise fully disclose. The idea behind it was that if the 'big picture' was worth a thousand words, a snapshot would provide a brief description. Doc looked down at his clasped hands for a moment and then nodded to himself. He looked up.

"All right," he conceded. "Listen. Everything Angela told you is the truth. She told no lies. Marcus Gowan isn't a terrorist. He was building a spacecraft. At the time that the Destiny was preparing to launch, Major Manning and his team became trapped within the mine. They were taken aboard for their safety. I assure you, that they *are* fine. And yes; they are in space. A malfunction in the propulsion systems occurred and the Destiny traveled out further than intended. They'll be returning to orbit within a few days and should be planet-side soon after that, where they'll be taken to a neutral country and returned to Canada."

Listening to the explanation given by her ex-boyfriend, she realized he was telling her the truth and that if he had, indeed, lied, she would know it. She knew him too well.

"Are you implying that all the evidence I've heard, was designed to make Gowan look like he was a threat?"

"Sheila," Doc said giving her the 'look' she hadn't seen in years. "I'm not implying it. Consider it a counter-accusation. The evidence before you, is a work of fiction."

"Tom, please. Who would do that?"

"Those, who would hold power and those who have possession of the same technology that we currently have," Thorpe stated matter of fact.

"Tom. That's unlike you," Chancellor Conway said, making light of the conversation. "You sound like a conspiracy theorist."

"I know what this sounds like, Sheila," Doc admitted. "Believe me. If the roles were reversed, I, too, would be skeptical. I don't envy the position you're in, right now."

"And that is?" she inquired.

He asked her to do something she didn't want to do.

"Turn off the recorder. For your political and personal safety."

Chancellor Conway hesitated but reached for the keypad on her desk and entered a series of numbers anyway.

"Done."

"The position you are in is that one; yes, you have sovereignty issues to resolve. Two; people other than yourself or your office, are making national decisions. Three; people are deliberately withholding critical information from you. You're not getting the big picture."

Chanecellor Conway just stared at Doc and as she was about to ask for details, he continued.

"That is all I'm prepared to say about it. You deserved to know. You can turn the recorder back on, now."

"I'd like to recall my staff, if that is all right?" she asked.

"Certainly," he said as he gestured for Angela to rejoin him.

"And Tom," getting his attention. She paused, looking him directly in the eyes, "Thank-you."

He nodded, saying nothing more.

After the recorder was turned back on and everyone re-entered the office, the atmosphere became more formal. She addressed her senior staff.

"Gentlemen. Mr. Thorpe and I have some history. During my days at the Federal Canadian University, we dated for three and a half years. Mr. Thorpe has assured me that our people are safe and will be returned to us."

"Would you like to speak to the Major directly, Chancellor?" Doc offered.

Taken aback yet again, Chancellor Conway shot a look to Doc. "You can do that?"

"Of course I can," he said as he looked to Angela. "Contact Destiny and ask Joni to page Major Manning to the flight deck." He looked back into the monitor, "This will take a few moments as I'm not sure as to his location on the Destiny."

"Just how big is this spacecraft?"

"Oh, its fairly large Chancellor, believe me. Two hundred meters, beam is eighty-five meters. Displacement is 10,000 metric tons. There are eight decks and she compliments a crew of fifty."

"How did they get something that big and that heavy into space?" one of the Chancellor's staff asked another. Chancellor Conway looked over to the group of men, back to Doc and raised her eyebrows as she knew he had heard the question.

"Actually, I can't reveal just how thats possible," he replied. "It's top secret."

The Chief Aid stepped forward.

"To whom, Mr. Thorpe. You're a loyal federal citizen, correct? Again I ask, top secret to whom?"

Doc smirked at Chancellor Conway and then answered the Chief Aid directly.

"Sir, the technology involved would be top secret to everyone in the world. It has the potential to be mis-used. The world isn't ready for it, yet. It is the property of the Pacifican government. And, for your information, I am no longer a citizen of Canada. I am now a citizen of Earth and a Pacifican citizen, second."

"You're not renouncing your Canadian citizenship?" Conway asked, shocked.

"I'm afraid I am, Chancellor," Doc confirmed.

"I see," she said. For the second time in her life, Sheila Conway realized that someone from her past was truly following their life's path.

"Who better to make that declaration, than to an old friend," Doc said smiling at Chancellor Conway. "Listen, Chancellor. I would like to keep the lines of communication open between our two governments. In the next little while, this government will be in need of an unbiased link to the rest of the world, once we declare our existence. Would your office be willing to do this?"

Chancellor Conway was speechless. She didn't quite know what to make of the offer being suggested. She looked over to her staff, blankly, for a moment. All sorts of diplomatic protocols came to mind and had to be discussed before such an endeavor was to be seriously contemplated.

"As long as we get our people back and…why us?" she asked.

"Canadian political heritage has always been one of peace and diplomacy. Historically, co-founding the United Nations. Conceiving the idea of the UN peacekeeping forces. Even after Canada entered into the pact of the Continental Security Agreement with the United States. Helping other nations to facilitate their independence from dictatorships to democracies. Providing them with a voice on the world stage. Look at the good Canada did for Cuba during its transition from Communism. A lot of lives were saved. And now, it's the pearl of the Caribbean."

"Tom," she began. "I reserve the right to discuss this with my staff, thoroughly and I promise to give you an answer in the future."

Doc nodded, "Fair enough." He looked off camera for a second and nodded, presumably to Angela Teslin. "Chancellor, Ms. Teslin tells me that Major Manning is now available to speak with you. Talk to him for as long as you like. The link will not be severed until you break off. And, I promise you, that you will have complete privacy. I will be terminating my link now, which will be replaced by that of Major Manning."

He could be seen reaching for something when Chancellor Conway interrupted him. At the same time, Federal Defense Minister Boudreaux stood up from his seat on the sofa to stand by her office door, out of sight of the video-phone camera. Clearly he did not want to be seen by the soldier who was about to appear.

"Tom. It was good to see you…again."

Doc smiled back, "The pleasure was all mine, Chancellor." He broke his link and an image of a thin, older man with military-cut grey hair and a goatee and moustache appeared on the large monitor. Behind him, could be seen the large size of the flight deck and the large windscreen and a large, red orb beyond.

"Chancellor, I am Major Dennis Manning. Commanding the Canadian Anti-Terrorist Team," he announced.

"Major," Chancellor Conway began. "Can we speak freely?"

"Yes, Chancellor," he said looking around, just to make sure. "I am alone on the bridge."

"Can you confirm, for me, that you and your people are on a spacecraft and in space?"

Making eye-contact with the Chancellor and with all seriousness, he replied, "Yes, Chancellor. I can confirm that."

This brought back hushed murmurs among the staff members in her office. Manning could be seen reacting to them, by looking at the bottom corner of the monitor.

"People!" Chancellor Conway said, hushing her staff. They stopped abruptly and turned their attention back to the screen.

"Are you and your people being held against your will?"

"On the contrary," he began. "We are being treated as guests and have been told as much. We have complete freedom of movement aboard the spacecraft. The flight commander even took Lt. Stuart and I, for a spacewalk to help convince *me* that we were, indeed in space."

This time, the Chancellor's staff looked at one another, incredulously, silently.

"You've walked in space?"

"Went for a walk on the ship's hull, actually." Manning confirmed.

Chancellor Conway could hear whispers now from her staff.

"Can you confirm that this spacecraft is about two hundred meters long by eighty-five meters wide?"

Thinking for a second, "Sounds about right. It *is* a large spacecraft, Chancellor. As for the technology we've seen, I've only seen this stuff in the movies. Its sophisticated."

"Advanced?" she offered.

"Beyond even that, Chancellor," Manning stated flatly.

Chancellor Conway acknowledged what Manning was saying by simply nodding.

"I understand you suffered injuries amongst your team?" she asked.

"Yes, Chancellor," Manning confirmed. "Two of my troopers suffered broken bones. One of which, had a compound fracture of the left leg and he was hemorrhaging. He was taken immediately to the ship's infirmary where it was repaired. The other was a broken arm and it was set and also repaired shortly afterwards. Both soldiers are resting and stable. Their medical technology is pretty impressive as well."

"That's it for injuries?" she asked.

"The rest of us just suffered bumps and bruises. We're fine."

"Good," she said, satisfied. "Who is the Captain of the spacecraft? Is it Gowan?"

"Yes, Chancellor," he nodded.

"What are his intentions for the purpose of the spacecraft?"

Implicitly aware of what she was asking, Manning mulled the question for a long moment before answering.

"Chancellor, as far as I can and have determined, the Destiny is either a ship of exploration or space mining, or both. I have been given the grand tour and have virtually unlimited access to the entire vessel. We have seen no military hardware and I doubt there ever was any."

From the shadows, the Defense Minister whispered to Chancellor Conway.

"Can he commandeer the ship?"

Chancellor Conway looked over to him, wondering why he, himself didn't ask the question. Then again, this was her show.

"Major," she began still looking towards Boudreaux and then turning to the image of Manning. "have you entertained the idea of taking the ship by force?"

""We did, Chancellor," he replied. "That was before we found out where we were. I decided that to, continue, Canada would be breaking diplomatic agreements and international law set forth by the United Nations."

Chancellor Conway could see, out the corner of her eye, Boudreaux take a step forward to protest.

"Gowan should be arrested," he hissed, urging the Chancellor.

"Minister!" she shot back, gesturing with her hand for him to stop. "I'm inclined to agree with the Major on this issue. Do you want to be the one to answer to the World Court at The Hague about treaty violations? Hmm? I know I wouldn't."

Boudreaux quietly stepped back into the shadows.

She turned to the monitor, "Good call, Major."

"Thank-you, Chancellor," he replied.

"When should we expect your return?" she said, changing the subject.

"Commander Gowan says we'll be underway in a matter of hours. He says that he is waiting to hear from his scientists to confirm a system analysis on the propulsion system. He said that once we are in orbit, a suitable neutral country will be determined to drop us off and that you'll be notified as to our whereabouts," Manning explained.

"So, he's keeping you updated on a regular basis? Not holding back, anything?" Chancellor Conway asked.

"Actually," he said raising his eyebrows. "Commander Gowan and his crew have been quite open about their onboard operations. And in return, we have caused him no problems."

"Can you provide us a list of personnel that are with you so that we may compare with a list of the missing?" Chancellor Conway asked.

"Yes, Chancellor," Manning replied as he brought out a notepad from his right breast pocket. He began stating the names as one of the Chancellor's staff checked them off from a clipboard. Once the names were read aloud, the staff member confirmed that everyone was accounted for. Manning expressed concern for his troops left behind. Chancellor Conway informed him that there were no injuries or casualties sustained on the ground.

"Now," Chancellor Conway went on. "Can you provide me with the names of the crew?"

"Well, there is Flight Commander Gowan," he started. "The pilot, Mackenzie Marsh. Operations specialist, Joni Edwards. There are the two engineers, Bruno Kravakis and Joe Kyras as well as a mechanic by the name of Ron Kane."

She looked over to her Chief Aid and asked him to do background checks on Gowan's crew. She turned to the image of Major Manning.

"Major," she began. "Can you trust Gowan?"

"With our lives, Chancellor."

CHAPTER TEN

SHIPWRECK

Marcus sat at the Commander's Station for hours going over, once again, the data that his fellow scientists, on Earth, had sent him. The technology was still new enough that he had to admit to himself, was not fully understood. He and his colleagues had to keep reminding themselves, that they had to stop thinking inside the box. At times, they had to keep going back to their computers, go over the data and re-run the simulations. Marcus had insisted on a 0.35 % margin of error nine times out of ten. He, Kyras, Kravakis and Joni went over the data several more times before formulating a mission protocol for returning to Earth. Still, he felt a need to go over the data once more and then a second time.

He did manage to get about six hours of sleep after the exhaustive meeting. In the end, they came up with a cautious, yet direct flight plan. Power utilization would be increased in increments, termed as stages. Six in all. Power to the projectors would be increased from the Engine Room as called for by the Flight Deck. At any time, if a problem arose, Kravakis could shut down the reactor-quad without notice.

He began going over the flight plan that would take the Destiny the twenty million miles back to Earth. Earth's and Mars' orbital path around the Sun were at their closest. When one looked up, with the naked eye from Earth, one could see the red tinge of Mars in the open, night sky.

Conventionally, a spacecraft would normally achieve escape velocity of Mars and then head off towards to a point in space where Earth would be at a specific time, months later. As a spacecraft gets closer to the target destination, speed is reduced and course corrections made to better facilitate a smooth transition into the planet's gravity well. However, with the Destiny, it would be, 'point the nose towards Earth and then pour it on.'

Well, not really. What they had all agreed on, was that at first, the Helium3 thrusters would be fired for 13 seconds to break out of the Mars gravity well; Stage 1. Stage 2; as the Destiny coasted out, power to the GD-field projectors would be set at 1%. Stage 3; With Joe Kyras, monitoring the plasma feed though to the amplifiers and then the projectors and the tachyon build-up in the accumulator, Bruno Kravakis would give Marcus the 'thumbs up or down' to continue. They would also advise Marcus what next percentage of power best would get the Destiny to Earth, safely. Speed at this point, was not a factor. Stage 4; once the crew was satisfied that the propulsion system was working within the new distribution protocols, power would be increased to the GD-field projectors, therefore increasing Destiny's speed towards Earth. Stage 5; after everything, hopefully, as Mac Marsh commonly referred to as 'no hiccups', the crew of the Destiny should find themselves parked approximately, 2000 kilometers above the Moon's north pole. Stage 6; use the Helium3 thrusters for Earth orbit insertion and make preparations to enter the atmosphere and land in Pacifica.

Marcus heard the flight deck door cycle open for Joni and Marsh to enter. Both had travel-mugs of coffee in their hands, Marsh had two and was telling Joni one of his many flying stories.

"...so you can imagine, this twenty foot long container onboard this Boeing 848, descending from 40,000 feet only had a wide-open, half inch pressure relief valve. We were descending faster than the air onboard could enter the interior of the steel container."

"Oh, my God!" she turned to say to him. "You mean...."

"Yup," he confirmed. "Squashed like a beer can. I thought a bomb had gone off. I could still feel the vibration through the flight controls for 30 seconds afterward." Then he smirked, handing Marcus the second cup of coffee, "Thought I soiled myself, too."

Joni, who had been taking a sip from her cup, blew coffee out through her nose and burst out laughing. Then she slapped his chest.

"You do that every time," she said as she sat down at her station.

"What?" he said stopping his descent to the lower flight deck.

"Deliver a punch line when I'm taking a drink."

"Rats! My secret is out," he chuckled as he turned and continued with Marcus down the steps. "I take it, you've been going over the new protocols and the flight plan?"

Marcus nodded as he took his station, "I did."

Marsh shook his head, "Do you ever get any sleep, mate?"

Marcus chuckled without looking up from his panels, "As a matter of fact, I got about 4 hours."

"Are we still a go, on this morning's run to Earth?" Marsh asked.

Marcus handed Marsh the hardcopy print-outs. Notations were clearly marked, "Yes, but I want to keep an eye on any possible fluctuations or variables in tachyon flow to the projector emitters."

Joni, overhearing the conversation from her station, turned her chair to face the two at the bottom of the stairs.

"Joni, I've set that up at your station and I took the liberty of re-aligning the targeting scanners and recalibrating the projector's guidance actuators."

"Thank-you, Sir," she said as she gave Marcus a half attempt at a salute. "You probably saved me about an hours worth of work."

Marcus winked at her, "You're welcome, kiddo."

Marsh had taken his station and began checking his displays before he and Marcus would begin going through their pre-flight checklist.

"Where are Ron and Major Manning?" Marcus asked.

As Marcus took the Flight Commander's station, Joni spoke up from the 2nd tier, "He thought that it would be a good idea for Manning's troops to take seats in the forward observation lounge for the journey back. He's settling them in for that and then they'll both be here."

"That's a good idea," Marcus said. "I wish I thought of that."

"You did," Marsh offered. "Ron's doing it on behalf of the Destiny's Commander."

Marcus smiled and looked over to Marsh, "I take it back, then. I'm glad I did think of it."

Marsh smiled back, "Such a thoughtful guy."

"Ok, lets get down to business," Marcus suggested as he started checking his displays. "Joni. Give me a reading on the Helium3 storage tanks, please."

"Helium3 storage tanks are 150 metric tons with a temperature holding at minus 269 degrees Celsius. Pressure is holding at 100,000 kilopascals," she read from her displays. "Booster pumps to the RCS thrusters are online and status is in the green. Pre-heaters are online. "

"Supply lines are pressurized?" Marsh asked.

Joni quickly looked to her display and replied, "They are. Thruster control, at your discretion."

Marsh looked over to Marcus, "I figure at .02% thrust; about 20 Kps, we'll need a burn-time of 13 seconds to make escape velocity."

"That's a little more speed than we need, isn't it?" Marcus questioned.

"Depends on how quickly you want to get home."

Just then, the hatchway door opened and in, entered Ron Kane and Major Manning. Kane took his seat at the operations station. Earlier he had a second chair inserted to the chair-track in the floor so Manning could sit beside him. He invited him to take a seat. Kane smirked as he watched Manning put on and fasten his seat belts.

Manning noticed Kane and felt a little self-conscious, "What? You're not putting yours on?"

"Don't get me wrong, Major. If you feel safer with it on, by all means, please do," Kane explained.

"Do you hold a rank, Mr. Kane?" Manning asked, finishing belting up.

Kane looked puzzled for a moment, "Well, I am a mechanic/machinist/millwright. Being that we are at the Flight Console, I could be a flight-specialist." Then he leaned over to the Major and whispered, "Means I'm a low-life."

Manning chuckled at Kane's sense of humor.

"Hey low-life," Marsh called out from the lower fight deck. "Lets run through the Ops Checklist."

Going through the Ops checklist took 5 minutes and then the Engineering/Systems checklist with Joni, Kravakis and Kyras took another 10 minutes. Manning was amazed at what he was witnessing. It was a moment in time he would never forget. It was, for him, a perfect moment. So surreal, being a part of everything, that happened, yet, having the perspective of being the observer. There were only a few times that he had had that experience. This was one of them.

Then, he had an epiphany. Because Marcus Gowan trusted him, his crew trusted him. They had accepted him and his troops, unconditionally. This un-nerved him a little bit. Then the thought entered his mind that if a person could be so trusted, that person could, take advantage of such a situation. He gave his head a barely noticeable shake knowing that Gowan would take steps to ensure that the technology onboard the Destiny would not fall into the wrong hands. They wanted him to see everything they were doing. He guessed, to prove to him that they were doing everything to get back to Earth.

Marsh looked over Marcus, "We are 'Go' for spatial orientation."

Marcus did a cursory check of his displays and nodded, saying, "Proceed."

Marsh flipped a few switches and then took hold of the flight-control yolk which was similar to that of a large aircraft that he had seen; only more elaborate. The view out the flight-deck wind-screen changed as the pitch and yaw of the Destiny's nose pointed towards Earth. Mars had moved from the port-side of the wind-screen to the high starboard-side. Manning could hear, somewhere within the Destiny, the noise from the reaction-control thrusters.

"Spatial orientation, set. Course is set and locked," Marsh announced.

"Uplink to the inter-planetary positioning system is strong and holding," Kane added.

"Confirmed. Flight; please notify Pacifica we are about to proceed," Marcus said and opened the ship's intercom, which sounded an audible warning, first. "All hands! Stand-by for Stage 1. Stand-by for Stage 1."

Marcus then began polling for status on the Flight deck.

"Helm, go/no go?"

"Green for 'Go', Marsh replied, ready.

"Flight, go/no go?"

"Status is 'Go' and Doc says he is awaiting our return," Kane responded after double-checking his displays.

"Systems, go/no go?"

"Systems is a 'Go', Joni replied.

"Engineering, go/no go?" Marcus finally said into the intercom.

Bruno Kravakis replied, "Engineering systems are showing green across the board. We are 'Go'."

"Flight Commander concurs with crew. We are 'Go'," Marcus said looking at Mac Marsh. "Proceed with Stage 1."

Marsh began activating certain systems to initiate the 13 second burn time of the reaction-control thrusters.

"RC-Thrust-levers are set to .02 percent maximum. Igniters armed," He took a light hold of the control yokes with his finger-tips and placed his right hand over a button just behind a set of levers on a center console between him and Marcus.

"Enable ignition sequence," Marcus gave the command and Marsh pushed the button and closed the clear plastic button protector. The levers on the center console automatically moved all the way forward and Manning could hear from somewhere in the ship, a high pitched whine. He looked around to identify where it was coming from.

"H3 booster pumps are cycling. High temperature H3 is within specs," Joni announced. "Pressure is good."

Marsh called out, "Pre-programmed ignition firing in; 5…4…3…2…1. Now."

Manning heard the thrusters ignite and was able to perceive a slight acceleration, his body being pushed into his seat which did not continue. The only other stimuli he could rely on that the Destiny was actually moving, was by looking out the forward windscreen of the flight deck.

Manning looked to Kane who was watching his displays.

"What speed do we need to reach?" he asked.

Without looking up, "For escape velocity, we need only 5 kilometers per second to climb out of the Mars gravity well. That's about 18,000 kilometers per hour."

Manning thought for a moment.

"Well, with speed limited to .02 percent thrust, couldn't we still get to Earth within a relatively short period of time?"

Kane ceased monitoring his displays, blinked twice and stared at Manning. The high-pitched whine of the Helium3 pumps stopped and the thrusters cut out.

"Stage 1, complete," Marcus announced through the ship's intercom. "Standby for Stage 2."

"What?" Manning said, looking back at Kane.

"Major," Kane began. "Few people would have realized that the Helium3 onboard would be sufficient to get to Earth. However, we also need what we do have, for a controlled re-entry and safe landing on the planet surface."

"I thought that was the point of the main propulsion system?" Manning asked.

Kane reached over to a display in front of Manning and touched its screen, "Oh, it is but, it operates best at the higher speeds. Usually, we use the Helium3 thrusters for take-offs and landings and for station-keeping while in space. With the new capabilities we've discovered with the propulsion system, we have to re-write the books and that means proceeding cautiously."

"Projector targeting scanners aligned and focal point is set," Joni announced.

"Understood," Marcus replied. "Engineering; flight deck. Stage 2. One percent power to the GD Projectors, please."

Again, Manning felt a barely perceptible acceleration against his body.

"Flight, velocity?" Marcus asked.

Kane looked over to one of his other monitors and replied, "Velocity is 9400 kilometers per second."

Marsh, with a big grin, looked over to Marcus.

"Warp-speed, Commander?"

Still looking forward, Marcus grinned and then chuckled as he looked down at his displays.

Marsh tilted his head, "Sorry, couldn't resist,"

"That's funny. Engineering; Stage 3 status report."

There was a long pause before Kravakis answered.

"We're good here, Flight Deck. We're not getting any anomalous readings from the reactor-quad or through to the projector system. High energy plasma flow from the accumulator is consistent with the simulations. Linear mitigaters and the nodes are performing as expected. Regulating sequencers are holding. Tachyon particles in the buffer system is building and the injector system is online. If my calculations are correct; we suggest an acceleration setting of 24 %. That would give the Destiny a speed of 4 times the speed of light and a transit time of 2.5 minutes."

"Energy efficiency is currently holding 89.59 %," Joni added.

"Thank-you," Marcus said. "Engineering; Stage 5. You can proceed with increasing power to the distortion amps. to 24 % but, in 1 % increments every 3 seconds."

"Understood, Flight Deck," Kravakis replied.

With each passing second, the Destiny was moving further and faster from Mars. In fact, if one were to be looking out one of the many windows onboard, they would see the red planet shrinking fast. On the flat-screen monitors before him, Manning saw a digital representation of the Mars gravity-well and the Destiny slowly climbing out of it. And the Destiny was accelerating. The Destiny's own gravity-well projected and focused before her was trying to pull the ship to it's event-horizon. It wasn't an artificial black-hole but, the principle was the same. The smaller and deeper the focal-point, the stronger the gravitic attraction, the faster the Destiny was able to move through space. Any other matter, free-floating in space that was being pulled into the same gravity-well, that could potentially endanger the Destiny, was being repelled by her own magnetic field, like that of the Earth's. After 18 seconds, the Destiny again, crossed the lightspeed-threshold and visually, disappeared. After 72 seconds, she was traveling at four times the speed of light.

Looking forward through the flight deck windscreen, Manning witnessed the Destiny travel through a sort of spatial tunnel. It was like watching oneself being propelled through a tunnel on a subway system, only faster.

"Why is that happening?" Manning asked Kane.

Kane, who had been busy monitoring his displays, looked up at the tunnel-effect outside the windscreen and smiled, before looking back to his displays, "I will never get tired of that."

"What's doing that?"

"We've left normal space and entered 'phased' space. The effect you are seeing is from the event horizon being projected directly in front of the Destiny and the various elements streaming by in normal space."

"Oh," Manning said. "Like 'warp speed'."

Kane looked up at the tunnel-effect for a second, to his displays and then to Manning.

Shaking his head, Kane looked to Manning.

"Uh, No. This is quite different."

Manning continued watching the tunnel-effect. He hadn't noticed that someone had lowered the light level on the flight deck. He was completely mesmerized by the effect. Before he knew it, the show outside was about to end.

"Standby for transitory exit," Marcus announced.

This brought new activity from Kane and Joni on the upper tier. It was obvious to Manning that they were getting ready for yet another stage of the flight. Kane's hands flew over displays and buttons and switches. Manning looked at the only monitor that Kane had not touched. It displayed a map of the Earth and Moon and Mars in space and a highlighted course that the Destiny was taking. There was also, a representation of the Destiny as it traversed its way back to Earth.

"Engineering, standing by," was the response from Kravakis.

"Ops?" Marcus asked.

"Standing by," replied Joni.

"Flight?"

Kane's hands were still flying over his controls before finally responding.

"Ready."

"Transitory exit in ten seconds. Mark," Marcus declared.

Manning instinctively braced himself against the workstation console. Kane gave him a quick sideways glance, turned back to his duties and allowed himself a barely noticeable smirk. Manning noticed this, became a bit self-conscious and then put his hands back in his lap. Paul Kane's smirk got larger.

Then, suddenly, the spatial tunnel effect, ceased.

"Exit," Mac announced, "successful ."

Marcus clicked on the ship-wide intercom, "All hands. Stage 5 complete. Land-ho."

Mac stifled a chuckle.

"Projector alignment deviated 0.0002 degrees while in 'phased space'," Joni added. "I have made the necessary corrections to prevent a re-occurrence."

Manning looked forward and saw for the first time in his life, his home planet from space. Half the planet was bathed in daytime sunlight and the other half was covered in night-time darkness against the back-drop of deep space. Sunlight was streaming into the flight deck, giving it an eerie glow.

"Wow," Manning said quietly to himself, admiring the view.

"Wait," Marcus said, looking back at the awed Major. "Mac. Pitch 90 degrees forward, please."

Manning could see Mac working his flight controls as the view outside the forward windscreen slowly changed. The view of the Earth was replaced with that of the half-lit Moon. The terminator between the light-side and the dark-side was clearly defined. The brightness astounded him. The detail and number of craters visible, amazed him. Seeing the Moon even at this close distance, stirred a sense of awe, deep inside him. It felt almost instinctual.

"This is amazing," Manning said taking in the view.

"Ok, Mac," Marcus said after moment. "You can bring us back."

Mac did so, pointing the nose of the Destiny toward the Earth.

Marcus keyed the intercom, again, "All hands. We are about to begin the last leg of our journey home. This should take about 30 minutes. We'll then be entering a equatorial orbit and re-entering atmosphere above the Indian Ocean. Within the hour, you'll be enjoying the warm air of the South Pacific. So, sit tight and enjoy the ride of your lives."

Mac looked over to Marcus who, nodded back as he keyed-off the intercom. Mac immediately got to work and in no time, the Destiny began her approach to the Earth. Manning could barely perceive, through the windscreen, the Earth, getting larger. If he looked away for 30 seconds, he could definitively see evidence of it.

"The 'Fence' is coming up quick," Kane announced. Manning looked at the display Kane was watching. He could see the image of the Earth and a representation of a grid system encircling the planet and a small image of the Destiny as it quickly approached it.

Still monitoring his displays, without looking back, Marcus acknowledged Kane.

"I know. We are going to have to cross it and hope they won't have enough time to do anything about it."

The Senator was in his office sipping on a cognac, reading some briefs concerning a bill that had been proposed by the President. He was planning on voting against it since the bill would indirectly affect his constituents. He liked the President. He just didn't like his politics.

The intercom of his phone buzzed and he pushed the button.

"Yes," he answered.

"Senator," the receptionist announced. "Air Force Colonel, Brunson from the Pentagon is on videoline 2. I told him you were busy studying a brief for an upcoming bill. That you were not to be disturbed. He says that if it was important enough, you wanted to be informed."

Looking off into empty space, the Senator recalled his instructions to the Colonel. Realizing something big had occurred. He put down the brief, put aside his cognac and sat up.

"Its Ok, Leslie. I'll take the call." He pressed the flashing button that activated his vidphone. "Colonel. Is this a secure line?"

"Yes, Sir. It is."

"What do you have?" The Senator asked.

"Approximately 10 minutes ago, the Outer Satellite Surveillance Network picked up an object heading inbound to Earth. The object velocity has been calculated to be three quarters of a million miles per hour. ETA to Earth is roughly 20 minutes."

The Senator was astonished at the speed of the object.

"Is it an asteroid?"

"No Sir. It is not an asteroid." Brunson paused. "I asked NORAD Space Command to task one of its satellites to track this fast-mover. I had this request listed as 'above top-secret' trough the National Security Agency."

"Gowan." The Senator murmured.

"There is no definitive proof as we have yet to identify the object."

"When will you be able to confirm I.D. of the object?"

"In another ten minutes, Sir," Brunson replied.

"Where are you now, Colonel?"

"The Special Projects Situation Room at the Pentagon, Sir"

"We have Orbital Marines in orbit right now, do we not?"

Brunson paused again. His hesitation was, to the Senator, an indication in the affirmative.

"Senator," The Colonel began. "How did you know about the current OMARR mission?"

The Senator chuckled. OMARR was the acronym for Orbital Marine and Rapid Reaction System and was part of the U.S. Marine Rapid Reaction Force. It involved a 2-stage system; the carrier, essentially, a modified C9E Titan cargo-plane which launched an orbital lander from the top of its fuselage at high altitude. The lander was the same size of the current generation of space shuttles. Only sleeker and meaner looking. Onboard the lander, was a Marine squad outfitted complete, with gear and equipment. In emergency missions, it was, traditionally, the Marines who were the first ones to be called. That tradition continued. They even referred to themselves as the 'Dogs of War' and their motto of 'Semper Fi', was accompanied by 'Deliver Oblivion'. The purpose of OMARR was to insert, into a hot combat zone, Marines directly from orbit without ever crossing the airspace of another neutral or hostile country. Once in-country and mission successful or not, the lander would take-off like any other aircraft with the use of its hypersonic, hydrogen ramjet engines for the journey back to the United States.

"Son. If its in orbit, I know about it."

Again, the Colonel hesitated before answering.

"We have three Eagles in orbit awaiting the green lit for a mission in the United Republics of Central Africa. Two have contingents of Marines and the other is a support vehicle stocked with ordinances."

"What kind of ordinances?" the Senator asked.

"Mainly, Orbital to surface bombardment systems. Electro-magnetic rail launchers with re-entry warheads, Orbital-Strike missiles with plasma warheads. Anti-aircraft missiles."

The Senator thought for a moment. He knew the Orbital Marines were on an important mission. To re-task an important mission such as this, would raise too many eye-brows. However, the support Eagle…..

"Colonel. Can you re-task the support Eagle for one job?"

Another moment of hesitation.

"Depends on the time-frame, Senator," Brunson replied.

The Senator smiled at the image of the Colonel, "All I want is one shot."

Half sitting and half leaning against the conference room table, Doc Thorpe had been monitoring the progress of the Destiny's journey back to Earth along-side Angela Teslin. He noticed that Angela had a nasty habit of biting her fingernails. He looked over to her and she looked back. Aware that he noticed this, she quickly crossed her arms across her chest to watch the large wall monitor. They both had been listening to the voice conversation on the flight deck via the Quantum Hyperlink. They listened intently as the Destiny increased velocity using the RCS thrusters. As the main propulsion was engaged and the Destiny accelerated beyond the speed of light, all communication; voice, data and telemetry was lost. Angela gave Doc a worried look. He looked back at her, raised his eyebrows and tilted his head as if it was all perfectly normal. She continued biting at her fingernails.

After about 2 -1/2 minutes, the Inter-planetary Positioning System detected the Destiny exactly where she was expected to be. Voice, data and telemetry communication was restored. Doc went to his laptop computer, entered a few keystrokes and looked up to the wall monitor just in time to see the projected course of the Destiny' approach to Earth orbit. It's course would take it into a equatorial orbit. He returned to his place beside Angela to watch the next stage of the flight.

"Should be about another 20 minutes to orbit," he postulated. "They should be landing within the hour."

"I would love to do what they are doing," Angela whispered. "To be able to take a short trip to the Moon and back."

Still watching the monitor, "We'll all be able to do that sooner than you think."

She continued to stare at the wall monitor as well, "Oh I know. It's just that I wish I could experience what they are, as they approach Earth."

Doc smirked, "Give it a year." Then he looked at her, "Then you'll be able to have that experience."

"I thought that everything would be on hold since we had to move up the 'Exodus'?" she replied.

"Not according to Marcus," Doc informed her. "In fact, we were talking about bumping up the schedule since we had to evacuate early."

"The entire plan or partially?" she asked.

"The whole, damn thing," he informed her.

The plan was, he explained, once the infrastructure and the economy was well established, once the population was 'settled-in' and the existence of Pacifica was declared to the world, that's when committed forays into space would begin in earnest.

Firstly, the completion of the space-flight center twenty kilometers south-west of the capital, Fresco City. Immediately after that, construction and assembly of a high-orbit space station would begin. During this of course, construction of the space-craft manufacturing facility for mining and exploration as well as cargo vessels would be in full swing. All the while, construction of the moon base would begin at the same time as the regolith mining facility. There was also the planned construction of the optical and radio telescope observatories on the dark-side of the moon. As well, there would be the water processing facility at the crater on the dark-side of the Moon, near its south-pole. He explained also, that there would be a massive open-air resort facility where tourists could enjoy the reduced gravity of the Moon.

"Imagine playing golf or human-powered flight on the Moon," He said.

"Fly?" she asked. "How?"

Doc smirked as he looked back to the wall monitor, "Why, like a bird, of course."

"I don't understand."

"Well, imagine wearing a jump-suit that has fabric-like flaps from your wrists to your hips. You jump off a platform, much like that for bungee-jumping and you glide through the air. Flight-time would be 30 to 60 seconds, depending on your experience."

"I dunno," Angela began. "I think I'd rather try gol....."

Doc had suddenly launched himself from his leaning position on the conference table, raised his hand to signal Angela to wait and approached the monitor as if to see something more closely. Angela couldn't see what it was that got his attention. She thought he noticed a problem with the Destiny.

"What is it, Doc?" She asked.

He walked right up to the monitor and touched it, on the spot of three small dots in low-Earth orbit. The wall-monitor display changed to zoom-in on the dots. In orbit were three space-craft flying in formation. The computer identified them as Orbital Marine Eagles. One of them had broken that formation as the other two, continued on. It looked to him as if the one had also changed its orbit. Doc quickly turned and walked briskly to the other side of the large conference table to his laptop. Entering a few keystrokes, the Orbital Marine Eagle's course was projected on the monitor. It was a direct line to the Destiny.

Angela looked back at Doc with a horrified expression.

"Are they trying to intercept the Destiny?"

"They can't," he replied. They wouldn't have the fuel."

She looked back at the monitor, realizing he was right.

"Then, what?"

Doc stared at the monitor for a moment

"I have no idea," he replied. "but, we have to warn the Destiny."

CHAPTER ELEVEN

The Dogs of War

The US Marine Orbital Transportation Shuttle(MOTS) or Eagle as was commonly referred to by the 'Corps', floated in its orbit around the Earth at 18500 miles per hour, pointed towards the Moon. Reaction-control thrusters firing, infrequently, to maintain its position. The Eagle was mostly military grey with the exception of the black-colored ceramic tiles on it's underside for re-entering the atmosphere. Its fuselage and wings incorporated the newest uni-body design. The twin-tail stabilizers were accompanied with vertical stabilizers at its delta wing-tips. It was a sleek spacecraft, designed also for high-speed, hypersonic flight. Silently, waiting for the arrival of it intended prey.

Colonel Jason Lowry watched the radar monitor on his instrument panel. He could see the object moving towards them at high velocity. He and his crew were informed two minutes prior, from NORAD, that an asteroid was spotted over the north-pole of the Moon and would pass closely to the Earth and was in danger of impacting the surface. Their orders were to fire at least one, possibly more Orbital-Strike Missiles(OSM), referred to as 'Awesomes', to knock it off it's current trajectory, thereby missing the Earth. He thought how fortunate it was that his squadron just happened to be in orbit to assist in saving lives in a hostile country and now, they had revised orders to save the Earth from a devastating meteor impact.

"Damn it, Samson," Lowry called out. "Where's that firing solution?"

"Almost there, Sir," came back the reply over the intercom from the lower compartment.

Lowry frowned to himself and briefly looked out the forward window, trying to spot the rock he knew was inbound. He couldn't see anything except the Moon, knowing radar had already detected the object.

Oh, he could just lock onto it and fire but, their orders were to knock it off course and not just obliterate it. And by doing so, was no guarantee that it would even scratch the surface.

"I wanna' be able to program the guidance systems before I fire the damn missiles," Lowry complained.

"Aye, aye, Sir!" came the reply through the head-set.

Lowry's co-pilot, Major Albert Grant was watching the instrument panel as well and noticed the velocity of the rock.

"Geeze! That thing is really movin'," Grant called out. "I thought these rocks traveled at velocities slower than that?"

Lowry looked down briefly at the telemetry data coming in from the satellites that were tracking it. It *was* moving fast. In his mind he tried to figure out the physics that would cause a rock to move that fast and then explain it to his co-pilot.

"Coulda' been knocked out of the asteroid belt which sent it on a trajectory, which may have sling-shot it around one or more of the planets and since it's heading towards the Sun… Earth just happens to be in the way."

He wondered if he was trying to convince his co-pilot or himself. It didn't matter, he thought. A few moments after launching, the plasma warheads would detonate on the underside, the gaseous, superheated plasma, would push it well out of Earth's gravity-well.

They could both tell, on the radar monitor, that the object wasn't very big. In fact, it seemed to Lowry to be fairly unremarkable. He couldn't really understand how an astronomer managed to detect it in the first place. Then again, that wasn't part of his job. He followed his orders and he did it well. In his duties, he relied heavily on facts and intelligence, not imagination.

"Colonel, Sir?" Samson said over the intercom.

"You done with that firing solution, Lieutenant?" Lowry asked.

There was a pause before Samson replied.

"Uh, no Sir. I can't," came the reply.

Lowry looked over to Grant with a puzzled look.

"Why the hell, not?" Grant said over the intercom.

"Damn thing keeps changing course. I can't keep up with the changes."

"So," Lowry began. "it's no longer heading for Earth, right?"

"Oh, yes it is. Even with the constant course changes, it's still heading for Earth. And its velocity is decreasing."

"That's not possible," Lowry said. "Check that again."

"I did, Sir," Samson replied. "Three times."

"So much for that idea," Grant said to his commanding officer.

"Yep," Lowry agreed. "We get to blow something up in space this time." Combat tactics called for changes to the mission. Even though, they could no longer change the rock's trajectory.

Samson came back on the intercom.

"Object will pass over top of us by 800 kilometers. At its current velocity, it will be in range for approximately 3 minutes before we loose line of sight over the horizon. "

"Reprogram one plasma warhead for maximum yield," Lowry ordered. "The only thing I want raining down on the planet is space-dust."

"Aye, aye, Sir!" came the reply.

Grant then got Lowry's attention

"Hey! Its changed course, again."

Lowry looked to the radar monitor quickly and watched the screen. The changes were more frequent and erratic. At times, the object would increase speed and then decrease and then increase. The changes seemed, evasive. He was beginning to understand why Samson couldn't come up with an effective firing solution.

Lowry postulated, "Could it be tumbling?"

"Can't tell at this distance," Grant replied. "Give it 2 minutes."

Lowry looked out the forward window and could see a faint reflection of light, slowly moving against the backdrop of stars. That had to be it, he concluded. He looked down at the monitor and back up again but, lost sight of it. Looking back down at the radar monitor, he was relieved to see that the object could still be detected.

"Samson," Lowry called out on the intercom. "Make sure the guidance system is working five by five. Including the optical tracking system."

"Aye, aye, Sir," Samson replied. "Already done, Sir."

""Get Command on the line," Lowry ordered. "I want to know if they are getting the same radar returns that we are."

Grant immediately activated the radio and was busy talking to the mission controller. In the mean time, Lowry checked over the instrument panel, making sure there were no glitches. After a moment, Grant looked over to Lowry, explaining to him that although the ground stations were seeing the same things there were, their orders still stood, adding that in the event that they could not alter the asteroids trajectory, it was to be destroyed by all necessary means.

Lowry took that to mean that the impact must be somewhere in the US.

'Not on my watch', Lowry thought to himself. "Samson," Lowry said calm into the microphone of his headset. "Warm up the other eleven 'Awesomes'."

"That's our entire inventory of plasma warheads, Colonel," Samson replied as if Lowry didn't know that fact.

"I know that, Lieutenant," Lowry began. We've received updated orders. I want the warheads armed as soon as they leave the payload bay. How much time will it take to get ready?"

There was a pause from the payload weapons officer before he replied, excited.

"Aye-aye, Sir. Already working on it. We'll be launch-ready in three minutes." Samson had forgot to click-off his microphone and the two pilots could hear him say to himself, "This is gonna' be a blast."

"Very well," Lowry acknowledged as he smirked to himself. "Al, make preparations for the rocket-motor wash pushing against the payload bay and to counter-act it."

"Aye-aye, Sir."

His eyes looked down at the radar monitor to check the intended target's position. He could, indeed, see that it was constantly changing course. Speed increased and then decreased. As he continued to watch the object, he witnessed it once again, change course. This not only puzzled him, it alarmed him. For a piece of left-over, from the formation of the solar system, it was breaking all the laws of physics. Somebody or... something was piloting that rock.

Major Grant, who was also watching the same monitor, announced, "That's no asteroid."

Lowry declared without agreeing, "I don't care what it is. We have our orders. We're Marines, the 'Dogs of War'," he looked up to his subordinate. "Deliver oblivion."

Grant smiled back, devilishly, "Semper Fi."

Lowry looked out into space and replied, under his breathe, "Hoo-Rah."

Mac Marsh was really giving the flight controls and the Destiny a work-out. Marcus could see that he was flying by instruments alone. Marcus had looked up, through the forward windscreen and became slightly dizzy. He looked back down at his own instruments. Minutes earlier, the Destiny had crossed the 'Fence' and he knew that they had been detected and they were now being tracked. Before that, Doc Thorpe had contacted them, to warn them, that a US. Orbital Marine Eagle had altered its orbit to either intercept or observe them. Joni went to work to scan the US spacecraft.

"Their RADAR is still passive," Joni announced. "I think they're waiting till we get closer."

"Are they moving toward us?" Marcus asked

Joni rechecked her scan of the Eagle for a moment, and then checked another monitor before answering.

"Nope. Its just floating along in its orbit with its nose pointed in our direction."

Manning looked over to Joni, "You can tell that at this distance?"

Joni nodded as she looked back at the Major. "From the short-range scanners? Oh, sure. And from much further out, actually."

Manning couldn't imagine that at this distance, the capabilities of the technology, these people were demonstrating. He felt like pinching himself to prove to himself he wasn't in some science fiction movie. He watched the two men on the tier below, piloting the massive craft through its maneuvers. He couldn't help but, look out the forward windscreen, whereby he immediately became disoriented.

Kane who witnessed this, smirked, "Try not to look outside, Sir. Just keep your eyes on the consoles or anything not moving on the flight deck."

Joni, who was studying her scan of the Marine Eagle, half turned in her chair.

"Marcus. According to my scans, they just powered up a bunch of missiles. I think they're getting ready to fire."

"What kind of missiles?" Marsh asked.

Joni looked back at her scans, "I don't know but, there's twelve of them."

Manning looked over to Joni.

"Can you transfer what you're seeing to this station? Maybe I can identify them."

Joni looked to Marcus on the lower tier of the flight deck, who looked back up to her and silently nodded, his agreement. She looked to the Major, smiled and turned to her console.

"Transferring now," she said.

One of the monitors came alive before Manning with an electronic representation of the Marine Eagle. The scan was impressive and thorough. Manning could see that every system could be identified as well as the number of souls aboard.

"Ms. Edwards. Can you show me the weapons systems?"

Joni nodded, "Of course, Major."

The scan changed to reveal the weapons onboard the Eagle. Most of its weapons were inactive. The scans indicated that 12 missiles were active with power from the Eagle, its own, on-board power and he could even tell that they were receiving data from the Eagle's main computer.

"Can you scan the warheads?" Manning asked.

"On the way, Major," Joni complied.

It took a few seconds for Manning to recognize what he suspected. And he didn't like what he saw.

"Awesomes," he whispered to himself.

"What's awesome?" Kane asked an unsettled looking Major Manning.

Manning sat back against the back of his chair and looked to the ceiling of the flight deck as if lost in thought.

"Awesomes, OSM. Orbital Strike Missiles" he repeated. "This can't be good."

Looking at the same display as Manning, Kane asked, "Those aren't nukes, are they?"

Looking back down at the monitor, Manning replied, "Worse."

These, Manning knew, were the new weapons of choice of the US military. They were officially called Orbital Strike Missiles, code-named 'Awesome' and were meant to replace the US nuclear arsenal, even though they were still kept stockpiled. An OSM could be launched from any platform, circumnavigate the entire planet, fly well past its launch point and still vaporize its target. As valuable as nuclear weaponry were to the US military, it was realized that some point that they would have to be phased out eventually in favor of the more reliable, low maintenance, non-radioactive components of the new plasma warhead. As powerful as a nuclear detonation without the nasty radioactive fallout to deal with, for thousands of years.

Manning had heard that one could increase or decrease the warhead's explosive yield, from a blast that could, at temperatures of between 18000 to 25000 degrees Fahrenheit, vaporize an entire city block or the entire city itself. He could understand the Eagle using one of these warheads against the Destiny but, he couldn't fathom the reasoning for the use of 12 such warheads.

"Commander Gowan!" Manning began. "You should be aware, that the missiles, Ms. Edwards scanned, contain plasma warheads….and I think they're preparing to launch the lot of them."

"You can't be serious!" Marcus looked back up to Manning. "How certain of that, are you?"

Manning locked his eyes onto Marcus'. "I assure you Commander, I am quite, serious. As to my certainty, I may be wrong. However, the next thing they'll do, is obtain radar-lock. They have 12 'hot pickles' and we're the only pickle-barrel in sight, right now."

Marcus immediately understood Manning's warning where military pilots routinely referred to their armed missiles as 'hot pickles' and the targets being inside the, 'pickle barrel'.

"I thought they were used primarily against ground targets?"

Manning frowned and tilted his head, "Obviously, not anymore, Commander."

Marcus looked to the floor for a brief moment as if lost in thought and then looked back up to the upper tier to Manning, nodded once as if saying, 'thank-you', before turning to his co-pilot.

"Mac. Can you out-fly those things?"

Marsh, busy with the flight controls, paused briefly before answering.

"I can if its one, two or three, tops. But, if they fire all twelve, that would be too much, even for me. Would be better to out-run them."

"You think you can do that, with them between us and the planet?" Marcus asked.

Marsh considered the question for a half-second.

"If we enter the atmosphere over the North Pole and traverse the length of the north and south Atlantic, come over the south pole to land in Pacifica. By entering at a shallow angle, they'll burn up trying to follow us in."

Manning looked to Kane, "We'll burn up, too."

Kane just smiled again and shook his head, "Nope. We won't. Duralloy hull. We could fly almost all the way to the sun, catch some rays, and have a few ice cold brews before we would have to find some shade."

Manning looked over to Kane for a moment before looking forward, "Interesting analogy."

Marcus looked over to Marsh, "Make preparations for the run over the North Pole."

Marsh, nodded, "Very well. Prepping for pole to pole run."

Marcus looked back up to Kane, "Ron, calculate a high-speed, shallow atmospheric insertion. Try to stretch it out for as long as possible. They'll either disintegrate or we'll lose them in our ionization trail."

Kane nodded in agreement the whole time, listening to Marcus' instructions as he began working, then stopped and looked up.

"Where shall we make our final approach to Fresco City?"

Marcus looked over to Marsh, who looked back to Marcus and shrugged before returning to his duties of flying the Destiny

Marcus looked back up to Kane on the upper tier of the flight-deck

"Make our 'final' over Antarctica."

Kane got to work immediately. Calculating the required trajectory, it took him a moment to input the data before sending the information to Marsh's console.

"That's the course you'll want to take, Mac," Kane called down.

Both Marcus and Mac briefly looked at the data before nodding to one another and returning to their own instruments. Mac pointed the nose of the Destiny at the planet's North Pole and then, increased speed.

Then, from Joni's console, an alarm sounded.

"Oh, my God!" Joni exclaimed. "They're firing. I count 2, 8, 10…they fired all 12 missiles!"

Manning was now looking at the power readings of the warheads.

"All warheads are set to their maximum yields."

Mac reacted by increasing the Destiny's speed to the insertion point, over the North Pole. He knew he couldn't increase it too much or the large spacecraft would violently bounce off the atmosphere.

"Thermosphere in 10 seconds," Kane announced.

"I guarantee, there will be no impact," Mac muttered.

Manning spoke up, "Those warheads are equipped with proximity sensors. All they have to do is get close."

Marcus looked to Mac, "Guess you'll have to stay one step ahead."

"No worries mate," Mac smiled devilishly.

"All missiles are locked on," Kane announced.

Mac pushed a button on his console and the Heads-Up Display (HUD) appeared on the windscreen. On it was a graphic representation of octagons extending to the horizon of the Earth. It was a flight path that Mac maneuvered the Destiny to follow. He aimed the nose of the Destiny for the center of each successive octagon as it flew through each. The computer-generated octagons on the HUD began to twist as the ship descended closer to the Earth's atmosphere. Mac maneuvered the Destiny with the twisting octagons.

"A pair of missiles are getting close," Kane announced.

Just as the Destiny made contact with the upper mesosphere, over the North Pole, 2 violent jolts shook the spacecraft. Warning alarms sounded and Mac continued to fly his course

"Take us down deeper, Mac," Marcus ordered as he activated the ship-wide intercom. "All hands! Take your seats and fasten your seat-belts. We're going in hot!" He could imagine the view from the perspective of those in the Forward Observation Lounge. The wide, expansive window and the view of the Earth filling it up, fast.

"You think that by entering at a steeper angle, those 'Awesomes' will burn up a lot more quickly?" Mac said, without looking away from his instruments.

"That's what I'm hoping for," Marcus replied.

"You know they have shielding for re-entry, don't you?"

Marcus nodded, "Designed for free-fall. At this speed, it won't last long."

"Well, watch this, mate," Mac said as he cut power to the projectors to let the Destiny coast into Earth's gravity-well.

Manning watched Kane's display. There was a cluster of eight missiles closing in behind the Destiny followed by the last two. At the bottom of the screen, were 2 sets of numbers that were counting down.

"What are those numbers," Manning asked Kane.

"The top numbers is the distance of the lead missile from us and the bottom set is the indicator as to when the proximity sensor will detonate. Those numbers will turn red when the sensor goes active."

"Amazing," Manning whispered as he witnessed the numbers, indeed turn red.

"Proximity sensor is now active. Cluster of eight, now in a tight formation," Kane called out.

"We see it," Mac and Marcus said in unison. Just before the red indicator numbers zeroed out, Mac gave power to the throttles by pushing them forward, just in time as the lead missile exploded. All felt a slight 'kick' from behind and a low rumble as if distant thunder rolled through the Destiny.

Watching the display, Manning could see that the one missile had taken out the other 7 missiles but, the last 2 were still closing the distance. The numbers at the bottom of the screen began to countdown. Again, Mac cut power to the throttle controls, watched and waited. This time, he brought the upper-hull Helium3 thrusters online.

"Let's see if they can handle a sudden upper atmosphere course correction," Mac offered.

Marcus thought for a second, "By decreasing altitude on the Z-axis."

"That's what I'm thinking," Mac confirmed. "We'll have so much ionization around us, they won't be able to lock onto us."

Marcus nodded his acceptance, "All right, proceed."

Mac immediately began making preparations to engage his maneuver. Once ready, he watched his displays and waited. Manning could see that these pair of missiles was closer than the previous ones and he could tell that the flight-deck crew had noticed this as well.

"Uh..Mac.." Marcus began, watching his display.

Mac reacted instantly by engaging the RCS thrusters and the Destiny was pushed deeper into the atmosphere. Immediately, ionization flared, intermittently at first, over the leading edge of the Destiny, with the red-white glow illuminating the flight-deck. The automatic-tint of the flight-deck wind-screen reacted to temper the lightning-like flashes. Manning again could hear the RCS thrusters firing from Mac's inputs from his flight controls.

Then, there was a brief, bright flash and the automatic-tint of the wind-screen reacted by totally obscuring any view from the outside. A half second later, there was a loud 'thump' as the entire ship shuddered violently. To Manning, it felt like being in a falling elevator. As the automatic-tint of the wind-screen lessened and all could see that the ionizing gases were now constantly, flaring against the hull. An alarm sounded on the engineering monitor and Mac announced that the ship's thrusters were offline.

"Engineering?" Marcus called out.

Bruno answered immediately, "That last blast knocked out power to the distribution manifold to the H3 Cyclers. We're trying a bypass."

"Can we use the GD-projectors to slow our descent or at least hold our altitude?" Marcus asked quickly.

"With the amount of ionization on the hull, at this rate of free-fall right now," Bruno explained. "I would, seriously, **not** recommend it. We don't have enough hands down here. We need to reconfigure power utilization to the projectors. We're gonna need Ron, down here."

"He's on his way. Keep working on the RCS thrusters," Marcus ordered as he flashed Kane a quick look back. "I don't want the ship to start tumbling out of control."

Ron un-latched his seat-belt, patted Manning on the shoulder and said, "Save my seat, would, ya'."

Kane patted Manning twice again on the shoulder, turned and left the flight deck.

Agent Tobin made his way to the exits of the airport terminal. He noticed that it was not as busy as an American airport. There were still a lot of people here but, he also noticed that there were no individuals loitering around in long lines to board flights, which was common in U.S. airports. He had heard that international airports, the world over, had introduced some rather draconian security measures in airports, train stations and even bus terminals. For those meeting arrivals, this had to be done at an off-site building, away from the main terminals. The philosophy was; that in such places, you were either coming or going and if you were waiting for a late flight or a missed connection, you were to wait in a secured holding area. If you weren't leaving the terminal fast enough, terminal personnel would try to usher you out and if they were to become suspicious about any of your answers to their questions, you would be either escorted under armed guard out of the terminal or detained for further questioning. Entering a terminal was just as arduous. One had to arrive with an already purchased ticket from an offsite ticket-agent before one could even enter the doors of the terminals. Once inside, one could expect to go through as many as 6 internal check-points before getting to the intended gate to get on a commercial airliner. And the whole time, facing repeated questioning from terminal personnel as to destination, nature of your travel, length of stay at your destination, travel companions, etc. Questions designed to indicate inconsistencies in one's previous answers. It was rumored that security personnel at international airports, out-numbered travelers, 2:1.

It was a system first developed successfully by the Israelis' who, after repeated hi-jackings of other commercial airliners, decided to implement these measures to weed out terrorists from regular, everyday passengers. Since the Israelis' first implemented these measures, all flights in and out of the small country have been 'hi-jack free'. It took a number of years and several hi-jackings for the whole world to take notice, the beginning of which was the Sept. 11, 2001 terrorist attacks on New York and Washington.

Tobin looked to the terminal representative who met him in the hangar when the CSA Dept. jet arrived. Her job was to escort him through the many check-points to meet an awaiting car. As they approached each check-point, she revealed paperwork declaring his exemption and he displayed his CSA credentials. It was obvious to Tobin that the well-armed police and military security personnel rarely witnessed such exceptions. They were trained to observe and that, they did. Between each of the checkpoints, his escort waived off the questioning terminal personnel.

Once outside, his escort brought him to a black colored limousine with blacked-out, privacy-glass. There was a chauffeur standing beside it, holding a placard with Tobin's name printed on it. After showing the chauffeur his identification, the door to the rear of the vehicle was open and Tobin hesitated before entering. He sat down on the back seat, facing forward, looking into the face of the man facing the rear of the vehicle. He extended his hand in greeting.

"Agent Tobin. I'm Federal Defense Minister George Boudreaux," he said with noticeable French accent. "You may refer to me using my title or you may use, 'Sir'."

That, made Tobin raise an eyebrow as he hesitantly, took his hand and shook it. Tobin's first impression of this man was that he fit the description of a typical politician; pompous, "You're my contact, Minister?"

Boudreaux gestured for his driver to drive and then pushed a button on the console beside him to extend the privacy glass.

"I am. Our mutual friend, the Senator, asked me to meet you and to provide you with anything you require."

Tobin nodded, "It's appreciated, I assure you." Tobin looked outside, noticing a vehicle checkpoint in the opposite lane, leading to the airport. "Are we both to question Glenn Gowan?"

Boudreaux shook his head, "I cannot. My driver will drop me off and he'll take you to your meeting with Glenn Gowan. There are some security issues I must attend to dealing with the possible annexation by your government of our most western province."

"British Columbia, right?" Tobin asked.

"Yes," Boudreaux hissed accompanied with a facial scowl. "You know, your government could have the decency to politely decline the request for annexation. We both know the only thing your government wants, is the resources that province has to offer. It is not about politics."

Tobin recognized that he had hit a nerve with the defense minister. It appeared to Tobin, that he resented the fact that the US Government would entertain such an annexation from an ally.

"With all due respect, Sir," Tobin began. "I am not an expert on Canada/US relations but, your government passed laws and criteria several decades ago, to prevent any of the provinces from seceding from Confederation on their own."

"What do you know of Canadian politics?" Boudreaux's contempt of the man in front of him, now more evident.

"Its public knowledge, state-side, and of great interest to the CSA, since it would mean the US would be in control of the ports there," Tobin began as he continued his gaze out the window. "Now, I believe it was a result of the Quebec province's repeated and failed referendums to secede from this country to become its own, stand alone nation. With all the concessions demanded by the province of Quebec, this was inevitable. No one in your country even entertained the possibility of the crisis you're facing, today. There is no law forbidding it. Quebec will be its own nation but, at the cost of one nation and the benefit of another."

Boudreaux glared at the CSA agent seated across from him, "Is that the official view of the United States Government?"

Tobin looked the Defense Minister in the eye, "No Sir. Just mine."

"Well, you may be wrong in your, personal assessment," Boudreaux said dismissively. "The Federal Dominion of Canada *will* endure."

"As a guest in your country, Minister, I find myself conceding to your point," agreeing to avoid a confrontation.

There was a brief moment of awkwardness between the two when Tobin strategically and quickly changed the subject.

"Now, what can you tell me about Glenn Gowan that was not in his file?"

"I am unsure as to what it says in *your* intelligence files as opposed to our own," Boudreaux said venomously. "However, he is an extremely intelligent and shrewd businessman. He is a master chess-player. From what I've heard, he is a talented risk-taker, debater and negotiator."

"Does he resent his brother?" Tobin asked. "I mean, there must have been some tension between the two over control of their late-father's company."

Boudreaux considered the question's possibility and quickly answered, "I don't know. News reports suggest Glenn and Marcus feuded over control of their late father's company. A battle which, involved the Board of Directors, who sided with Glenn."

Tobin nodded, "That's good to know."

Boudreaux agreed, "Especially with what we know, now. It makes sense."

Tobin shot a look at the Defense Minister, "What are you talking about?"

Boudreaux stared blankly at the young CSA agent before a look of realization could be seen washing over his face.

"Of course. You've been airborne and out of communication," he began as he filled Tobin in on the meeting in the Chancellor's office and the video-phone call from a place called Pacifica and from space.

Hearing Boudreaux tell him the first-hand account of what happened in the Office of the Chancellor; Tobin couldn't help think that this was what it was all about. He also sensed that Boudreaux took pleasure in knowing something that he did not. At issue, it seemed, was not some suspected insurgent but technology used to get a spacecraft into space. He took comfort in knowing that the Senator would finally give him full disclosure.

"What was Glenn Gowan told about the purpose of this meeting?"

Boudreaux stared at Tobin, eyes narrowing, "That the CSA has received information that his brother has been conspiring to over-throw the Canadian Government, using the crisis in British Columbia as a spring-board for civil-war and has been stock-piling weapons for just such an insurgency. That the CSA is investigating the allegations and requires any and all evidence he can provide."

Tobin nodded, "You realize, we have no such evidence to support those allegations."

Boudreaux responded, angrily, "We are the *Federal Dominion of Canada* and we can do damn-well what we please, within our borders. The CSA has made up 'trumped-up' charges under the Continental Security Agreement to detain Marcus Gowan. The charges alone make him dangerous. We just extrapolated the charges. The CSA started this mess in the first place. And now, the Chancellor may suspect that she has a mole in her inner circle."

Tobin looked back, relaxed as the Canadian Defense Minister unloaded his personal feeling upon him, before responding. It was obvious that this man had absolutely, no people-skills and must offend a lot of people making such off-hand, comments. It was almost, surreal to him.

"Mr. Boudreaux," Tobin said with a smirk on his face. "Believe me when I say, I am not offended. Now, your country has laws requiring its people and businesses to register with your government and get permits for building and flying spacecraft, much less an aircraft. Your nation has even signed UN treaties and bi-lateral agreements agreeing to such. The reasons for this, goes back to the 'Cold War'. Everybody knows what everybody else is up to. Especially, it citizens. Don't lecture me about policies of an organization of which both our countries are committed partners. You understood the risks when you accepted your association with us. I suggest you deal with it."

"You can't talk to me like that," Boudreaux complained. "You don't have the right."

Tobin countered, "And you haven't the right to talk to me the way, you have. I am a professional, an expert. You? You may not have the same job in 5 years. As an *elected official.*"

Boudreaux seemed to deflate a little in his seat and rubbed his forehead with his right hand, "I'm sorry, Mr. Tobin. I have been under a lot of stress, today. Please forgive me."

Tobin took a conciliatory tone with Boudreaux.

"Look, we are allies. Let's work together on this. It *is* to our mutual benefit. With what you told me about what happened in the Chancellor's Office, you were able to see a bigger piece of the jigsaw puzzle of which, I have only been able to see individual pieces. That's valuable intel."

The limousine pulled to the curb, stopped and the driver got out, opening the door for the Defense Minister. He stepped out and turned and bent over to talk to Tobin, "I hope this conversation can stay between us. I don't see the point in repeating all this to the Senator. Can I ask that of you?"

Tobin smiled back, "Why certainly, Defense Minister Boudreaux."

Boudreaux seemed relieved and genuinely pleased that someone addressed him by his title, smiled and again shook Tobin's hand, "Thank-you."

The door closed, the smile was replaced with a disgusted look and Tobin quietly cursed under his breathe, "Weasel."

Zhong Xiao(Lieutenant Colonel) Jin Mah knew one thing. No matter how much rice wine one could drink, it was still cold inside the all-terrain vehicle he was riding in. And he needed to urinate. For 6 hours, he was bouncing around on his seat, traversing the length of a 200 mile glacier, slowing every once in awhile to cross a wider crevasse. He was looking at an additional 2 hours before finally returning to the main base. The vehicle was as large as bus but, wider and had 8, six-foot tall tires which was capable of adjusting along the length of its chassis to better traverse crevasses. It could carry cargo and about 15 personnel. As commanding officer of China's lone scientific research base in Antarctica for the previous 6 months, he had decided to break-up another-wise boring day, to accompany the weekly supply shipment to the outpost survey station and back. He had decided to take this assignment to better promote his career. He was regretting his decision. The People's Army had been for years looking for well-rounded officers who had a wealth of experience in all fields. Whether it was commanding an elite special operations force or babysitting a bunch of scientists on the ass-end of Earth.

However, these were no ordinary scientists. They had been selected to study the long-term effects of isolation of a deep-space voyage to and from Mars. The best place on Earth to do this was in Antarctica. Even though, China had made it to the Moon and set up a base, it was only semi-permanent. At best, the longest they had been able to stay was 3 months. The spacecraft, 'Chairman Mao' still made it's customary flights to and from the Moon but, only to keep up appearances to the world community that they still maintained a permanent presence on the Moon. Mah knew that the national leaders would only do this for so long. What they really wanted was another propaganda-coupe to top the high-tech accomplishments of the United States of America and its allies.

The Chinese Polar Research Station was the second largest in Antarctica. Second only to the US McMurdo Station. Publicly, the Chinese station touted 300 personnel but unofficially, 50 were well armed soldiers of the Ministry of State Security. In case, the scientist decided to change their minds about their work in such a remote and desolate place. Worse was the prospect of defection. The work here was considered top secret. Officially, China announced to the world that they wanted to study the effects of global warming. Unofficially, there were collecting data on the psychological effects on personnel for long-term isolation for the Chinese mission to Mars. And through liaisons with other scientists of other research stations, spying on them, as well. The best place to do this was the South Pole.

Looking forward, through the vehicle's windshield, he could see that Sappers Ridge was approximately 20 kilometers away. On the other side, 3 kilometers beyond, was the research station. Mah knew they were about 2 hours from arrival. He debated himself whether to order the driver to climb the gentle slope or let him drive the customary snow-carved roadway. The climb up and over the ridge would only shave off about 30 minutes of travel-time and probably use up all their remaining fuel before they reached the top. He decided against the order.

Above the ridge-line, he spotted flashes of light. He watched the same spot for a moment, and then saw another faint flash. He lowered his sunglasses and although he didn't see anything, he convinced himself that he was seeing sun-reflective ice-particles, high in the cold Antarctic air.

Raising his sun-glasses to his eyes, he was able to make out a contrail high in the upper atmosphere, accompanied by 2 more flashes. He instructed the driver to stop the vehicle as he turned to retrieve his field-pack. Kneeling down, he had to brace himself against a jump-seat as the vehicle came to a sliding, sideways stop, while he hurriedly, and dug out his binoculars. The other personnel inside the vehicle had watched him head to the vehicle's emergency escape hatch on the ceiling and open it. He climbed out and was immediately followed by a few including the driver. Others had exited the vehicle and stood on the ice. They too, each had a pair of binoculars, wanting to see what he had seen. One of his men had a video camera. Mah grabbed him by his parka and told him to look at the vapor trail above the ridge to the North.

"Film that!" he ordered.

"Is it an asteroid?" the young soldier asked.

Mah paused for a moment and wondered if it was a comet or asteroid. If large enough, they were as good as dead. Knowing full well, that the closer whatever it was got, and if it reacted explosively to the atmosphere, there wasn't anywhere they could hide.

"If it is an asteroid, it will be of great value to our scientists," he looked at the soldier to make sure he was filming. "If it is a comet, we are dead men because it will explode in the atmosphere like a nuclear bomb. Just keep filming and pan-out when it goes behind that ridge to the east."

Understood, Comrade-Colonel." The soldier complied.

All personnel continued to watch for a moment. The descent of the object appeared to be slow. Mah realized that it must still be high in the atmosphere and that its entry was steep. It was still apparent to him that the object would still make touch-down in the valley beyond the East

Ridge. They too, witnessed the object change direction, ever so slightly, to the West and back again. Mah noticed some of the personnel look to him from ground level; they saw it, too. Mah looked to the man holding the camera.

"Did you get that?"

"Yes, Comrade-Colonel," he replied, excited. "it is maneuvering."

Mah speculated that it must be an aircraft. Perhaps, the high-altitude, hyper-sonic USAF 'Icarus' spyplane. The aircraft was known to fly the upper reaches of the atmosphere at a rumored speed in excess of MACH 10. Any salvageable technology from such a crash-site could yield a valuable intelligence and propaganda coupe for the Communist Party of China. He and the others with him would be 'Heroes of the People' and have their choice of postings/assignments, anywhere.

The descent was faster now and the longer they all watched, Mah began to have serious doubts as to whether the aircraft would clear Sapper's Ridge, to the north, if at all. He wondered what kind of crater it would leave if it impacted the slope on the far side.

Mah didn't have to wait long as the fiery object barely skimmed the top of the ridge, kicking up wisps of snow and ice in its wake. Following the terrain of the slope as it continued to descend, fire seemed to leap from the front, steam and vapor, further obstructing their ability to identify just what kind of craft it was. And then, because of the slope of the glacier and the distance from the ridge itself, the object was no longer in sight. A loud 'crack' sound was felt more than heard reverberating through the glacier. Seconds later, sound from the impact, reached the group and Mah, from his vantage point on top of the vehicle could see plumes of snow, ice, and water vapor rising into the air. It was a few seconds before the group was able to see a large craft, at a distance of about 3 kilometers, come skidding past them at approximately 800 kilometers an hour and decelerating fast. Then, it was out of sight and the vibrations, ceased.

Mah looked down to his personnel on the ice, who were talking excitedly amongst themselves. To get their attention, he knelt down and loudly banged his binoculars against the roof of the vehicle. They all looked up in his direction.

"Everybody, get aboard," he ordered. "We are going to the crash-site."

CHAPTER TWELVE

ILLUSIONS

Glenn Gowan was signing his name to documents, furiously. As he finished one set, his assistant, Helen Schuler would take that set, to reveal another below.

"And this is to finalize the payment of taxes to the government," she declared.

"You means the 'kickbacks', don't you?"

She looked at him seriously for a moment before replying.

"No. Those Members of the Federal Parliament were paid as demanded."

Glenn shook his head, "Oh, that's right. I forgot. I'm sorry."

Once he said that, she looked at him more closely and noticed a stressed look she hadn't seen since his father's death.

"Where have you been?" she asked, concerned.

"Nowhere," he replied as he put his left hand as he signed the tax forms with his right. "Just….off in hyperspace."

Helen nodded, understanding. "I'm sure Marcus is fine. Doc would have called if something happened."

Finishing the last of the tax forms, he handed them all to Helen, "I'm sure you're right. Is Agent Tobin getting impatient out there?"

Helen looked up and stared at the closed office door for a moment and then looked at boss.

"I don't think so. I'm actually quite surprised he hasn't barged in here."

Signing off on the last form, he dropped the pen, sat back in his chair and sighed.

"Well, give me a moment. I'll buzz you and then, I'll see him."

"Will do," Helen smiled as she gathered up the form and placed all the forms in a beige file folder and left the office.

Glenn turned his chair to face the large, expansive office window that gave him a spectacular view of South-West Toronto. His corporate offices were on the top 5 floors of the 160-floor, Huron Tower Plaza. The base of which took up 4 blocks. Sometimes, on clear evenings, he would stay late to watch the setting Sun and look down on the city, already cast in darkness. He daydreamt for a moment, remembering the vivid colors of reds, pinks and yellows, from his last observation before coming back to reality. He slowly spun his chair back to his desk, allowing the mental image to slowly fade from memory. He clicked on his intercom on the panel imbedded into the surface of his desk.

"Helen. You can send in Agent Tobin, now."

A moment later, Agent Tobin entered the office to find Glenn Gowan, standing behind his desk, with his arms behind his back, smiling.

Agent Tobin," Glenn began. "How may I assist the Continental Security Agency?"

Tobin was taken slightly taken aback. Unsure, how to respond. He said the first thing that came to mind.

"By telling me what your brother is really up to," shocking himself, amazed he had even said that.

Glenn raised an eyebrow to the response he had received, smiled more broadly and offered his hand to shake Tobin's, which was accepted. Glenn held on to Tobin's hand until the two made eye-contact.

"I thought you spy-types liked foreplay before getting to the point?" Glenn let go of Tobin's hand and gestured for him to sit in one of the chairs in front of his desk.

"I have to admire that about a person. Blunt and/or direct."

Tobin took stock of the man before him. Glenn Gowan was perhaps, 10 years younger than he. Still had a slight build and a bit of a baby-face. He seemed too young to be the head of a multi-national corporation.

"To set the record straight," Tobin began. "I am not a spy. I am an employee of an agency funded by both our governments."

"Then why pose as a Canadian military investigator at White Alice?" Glenn countered, not being able to conceal the smirk on his face.

Tobin just stared at Glenn, not saying a word.

"You're wondering, how I know that," Glenn announced. "Lets just say that I have some friends in Parliament who know you were there and are not happy about 'cross-border' transgressions."

"Ok, Mr. Gowan," Tobin admitted, not wanting to get into the fact that he was ordered to investigate the site, first hand. "you have me over a barrel. It has been suggested that your brother is planning an insurgency against the federal government. That, for the past few years, he has been collecting weaponry to arm a small insurgent army to overthrow the Federal Parliament in order to prevent the annexation of British Columbia by the USA."

Glenn watched the CSA agent very closely. He could tell, almost immediately that this agent had doubts about the accusations. He allowed himself a slight smirk which bordered on annoyance. Glenn realized that Tobin mustn't play poker because, a big 'tell' was revealed.

"You don't believe the accusations, though?" Glenn pounced.

"It's not important what I believe," Tobin countered, realizing he had been read. "I was sent to interview you as part of my investigation in the hope of finding out what is really going on."

"And what *is* really going on, Agent Tobin?" Glenn asked, sitting up with hands clasped before him.

Tobin locked eyes with Glenn. Before him was a young man who played major-league hardball.

"You're brother has been deemed a threat by some very powerful people. People who have in their possession, powerful technology that they have spent a great many years hiding from the eyes of the world. The same technology you're brother used to build a spaceship. Since they are unable to dissuade him from 1; using it and 2; making it public knowledge, it was easier and more beneficial to them, to label and discredit him, capture and then silence him."

Glenn listened to the explanation provided by Tobin. For the longest moment, Glenn stared past Tobin, assessing the commentary.

"You mean, kill him," Glenn countered.

Tobin answered with only silence.

"That doesn't sound like an official assessment of the CSA, Agent Tobin."

Tobin brushed some lint off his lap, "The assessment is my own, however, I will include it in my final report."

"Plus any relevant intel I can provide, as well," Glenn quickly added.

"This is true. Now, we had heard that there was some friction between you two in relation to control of your corporation. We had heard rumors that the two of you fought over the direction this company should take. That you, with the help of the board of directors, forced your brother out."

Glenn simply nodded, saying nothing. Again, he stared past Tobin and then he slowly turned his chair to briefly look out onto the city before turning back to face Tobin.

"Agent Tobin, the same people you work for, have undoubtedly, been the same group that has been hounding my family for as far back as I can remember. I will not provide you with what you need. I think it best that your superiors fill in the blanks, as they already have. Marcus is my brother and I love him very much. What happened between us, is private. If he had, perhaps, committed a crime, I would have been the first one to turn him in."

"Is he a threat?" Tobin asked.

Glenn let a single laugh burst out, "Marcus is no more of a threat than you or I. He is a futurist. A researcher, scientist and above all, he's an idealist."

"Perhaps, that's why he's perceived as a threat?"

"Possibly," Glenn conceded.

Then Tobin set about surprising Glenn Gowan and watching for his reaction.

"What can you tell me about Pacifica?"

Glenn gave Tobin a puzzled look, "Isn't that a municipality in California? We have had no business dealings in that part of the States."

Tobin, satisfied that Glenn Gowan was indeed, being honest, continued, "It is apparently, the name of the island your father discovered."

"Agent Tobin, all I ever knew it as, was 'The Island'. And I have never been there so I can't tell you much." Glenn sat forward in his chair. "I know that after the first upward thrust and resulting tsunami, my father set about preventing any more damage around the Pacific Rim coastlines. My focus has always been this company."

"You mentioned a group that has been 'hounding' your family," Tobin inquired. "What group is that?"

This time it was Glenn's turn to watch for the reaction of the man seated on the opposite side of his desk.

"The NSA for one and now the CSA. Under the direction of a certain United States Senator."

Tobin looked into the eyes of Glenn and knew he had given Glenn exactly what he was looking for; recognition.

"I'm not sure I understand," Tobin tried to recover. "Can you be more specific?"

Glenn smirked, "Come on, now Agent Tobin. As soon as I mentioned the Senator, I saw that spark in your eyes. You know exactly of whom I speak of. The same man who has been pulling the strings for damn, near 40 years."

Tobin allowed himself a small chuckle, "Come now, Mr Gowan. Your not accusing the CSA of 'conspiracy', are you?"

With a serious look, Glenn replied, "About 35 years ago, Corporate Security apprehended an intruder who gained access from the rooftop. Total elapsed time from when he first set foot on the roof to his apprehension was ; 2 minutes, 38 seconds. He was armed with a single, silencer-equipped pistol. His orders were to hide and lay in wait for my father to return to his office the next morning to assassinate him. My father had him held for 12 hours and even questioned him, personally. In the end, my father was able to learn everything about this man, his entire life, his mission, job *and* his employers. The entire confession was recorded."

"And he was able to do this how?"

Glenn smiled back. "My father built a device that once attached to the forehead of an individual, is able to reach the sub-conscious part of the mind. It's actually quite amazing how receptive the subconscious mind is. And just as amazing, how easy it is to reach it and to retrieve information, without any adverse effects. His short-term memory was erased from his mind and he was released. His only recall of the incident was that he was caught and then being escorted out of the building by my father who, had returned his weapon to him, minus the bullets, of course."

Tobin thought for a moment and then looked to his watch. 5 minutes since he first entered the office.

"How do I know you haven't done the same to me?"

"Because I don't have the device my father had," Glenn revealed. "And quite frankly, he destroyed it before he died."

Tobin relaxed for a second.

"You and your brother couldn't run the company, together?" Tobin asked.

Glenn smiled at Tobin's persistence.

"Again, Agent Tobin. I will not reveal private matters to you or your organization. However, to throw you a bone, I'll say only this; in the real world, the world of business and high finance, when 2 managers are vying for the same top position, the unsuccessful one, always bows out and resigns."

"Was he compensated for doing so?" Tobin inquired.

"Of course, he was," Glenn replied. "That is a matter of public record. It is also the reason why this company is going through, financial restructuring. People have been 'laid-off', inventory has been reduced, costs have been lowered and our profit margin is once again, up."

"I see," Tobin said. "So, what are your brother's intentions, in regards to the use of this technology?"

Glenn just stared at Tobin for a second. It was perhaps the best poker-face, Tobin had ever seen.

"Agent Tobin that is something you will have to ask my brother, yourself. I haven't seen him in almost a year, so, I couldn't tell you. Whatever his plans, I was not privy to them."

Tobin realized that this interview was getting him now where. He was hoping to take advantage of any bad blood between the two brothers. If there were any, Glenn was holding those cards close to his chest. He decided it was time to leave. He stood up.

"Well, thank-you for your time, Mr. Gowan," Tobin extended his hand to shake Glenn's and the gesture was returned.

"I'm sorry I couldn't be of more help," Glenn replied.

"Apologies are not necessary. If it were my brother, I too, would be reluctant to reveal private, family matters."

"Thank-you, Agent Tobin," Glenn said. "I appreciate that. Good day to you, Sir."

Tobin turned and left the office and Glenn, turned to the window to look upon the city once again. And then he looked at the item that was in his left hand. It had been many years since the device had last been used. He placed in the left pocket of his suit and then retrieved the quantum hyper-com-link head-set from his desk drawer and placed it to his ear to wear. The device prompted him to say who he wanted to contact.

"Contact, 'Doc Thorpe', he replied.

Agent Tobin had taken the elevator to the main floor and was walking toward the building's exit when he checked his watch. He was perplexed that it had stopped. As he exited through the revolving doors, he shook his wrist and then raised it to his ear to see if he could hear the mechanism working inside. With the noise all around him, he realized it was a futile attempt at best. He spotted the Defense Minister's chauffeur and limousine. As he approached the vehicle, the chauffeur opened the rear door for him. Tobin stopped before entering.

"My watch has stopped working," he began. "Do you know what time it is?"

The chauffeur raised his own wrist to look at his watch, "4:25, Sir."

Tobin was puzzled for a moment. He hadn't realized he had been in the building for so long. He mentally, tried to figure out if he was in a different time-zone and then, he realized, he wasn't. Doing some quick math, he figured he had been waiting for Glenn to see him for 30 minutes with the interview not taking more than 10 minutes. That left him with the inability to account for 20 minutes. He looked out the passenger door window toward the upper floors of the building as the limousine pulled into traffic.

"Son of a bitch!"

The lights on the flight-deck were out and the emergency lighting had kicked in. flat-panel displays were flickering. Marcus was the first to raise himself from his seat, as did Marsh.

"You ok?" Marcus asked.

"I'm ok," Marsh replied. "Are you ok, mate?"

"Fine," He looked up to the second tier, not able to see Joni at her station. "Oh, my God…." He said as he raced up the steps, with Marsh close behind. The two reached the second tier of the flight deck at the same time to find Joni kneeling over an unconscious Major Manning. Stunned at the sight before him, Marcus reached for the first-aid kit on the wall beside the Operations workstation.

"What happened?" Marsh asked.

Joni looked up, "Ceiling monitor unlatched and swung down on impact. Hit him on the forehead.

Both men looked to the hanging monitor. The Duraglass face was unbroken.

Marcus opened the first aid kit to retrieve the smelling salts, "I thought he was strapped in?"

Joni accepted the smelling salt from Marcus, "I un-strapped him and laid him out here. No neck injuries but, quite the goose-egg on the forehead."

Cracking open the smelling salt, Joni moved it to under Manning's nose. It took about 3 seconds before the three witnessed a reaction. Manning hacked and coughed, even made a face as he regained consciousness. The three helped the Major to his feet and then to one of the chairs.

"I'm ok," Manning said while lightly touching his forehead.

"How do you feel?" Marcus asked.

Manning shook his head a little then touched the bump on his head, looking up to the device that struck him.

"Must have a thicker skull than I thought. It's only the skin that hurts."

"Here," Joni said handing him an activated, instant ice pack. Manning, putting it to his head.

The door to the flight deck opened and Paul Kane rushed in, stopping abruptly, followed by Bruno Kravakis.

"Is everybody, Ok?" Kane asked.

After everybody agreed that they were, Marcus asked for a damage report from Kravakis.

"Quite honestly, Marcus," he began. "Our first priority was to check for injured...haven't had the time nor the luxury to think about damage to the ship."

Marcus nodded. "Fair enough."

"However," Kravakis added. "I am interested in finding out how the superstructure of the under carriage held out against the impact."

Marcus nodded again, "Lets focus on the internal systems and bulkheads for now. If everything checks out, we'll move towards checking that out."

Kravakis turned on his heels saying, "I'm on it." Then, he left the flight deck.

Manning looked to Joni, "I'm alright, dear. You can attend to your duties."

Kneeling before Manning with the open first-aid kit, she put her hand Manning's

"Are you sure, Major?"

"Yes of course. Really, I'm fine," Manning replied.

"Well, I don't want you to move from this seat, without assistance. At least, for a while," she ordered.

Manning gave her a re-assuring smile, "I promise I won't make a move without you."

With that, Joni closed up the first-aid kit and returned to her station. Marcus and Marsh looked to Manning.

"I think she likes ya, mate," Marsh commented as he turned to Joni and winked at her. She stuck her tongue out at him. That made Manning chuckle *and* blush a little.

Marcus broke it up.

"Alright, let's get to work restoring power to the main systems and find out what kind of damage we're dealing with."

Manning sat quietly and watched as the bridge crew worked for about 20 minutes restoring all the workstations. Occasionally, calls were exchanged through the ship's intercom between the flight deck and engineering, coordinating the restoration. Manning was surprised at not only the professionalism but, the expertise as well. Marcus Gowan was clearly the man in charge and by what he observed, he was a fine command officer.

Joni left her station and approached the Major

"How do you feel, Major?" she asked.

"I feel fine," he replied taking the cold compress away from his forehead. "How does it look? Am I still handsome?"

She looked up to his forehead and smiled, "Off course, Major."

His turn to pause, smiling back, "You didn't answer right away, I noticed."

"I'm sorry, Major," Joni replied, grinning devilishly. "I'm not very good at subtlety."

He chuckled to himself, "Wanna bet?"

Marcus approached the two, taking particular notice of Manning's forehead.

"Doesn't look so bad, actually."

Manning, tenderly touched the bump on his forehead with his fingers.

"Major," Marcus began. "Ron checked with your personnel. Everyone is fine. There were no injuries. Lt. Stuart was notified that you were injured. He is on his way here, now."

"Where *is* 'here', by the way?" Manning asked.

"In Antarctica, approximately 800 kilometers inland, from the Atlantic coastline."

What is the damage to your ship?" Manning asked.

Marcus sighed and then leaned against one of the consoles, "So far, minimal to the onboard systems and we are about to start a cursory structural inspection."

"Well, If myself or my people can be of any assistance, let me know."

Marcus looked to Joni and then Marsh, who stopped what they were doing and looked back. Marcus smiled and made eye contact with the Major.

"Thank-you, Major. I just may do that but, I think you should take it easy for a while."

Manning shook his head, "Pish-posh! I'm fine." He then stood up.

Marcus nodded. "Ok, Major. I won't argue with you. However, remember this is twice now, you've been knocked out in 96 hours."

Manning had opened his mouth for a rebuttal and then abruptly closed it. He had forgotten completely about the previous incident.

"'Hmf'," he sort of grunted. "Right."

Lt. Stuart entered the flight deck and went immediately to Manning's side, "You alright, Sir?"

"As I was telling our hosts, I'm fine," He nodded. "However, I'll entrust you to keep an eye on my health to satisfy their concerns."

"Of course, Major," Stuart nodded.

"Sit. Rep., on the troops?" Manning asked.

"Everyone is fine. Although some of us thought we were gonna burn up on re-entry. Me, included. It was the best show in the house, though."

Manning who had been looking down, looked up to make eye contact with his sub-ordinate, "Oh, I don't know about that."

Stuart looked to the flight deck windscreen, "I'll give you that."

Then, a soft alarm sounded on one of the panel monitors on the Ops. workstation. Joni approached, sat down in the chair and accessed the information.

"Marcus," she said calmly. "You should see this."

Marcus, who had gone back down to the lower tier of the flight deck, returned to the top tier and looked over Joni's shoulder, reading the information. 6 kilometers away, a vehicle was approaching at an average speed of 20 kilometers per hour. It would slow once in a while and then pick up speed.

"What have we got?"

"Company," she said.

The word 'company' got Manning and Stuart's attention.

"Company?" Stuart asked. "Here?"

"Looks like it," Marcus replied. "Seems to be one of those vehicles meant to traverse glaciers. Heading straight for us."

"Must have seen us comin' in," Marsh said referring to the crash landing. "I wonder what that must have looked like?"

Marcus had a hunch, "Joni, bring up the topographic map of Antarctica showing our location and the known scientific research stations."

It took just a second for her to do as she was asked and in no time at all, they could all see that the Destiny had crash-landed near the Chinese station.

"Now scan the vehicle," Marcus asked. "How many onboard?"

Joni switched screen to access the appropriate program and began to scan the vehicle. It was obvious to all that the scanner was experiencing technical problems. She made a few quick adjustments.

"There are 11 people onboard," Joni announced.

Marcus stood up straight, rubbing his chin and jaw.

"Now scan for weaponry."

Another second later, they had their answer. Manning was the first to recognize and respond.

"Whoa!" he exclaimed. "Since when are scientists issued tools like that?"

"With that much firepower, we could out-fit our 2 sections," Stuart offered.

"Scans indicate 7, are arming themselves. 2 are not." Joni added. "Aren't they violating some UN treaty, or something?"

"Probably. Those 2, are the scientists," Marcus commented as he pointed at the monitor.

"Scientist don't have weapons as part of their standard equipment," Manning agreed. Manning turned to Lt. Stuart.

"Assemble the troops in the Mess Bay. We have a ship to defend."

Marcus intervened, "Major. I'm sorry but, I can't allow that."

Manning gave Marcus a puzzled look, "You gotta be freaking, kiddiing. Your scans show they're armed with Type 34 heavy assault rifles. They intend to take this ship. Rumor has it, they only take prisoners if it suits them."

"Major, the Destiny is Pacifican property. You and your people are under no obligation to defend us or this ship. *Your* safety is paramount. If it comes down to it, I'll destroy the Destiny to prevent its seizure. I'm sorry, Major. I have to order *you,* to stay out of it."

The 2 men stood silently, keeping eye-contact for the longest time and then Marcus gave the Major a wink of his right eye. It was one thing to take that kind of order from his superiors but, from someone who wasn't his commanding officer. Subtle realization washed over Manning's face.

"All right, Commander. I will, of course, abide by your wishes. I need to go and brief my people about the situation."

"By all means, Major," Marcus nodded and watched as the 2 army officers left the flight deck.

Mac Marsh approached and stood beside Marcus.

"Your slick, mate," he commented.

Marcus turned his head and smiled at Marsh. Joni, who was not 2 feet away, looked at the 2 men with a puzzled look.

"OK, you two," she began. "I missed something, didn't I?"

Marsh looked to Joni, "Marcus ordered the Major to stand down. However, that doesn't include any orders the Major may give to his soldiers."

"Ohhh," Joni said, grinning at Marcus.

Marcus turned to Joni, "Contact Doc. Let him know we're Ok."

Doc was seated at the Conference Room table looking at the image of Canadian Chancellor on the wall-sized monitor.

"And you are certain, they are Ok?" the image of Sheila Conway asked.

Doc nodded his head, "I assure you, they are. We are in almost constant contact and near as we can tell, the Destiny is virtually intact although an extensive inspection of the hull has yet to be done."

"How can I speak to Major Manning, on my own, directly?" she asked.

"I'm sorry, Chancellor," Doc began. "Unless you have the same technology we use, you won't be able to. However, any time you wish to contact him, I will connect you through us, to the Destiny. Did you want to speak with him, now?"

Sheila Conway shook her head, "Not, right at the moment." She looked down to her hands in her lap and without moving her head, made eye contact with Doc and smiled devilishly. "I needed to test you about the truth of what you said about having contact with the Destiny. I needed to know if you were stalling for some reason."

"Why?" Doc asked. "You know me better than that."

"Correction, Tom," she corrected. "I *used* to know you."

"Nothing's changed," he countered flatly.

"Tom. I am being told some very contradictory things about the fate of the Destiny," she began. "Things that, shake my trust of you and your words. I have been told that she was not only blasted out of orbit but she also burned-up on re-entry."

"Who told you that?"

"My Defense Minister, for one," she replied.

"And he acquired that information, *how?*"

"He told me he was notified by the US. Air Force, through NORAD Space Command and some advisor to the President of the United States. That the Destiny, was in the same orbital path and altitude as one of their Eagles. Attempts were made to warn off the Destiny, to change its orbit. All attempts at communication were unsuccessful. An, on-board command decision was made to fire upon and destroy the Destiny. The cover-story is that they fired on an asteroid and a piece of it fell to Earth."

Doc sat forward in his chair, looking down at his own reflection in the highly polished surface of the conference table, shaking his head.

"Chancellor," he said looking up to the monitor. "Anytime you wish to speak to Major Manning or any one else, just say so and I will put you through, immediately. Either your Defense Minister has been given erroneous information or *he* is feeding you, erroneous information."

Doc could tell that his old flame was considering his words, although she said nothing.

"If something dire had happened, I would have been forthright about it. There is no deception, here. Again, Chancellor, would you like to speak to him, *now?*" he asked.

"No, that won't be necessary," satisfied with the answer. "However, I would like to be updated on any new information you may have,"

"Allright," he began. "This is what I know, personally. As the Destiny approached the Earth, a US Marine Eagle changed its orbit, locked onto her while she was still eight thousand kilometers out and at 800 kilometers, unloaded its entire payload of 12, plasma-tipped Orbital Strike Missiles."

"12 of them?" she gasped.

"Every single, last one of them."

"Just so I can understand this, Tom," Chancellor Conway said, slightly embarrassed. "How did the Eagle change its orbit, exactly?"

Doc couldn't help but let a smile of familiarity spread across his face.

"You always did have trouble with science," he commented.

Sheila Conway smiled back, "Like you did with politics."

Doc nodded his head and then continued, "A spacecraft changes its orbit by decreasing or increasing its velocity, thereby changing its altitude. In the Destiny's case, by going to a higher orbit, they were able to increase the time they had line of sight of the Destiny to fire the missiles."

Chancellor Conway paused for a moment.

"Perhaps there *was* a possibility of an orbital collision?"

Doc shook his head, "I'm afraid the Eagle's orbit was equatorial. The Destiny was aiming for a polar orbit."

"Oh…" pausing. "You said that you knew this,'personally'. How?"

Without missing a beat, "We have the capability to scan objects in orbit around the Earth at short and long range. I was able to warn the Destiny of the Eagle's change in posture and we were able to receive real-time telemetry from the Destiny. The Destiny then changed her course away from the Eagle. The Eagle threw the first punch."

"I wish this information could be verified, Tom," She sighed.

"I know that all you have is my say-so," Doc began. "We intercepted ground-to-Eagle transmissions. However, you know me as I know you. You once told me I was a 'tell it like it is' sort. I have given you the information you asked for and will continue to do so, concerning your military personnel. I am not asking you to believe me. Just, make up your own mind."

Sheila Conway nodded but, said nothing. His words seemed to calm her insecurities. He always did have that effect on her. Someone off camera distracted Thorpe, addressed him as 'Doc', and handed him an electronic data pad. He, excused himself, looked at it and then took the stylus-pen, initialed it and handed it back.

"Why did he call you 'Doc', Tom?" she asked.

Doc smiled as he looked down. He nodded his head slightly four times before he looked up.

"Well, that is a funny story, Chancellor. Years after our mutual break-up, I studied political science. I also studied theology and philosophy. I hold a PHD. in all three."

The impressed expression on Sheila Conway's face bordered on shock. When they dated, he was a business major who was uninterested by politics and her rants about what was wrong with the politics and laws of the day. The two always had healthy debates about this or that, political process. He always saw the other side to what-ever point of view she held and it always helped her to hone her craft.

"So what's next?" she asked.

"As we speak, rescue and salvage teams are being organized. Major Manning and his teams will be airlifted out. Then, we go to work on either recovering the Destiny or we may have to destroy her."

"Why would you destroy the spacecraft as opposed to salvaging it?" Sheila Conway asked.

Doc stared blankly into the image of her eyes, briefly, before telling her why.

"There may not be time to salvage the Destiny. At this moment, Chancellor, armed personnel from the Chinese Antarctic Research Station, are approaching the Destiny. Marcus Gowan won't allow the Destiny to be stolen and turned into a weapon. He will see to it, that the Destiny is destroyed to prevent that."

"And what of Major Manning and his people?" she inquired.

"Knowing Marcus as well as I do, he has probably told them to stand down and stay out of harm's way. That this is *not*, their fight, Chancellor."

Sheila Conway nodded and then sat silently, looking down at the table-top before her. Doc could tell that something was on her mind.

"Hey," Doc began. "Where are you?"

She gave her head a slight shake, losing her train of thought.

"Oh, I'm sorry. My mind's been on the BC. Vote for US annexation. And now there are grumblings from the other western provinces to go the same route. Honestly, Tom, if BC's request for annexation by the US is granted, Canada is lost."

Doc nodded, "Would the US Congress decline BC's request?"

"Why would they?" she began. "They would gain two more major seaports, the natural resources BC has to offer, not to mention an uninterrupted coastline from Arctic Circle to the State of Baja. My aides tell me that the polls are showing an overwhelming 'yes' and that yes, Congress *will* grant annexation."

"Then what, Chancellor?" Doc asked.

Sheila Conway let out a sigh, "That is the day I offer my resignation to the Executive-General of the Federal Parliament so that a new election can be called."

"I really wish you the best of luck with that, Chancellor," Doc sincerely offered.

"Thank-you, Tom," she replied.

"When is the referendum, by the way?"

She sighed, "In a month."

"Well, you know as well as I do, that in Canadian politics, that is a long way off," Doc stated. "Things could change."

"I know," she agreed. "However, imposing the Civil Security Accords, 30 years ago, hasn't helped matters much. Demonstrations have increased. The media reports of military and police abuses are piling up with each day. They have become too powerful. If they get wind of Parliament attempting to rescind the Accord, they'll resort to fear tactics to gain political, media and public support. All in the name of safety and security. Former Prime Minister Uretsky left a hell of a mess severing all ties to the British Monarchy. Getting assassinated because of it, only made matters, worse."

"Look," Doc began. "This is your time to shine and become the leader of the free Canada you always wanted it to be. The Federal Dominion of Canada has become a police-state. Only in your position, can you undue the damage that has been done by your predecessors? Political reforms take years but, you have to remember, not all the Members of Parliament and Senators are corrupt. There will be those who will support your reforms to return the country to freedom and liberty. Then, all you have to worry about is the corrupt bureaucrats. However, I have to admit, it will be a long road back to democracy."

A smirk appeared on Sheila Conway's face, "Geeze, Tom. You make it sound so simple. Thank-you, for putting it into perspective for me."

"Anytime, Chancellor," Doc nodded, smiling. "Well, I must get my teams ready. I will call you back when I have an update. Now, are you sure you don't need to speak to Major Manning?"

"I'm sure, Tom. I trust you, really."

"Well, its about time," he said as he smiled broadly, gave a slight nod and terminated the video-link.

Diego awoke abruptly to the sound of the fog-horn of the Majestic Empress. He had sat up and then fell back to the bed and pillows. The patio-doors to the suite were open and a light breeze made the sheer-curtains flutter and wave. He felt well-rested and relaxed. A feeling he hadn't had in years. He watched the ocean waves from his view from the bed. Through the veil of the sheer-curtain, he could see a pair of legs stretched out on the plastic-resin, patio lounge-chair on the balcony. He laid there, admiring the sleekness of the upper thighs which were connected to the petite knees, the sleek almost aerodynamic calves and the slender ankles and feet.

The woman got up from the chair, left the balcony with the intent to silently enter the cabin as if she were a thief in the night. Wearing the dress-shirt he had on the night before, she slowly pushed aside the flowing sheer curtain to find her lover smiling back at her, awake. She smiled mischievously and then leapt onto the bed beside Diego, kissing him aggressively, passionately. He held her tightly.

"Good morning, sleepy-head," Annette said as she pulled away to look into Diego's eyes.

Diego looked back deeply into her eyes.

"I could get used to wake-up calls like that."

Smiling mischievously, "I have many different kinds."

"I bet you do," he replied and then he pulled her closer, kissing her softly to which

she responded by kissing him harder.

As the two cuddled on the bed, Diego noticed that Annette had brought in with her, the magazine she had been reading on the balcony. He reached for it and began flipping through the pages that showed the different decks of the cruise-liner.

What have you been reading?" he asked.

She shifted her position to look at the magazine with him, "Oh, nothing, really. I was just checking the lay-out of the ship. I've always found such things interesting."

"See," he began and cuddled tighter to her. "I knew it was a good idea to hire you."

Annette shifted and looked into Diego's eyes and felt his forehead, "How do you feel? You don't have a hangover, do you?"

"No, of course not. I feel fine," he smiled at her appreciating the caring soul before him. "I didn't have *that* much to drink. I'm surprised you only had one glass of wine."

"One was enough," she replied. "Being a former drug-addict, it's relatively easy for one to substitute one addiction for another."

"Even after your successful treatment?" he asked, sitting up.

"Well, I'm not sure about that but, I don't want to tempt fate."

"What about sex addiction?" Diego smiled.

"With you?" she said as she straddled his legs, facing him, giving him a light kiss on the lips. "I think I can handle it. Can you?"

"I don't know. I'm willing to investigate the theory, though."

They both laughed and rolled on the bed in a tight embrace, kissing passionately until they stopped at the ship's Captain making a ship-wide announcement over the intercom.

"All passengers and crew. This is Captain Kelly. We are within sight of land and our destination. We are due in port in approximately 2 to 2 ½ hours and dock-side in 3. It has been our pleasure to have you all aboard. If any of you have questions or require assistance concerning departure, the Purser's Office will be happy to accommodate you. May your new lives bring you happiness. Godspeed."

They looked into each others eyes and smiled devilishly, together.

"We have 3 hours," Diego said finally.

"I like how you think," she said.

They embraced and then took an hour to make love. After, Annette had gone into the room's small shower and Diego, sitting on the balcony, waited his turn. He was watching the pilot and tugboats approach the cruise liner, when she came out from putting on her make-up. Diego thought she was the most beautiful woman in the world as she sat in his lap. She put her head next to his.

"You seem distant," she began. "What are you thinking?"

He thought for a moment and then looked again, deeply into her eyes.

"I was thinking, 'what a woman, as beautiful and kind and as incredibly sexy as yourself, could possibly see in an old, broken-down and balding, techno-nerd as myself'?"

She looked away to the tug and then quickly back to Diego.

"That night you called, it was love at first sight," she explained. "I still didn't know if you or I would have the chemistry but, after arriving on the ferry, after a few moments, I knew we had a …connection."

"After losing Rosa, I guess I'm in shock that such a beautiful woman would find me attractive, is all," Diego stated.

"Oh, Diego," she said caressing his face with her hand. "I know how much you loved your late wife. I don't want you to ever forget her. But, I think you should live life and enjoy it, too. I want to help you, with that."

He pulled her away, paused, looked into her eyes and smirked.

"I'm not that bad, am I?"

"No. Of course not," she replied. "But, I have seen that forlorn look on your face twice, now."

"I'm sorry," he said looking down to his chest, knowing she had seen him thinking about his late-wife. "I was just thinking that perhaps it is time that I do, indeed, move on. She wouldn't have wanted me to keep grieving after all this time."

"I can understand the pain of losing her," she began. "Seeing you in pain, breaks my heart and I just want to hold onto you. To let you know it's going to be ok."

Diego pulled her close and kissed her. They sat there, on the balcony, watching the ocean waves for many minutes.

"What do you say, we go to the forward lounge, have breakfast and some coffee, enjoy the view as we approach the harbor?"

"I think that's a wonderful idea," she said as she got up, holding Diego's hand. "But you, need to get showered and dressed. Can't have you walking around the ship, half-nude."

Diego stood up and looked at himself. He was wearing nothing but his underwear and a robe. "I suppose not. There's nothing more terrifying than a middle-aged, balding, fat Hispanic man roaming the corridors in his underwear. Might create a riot."

Annette burst out laughing. She embraced him, kissed him on the cheek and patted him on the butt. "Get going, you tease or we'll never make it out of this room."

20 minutes later, Diego came out of the shower in his towel to find the room empty. A folded note attached to the mirror, with Annette's lipstick-impression lips, clearly visible, was addressed to Diego. He unfolded the note and read it;

Diego, my love,

You are cordially invited to join me at the café on the forward observation deck for breakfast and coffee, where we will enjoy each other's company and we can both speculate on the future of our lives in a new land.

Annette.

Diego first, smiled and then blushed as he folded the note and put it away in his bag. It was his intention to save it as a keep-sake. He got dressed, left the room and headed forward. He passed a few people who he recognized from the ferry out of LA.

After entering the elevator, he was joined by other passengers and couldn't help but overhear their future plans and the prospect of their new lives. The excitement was contagious. Diego began to think of the possibilities before him. The misery and grief of the last few years seemed to fall to his feet like a handkerchief, to the floor. He realized, it felt like it weighed a ton and was replaced with a feeling of warmth and affection that words could not come close to describing. He was filled with an irresistible urge to find Annette and tell her how and what, he felt.

As the elevator doors opened, he excused himself as he rushed past the others and walked very quickly to the café. As he entered the café and looked around, he found her sitting at a table, observing the landmass the cruise-liner approached.

Just then she turned her head towards Diego and smiled almost angelically at him. He approached her and leaned over to kiss her on the cheek before seating himself next to her.

"What a view, huh?" she said looking towards the island.

"More than you know," he replied without taking his eyes off of Annette.

She looked away from the island and towards Diego and blushed.

"What?" she said.

He reached for her hand and looked into her eyes

"I have to tell you something," he began. "These past few years….I have locked myself away from the world. Thrown myself into my work and my business. Anything to prevent me from thinking about the horror of that day. Of losing the best thing that had happened to me. Of Rosa, dieing alone. After justice was served, I still felt no relief from my pain. I, more or less, became a hermit. And a prisoner to my grief. As time passed…I found it easier to not think about that day. However, there would be times…at night…when there was nothing else to think about…when I found myself replaying the events of that day in my mind's eye."

Tears welled up in his eyes and he had to look away. Tears welled up in Annette's eyes at hearing of his pain. She held his hands tighter.

"Diego…sweety…its all right. You don't have to…"

"No," he interrupted. "I have to say this. To tell you, what your affection and love has done for me and what it means to me. I feel young…I feel drunk in your presence. Forgive me for making this analogy but, I feel addicted to you. I feel alive. And, my dear Annette, I feel love, for you. I never, *ever,* thought that…I would be capable of giving my heart to anyone after that. So, I am here with my bare soul and an open heart. I love you."

"Oh, Diego," she replied, tears streaming down her cheeks. "I love *you*."

"I'm sorry, my love," he said. "I didn't mean to make you cry."

"No, no. They're tears of joy," she explained. "All my adult life, because of my addiction, I was exploited, used and, at times, abused. As a junkie, I was treated with....contempt and discarded. I have never known anyone to confess their affection and love, before."

Diego was looking down at her hands as he caressed them, nodding as he listened to her quivering voice.

"Until now," he replied.

"Until now, my love," she agreed.

They both kissed and then quietly ate their breakfast as they watched the ship approach the coastline of the island. Soon they began speculating about what they were expecting to find in the form of quality of life on the island. Diego told Annette that he would be heading up a new robotic manufacturing company with an exclusive government contract. After ten years, he explained, it should be quite the operation. That's why he wanted to hire her as his chief designer. Falling in love with her was an added bonus.

CHAPTER THIRTEEN

HAI, HAI..

Colonel Mah was the first to open the door and descend the steps of the glacier vehicle followed by six of his people. Everyone was armed with assault rifles hidden beneath their cold-weather parkas. The vehicle was parked in such a way the he and his people needed, if necessary, use it as a shield. Moving to the front of the vehicle, he peered around the treads of the massive 6 foot tires. He could see no movement. He indicated, with hand signals to his personnel that the approach would be in loose V-formation. That, at the count of 3, by hand, they would all move-out.

When they began their approach, a few had made verbal comments of how large the aircraft was. Mah cursed them to remain silent. The craft was, indeed, large. In fact, it towered over the icescape. And it was long, as well. He couldn't take his eyes off of it. The only time he had seen anything that big, this close, were the Jin-class nuclear ICBM submarines in drydock at the Hulatao Naval Shipyards. This, however, was no submarine.

At 50 meters away, he could see their reflection in the mirrored surface of the aircraft's polished surface. He clearly knew this was not the USAF, Icarus spyplane. This was different. This was bigger. He realized this, might be a spaceship. He saw no external markings, no hatchway, no windows.

He ordered his people to fan out in formation and then, continue to approach the massive vessel. He could see now, steam rising from the base of the ship. The hull seemed to be hot, melting the ice of the glacier it was resting on. Further evidence, that it may have possibly been subjected to temperatures not unlike those from spacecraft re-entering the atmosphere.

Then, without warning, an opening appeared, approximately 6 feet above the surface. Internal lighting shining almost blindingly bright in the shadow of the craft. They all saw movement from inside and they reacted by stopping and bringing their weapons up and ready. External lighting came on and a set of stairs began to extend to the glacier surface with a mechanical sound. Mah's people watched him for his reaction and any orders he might give. He lowered his weapon and began making his way to the open hatch. They followed suit and began tightening up, in formation. In Chinese, he advised them all to remain passive and to 'keep their eyes open'.

Initially, 4 people descended the stairway with equipment cases and began working along-side the craft. They seemed more concerned with the hull than with the welcoming party that was approaching. Then, many more people began to descend the stairway. They were dressed in military, cold-weather parkas and they were armed with automatic rifles. These were clearly, soldiers. Mah advised his now nervous personnel to remain at ease.

Obscuring the view of the first 4 people who exited the craft, about 10 soldiers came out in an inverse V formation to meet Mah and his group. Mah recognized this tactical ground formation. If they were perceived as a threat, the inverse V allowed all to concentrate their fire on a single target or multiple targets in a tight group. Mah recognized that he was at a disadvantage. He mentally admonished himself for it.

The group stopped and remained stationary, watching them. Mah stepped forward.

"Who commands, here?" Mah shouted in almost fluent English, over the howling Antarctic winds. For a second, there was no reply as he looked around. Then a single, individual broke rank and approached him.

"I do," he said as he pulled the hood of his parka back, off his head and offered his bare hand in the cold air. "I am Major Manning. What can I do for you people?"

Mah took out his hand from his glove and shook Manning's.

"We witnessed your crash-landing from the other side of the glacier. We came to offer assistance. Has anyone suffered injuries, Major?"

"Who are you?" Manning asked, not letting go of Mah's hand.

Mah felt slightly embarrassed at not introducing himself, "Forgive me, Major. I am Lieutenant-Colonel Jin Mah. I am base commander for the Chinese Antarctic Research Station. Do you require assistance?"

"No, I think we're doing fine, thank-you." Manning replied as he let go of Mah's hand.

"But, we saw you crash-land," Mah said. "We thought we could render assistance and perhaps rescue any survivors."

Manning looked at Mah with a quizzical look and then smiled.

"That? Oh no. No. That was nothing. That was… a controlled, wheels-up landing. We meant to do that. We were testing the structural integrity of the hull on frozen surfaces," he shrugged. "It's a Canadian thing."

Mah gave Manning a strange look. He couldn't tell if the man was joking or not. The Major was clearly serious. He looked over to his own men and in Chinese, told them to put away their weapons, which they did. Mah turned back to Manning.

"Maybe, we could help you contact your government, to let them know that you have, put down, here."

"Really, Colonel. That won't be necessary," Manning paused. "As I said, this was a controlled and planned landing. My government is well aware of the situation and our exact location. I am, however…a little concerned."

"About what, Major?" Mah asked as he looked past him at the crew working along the hull.

"That, you and your people have arrived at what you perceived as a crash-site to, as you say, render assistance…" he looked around at Mah's people. "..only, you show up armed with Type 34 rifles." Manning now looked at Mah directly, eye to eye, and with all seriousness to make his point with him. "Did you really come here to do that or were you hoping to seize this vessel?"

"Major," Mah began. "We didn't know what to expect. I thought that if there were any survivors, they would have to be extricated from the wreckage and protected against the cold."

Manning took a step back, turned completely around slowly, only to face Mah once again. *"You* didn't expect to find survivors," he accused with a smirk. "And I'll just bet that any survivors you *did* find… would have to be eliminated for you to extract any useful technology to take back to China. It would be hard enough to identify the difference between systems damaged in a crash and those ripped out of its mountings."

Mah displayed shock on his face. Not at the fact that he was being accused of subterfuge but, at the fact that this man had read his intent so well.

"Major, we really came to render aid," he lied.

"Then, why the heavy artillery, Colonel?"

"I am their commanding officer," he shrugged. "My people were concerned for my safety."

"Against what, Colonel?" Manning asked tersely. "Penguins? I don't know about you but, I don't think there are any dangerous penguins within a thousand kilometers of here."

Mah stared blankly at the Canadian for a moment. He read Mah like a book and that un-nerved him. This was the first person, in years, who was able to read him so well. Mah maintained eye contact with Manning but, said nothing. For a brief moment, the idea of ordering his people to attack, flashed in his mind. It was quickly discarded. Again, Mah knew he and his people were at a tactical disadvantage. They might take out a few but, in the end, he and his people would be dead.

From behind Manning, an individual approached calling out his name. Manning turned to see who was calling his name. Looking at the man, the man waved for the major to come over. As Manning turned back, Mah witnessed him roll his eyes.

"Damn techs," Manning spit. "They think everything is important. Listen, hang tight. I'll be right back."

Manning turned on his heels and Mah couldn't help but notice the rest of the Canadian soldiers had not taken their eyes off him and his men. Mah had returned his gaze to Manning and the technician. Although, he could not hear what the discussion was about, there was something odd about the body language and the gestures of the 2 men.

As he watched, he realized the technician was familiar. This man was featured on some of the NEWS feeds he had seen at the base. That man was famous, he thought. Mah tried to recall the exact details but, it eluded him. It had something to do with the fact that he had inherited a vast amount of money and that it was speculated that he was fighting his embattled brother over control of some company.

Mah looked back to his vehicle, knowing that the 2 scientist he had ordered to stay inside were using the vehicle's surveillance equipment to record their approach to the vessel. He knew the camera would be trained on him and without saying a word, with facial gestures alone, he directed

257

the 2 inside to train the camera on the Major and the technician. After a few seconds, the camera changed positions.

Mah turned back to Manning, who after a moment, was finished speaking to the technician and approaching him.

"Is there a problem, Major?" Mah asked.

"No," Manning replied. "No problem. He just wanted to know where to set up the barbeque."

Mah stared at Manning, "Its minus 20 Celsius, Major."

Manning paused and stared back at Mah, "Yeah, it's a Canadian thing."

Mah knew first hand, how harsh Canadian winters could be. Once, traveling from the Chinese Consulate in Ottawa to China, he had a 24 hour lay-over in Edmonton during a prairie blizzard. A storm system had moved in from the North Pacific, carried by fierce (to him) Arctic winds and dumped large amounts of snow, forming snow-drifts. While he was there, he had heard that parts of Canada could get as cold as Siberia.

"Major," Mah began. "If you do not require our assistance, I must return to our research station. We have an outpost some distance up the glazier. We will be passing by here repeatedly. We will check on you."

Manning looked at Mah and considered what he had just said. Now, he knew to expect the Chinese or Mah was giving himself an opening so the 'dumb' Canucks would let their guard down every time they approached.

"Alright, Colonel. Maybe, we'll have you over for a barbeque, too," Manning said and then saluted his Chinese counterpart.

Mah returned the salute, "That is kind of you, Major. I would be honored." With that, Mah turned and gathered his men to return to his vehicle.

"Colonel!" a voice called out.

Mah turned to see Manning standing, feet apart, hands on his hips facing him, flanked by his own men.

"Leave the weapons, behind!" Manning shouted.

Mah looked at his own men, some of which understood English, the rest who didn't. He looked back to Manning, gave a quick 2-fingered salute and resumed his trek back to the vehicle. By doing that, he gave himself a mental pat on the back for being clever enough to not really agreeing to Manning's terms. He even smirked to himself.

Mah's group remained silent as they walked back to the glazier vehicle. Once the vehicle was powered up and on its way back to the research station, he went to secure the surveillance recording by personally removing it from the equipment and putting it in his jacket's interior breast pocket. As he made his way back to the rear of the vehicle, none of his people said a word. He found his back-pack and began digging through it and found the small portable play-back unit that he purchased before leaving China. The headphones were already plugged in and wrapped around the unit. He un-wrapped the headphones, put them in his ears, inserted the recording and lit a cigarette. He then, turned on the player and cued up, the moment the technician called out to the Major.

"Major," the technician said. "If I'm not mistaken, I thought I ordered *you* not to confront these people?"

"Commander," Manning replied. "I told that Colonel, you were just a tech. Follow my lead." He looked behind him and then back to the man before him. "And yes, you did but, you didn't order me to not order my men to hold these people back."

"Then what are you doing out here, Major?"

"Supervising," Manning replied with a smile.

"You could have done that from inside, Major," the man facing the camera said.

Mah could here Manning chuckle, "I had to come out here to delegate, Commander. And while I was out here, Colonel Mah asked for the CO. I answered. Better me than you."

Mah watched the screen more intently, now.

"Semantics, Major," the man conceded. "Promises were made to Chancellor Conway that you would not be put in harm's way."

"Consider it, the Major's perogitive," Mah heard Manning reply. "Look, Commander, everything is under control. We've made a strong show of force. They're backing down and hopefully, we won't see them again."

Mah watched the man look over Manning's left shoulder and then back.

"All right, Major. I will leave this in your capable hands. Shall I wander back inside, with my tail between my legs?"

Mah thought he heard Manning chuckle, once again. "That would be the Commander's perogitive."

The man smiled, "Thy will be done."

Mah watched the man leave the frame of the screen as Manning paused before turning and approached Mah.

Mah turned off the playback device and took in a deep draw from his cigarette. His mind raced. He had been cleverly duped by Major Manning. Manning had addressed the 'technician' as 'Commander'. Mah was impressed at Manning's cunning.

Mah, in the same situation, would have done the same to protect a commanding officer. He decided to replay the recording and did so several times. After several cigarettes, he realized the 'technician/commander' was not Manning's superior officer. The man was concerned for the Major's safety and Mah realized he had made a promise to the Canadian Chancellor that the Major would not be asked to be put in this very situation.

There was something that was not quite right. This man clearly did not act like Manning's commanding officer and having made a promise to,(not ordered by) the Canadian Chancellor to keep the Major safe, it seemed to Mah, that he had come over to admonish Manning for being outside in the first place. The chain of command was not followed, here.

On his play-back device, he had freeze-framed the image of the 'technician/commander'. His thoughts turned to the identity of the man. Who was he? What current events occurred that propelled him into the news media? He knew he was important, maybe even famous.

Once they returned to the research station, Mah knew he had to have a meeting with the station's Intelligence Officer to figure out this puzzle. He had some misgivings about this, since the man was a self-important, pompous ass. However, he was good at his job and was quite knowledgeable about current international events. The Ministry of State Security may even have to be contacted, as well.

After putting the play-back device into his back-pack and securing it, he stood at the forward end of the cabin and addressed the personnel on the vehicle.

"I know that what we saw was exciting," he began, pausing. "And I know you all would like to talk about it. I am giving you permission to do so. My reason for this is simple." He now had the attention of everyone on the vehicle, including the driver and co-driver. "I want you to keep this incident fresh in your minds so that it will be easier for the Political and State Security Officers to facilitate our debriefing in greater detail."

Mah could tell that some were not happy about that prospect. The rest nodded in agreement. "However, once we arrive at the research station, you are not to talk to anyone about what we saw out here, today. Not even amongst yourselves. Do I make myself clear?"

He received nods of agreement from all. One of his men raised his hands to speak. Mah permitted him to do so.

"Colonel, Some of us noticed that those soldiers had red leaf shoulder patches," he looked around to the others. "Those weren't Americans, no?"

Mah, looked down to the floor and shook his head twice, "Possible. As some of you know, I spent 2 years at the Chinese Consulate in the Federal Dominion of Canada. Those were Canadian uniforms."

Another man commented, "The Canadian's are flying ships like that? How far behind are we?"

"I wonder if they were Americans dressed in Canadian uniforms," another said.

Another added, "Only the Americans would have the technology to get something that big, off the ground."

"And the Russians," another said.

One of his men, who was sitting to the rear of the vehicle leaned forward to make eye-contact with Mah, "Colonel. Was that an aircraft or a spacecraft?"

All eyes were on Mah, "Honestly, I don't know. I have never seen anything remotely similar for either craft. I do know this, whatever it is, such a craft would be of great value the People's Republic of China. By taking advantage of this unique situation, we would *all* become heroes of the People.

At that, they all looked around to each other, realizing the implications of his proposal. The prospect of new and better postings, recognition, and more money, got them all excited. By suggesting this, he was able to entice their greed and enlist their support.

"Wouldn't the Central Committee have to approve such a seizure," one of the scientists asked.

Mah turned to the man, "Oh yes. And once they review the video recordings, I have no doubt; such a seizure would be approved."

Marcus leaned against the window-sill of the Observation Lounge, looking out towards the setting sun on the valley ridgeline to the North-West. Manning was seated in the front row, leaning forward, head down, elbows resting on his knees and hands clasped.

"What are the odds that they won't?" Marcus asked without turning around.

Manning looked up and sat back in the lounge seat. He paused for a moment while looking up at the ceiling.

"Remote," he answered. "I once read reports of numerous incidents of Chinese attempts to acquire whatever high technology, where-ever possible, by any and all means possible."

Marcus turned towards Manning, "I wish I could say that you're just being paranoid, Major but, I'm inclined to agree with you."

"Thought you might."

Marcus looked North to Sapper's Ridge, lost in thought for a moment.

"How do you think this'll go down, then?"

"The Chinese officer went out of his way to mention that he would be passing by, to an outpost at the other end of the glacier. He mentioned this, so we wouldn't be alarmed by their approach. So, we would let down our guard."

Marcus spoke up, "However, they know there are at least 10 well armed soldiers."

Manning countered, "Who, would be ineffective if they're caught un-prepared for a confrontation. They'd be slaughtered."

Marcus nodded. He knew Manning was right. For years he understood how and why adversaries in the business world would try to steal this trade secret or that technology, through corporate espionage. He understood, vaguely, how governments would also do the same thing by covert and/or military means. Marcus understood, very well, that Manning was providing him, a crash-course in the art of a very, hostile take-over. In the back of his mind, was the hope that the Chinese would not try to seize the Destiny as Manning was anticipating. Manning continued.

"One of 2 things will happen;

1. They'll approach as they said before. Make some excuse to stop by to check on us and attack then.
2. They'll approach on their way *back* from the outpost, checking on our progress and attack then. Either directly or by diverting our attention first and then attacking us from another direction.

I'm hedging my bets on number 2"

Marcus, still silent, just nodded. He had read or heard in the News Media that the Chinese Government had become more aggressive and ruthless when it came to acquiring technology, property and territory. He knew that no matter what government happened to stumble across the same opportunity, they too, would contemplate the same action. His father faced the same but, subtle, covert situations, many times before. He and his brother, Glenn, were witnessed to that.

"What do you propose, Major?" Marcus asked.

"We should never have more than ten of my people visible, outside, at any given time. You and your people can, of course, go outside and do whatever is necessary to get the Destiny, airborne. I will have the rest of my troops placed in areas that the Chinese will figure is an opening for them to attack. I have studied their infantry tactics, before. They'll see that opening and exploit it."

"I'm concerned about a nasty fire-fight and the potential for lose of life, on both sides," Marcus revealed.

"I can assure you, that the Chinese will not be," Manning replied. "To seize this ship, the only valuable people, will be the crew."

Marcus began smirking, "I thought I ordered you to stay out of this? Have you decided to accept my offer?"

"You did and as you are not *my* commanding officer, I am ignoring that order in this case. And the jury is still out on your offer."

Marcus had a serious look on his face, "Then, why protect us and this ship?"

Manning sat forward, "I've come to realize that your fears of the misuse of this technology are true or becoming true. By protecting the lives of you and your people and this ship, I am, really, protecting my own people. The last thing they'll expect are 2 fully-equipped sections of the Federal Canadian military. Now, I think a show of force is in order. One; they'll be so shocked, they'll think twice about their intended actions. Two; If they actually get over that, they'll be facing-off against 30 well-armed people who'll have a distinct tactical advantage over them. Their only option, will be to back down. I'll only authorize my people to use force in retaliation. Is that satisfactory?"

"Yes, Major," Marcus said smiling back. "Thank-you."

"Now, If you'll excuse me, its time for me to get to work," Manning said as he stood up.

Marcus left the Lounge as well. Not to follow Manning but, to head up to the Flight Deck for a meeting that was waiting for him. He had been heading there, when Manning had intercepted him. They had something urgent to discuss, Marcus recalled Manning saying. So, Marcus told his staff to wait 5 minutes.

Upon entering the FlightDeck, Marcus found everybody occupying all the seating there. Mac rose from his seat for Marcus to take. Marcus gestured for him to remain seated as he leaned against the hand-rail and stood on the steps at the halfway point between the two levels of the Flight-deck.

"So what do we have?" Marcus asked Bruno, referring to the structural inspections.

"Structural integrity is intact," Kravakis declared. "Minimal damage."

"So, we are still air and spaceworthy?" Marcus asked.

Mac spoke up, "Not as long as we're stuck to this block of ice, we're not"

"Can't we just use the vertical G-D projectors to pull use free, out of the glacier?" Joni asked, looking around.

"So much of the hull has melted," Kravakis explained. "into the glacier that no amount of pulling, will free the ship."

Kyras piped in, "As strong and secure as the projector mounts are, we'd probably end up tearing the projectors off their mountings, causing them to rocket right through the ship before they lost power."

"I have an idea," Kane announced.

Marcus looked over to Kane, "You have the floor."

"Well, I was thinking what if we excavate a large chamber deep below the Destiny, using the MOMEE. We could then 'laze' drainage holes connected to the surface, underneath the ship and again using the MOMEE, melt the ice from the hull."

Joni stared at Kane for a second and then she looked around before looking back to Kane.

"What do you do with the water from the deep chamber?"

Kane chuckled, "Why we vaporize it, dear Lyla, dear Lyla."

"Ahh," Joni said as she made a face toward Marcus and said "Duh!"

Everyone chuckled.

"Ok, Ron," Marcus agreed. "Fire up and roll out the MOMEE. I want you to get started right away. We'll be out side helping wherever we can."

Kane stood up quickly, "I'll get on it, right now."

"Just a minute, Ron," Marcus interrupted. "I need to discuss with all of you the conversation I just had with Major Manning in the Observation Lounge."

"What did he say?" Mac asked.

264

"He is concerned that the Chinese will return to take this ship by force. That those deemed a liability, will be killed. Any one of *us,* who are captured, would likely be interrogated until we lived out our usefulness."

"I thought we left that party?" Kravakis asked rhetorically, shaking his head.

"Get used to it, mate," Mac offered. "From now on, the enemy will *always* be at the gates."

"I hear ya," Kravakis agreed.

"If they do show up, we could just hole up inside until they leave," Kyras offered.

Marcus looked to him and countered, "Until they use enough high-explosives to gain entry to the ship at which point the Destiny may be un-flyable."

"I see your point," Kyras conceded.

"Major Manning says he'll have ten of his soldiers, outside with us at all times," Marcus explained. "He believes, that they will approach, check-in with us before continuing to their science outpost. They may mention that they'll check in with us again, on their way back. The Major believes that this is when they'll strike from the opposite direction."

"So you want to continue with the excavation, then?" Kane asked.

"I do," Marcus replied. "And when it hits the fan, I want everybody to stay low and out of the way."

"How soon do we want to be in the air, Marcus?" Mac asked.

"48 hours," Marcus replied. "That should give us plenty of time. Just make sure everybody dresses warm. Temperature outside tonight is going down to -35 Celsius."

Everyone nodded as he looked around.

"Well, lets rock."

Tobin was walking slightly behind the Senator as they left the Oval Office. He could understand the President's dismay about the the events of the report they just briefed him on. What he didn't understand was the NSA Director's anger of the events. It was like someone had let out the biggest secret and told the entire world. The NSA Director expressed the view that a mole may involved in his agency. The Senator presented clear evidence that this was not the case. The President seemed unusually calm about the entire briefing. To Tobin's relief, it had gone surprisingly well.

"How long has the President been a committee member?" Tobin asked.

The Senator flashed Tobin a quick smile as they continued, "The day he took office."

"And the NSA Director?"

The Sentator kept walking without turning, "Never has, never will be. The man is a Nazi. If he had his way, any non-productive, able-bodied member of society, with the exception of children or the elderly, would either be enlisted in the military, work-camps or in jail. Any serious criminals would be executed immediately upon conviction. In order to save taxpayer dollars. Any naturalized American convicted of committing a crime, any crime, would face automatic deportation."

"That sounds like the President's proposed Bill," Tobin mentioned.

"It's the price the President has to pay, for getting to the White House," the Sentator stopped and told Tobin, in a hushed voice. "Doesn't mean the 2 Houses will pass it, though." The Senator looked off into space for a moment and added, "Then again, with the problems the nation has been facing all these years, they just might."

"Senator," Tobin began. "I have to tell you something about my meeting with Glenn Gowan that I left out of my report."

The Senator looked at him hard, "Oh?"

"I can't account for approximately 20 minutes of my meeting," he revealed.

The Senator grabbed Tobin by the arm and took him into an adjoining but, empty hallway.

"Go on."

"All I know, is that I cannot account for 20 minutes," Tobin explained in a hushed voice, visibly worried. "I can't even figure when, during the whole meeting, that I could be missing time. As far as I can recall, the whole thing went pretty well, seamlessly."

"From start to finish?" The Senator asked.

Tobin nodded, "I think I may have compromised the agency, Sir. This device that Glenn Gowan described as once being owned by his father, I think he still has it. And I think he used it on me."

The Senator began to pace the hallway, saying nothing.

"20 minutes is not enough time," he said to no-one in particular. "to gather in-depth intelligence but you could have inadvertently revealed my involvement and that of the committee."

Feeling bad, Tobin offered, "He did mention 'a senator'. However, I can't say it was from me or his father. If you prefer, I'll resign immediately, Sir."

The Senator stopped mid-step in his pacing and just stared at Tobin, blankly.

"No. No, son," The Senator began. "I'm sorry, Agent Tobin. I was just thinking. It's not your fault. Obviously, you had no control over what happened. In fact, I've seen this happen before."

"What do we do about it?" Tobin asked.

The Senator came very close him and spoke very quietly

"Not a thing. Keep it under your hat. We won't discuss this ever again. Agreed?"

Tobin nodded and they continued to the exit.

"What about Gowan?" Tobin asked.

"Hopefully, he and his ship burned up on re-entry and that's the last we've heard of him."

"Do we know for sure, though," Tobin asked.

"No and we won't until I can send a pair of eyes, *you,* down there to confirm the crash-site," the Senator replied.

"Where?"

"Antarctica," the Senator said as he approached the opened door of the awaiting limo.

If Tobin didn't know any better, he'd think the Senator hated him.

CHAPTER FOURTEEN

STEAM MACHINE

36 hours had passed and the work was almost done. The Destiny was now supported by four pillars of ice at each quadrant of her hull. Underneath her, a large cavity had been excavated with the MOMMEE and below that, another large chamber, 200 meters below had been cut as well and was now full of water. For 2 hours they had to cease operations as one of the pillars had begun to shatter under the sheer weight of the ship. Bruno Kravakis' idea of using the vertical G-D Projectors to 'lighten' the Destiny was working and work continued. 6 hours after they began, a lone Chinese glacier vehicle slowly drove by; its occupants, waving. Joni, had scanned the vehicle and discovered that there were only 18 people, total, onboard. Marcus informed Manning that the game was now, 'in-play'.

Manning immediately went about implementing his defensive plan. Even enlisting the young Ron Kane and his MOMMEE to cut, into the ice, a series of fox-holes with inter-connecting trenches that led all the back to Destiny. He walked to and inspected each position. There was no way that anyone could spot his people lying in wait. The trap was set.

It had taken the Chinese vehicle another 3 hours to reach the outpost and four hours after that, Joni informed all, that the vehicle had fired-up and were now on its way back. That was almost 3 hours ago. Manning informed Marcus of how he suspected that the confrontation was going to go down.

The main Chinese force would be dropped off further down the glacier and approach, on foot and in the dark, slowly towards the Destiny. This would keep everyone's attention on the vehicle as it approached the Destiny on their way back to the main research station. A diversion specifically designed as the main force sneaks up from behind and attacks. Manning had even gone up to the Flight Deck to see if Joni could scan and detect anyone else on the glacier. She explained that she could not. The scanner was damaged somehow in the crash and could not scan more than one target at a time. She even had her workstation dismantled, working on the problem. She explained that if the Chinese soldiers were out there, they must be wearing the commonly used, winter thermal-abatement clothing and that if they were, the insulation would be too thick to get a life-sign reading. However, she informed him that there were 5 portable, hand-held units, used for mineral scanning, in the equipment locker in the Tool-Bay but, they only worked up to 500 meters.

Manning knew they were out there. He could feel them. His gut told him so. Marching, crawling slowly if they had to. Closer by the minute. It was a feeling he had relied on, many times before. Through the hyperlink headset that Marcus had provided, Joni informed all that the ETA of the recovery team was within 30 minutes.

Wearing his night-vision goggles, Manning checked each hidden position. The wind had picked up and he wanted to make certain that his people were staying warm. After spending time to speak with each group and provide words of encouragement, going over the plan and handing out 1 of the portable scanners to each clustered group, Manning stood and looked down the glacier to see if he could see any hint of the Chinese approach. Manning found the position that Lt. Stuart had found and jumped in.

"Sir," Stuart greeted his superior.

"Take a gander at this," Manning handed the scanner to Stuart. "Works to about 500 meters and we can network the other 4, I just handed out."

"This is cool." Stuart commented. "I wish we had these. We can see everybody."

"Certainly gives us an advantage," Manning replied as he continued to watch across the glacier. There was a long pause.

"You don't think.." Stuart began to suggest. "..that we could take one and.."

Manning sternly interrupted, "Lieutenant. I know what your suggesting and the answer is absolutely, **not.** Besides, even if we did, I seriously doubt

269

it would be in our position for very long. It would simply disappear like the White Alice Mining Station."

Stuart nodded and chuckled, "True…"

Stuart's field radio crackled to life.

"Movement! We see movement!"

The other 4 positions were spread out in a straight line, 50 meters ahead with the ends curved slightly forward to maximize the interlacing field of fire of their heavy machine-guns. The position that Manning, Stuart and 2 other troopers occupied was behind the middle 2. Stuart cocked his weapon and handed the scanner to Manning. Manning studied the scanner and it hadn't picked up anything yet but, networked into the others, he could. There were 5 glacier-vehicles, without lights, lumbering slowly towards them with 20 people each, walking amongst them. He couldn't tell it they were armed but, he knew they would be.

At 300 meters out, the vehicles came to a stop. This perplexed Manning for a moment. No one exited the vehicles. They just sat there. Had they spotted the trap? Manning instructed Stuart to send, via the section radio, to 'hold-fire'.

"Ms. Edwards," Manning called on the headset. "Where is that outpost vehicle?"

"Major, its a kilometer away and it just increased speed. It'll will be here in less than 5 minutes."

Manning did a quick calculation of when he surmised the action was to begin.

"Tell Commander Gowan, this is going down now."

On the other side of the Destiny, Captain Svanda ran up to Marcus with a slight limp. Marcus assumed his leg hadn't completely healed, yet.

"Commander!" He yelled over the noise of the wind. "You people need to take cover. Hostiles inbound, Sir!"

"I heard!" he replied as he waved for his people to follow. "We're on our way inside."

Just then, 4 bullets ripped into Captain Svanda's upper body, followed by the sounds of automatic weapons fire. Svanda dropped where he stood and Marcus dove to the ice beside him. Svanda, to his relief, was still alive and conscious. With labored breathing, he cursed between his teeth. Marcus could hear the other 9 CAT Team members respond on the port-side of the Destiny to the fire they found themselves under. Marcus checked Svanda's wounds. He realized that although Svanda had been hit diagonally across his chest, he was wearing his body armor. Svanda sat upright and grabbed his heavy machine-gun, unfolded its tripod and positioned it on one of the equipment crates and began firing at the headlights and spotlights of the now, approaching Chinese vehicle. It stopped.

By this time, Kravakis, Kyras and Mac joined Marcus behind Svanda's position.

"We gotta' get outta' here!" Kravakis yelled above the loud chatter of the machine-gun. Ice chips exploded around them as the Chinese fired back.

In between bursts of firing, Svanda replied, "Go ahead!" He let loose a burst of 10 rounds without looking back. "I got your backs! Crawl back on your stomachs as fast as you can! GO!"

To cover them, Svanda laid down an intense and relentless rate of fire on the Chinese positions and vehicle as did the other 9 nine troopers. The Chinese retreated to behind the large glacier-vehicle and began throwing grenades over it which didn't even come close to the CAT team. Then a flare, a red one, was fired, straight into the air from behind the vehicle. Svanda knew then, that this was the signal for the 2nd contingent of Chinese to begin their assault on the starboard-side of the Destiny. His orders were to hold position, here.

The vehicle began reversing slowly, away.

"Hey!" Svanda yelled out, firing again. "Where you guys goin? This is your party!"

Before entering the port-side hatch, Marcus looked back to see that Svanda had begun firing again. Once inside the four split up into 2 groups; one heading to Engineering and the other to the flight deck. Marcus and Mac found Joni directing her scans on the north side of the Destiny and advising Manning.

"Yes, Major," she said as she looked up at Marcus as he and Mac literally ran through the hatch-way. "Captain Svanda and his group are holding their positions. The Chinese to the South are retreating."

"Major," Marcus asked. "Are you under attack?"

"No. But the 5 vehicles are now advancing on our positions," Manning replied on the headset.

"Major, we're powering up the propulsion system," he explained. "When you and your people are ready to retreat, we'll have the cargo-bay ramp down."

"Will do," Manning replied. "Any word from Kane? Is he done, yet?"

Marcus looked over to Joni who, shook her head.

"Not yet, Major. We should hear from him soon."

"We'll hold the line as long as we can," Manning replied.

Ron Kane was finished carving the ice tunnel and began to drive the MOMMEE to the surface. He shunted residual energy back to the generator from the buffers. He used the last of the power in the buffers to create vertical trench in the ice ramp as wide as the tunnel that dropped 10 meters; a dead end to those seeking quick exit to the surface. While doing so, he looked out at his creation. The glare from the MOMEE's headlights and spotlight gave the tunnel, an eerie glow. Kane wished he had a camera. *A work of art,' he thought.*

As the MOMEE lumbered up through the tunnel, Kane had to gear-down the transmission for the wheels to regain traction. It was slow going but, 3 minutes later; the vehicle emerged from the tunnel at the surface

At first, Kane didn't understand what he was seeing in the dim twilight. It looked like there was a bunch of photographers flashing off their cameras on the port side of the Destiny. Then, when he saw the explosions, his heart began to race. He had emerged 5 kilometers left of the 5 Chinese glacier vehicles and he immediately, shut off the headlights of the MOMEE, turned on the thermal imaging cameras and activated its monitor. Sitting there, watching the monitor, he got a sense of what was going on. As per Major Manning's request, Kane used the MOMEE to create a series of 'fox-holes'. Kane then used the drill/laser to cut an inter-connecting trench, linking all fox-holes, including an escape-route to the Destiny.

Manning and his people hadn't opened fire yet, on the approaching vehicles. Kane could see, armed people walking amongst and alongside the vehicles. Their approach was slow and seemingly cautious. Kane suspected that they didn't want anyone to detect the noise that the vehicle's diesel engines would produce. He switched the generator back on and let the plasma energy build back up in the buffer. The power to the charger-coils was on a slow build-up and he disengaged the drill-emitter safeties.

If the 5 vehicles succeeded in getting too close to Manning's defensive positions, it was Ron Kane's intention to use the drill-laser to cut them in half.

He was hoping that the combined weight of the vehicles would collapse the roof of the tunnel he had used the MOMEE to cut below the surface of the glacier, effectively creating an inescapable vehicle trench. He had even made sure that those who would have fallen in, had a way to the surface; 15 kilometers North-East.

He had 5 minutes to full power.

Manning watched the approach of the vehicles. He could see the slow rotation of each vehicle's 8 massive tires and the Chinese soldiers walking beside them. It almost seemed comical as he compared their small stature to the vehicles. It made the vehicles look much larger than they were.

Manning became aware that those in the cabs of the vehicles might, from their higher vantage points, be able to see the fox-holes and the connecting trenches. He ordered his people to take cover. On the radio, he received acknowledgment. All four groups watched the small scanning devices in their possession. They could all see the approach and then the vehicles seemed to stop about 200 meters away, just before the tunnel Manning had asked Ron Kane to build. Manning had wondered if there was something wrong with the unit or had they spotted Manning's trap.

Manning stood up and peered over the edge of his fox-hole. The sky was growing brighter and he knew that soon the Sun, once again, would be above the horizon.

Then, as he was raising his binoculars to his eyes, ice chips exploded less than a foot from the edge of the fox-hole. Manning instinctually dropped down to take cover. The first thought in his mind was how stupid he was for giving someone such an irresistible target. He looked at the smirk on Lt. Stuart's face, ice chips falling into the hole.

"Not a word, Lieutenant," Manning said shaking his head.

"Please, Sir," Stuart said with his smirk growing into an ear to ear grin, placing his hand on his superiors shoulder. "I have to say it."

Manning looked to Stuart and paused for a moment, "Alright. Go."

"Did we learn something from that? Hmmm?"

Manning chuckled, "I know, I know. I knew better. All right, you ready?"

Stuart nodded.

Standing and opening fire on the five Chinese vehicles, was Manning's signal for the rest of the defenders to return fire, which they did in earnest. The Chinese soldiers either flattened out on the hard, cold glacier or retreated behind the massive vehicles which had come to a stop. They were barely given a chance to respond. Their only recourse was to fire their grenade-launchers from their Type 34's over their vehicles, with no effect. And then the Chinese held their fire. Manning could hear yelling in Chinese and he instructed his people to 'Hold' their fire. He thought it sounded like Mah, although he wasn't certain. Lt. Stuart smirked and looked at Manning.

"Sounds like unit cohesion is a problem, over there."

"No doubt," Manning replied. Manning picked up the radio, activated it.

"Stay frosty, everybody. Once they regroup, they'll come at us, like a pack of wolves."

He switched channels and contacted Capt. Svanda.

"Cat One, this is Cat Two. Sit Rep?"

Almost immediately, Svanda responded.

"Two, One here," the odd rifle shot could be heard over the radio. "Fire is under control here. They retreated so far back, we're out of their range." There was a pause. "But, their not out of our range." And then he chuckled, "Orders, Two?"

"Hold fast, One," Manning ordered

"Holding, Two," Svanda replied accompanied by him firing his weapon.

Manning joined the other 3, peering over the edge of their fox-hole. The sky was now noticeably lighter. He could see the vehicles more clearly now, and the soldiers hiding behind them.

"Yelling's stopped," Stuart mentioned to Manning

"Wait for it," Manning cautioned. He looked over at the 2 other troopers. " Lieutenant, take one of these fine troopers and get set up 5 meters down the trench to the right. Lets set up our own little kill-zone."

A devilish grin appeared on Stuart's face, "Yes, sir." He patted the trooper closest to him on the shoulder and continued on.

"Rojas! You're with me!"

Manning watched Stuart and Rojas stop and set-up 5 meters away. The both of them made eye contact and nodded to each other. Manning looked to the trooper left with him. Private Rozinski smiled back and turned back to face the enemy.

"Get Ready, Corporal," Manning warned. "This will be quick."

"I'm always ready, Sir," Rozinski quipped without looking back.

No sooner had she replied, the engines revved and the vehicles moved forward. Manning could see soldiers on top of them and before he could broadcast a warning, they began firing. The rest of the soldiers came out from behind the vehicles, firing intermittently as they advanced alongside, trying to keep the defender's heads down.

Manning aimed for and fired at the lead glacier vehicle's front tires but, his rounds seemed to have no effect. Then one of the forward positions fired a 40mm grenade from a launcher at the exposed front axle of the forward vehicle, immobilizing it. The other vehicles continued.

Manning was impressed with Rozinski. With her weapon set on single-shot, she was using her scope to aim for the legs of the Chinese soldiers she was aiming for. If she missed, she succeeded in slowing them down.

Then, in between the firing, there was a loud sound of ice cracking accompanied with what sounded like, to Manning, shattering glass. Both sides ceased firing and then 2 of the vehicles fell through the ice, disappearing completely. A shudder could be felt through the soles of Manning's boots.

"3 down, 2 to go," Manning murmured to himself.

He noticed, though, that the other 2 vehicles had come to a halt and those that didn't fall into Ron Kane's hidden 'Tank-Trap', either retreated behind the 2 remaining vehicles or were checking on those who fell in. Manning instructed Fire-team 2 to hold fire while the Chinese attempted to rescue their own.

Ron Kane sat patiently in the warm cab of the MOMEE, watching the events unfold on the monitor of the thermal camera. His contingency plan was ready. He was just waiting to see if plan A would work. If the 3-ton Chinese vehicles didn't break through the thin roof of the tunnel, he had excavated, he was prepared to cut through it, to help it along. When he saw that 2 of the glacier-vehicles broke through the ice, he chuckled to himself even though the other 2 stopped dead in their tracks. He aimed the camera at them and saw that the remnant of the Chinese soldiers stopped their assault and had now taken refuge behind the 2 working and the 1 immobilized vehicle. A few had crawled to the edge of the holes to see what became of the vehicles and those that fell in. It took a minute but, the remaining vehicles roared back to life, black exhaust belching from the exhaust pipes. The attack began anew.

Kane sat up and began flipping switches.

"You numb-skulls don't know when to give it up, do ya?" he said to no one in particular. After he surveyed his panels, seeing the green status lights, he aimed the cross-hairs of the drill just above the side-by-side glacier-vehicles. He armed the drill and clicked off the safety on the joystick, following the progress of the advancing vehicles. He pulled the trigger and pushed the joystick forward.

Manning was keeping his head down. The Chinese were laying down intense fire on all the defensive positions. He took the opportunity to reload his weapon as Rozonski returned fire. When she knelt down to reload, he stood and began firing. Before he knew it, she joined him.

"I love my job," Rozinski said as she fired off a series of 3-round bursts, making the Major laugh. And she laughed too.

The Chinese were now almost upon the most forward, 'right-hand' position. He began to concentrate his fire there and he was able to drive them back before they returned fire, sending ice-chips into the air, around and into his fox-hole. This gave Manning's soldiers in the forward right-hand fox-hole, the opportunity to direct their fire on the Chinese; killing or wounding five of them. The glacier-vehicles continued.

And then, it happened.

A piercing and brilliant white, line of light appeared as if lightning, running East to West, just above the mid-section of the vehicles. Manning observed that line of light begin to descend to the surface of the ice. As it did so, it also began cutting through the vehicles like a hot knife through butter. Manning watched as the light reacted with matter; white-hot molten slag, falling to the icy surface, geysers of steam billowing skyward. Chinese soldiers running away as the vehicles combusted. One of the vehicles even exploded when the light came into contact with its fuel tank. In the end, both were cut in half and aflame. And the Chinese soldiers were in disarray and running. Then, the light, vanished.

Manning looked to the East and could see Ron Kane's MOMEE sitting by itself. The headlights flashed twice to answer Manning's 'thumbs-up'.

Manning activated his section radio, "Cat Two! Mop up!"

He surveyed the field of battle. He could feel the heat of the fires from the burning vehicles. The smell of burning diesel and melting metal. The Chinese who had not run and were injured were being attended to by there own or first-aid was being rendered by Manning's people, with guards. Then he heard several gunshots from the other side of the massive spacecraft.

Turning and activating the radio, he began walking toward the stern of the Destiny, "Cat One! Sit Rep!"

Capt. Svanda answered, "Hostiles are countering, Sir!"

"On my way," Manning replied as he broke into a flat run. It took him a few seconds to realize it but, there were several other pairs of boots, running with him. He turned his head; Rozinski, Rojas, Stuart and 3 others were with him. They reached the stern of the Destiny and Manning surveyed the scene by counting heads. All 10 were still firing. Manning took point and led his group for Svanda's position.

"Come to crash the party, Sir?" Svanda said as he fired off a burst of fire at the Chinese.

"Ours ended," Manning quipped. "How we doin', Captain?"

"Holding, as ordered, Sir!" as he let off another burst.

Manning motioned for Stuart and the others to take positions with the rest of the defending force. He watched as they strategically re-enforced the already established positions. They found and began firing on targets immediately. One of his troopers, with a .50 cal. sniper rifle, let off a shot. Manning witnessed a Chinese soldier being ripped apart in a spray of blood and body-parts.

One of his troopers yelled out, "He shoots, he scores!"

The Chinese, still a long way down-range, tried to return effective fire on the defenders. Manning's impression was that they were disorganized, afraid to get up close, still hiding behind the protection of the only surviving glacier-vehicle.

Then, the Chinese ceased firing and he could tell that the vehicle had come to a halt. He pulled out his binoculars, bringing them up to his face. The last of the Chinese soldiers were boarding the vehicle. And they weren't taking their time about it, either. He witnessed some of them, literally diving into the vehicle. Then the vehicle revved its engine, turn hard left, and take a course around and away from the Destiny. Manning was puzzled.

"Now, where do suppose, they're going?" Svanda said as he continued to track the speeding vehicle with his heavy machine-gun. "Something, spooked em'."

Manning, who was also tracking the vehicle with his binoculars, turned back to scan the area where the Chinese were, when they decided to leave. He could see, just over the curvature of the glacier, what appeared to be heads bobbing up and down. They were quite far away, and with each passing second, he spotted more and more heads appearing.

Then, it occurred to Manning, he was watching the approach of Gowan's recovery/salvage teams. He smirked to himself thinking that the Chinese were scared off by a bunch of engineers racing towards them on snowmobiles from behind.

Before long, Manning realized it wasn't just a 'bunch', it was hundreds of people on snowmobiles. He continued to watch the retreating Chinese vehicle as it continued around the Destiny. Manning ordered the Cat Two Teams to let it pass as he turned back to the advancing recovery teams.

The machines didn't sound right. Usually, one could hear the whine of a typical small-engine noise but, Manning heard a high-pitched, high-speed electrical sound. Not unlike that of a turbine or turbo-charger sound.

Another 30 seconds, and the snowmobiles came to a halt, in and amongst Cat One's defensive positions. One by one, the riders switched off their machines and dismounted. Gowan's people approached, identified and introduced themselves, even shaking hands with Manning's troopers.

To Manning, it almost seemed surreal. Nevertheless, he was relieved they showed up when they did. He knew they would be unable to sustain a prolonged fire-fight

Manning spotted a man, dressed in military-style winter-camouflage jacket, assault rifle slung under his left shoulder; approach him from the crowd. The man was still wearing his snowmobile helmet and black-tinted goggles. He had a big, ear-to-ear grin and as he continued towards him, he removed his gloves.

"Major!" the man called out. "It's good to see you again and safe, Sir!"

Manning looked to Svanda, who shrugged his shoulders. He looked back to the approaching individual. "Who the hell, are you?"

The man stopped a meter away and began removing his helmet and goggles. He tucked them under his left arm and showed the Major and the Captain, the respect they deserved. He snapped a quick salute with his right hand.

"Lieutenant Chen," Svanda said as he returned the salute. "I'll be damned."

Manning too, returned the gesture and held his salute a little longer. After releasing his salute, he offered to shake the hand of David Chen.

"You were spying on me," Manning stated with a smirk.

"No, Sir!" Chen countered. "I was spying on the Federal Dominion of Canada and the Continental Security Agency. My service under you was genuine."

"Semantics, Mr. Chen," Manning replied with a wink.

"Of course, Major," Chen acquiesced with an even broader smile. "Now! Did anyone sustain injuries?"

"None, whatsoever," Manning replied. "How many armed personnel are with you?"

"20, Sir." Chen replied. "And we brought extra ammo. The rest are all technical or engineering personnel."

The radio crackled to life, "Cat One. Cat Two." Svanda picked it up and answered it while Manning and Chen continued their conversation.

"I thought there was heavy equipment arriving as well?" Manning asked.

Chen nodded, "There is. About 10 klicks behind us. We took off ahead after receiving the distress call from Commander Gowan."

Svanda interrupted, "Major! Cat Two reports remaining Chinese force has retrieved their KIA's and WIA's and are bugging out."

He turned to Svanda, "Very well. Post guards, though. Once they link up with those other 2 vehicles, they'll be back." He turned back to Chen, "I think the Destiny is close to being freed from the ice. Everybody has been working for 36 hours, straight. With little or no sleep. You may not need that heavy equipment."

"No, we won't," a voice agreed from behind them. The three of them turned to see Marcus approaching. "I've ordered the heavy-lift salvage equipment back to their planes and I want everybody here, to load their equipment and board the Destiny. Lift-off, in 20 minutes."

CHAPTER FIFTEEN

TEARS OF AN ANGEL

The Destiny sat alone on the glacier, with the exception of the still burning, Chinese vehicles. All equipment and personnel were now aboard her. Then, her massive thrusters roared to life, sending exhaust and steam plumes belching into the air. Below her, the 4 columns of ice, immediately began to melt at the presence of thermal, radiant heat. The bottom of the hull snapped free finally, of the ice-columns, with the help of the G-D projectors, keeping the entire vessel stabilized in mid-air.

Ever so slowly, The Destiny rose higher and higher. As she did so, there was a slight glow to her hull, sunlight reflecting off her Duralloy hull. Below her, the hole in the glacier was filling fast with water.

3 kilometers away, the remaining Chinese vehicles were racing back to the scene, making a counter-attack. It didn't matter, really. They were still too far away. On all 3 vehicles, there was at least 1 soldier poised in the roof-top escape hatch firing their weapons in the hope of damaging the ascending spacecraft.

Over the North-Western valley ridge, a helicopter appeared and descended to the glacier surface. The helicopter, sent out under orders from the Continental Security Agency from the US McMurdo Sound Research Station had only 2 occupants onboard; the pilot and Agent Tobin. Upon spotting the rising spacecraft, 10 kilometers away, Tobin frantically began to dig in his back-pack for his camera. He ordered the pilot to level out so he could snap some pictures. He first found his video camera and then the digital camera, turned and sat with both. In one combined move, he switched on, both. Mounting the vid-cam on the dash, he began snapping off pictures with the digital camera. He asked the pilot to hover so he could use the vid-cam. When he did so, Tobin centered the spacecraft in the center of the camera's small monitor-screen.

Tobin spotted 3 vehicles approaching the rising spacecraft, seeing tracer rounds streaking from them, striking the hull. He snapped a few pictures of them, too. And when he turned the camera back to spacecraft, it was gone. The only evidence that it was ever there, was the still rising steam plumes from the glacier.

Tobin suggested to the pilot that they leave before they too, found themselves fired upon. The pilot reacted immediately by banking the helicopter to the right and gaining altitude.

Manning once again found himself on the flight deck of the Destiny, standing beside David Chen. They all watched as clouds flew by faster than any jet he had seen. At hypersonic speeds, the ship climbed higher and higher before leveling out.

"Where to, Commander?" Manning asked from the upper tier of the flight deck.

Marcus secured his station and climbed the steps from the lower tier, "To our new home."

Manning looked around to all on the flight deck. David Chen had a smile on his face which puzzled him.

"I..I don't understand," he replied. "I thought my people and I were being dropped off in a neutral country?"

"You will be, Major," Chen assured him.

"Before that, however," Marcus continued. "we would like to invite you and your personnel to enjoy some R&R as guests of the Pacifican Government, to help you and them 'wind down'. Consider the gesture a, 'Thank-you' for helping to defend us, this spacecraft and the technology."

In the old days, troops returning from overseas theater of operations, would first enjoy a stop-over in some tropical paradise to help facilitate the relief stress and any healing of minor injuries. Manning remembered those days. That didn't happen any more. Not since the Federal Dominion of Canada came into existence all those years ago. The government felt that training and indoctrination was its own medicine. His troops put up a good fight. They followed his orders. They stuck their necks out for him, without reservation. As the outgoing CO of the Canadian Anti-terrorist Team, he was going to reward them, damn it. He owed them that.

"On behalf of my troopers, Commander," Manning began, shaking Marcus' hand. "I accept your offer."

Marcus patted Manning on the shoulder excitedly, "Fantastic! You'll enjoy yourselves, I promise," he said as descended the steps to the lower tier.

Manning turned to Joni, "How soon before we're there?"

Joni smiled at Manning, turned to her work station, hit a few keystrokes on her keyboard and turned back to him with her hands folded in her lap. The largest of the monitors flickered to life.

We're almost there, Major."

Manning approached the monitor. The exterior camera, pointed to the surface of the Earth, only showed thin, high atmospheric cirrus clouds. He could tell the Destiny was moving fast. The thin, wispy and narrow bands of cloud partially obscured the surface. The longer he watched, the cirrus clouds began to thin out and before his eyes, a landmass appeared, filling up the entire monitor. Sunlight bathed the entire island from coast to coast, North to South. He could see low altitude clouds in the interior amongst the mountain range and the foothills. It looked almost beautiful to him. This realization surprised him.

"What's our altitude?" Manning asked.

Joni looked to her displays, "50 kilometers."

"Amazing," Manning whispered.

Manning could tell now, that the Destiny was beginning its descent. He turned to watch Marcus and Mackenzie work. The professionalism between the two was unlike anything he seen previously from the two. Communication between the Destiny and the airport tower in Fresco City was piped through the ship-wide intercom for all to hear. Doc Thorpe could even be heard, explaining that thousands were waiting at the airport for the arrival of the Destiny. He further explained that the exploits of Manning and his CAT Teams had now become public and a big party was planned for them. Manning blushed; feeling slightly embarrassed.

Joni saw this, "Major, are you blushing?"

Manning looked at Joni ready to deny it, then changed his mind, smiling.

"I am. However, if it leaves the bridge, I'll deny it."

With each passing moment, the Destiny descended ever closer to the surface of the Earth, to Pacifica. The spacecraft wasn't bleeding off speed but, actually using the G-D projectors to slow velocity. Soon, the Destiny was skimming the surface of the ocean, flying at supersonic speeds. 8 kilometers out, North of Fresco City, the Destiny climbed to a higher altitude and all could see, for the first time, the layout of the area. The airport was dead-ahead. Mackenzie brought the Destiny in for a low, slow pass, East to West over the throngs of people, waiting at the airport.

The crowds responded with cheers and whistling. Make-shift banners waving in the air. People jumping up and down, excitedly.

The Destiny looped back around for its final approach, coming in low and slow from the North, heading directly for the crowds. The Destiny came to a full stop, hovering 3 meters above the tarmac, when the landing-struts extended and before she touched down, Mackenzie side-slipped the ship so the port-side faced the crowd.

The crowd went wild with even more cheers, whistling and clapping hands. An all-female, tribal African vocal group was singing a traditional chant which soon infected and spread through the crowd.

The main personnel hatchway opened and the hatch-stairs automatically descended to the tarmac. The singing stopped and the crowd became silent, waiting to see who was to appear first.

Then, the man they had all waited for, appeared from the shadow of the hatchway and stepped out into sunlight. The crowd roared to life. Marcus Gowan waved to the crowd and then descended the stairs to the tarmac, followed immediately by his flight-crew. The cheering continued.

A utility-vehicle towing a trailer with a podium, drove onto the tarmac and stopped about 5 meters before the crowds. Doc Thorpe exited the vehicle and jumped up onto the trailer, stood at the podium and activate the wireless microphone.

"Ladies and gentlemen." Doc looked back at the approaching Marcus Gowan, who had a big smile on his face. He turned to re-address the crowd, "Citizens of Pacifica. Please welcome home, the man who has given us all, our new lives. Marcus Gowan."

By this time, Marcus was standing behind Thorpe. He shook Thorpe's hand, they quickly patted each other on the back.

Marcus stood at the podium, savoring the adulation from the crowd. It was several minutes before silence reigned.

"Wow, So much for sneaking in." The crowd responded with laughter and cheers. "Thank-you. Thank-you, **all,** for this incredibly, warm home-coming." He paused for a moment, looking at the crowd and then continued.

"I want to say first, that this dream of mine, first began with my father. Without him, he would not have sown the seeds that would become this nation and the people that inhabit it. Without your creativity, without your commitment, your *own* personal risk and without *your* determination; this nation, *this day,* would only be a dream. We come from all walks of life. A diverse mixture of cultures, skills and life experiences. Our lives before, seemed without purpose. For some of you, existence was day to day. A struggle. Through our individual tragedies, we each felt we had an unknown destination on this road to utopia. And believe me, It is good to see the smiles. It is *you,* who have shown *me* the way, of what we are and what we can become. It is *I,* who is grateful and in *your* debt. *It* is *I,* who applauds *you!*"

Marcus stepped away from the podium and began to clap his hands together. The crowd responded with even louder cheers and whistles. After a moment, Marcus returned to the podium. He turned to Thorpe and nodded. Doc Thorpe then turned to one of his aides to cue those waiting inside the Destiny to exit.

Very quickly, one by one, the 30-odd members of the Federal Canadian Anti-terrorist Team, fell into formation, at attention, to the right of the trailer Marcus was addressing the crowd from.

"Ladies and gentlemen," Marcus said as he looked at Manning's formation and quickly back to the crowd. "Allow me to introduce to you, the Canadian military personnel who put their lives; without being asked to, ahead of the crew of the Destiny and secured our safe return and helped us safeguard the technology of the Destiny."

Manning stepped forward, "Company! For-ward! Atten-tion!"

His people stepped forward in unison, and stood at attention.

The crowd went wild and after a moment, Marcus announced they had earned R & R and were invited as his personal guests on Pacifica for a week before being returned to Canada via an as yet, to be determined, neutral country.

Manning faced Marcus and saluted him. Marcus responded by 'holding and then releasing the salute. Returning to the microphone, he spotted Kyle Latavish on the same stage as the tribal musical group.

"I would like to announce, as well, tomorrow as a national holiday, so…let the music begin," giving the cue to Kyle Latavish who began a couple of quick guitar-rifts, to get the crowd's attention.

"They should hear this party, all over the world," Latavish began and the crowd went wild.

Three weeks later, Major Manning sat alone in the debriefing room at Department of Federal Defense. He looked straight ahead at his reflection in the one-way glass. This was just a formality; he knew his fate had already been decided. He had instructed his people to say they were following his orders. He was prepared to face the music alone. To sacrifice himself and fall on his sword, if need be.

A lone male entered the room holding a clipboard and sat down at the table across from Manning. The man didn't say anything at first; he just read the sheets on the clipboard.

"Good morning, Major," the man finally said. "I am Mr. Tobin. I have a few questions concerning your original debriefing."

'This ought to be good,' Manning thought to himself. "I understand."

"In your report," Tobin was reading from the clipboard. "You stated that you alone decided that, to seize control of the spacecraft, would not only place your government in danger of breaking international law but, endanger the lives of the personnel under your command. Is that correct?"

Manning smirked as he made eye contact with Tobin.

"You have the transcripts in front of you. You tell me."

Tobin raised his left eyebrow at Manning, saying nothing at first. "Do you recall your statement?"

"I do," Manning said flatly.

"You had orders to arrest and detain Marcus Gowan," Tobin said as he read from a separate sheet of paper. "Yet, you chose not to take the spaceship by force, as you and your men stated you were about to do. Was that the moment, you decided to disobey your orders, Major?"

Manning could see where this was going. Someone in the Federal Parliament didn't like the fact that a serving field officer could not only think for himself and consider the troops he served with, but think of the impact of an illegal action of the government he served. Manning sat in silence, staring at the man before him.

"I'm sorry," Manning said finally, "You're who, exactly?"

Tobin reached into the inside pocket of his suit-jacket and handed him a CSA business-card. Manning read it, sat back and smirked to himself.

Between 2 fingers, he flicked the card back to Tobin, spinning when it landed on the table.

"Mister Tobin." Manning sneered. "I exercise my rights as a serving military officer of the Federal Parliament, to refuse further questioning."

"And why is that, Major?" Tobin asked

"Don't take me the wrong way, Mr. Tobin. You're probably a real nice guy but, you're merely an agency analyst, a civilian. And protocol states, I don't have to answer your questions."

"It's just a few questions, Major," Tobin explained.

"No!" Manning stated calmly. "It's an inquisition." He sat forward, with his hands folded between them. "I will re-iterate my position so you will fully comprehend and understand this 'witch-hunt'. I...don't... answer...to you."

There were two knocks on the one-way glass behind Tobin to which, he immediately began gathering up his paperwork. Without a word, he stood up and approached the door which was opened for him from the outside. He stepped through and was gone only to be replaced by a portly-looking man in an expensive but, ill-fitting suit. He closed the door behind him. There was a quick, surprised flash of recognition on Manning's face, quickly replaced with a frown.

"Well that figures.." Manning said shaking his head.

"And what is that, Major?"

"You, pulling Tobin's strings. Its so,...*you."* Manning stated.

"You know nothing about me!" Minister of Federal Defense, George Boudreaux said loudly.

"Oh, I know enough," Manning stated with certainty. *"You're* the same manipulative weasel I blew the whistle on, 20 years ago, for blaming *his* training mistakes on soldiers who knew how to get the job down. You acted, criminally; I just forced you to face the consequences of your actions."

Still standing before Manning, Boudreaux's fists clenched.

"You got me court-martialed, old man." Boudreaux complained through clenched teeth.

Manning, with a stern look, replied, "And you thought it was the right thing, to have those under *my* command, court-martialed for your incompetence?"

"Well, now that I am the Minister of the Department of Federal Defense, I can have you court-martialed for disobeying orders."

"Congratulations Minister, you found your true calling," Manning replied sarcastically.

"You don't believe me?" Boudreaux asked, incredulously.

"Minister," Manning smiled confidently. "If you were going to court-martial me, you wouldn't be standing there; talking outta' your ass. You want to. Badly enough to satisfy your revenge. But, you don't have the support of the Chancellor nor that of the Federal Parliament."

"You pompous, arrogant old man," Boudreaux began. "I should have you arrested."

"You can't," Manning quickly countered. "I invite you to, though. I have the backing of the Chancellor. *You,* do not. If you did arrest me, you'd find yourself in the Office of the Federal Chancellor, explaining your actions and your behavior. Is she aware of our prior history? You might even be asked for your resignation. I invite you to, humiliate yourself, once again. I hear Labrador is wonderful, this time of year."

"You're an asshole," was all that Boudreaux could finally say.

"Minister, I have never denied that," Manning agreed. "However, I'm feeling charitable, today. Consider this, a small gift."

Manning stood up from the chair he was sitting on, so quickly, that the startled Boudreaux stepped back defensively and loudly banged into the one-way mirror. Manning shook his head as he began to remove his metal rank insignia and pins. Keeping eye contact with Boudreaux, he let the insignia and pins clatter to the table's surface one by one.

"Minister. I hereby resign my commission. Explain *that,* to the Chancellor," Manning announced as he walked out of the room.

Later that night, Manning stumbled through the front door of his government issued residence. Besides feeling free for the first times in years, he was a little drunk, too. He saw an official notice that had been pushed through the door's mail slot, lying on the floor. He bent over to pick it up, straightened up and drunkenly opened it.

Upon reading the notice, he laughed aloud and shut the door. Holding the notice before him, he staggered slightly, into the living room and sat heavily onto the sofa.

The federal government was evicting him because he resigned. They were giving him a week to vacate or the Security Patrol would be removing him and his belongings by force. He sat up and on the coffee table, made a paper airplane out of the notice. When done, he sat back and launched it across the room. The paper plane flying straight and true, was caught by a breeze from the open window, looped back around and landed next to the clear crystal cylinder on the end-table beside the sofa. Manning stared at the crystal for the longest time.

He had misgivings about what he was about to do. He had been drinking and by activating the crystal, legally, his judgment was impaired. But, hadn't he already made that decision before he ordered the first drink? He knew he had. He just felt uncertain about it.

"What the hell," he muttered.

He touched the top of the crystal with his index finger. It immediately glowed blue. A holographic image of Marcus Gowan was projected from the center of the top of the crystal.

"General Manning, my friend," the smiling image began. "This pre-recorded image of me has been activated by you. This recording can only be accessed by your DNA and can only be viewed once, after which this crystal, will disintegrate."

The image paused….

Epilog

Declaration to the World

People of the Earth, can you hear me?

For the past twenty-four hours, on the hour and every hour, an automated message has been broadcast via satellite, on all channels and frequencies in the electromagnetic spectrum. The purpose is intended to reach all peoples of all nations of the Earth in the hope, that the people of Earth could anticipate and prepare themselves to hear this important announcement. As I speak, my words are being transmitted and simultaneously translated into all the known languages and dialects of the corresponding regions of Earth.

For the third time in the history of the Earth, a civilization has the capability to not only achieve flight but, defy gravity and leave the confines of this planet. I won't bore you with the details of the previous two. Suffice to say, *we*, modern civilization, are the third.

As for our current civilization; since our earliest, recorded history, *we, Humans,* have always sought to explore and adapt to our surroundings. To risk life and limb to simply see and know, what was just over the horizon. To satisfy our curiosity. It is truly, in Humanity's nature to do this. We discovered new lands and new cultures and even, new peoples. It has taken literally thousands of years, for us to get to know one another, understand each other's cultures and not fear or be offended by what we don't.

As our knowledge progressed, so did our technology. However, our behavior did not. Our ancestors fought over land, resources, profit and petty differences. Human enlightenment was taking a back-seat. There *was,* a glimmer of hope and great promise during the twentieth century when Humanity could have fulfilled its greatest potential. But, in the end, we did not. During this same time period, we Humans, began to explore further from our home-world. We had reached for and achieved placing men on the Moon. Sent interplanetary probes in the hope, of understanding more of our own planet and star system. Other probes are now, traveling in deep space in the hope of making contact with alien races.

And as before, as our ancestors did, we began to fight over land, resources, money and our petty differences. Again, we lost sight of our potential. Humanity has had the resources and the means to become true caretakers and chief stewards of this planet for many, many years. *We,* are ruining this planet. Humanity is the dominant species on Earth at the moment. However, in a moment of time, we could, conceivably, face annihilation. Whether by our own hand or by natural forces, or, depending on one's belief, by God, Himself.

Today, that changes.

My name is Marcus Gowan. I am the interim Director of the nation of Pacifica and *this,* is a declaration of our nation's existence. Pacifica is a newly-risen land mass, first discovered by my father, Samuel Gowan, 40 years ago after the Great Pacific Tsunami. At the time, he possessed technology to hide the cause and effect of future tsunami's as the mass continued to rise from the depths of the Pacific Ocean. Technology that, this nation possesses. Technology so advanced, it has the potential, in the wrong hands, to be miss-used.

Technology, in any field, often translates into power. Power to change the environment. Power over life and death. Power over individuals. Power to influence the masses. And yes, power over nations. Even on a global scale.

Ancient Greek general-turned philosopher, Thucydides, theorized about the Peloponnesian War and determined that it was fought mainly because of power. Who had it and how one exercises it. Thucydides, was the first to recognize and postulate, the reasons why Sparta(an oligarchy) and Athens(a democracy) went to war. It had no bearing on which of the two, was the good or the bad power. Whoever exercised that power, was the evil one and the aggressor. It is a doctrine which dominates world politics even, today. It is a doctrine we wish to, and **will,** avoid.

We, wish to use this technology for peaceful purposes. Constructively, creatively. The greatest danger this technology poses to planet Earth, is to share it with the less-enlightened. Often, in the past, important discoveries were turned into weapons of war. Technology, becoming perverted into new and efficient ways to maim or kill our fellow human beings. To share this technology, even with the best of intentions, could not only prove harmful but, could also mean the annihilation of all life on this planet. Often, powerful nations seek to influence leaders of other nations. This is done through the perception of power and the power of technology.

However, it will not become the policies of this nation's governing system. We choose not to share this technology with the world, at the present time. When the people and the nations of the Earth have matured and united as one, then, can we fully disclose the extent of our technology. With the power of our technology, it will become our highest responsibility to use it wisely and with great caution.

It will become our highest law.

So, now that the 'cat is out of the bag', so to speak, we wish to declare our intentions;

1. Pacifica will **not** seek membership to the United Nations Organization. To do so, Pacifica would be subject to the same treaties and *restrictions* as other nations of the world. For Pacifica, we consider this, a *backward* step. We do not and will not seek to become the most dominant nation on Earth. We intend to go upward and onward. We will not interfere in the affairs of nations on Earth. It is none of Pacifica's concern and will become another of our highest laws.

2. It is our intention to achieve a clear and permanent foothold in space. To begin Humanity's claim on our birth-right to the stars. With the achievements in space exploration in the last half of the twentieth century, Humanity should have well been established, by now. Our plan involves setting up permanent colonies on the Moon, Mars and other planets and moons, within our star system. Ambitious mining operations will begin on asteroids and comets circling our sun. The people of Pacifica are committed to this.

3. We have a plan, as well, to clean up the Earth's environment. From the ocean's depths to low-Earth orbit. We have technology to construct oceanic and atmospheric processors. We anticipate that they will be online and fully operational within 3 years.

4. Droughts and famines have caused more deaths than in any wars. It is a shame that in this day and age, people; man, woman and child should suffer from the lack of food and drinkable water. For generations, first-world nations stood by at the plight of the citizens of the third-world or developing nations in these extreme emergencies. The Pacifican government will offer its assistance, in such cases.

5. Hazardous waste, in all forms, is the scourge of any modern civilization. It pollutes the land, the water, the air, the food-chain and us, as well. We propose to take in the world's hazardous wastes for recycling, neutralization, and if need be, disposal (meaning, we will take it, off-world). Soon, this nation will offer to take and will accept hazardous wastes in all forms, including nuclear

6. Last but, certainly not the least. This planet has faced many global catastrophes in its history. Some have been by asteroid or cometary impacts. All one has to do, is look to the Moon to see evidence of this. It is also a fact that the Earth has experienced numerous ice ages and that the next one, is already overdue. With the risen land-mass off the California/Baja coastline, and the rise of Pacifica itself, we can only speculate as to how common it is for land-masses to rise and sink. Even the ancient Atlantians couldn't prevent the demise of their civilization. An ambitious off-world evacuation plan is being devised so that Humanity would be able to survive such catastrophes of a global scale.

Humanity is far too valuable to let die out. *I believe* in the Family of Man. *I believe* in *our* humanity and *I believe* in our capability to do a great many things. *Incredible things.* Things much bigger than our individual selves. We often forget just how mighty we can be. To be champions, of our home-world. It is my belief, that at this point in Human evolution; we should have turned this planet into a true paradise. We are capable of astounding compassion. Even, in the face of disasters, whether by nature or from ourselves. The Human race has survived through all of these. Scientists have even speculated that in some cases, historically, by the skin of our teeth. It will be this nation's policy to ensure the survival of the Human race when this planet is facing extinction level events, such as the dinosaurs did, some 65 million years ago.

As Konstatin Tsiokovsky wrote in 1899. 'Earth is the cradle of Humanity but, one cannot live in the cradle forever."

This concludes Pacifica's declaration of existence.
Upward and onward.

Thank-you, for your time.

-TRANSMISSION ENDS-